THE ETERNA FILES

Tor Books by
LEANNA RENEE HIEBER

The Eterna Files
Strangely Beautiful (forthcoming)

THE
ETERNA
FILES

LEANNA RENEE HIEBER

A Tom Doherty Associates Book
NEW YORK

THE ETERNA FILES

A Tor Book
Published by Tom Doherty Associates, LLC
175 Fifth Avenue
New York, NY 10010

www.tor-forge.com

Tor® is a registered trademark of Tom Doherty Associates, LLC.

The Library of Congress Cataloging-in-Publication Data
is available upon request.

ISBN 978-0-7653-3674-3 (hardcover)
ISBN 978-1-4668-2925-1 (e-book)

Tor books may be purchased for educational, business, or promotional use.
For information on bulk purchases, please contact the Macmillan Corporate
and Premium Sales Department at 1-800-221-7945, extension 5442,
or write to specialmarkets@macmillan.com.

First Edition: February 2015

Printed in the United States of America

0 9 8 7 6 5 4 3 2 1

THE ETERNA FILES

PROLOGUE

The White House, April 16, 1865

The sanity of a bloodied nation hung by a precarious thread. Hundreds of thousands of bodies rotted in mass graves. Mountains of arms and legs lay just beneath the earth in countless pits of appendages. Thousands of young men had been torn into wingless birds, stunned, harrowed, and half whole. No one had gone untouched by the war; everyone was haunted.

A gunshot in a theater tipped the straining scales and the nation's battered, broken heart faltered and stopped.

This was the world in which twelve-year-old Clara Templeton grieved. She wept for her land with the kind of passion only a young, gifted sensitive could offer. When she was called to the side of the first lady, she did not hesitate.

Clad in a black taffeta mourning gown, Clara stood in a dimly candlelit hallway outside the first lady's rooms, awaiting admittance alongside her guardian, Congressman Rupert Bishop, aged twenty-five—though his prematurely silver hair gave one pause as to his age. He'd been silver-haired as long as she'd known him. When she'd asked about it with a child's tactlessness, he'd simply responded with a wink and a smile: "It's the fault of the ghosts." Soon after, Bishop took her to her first séance and Clara began to understand just how dangerous the thrall of ghosts could be. . . .

A red-eyed maid opened the door and gestured them in.

Inside the small but well-appointed room, a low fire

mitigated a cool draft and cast most of the light in the room. Mary Todd Lincoln sat on a chair in the shadows, staring out a small window, her bell-sleeved, black crepe dress spilling out in all directions. Only the ticking of a fine clock on the mantel and the occasional sniff from the weeping maid broke the silence. The congressman beckoned Clara forward, into the firelight. Her step creaked upon the floorboards as her petite body cast a long shadow behind her.

Finally the first lady spoke in a quiet tremor. "Do you know why I called you here, Miss Templeton?"

"I've a supposition," Clara replied quietly, nervously moving forward another step. "But first, Mrs. Lincoln, my deepest sympathies—"

"When your guardian here first brought you to visit the White House two years ago, you ran up to me, a perfect stranger, and gave me an embrace from my William. My dead William."

"Yes, Mrs. Lincoln," Clara murmured, "I remember—"

"I need you now, Miss Templeton," the first lady began with a slightly wild look in her eyes, "to give me an embrace from my dead husband."

Alarmed, Clara looked at Bishop, her eyes wide. The tall, elegantly handsome man lifted a calming, gloved hand and Clara attempted to gather herself

"I . . . well," she stammered, "I'm unsure my gifts can work on command, Mrs.—"

"Try!" the grieving widow wailed, turning to face the girl, her face drawn and hollowed. Clara rushed over and fell to her knees beside the first lady, removing her kid gloves to take Mary's shaking, bare hands into hers.

"I know that he is with you," Clara murmured, tears falling from her bright green-gold eyes. "The president is with all who mourn him—"

"Prove it," Mary Todd murmured. She snapped her head

toward the door. "Rupert. You're a spiritualist, have you not *trained* Miss Templeton since she became your ward?"

"Only charlatans cue up the dead precisely when the grieving want them, Mary, you know that," Bishop said gently. "And this is far too vulnerable a time to try." He shivered suddenly. "Too many things want *in*. We risk inviting malevolence, not comfort."

"No one should *ever* have to suffer what I have—" the first lady choked out.

"No, they shouldn't," Clara replied. "Never."

"The country can bear no more," Bishop added quietly, his fine black mourning coat making him almost invisible in the shadows by the door. "We must guard against the basest evils grasping for purchase—"

"What could be more evil than what I have endured?" the first lady exclaimed.

The last two years had taught Clara that Rupert Bishop coddled no one, even the grieving. She spoke before he could offer another example of his oft-sobering perspective. "Such a powerful seat needs protection," Clara exclaimed, squeezing the widow's shaking hands with innocent, sure strength. "Such a man should never have fallen. He deserved to have been made immortal!"

"Why . . . yes, child!" Mary Lincoln exclaimed, a sudden light in her eyes. "Do we not have resources, researchers, scientists, theorists? Should we not have granted a man like the president eternal protection while he bore the nation on his shoulders? My dear Congressman Bishop . . ."

The small woman rose to her feet and began to pace the room, skirts swishing and sweeping with renewed determination.

"I charge you," she said, bright gaze fastened on Bishop. "If you'll not bring my husband back to me in spirit or form, then you must do this. Take Clara's idea. For this bled-dry country. For the seat cloaked in immense power. Do this, Congressman, so no other wife in this dreadful house might go through such agony again. . . ."

"Do *what*, Mary?" he pressed.

She stared at him with steely ferocity. "Find a cure for death."

Seventeen Years Later,
New York City, 1882

"It was born of good intentions," Clara insisted in a choking murmur.

She sat on a bench in Central Park on a mild June day, beneath a willow tree, looking out over the southeastern pond. She could not move. Her breath was shallow against the double stays of corset and buttoned bodice; soft ivory lace and muslin ruffles trembled around her throat. Tendrils of dark blond hair, blown free from braids beneath a fanciful straw feathered hat, tickled around her streaming eyes. Her world was again cracking open.

"Wake up," she heard a voice calling. "Wake up." It was not a human voice but that of some ancient, cosmic force.

She had known there was something different about her since the age of nine, since she'd awakened in the middle of the night to see a wild-haired woman in a cloak sitting at the foot of her bed.

"You're special," was all the woman said before vanishing.

The next day, Clara's father, a prominent doctor to Washington lawmakers, died of tuberculosis. Her mother soon followed. They were buried in a Greenwood Cemetery mausoleum in their native Brooklyn. Clara was the marble sepulcher's most frequent haunt. The Templetons' will ensured that Clara would be educated at fine institutions and looked after by prominent figures.

Rupert Bishop, then a talented young New York lawyer, frequented the same Washington and spiritualist circles as the Templetons. A beloved family friend, he stepped in to graciously provide for the girl left behind. Bitterly estranged from their Southern families after the war, the Templetons hoped Clara's manifest spiritual talents would blossom under Bishop's care and guidance. She indeed flourished, until her gifts turned physically dangerous and had to be carefully monitored.

The visitor returned the night Bishop brought Clara to the White House the first time; Clara saw the creature watching her from the shadows. She had not seen the strange herald since, not even after that fateful second encounter with the first lady, a meeting that had set an unlikely destiny in motion.

Paperwork left on the slain president's desk established a "Secret Service" to investigate counterfeit currency. A tiny cabal, headed by Bishop, supposed the service might also, in some unnamed office, investigate immortality. Bishop assembled a team of occultists, mystics, and chemists and set them to work in a secret location.

Once Clara completed finishing school, Bishop gave her a key to a nondescript office on Pearl Street in downtown Manhattan. A county clerk's record office on the first floor served as a front. Clara's offices—and those of the colleagues she and Bishop hired—took up the top floor. Congressman Bishop became Senator Bishop. A quiet era of investigation and theorizing followed.

In 1880, Eterna theorist Louis Dupris secretly told Clara that he'd made a breakthrough in localized magic. The world had suddenly seemed full of possibility. But now . . .

The Eterna Compound had been born out of grief. At this moment Clara wondered if it should never have been born at all, for now it bore grief of its own.

"Something's wrong," Clara murmured, wanting to cry but feeling wholly paralyzed. "I can feel it. . . ." All of Clara that had ever been could feel it; a love torn from her like layers of skin.

Before her eyes, in layers of concentric circles stretching out like mirrors reflecting mirrors in dizzying multiplication, she saw lives. Her lives, those she'd had before. She was twenty-nine years old . . . with a soul a thousand years older.

Pried open in a painful awakening, she knew her life was far more than the boundaries and limitations of her current flesh, but at present she felt the pain of all those centuries all at once, things done and undone. The sheer, heavy press of it all was staggering.

A mockingbird alighted on a branch above Clara's head. It squawked and stared at her, then made the sounds of a police whistle, a bicycle bell, and some roaring, whooshing thing: the sound of something tearing.

And then there was a woman next to her. The visitor.

Though she couldn't turn her head, in her peripheral vision Clara saw skirts, gloves, and long hair that was scandalously unbound. The presence of the visitor confirmed what she was feeling; something terrible was happening. Clara tried to move again, to fight the gravity lashing her to the bench, wishing tears, something, anything could be set free.

"What is it this time?" Clara gasped.

"Hello, Clara," the visitor said quietly. One didn't mistake an ordinary person for the visitor, for it brought with it the weight of time itself. "It's been awhile." The visitor smoothed the skirts of its long, plain, black, uniform-like dress, something a boarding school girl might wear. "Have you been waiting?" the visitor asked.

"I'm not one who likes waiting," Clara replied.

"That's why I trust you," the visitor said, pleasure in its voice. "I last saw you when you impetuously gave the first lady an embrace from her dead son."

The mockingbird gave a raucous trill from the limb above

them. The woman adjusted what Clara thought was a hat—she still couldn't get a good look. The mockingbird had flown across the path and alighted on a limb at her eye line, trilling accompaniment to their conversation.

"You presage terrible things but I never know what," Clara growled.

"You've always been gifted," the visitor replied. "Sensitive."

"And we see what good *sensitivity* has done me." Clara choked out her words. "I'm a freak of nature. My 'fits' render any hope I might have had for a normal life or a place in society laughable. I curse my gifts for all the misfortune they bring." Embarrassing, traumatic memories paraded through her mind, her past lives staring on in pity. Clara hated pity. Perhaps it was best, then, that the visitor had none.

"Don't be ungrateful, child," the visitor chided. "You've two friends in a world of loneliness, you had a lover when many never know such pleasure, you've worked when hordes seek pay, you've had a guardian who dotes on you when countless orphans have no one, and you've money and a fine house in a city that denies both to thousands of its denizens."

Clara wanted to lash out at the creature. But it was right, which only sharpened her pain.

"Something terrible has happened, hasn't it? To the Eterna team?" she whispered, her throat raw as if from screaming even though she had loosed no such sound. "To my Louis? My love is among them. . . ."

An amulet of protection, tucked beneath her corset stays, was a knot against her shaking breaths. The amulet had been given to her by Louis, an item charged and blessed by his mother. Clara never felt she had the right to it, and now, he, who needed protection, lacked it

"I am very sorry for your loss," the visitor said solemnly.

"I must go," Clara insisted, trying to fight free but failing. "Maybe I can help the team—"

The visitor held up a hand. "It's no use. They're gone."

"Why can't you stop terrible things if you're aware of them?" Clara demanded. "Why can't I?"

"Not in our skill set," the visitor replied. "You've taken too much ownership of something that is not your responsibility, Templeton. What is your responsibility, is to—"

"'*Wake up?*' Yes, I hear it, on the wind. In my bones. What does it mean?"

The woman gestured before her, to Clara's iterations. "You see the lives, don't you?"

"Yes." Clara swallowed hard. "Do you?"

"Of course I do," the visitor replied. "I'm here to tell you that a great storm is coming. It will break across two continents; two great cities, the hearts of empires. Your team is gone and storms are coming. Weather them, find special souls and shield them. Second-guess your enemy. Find the missing link between the lives you see. Do this for yourself. And for your country."

Clara snorted bitterly. "Do I hear patriotism?"

The visitor shook its head. "I owe allegiance to no land."

"Then what are you here for?" Clara begged.

The visitor's voice grew warm. "I care about certain people."

"Why me?"

"*Show* me why you, Templeton," the visitor proclaimed. "You're at the center of the storm. Be worthy of the squall."

The mockingbird made the strange, roaring sound again and the woman was gone.

Clara's hands shook. The people she had been in her many lives turned and looked at her, male, female, all with certain similar qualities that she recognized as uniquely hers. Curiosity. Hunger. Restlessness. Intensity. Independence. A desperate desire for noble purpose. And lonely.

She was *awake*. But Eterna had died, taking with it the lover no one knew she had.

CHAPTER

ONE

London, 1882

Harold Spire had been pacing until first light, crawling out of his skin to close his God-forsaken case. The moment the tentative sun poked over the chimney tops of Lambeth—though it did not successfully permeate London's sooty haze—he raced out the door to meet his appointed contact.

Conveniently, there was a fine black hansom just outside his door. Spire shouted his destination at the driver as he threw open the door and launched himself into the carriage. He was startled to find that the cab already had an occupant: a short, balding man, immaculately but distinctly dressed; as one might expect of a royal footman.

"Hello, Mr. Spire," the man said calmly.

Spire's stomach dropped; his right hand hovered over his left wrist, where he kept a small, sharp knife in a simple cuff. Surely this was one of Tourney's henchmen; the villain was well connected and would do anything to save his desperate hide.

"Do not be alarmed, sir," the stranger said. "We are en route to Buckingham Palace on orders of Her Majesty Queen Victoria."

"Is there a problem?" Spire asked, maintaining a calm tone, relaxing his hand but offering up a silent prayer to whatever God was decent and good that the queen would not have interceded on the wretch's behalf. . . .

"No, sir. You are being considered for an appointment. I can say nothing more."

"An . . . appointment."

"Yes, sir."

"I'm afraid I cannot attend to this great honor at present, sir."

The man arched a preened brow. "Beg your pardon?"

"With all due respect," Spire continued, not bothering to hide the earnest desperation he felt, "I am a policeman at a critical juncture, awaiting receipt of vital material without which a vicious criminal might walk free—"

"And what shall I tell Her Majesty? That you're too busy for her?"

Spire set his jaw, looking anxiously out the window, seeing that they were heading in the opposite direction from where he needed to be at precisely seven. "Please tell Her Majesty that I'm about to stop a ring of child murderers and resurrectionists. Burkes and Hares. Body snatchers—"

"That will have to wait. Mere police work does not come before Her Majesty."

"I think highly enough of Her Majesty to think she'd deem this important."

"I am under orders to take you to the palace regardless of prevarication—"

"I wouldn't dare lie about a thing like this!"

"Once Her Majesty has determined your suitability, you'll be returned to your duties."

"You'll have to give the empress my sincere regrets. She may be able to live with one more child dead in her realm but I, sir, *cannot*."

With that, Spire opened the door of the moving carriage and cast himself onto flagstones slick with the foul mixture of the London streets. His heel turned slightly under him and he came down painfully; his elbow jarred against stone and his forearm cut against the brace that held his knife sheath. He jumped to his feet and ran—with a slight limp—veering onto a bridge across the busy, teeming, brown Thames and onward to a life-or-death rendezvous.

He'd likely be arrested for his evasion, but his conscience was utterly clear.

*   *   *   *   *

Spire's right hand hovered over his left forearm as he entered the damp brick alley, which was lit sporadically by gas jets whose light was dim behind blackened lantern glass. Even though the world was brightening with the gray of morning, sunlight didn't penetrate into these drear, winding halls of sooty brick, London having its labyrinthine qualities. He made his tread soundless on the cobblestones, his eyes aware of every shadow and shape, his ears alert, his nostrils flared.

While he doubted his informant was dangerous—it was all bookkeeping, really, he imagined the source was a bank clerk or the like—what the ledgers revealed was something else entirely. The proof itself was dangerous and many men would kill with far less provocation. If "Gazelle" proved trustworthy, Spire would recruit the man for his department.

He palmed the key Gazelle had left in the drop location at Cleopatra's Needle. If all had gone according to plan, Gazelle would have left enough evidence at this bookstore to prove without a shadow of a doubt that Francis Tourney was bankrupting charitable societies in a speculation racket that would make any betting man blush. That he was also involved in a child-trafficking ring of both living and dead young bodies was harder to prove, but far more damning.

The key opened the rear-alley door of the bookshop. A small lantern was lit somewhere within, casting a wan yellow light over stacks of spines. Spire knocked on the wooden door frame: three taps, a pause, and two more.

A quiet rap in response, from somewhere within the maze

of books, confirmed that his informant was waiting. Spire edged his way through boxes and stacks—one stray limb could cause the whole precarious haphazard system to tumble—toward the source of the light.

He turned a corner of books and stopped dead in his tracks. There sat a woman who had gotten him into a good bit of trouble—the prime minister's best-kept secret, his bookkeeper, one Miss Rose Everhart. Poised as ever, seated at a long wooden table; the lit lantern cast her scowl of concentration into sharp relief as layered bell sleeves spilled over a stack of thin spines. One ledger lay, open, under her hand; she ran ungloved fingertips over the pages.

She wasn't stunning, but unique; her full mouth, set now in a frown, gave her a gravitas offset by the few loose brown curls around her cheeks, an almost whimsical contrast to her fastidious expression. When she looked up at Spire, the intensity and razor-sharp focus of her large blue eyes made her intriguing, magnetic.

"You're surprised to see a woman," she said. It was not a question.

"Yes." Spire spoke very carefully. "Especially one I recognize." At this, she smiled, a prim, self-satisfied smile. "You made quite an impression, Miss Everhart. A cloaked female figure glimpsed wandering the halls of Parliament, only to disappear into a wall? I didn't buy the story that you were a specter."

"The too-curious Westminster policeman. So we meet again," she said with an edge. "The eager dog sniffing out a fox. My employers, who were granting me the easiest access to my job while hoping to avoid any national outcry, were not fond of you. And I confess, nor was I. It was bad enough to have to sneak about, then to be thought suspect for it when I am a patriot? Horrible."

"Yes, I was quite chastised about that by your superior,

Lord Black," Spire muttered, "so you needn't pile on." He wondered with sudden fear if that's why the queen wished to see him: more scolding. Spire's purview was Westminster and its immediate environs. When he'd stumbled upon Miss Everhart, he'd merely been doing his job. Tourney's speculation ring involved members of both the House of Commons and the House of Lords, so it was perhaps not surprising that Spire had thought that the prime minister's bookkeeper had access others did not.

At the mention of Lord Black, Miss Everhart smiled and warmed. She stood suddenly, as if on ceremony, gesturing for Spire to sit at the bench opposite. While she was primly buttoned in dour blues and grays, her skirts and bodice were tailored in unique lines and accented with the occasional bauble that made Spire think a subtle bohemian lived somewhere deep beneath her proper corset laces.

"We have enough on the racketeering for a compelling case," she said, handing several ledgers across the table.

"Good," he said, nodding.

"But it's *this* that will deliver the decisive blow," she murmured, and shuddered. She passed him a narrow, thin black book that she didn't seem eager to touch. The cover said, "Registry."

"What's this? Did you collect this from the banks?"

"No. From Tourney's study." At Spire's raised eyebrow, Miss Everhart clarified, "After I showed him the numbers, Lord Black arranged for Sir Tourney to attend some sort of speculators' gala. Black stamped a warrant and found this."

"Himself?" Spire asked, incredulous.

"Lord Black had been feted at the Tourney estate, so sending him in was the most efficient. He knew to look for anything out of the ordinary. And *this* is hardly ordinary."

Shocked by a lord's unorthodox method but impressed by the man's initiative, Spire opened the book. Small, dark marks and round smudges marched down the pages in boxes made up of thin graphite lines. A few letters—initials, Spire guessed— were penciled above each dot.

On one side of the page, the dots were dark red. On the other side, the small marks were black. At the top of each page was a single large letter: "L" above the red marks and "D" above the black.

Horror dawned, slow and sick, as Spire stared at the lines of dots and initials. Dots the size of a child's fingertip.

"Living." Spire's finger hovered over the "L."

Then he moved to the "D." "Deceased"

Oh, God. They were children's fingerprints. Swabbed in their blood. Or, if their bodies had been stolen when dead, their fingers dipped in ink and pressed to the page.

A registry of stolen children.

Used for God knows what.

"I . . ." Spire stared at Miss Everhart, whose face was unreadable. "I'm sorry you had to see this."

Her jaw tensed, pursed lips pressed thinner. "I am thirty and unmarried. I doubt I'll ever have children, so I do whatever I can. I owe it to those poor children not to flinch."

Spire nodded. He hadn't thought to place any women assets in his police force. But women could keep secrets, tell lies, deceive, and connive with an aptitude that frightened him. Women made *bloody* good spies. He knew that well enough.

Spire rose, sliding the ledger, breakdown, and "registry" into his briefcase. "Thank you, Miss Everhart. Please give Lord Black my regards, I was unaware he was involved. I'm not wasting any time on the arrest."

"I didn't imagine you would." Everhart rose and wove expertly through the labyrinth of books. As she disappeared, she called back to him. "Go on. I'll alert your squadron. I doubt you should go there alone."

He stared after her a moment, resentful of initiative taken without his orders . . . but it would save him valuable time.

* * * * *

Spire and his squad descended upon the decadent Tourney estate; a hideous, sprawling mansion faced in ostentatious pink marble, hoarding a generous swath of land in North London.

His best men at his side, Stuart Grange and Gregory Phyfe, Spire stormed Tourney's front door, blowing past a startled footman.

The despicable creature was having breakfast in a fine parlor. The son of a Marquis, descended of a withering line, seemed quite shocked to see the police; his surprised expression validated Spire's existence.

Spire was tempted to strike the man across the jaw on principle but became distracted by the thin maid, in a tattered black dress and a besmeared white linen apron, who cowered in the corner of the parlor. Entirely ignored by the rest of the force, she was shaking, unable to look anyone in the eye. Her condition was a stark contrast to her fine surroundings, which valued possessions higher than humanity. . . .

Shaking his head, Spire instructed his colleagues to secure Tourney in the wagon.

"I've all kinds of connections," the bloated, balding man cried as he was dragged away. "Would you like me to list the names of the powerful who will help me?"

"I think you're in too deep for anyone but the devil to come to your aid, Mr. Tourney," Spire called as the door was shut between them. Silence fell and he turned to the woman in the corner.

At his approach, the gaunt, frail maid began murmuring through cracked lips, "Please, please, please." She lifted a bony arm and the cuff of her uniform slid back, revealing a grisly series of scars on her arm. Burns. Signs of binding and torture.

"Please what, Miss?" Spire asked gently, not touching her.

"S—secret door . . . Get them . . . out. . . ." She pointed at the opposite wall.

A chill went down Spire's spine. He studied the wall for a long time before noticing the line in the carved wooden paneling. Crossing the room, he ran his hand along the molding, pressing until something gave. The hidden door swung open and a horrific stench met his nostrils.

The maid loosed a wretched noise and sunk to her knees, rocking back and forth. Spire raised his voice, calling to his partner and friend, a stalwart man who played all things carefully and whom Spire trusted implicitly, "Grange, I think there may be a . . . situation down here."

Without waiting for a reply, Spire was through the door and descending a brick stairwell, fumbling in his pocket for a box of matches. A lantern hung at the base of the stair; he lit the wick and set it back upon the crook. The flame, magnified by mirrors, cast a wan light over the small, windowless brick room.

It was everything Spire could do to keep from screaming in horror.

Six small tables, three on each side of the room. Each bore the body of a child clothed in a bloodstained tunic. Spire could not determine their genders due to their unkempt hair, pallor, and emaciated bodies. Strange wires seemed to be attached to the children.

Nothing in his investigation, even that dread register, had prepared him for this: these poor, innocent souls, helpless victims of a powerful man who was viciously mad.

He raised his gaze from the children to an even greater horror, if a worse nightmare could be imagined. An auburn-haired woman in a thin chemise and petticoat was lashed to a crosslike apparatus, arms stretched out and sleeves torn away.

Streams of dried blood from numerous puncture wounds stained her clothes, the cross, and the walls and floor. Below each of her lashed arms sat large bronze chalices, there was a basin at her feet. Spire knew in a glance that these were to collect the woman's blood. What horrific sacrifice was this?

Spire turned his head to the side and retched. His mind scrambled to block out the image of who that woman reminded him of, the reason he'd become a police officer. The trauma of his childhood sprang back to haunt him at the sight of that ghastly visage in a blow to the mind, heart, and stomach. How could the world be endured if such a thing as this had come to pass? He'd asked the same question when the victim had been his mother. Nothing answered him, then or now, but sorrow.

"I never believed much in the devil," came a soft, familiar voice near his ear, "or hell, but if I did, it would be this." Spire spun to see a cloaked figure at his side, the solitary lantern casting a shallow beam of light upon the face of Rose Everhart.

"Miss Everhart, you should not be here. I don't know how you got past my men," Spire murmured, thinking it an additional horror that she should see this. "This is hardly the place—"

"For a lady? Even for the lady who handed you the critical evidence needed to arrest Tourney? Do I not wish to see him marched to the gallows as much as you do?" she replied vehemently. "Don't I have a right to see my work completed? Don't try my patience with references to 'women's delicate sensibilities.' I've seen more death and tragedy than I care to relate. But, admittedly . . . never like this. Never like this." She raised a handkerchief to her nose.

Spire suddenly wondered whether she had heard or seen him retch. It would be embarrassing if so.

"What are those wires?" she asked. "What are they for? Is this some sort of terrible experiment or workshop? Ritualistic, yes, but . . ."

Spire stepped forward, preparing however reluctantly to examine the bodies, when something lurched out of the darkness behind him with a clatter of chains and an inhuman growl. It grabbed him around the neck, grunted as it tightened its grip, and dragged him backward.

"Grange!" Rose shouted as Spire gasped for air and struggled to reach his knife. "If you're a victim, we don't want to hurt you," she called in a softer tone, lifting her lantern and directing its light toward the scuffle. "Let the officer go, he's with the police, here to help—"

Officer Grange tore down the stairs, arriving in the hell-hole just as Spire managed to grasp his weapon and cut at the arm holding him. There was a wretched sound of pain from his captor and Spire felt a warm liquid trickle over his hand. Released, he staggered away and fell to his knees. Grange fired, the report of the gunshot exploding loudly in the low stone space. Spire's assailant recoiled with a shriek. Stumbling back against the wall, it shuddered before collapsing.

Grange stood at the base of the stair with his gun raised. Rose stepped forward so the light from her lantern reached the back wall. Still gasping for air, Spire turned to view his attacker: a gaunt, muscular man with chunks of dark hair sprouting in uneven patches upon a scratched pate. The man's skin was carved with strange markings, his eyes black and oddly reflective. Blood pumped thick and dark from the bullet wound in his shoulder, looking old and half-congealed though the injury was fresh. One arm was shackled to the wall. A guard, then, but not one to be trusted freely.

With a strange gurgling noise, a convulsion, and a wave of foul stench, the creature's mouth sagged open and the thing expired. It then seemed as though an obscuring shadow rose from the body, then spread across the room as if it were a dark, heavy storm cloud, precipitous with dread terror.

Turning to look after the miasma as it passed, Grange, Spire, and Rose took in a startled breath at the same time. Grange cursed.

The mouths of the dead children, previously shut, were suddenly open.

As if screaming.

Silent, terrible moments passed before Spire, trying not to breathe the fetid air, stepped toward the tables, peering closer at the small, lifeless bodies. "From what I know of the telegraph and those new electric wires," he stated, clearing his raw throat, "it seems similar. Something to convey a . . . transmission or charge."

"But where do the wires lead?" Grange asked, looking at the ceiling, where the wires formed a latticework grid on the low timber-beamed ceiling. Many hung loose in gossamer metallic strands. "It seems they don't continue on to the upper floors."

"Go and see," Spire commanded. Grange nodded and trotted back up the stairs.

Rose was writing upon a small pad of paper. This commonsense act—usually the first thing Spire himself did upon entering a crime scene—recalled him to himself. For an instant he was flushed with shame that this unprecedented discovery had caused him to falter in his work. He forced himself back under control; he would not allow the dead woman across the room—and what she represented—to derail him.

Though the room was cool, perspiration coated Spire and he could smell his own tension. He took out his notepad, replaced the lantern on the hook at the base of the stairs where he'd found it, and set to work. Each child's wrists had puncture marks. Each arm bore odd carvings. He'd have to get one of the department sketch artists to accurately reproduce the

markings. He wished a daguerreotype was possible, not that
he wanted to subject more people to these horrors but only
for the purpose of detail.

They held the man responsible, but Spire knew Tourney
was not operating alone. The sheer gruesome spectacle of this
would be enough, the policeman hoped, to indict any of the
influential people Tourney worked with in this ghastly enter-
prise.

Spire turned his attention toward the woman at the back.
His head swam. His mind was filled with the sounds and sights
of his childhood trauma; the images superimposed over the
present moment like a screen lowered before his eyes. He had
to steady himself on one of the tables, hand fumbling over a
small, cold foot.

A sloppily painted symbol on the woman's tunic appeared
to be a crest: red and gold with dragons. He couldn't look at
her face. He was already haunted enough by the vision of a
beautiful, auburn-haired woman being bled before his eyes.

He felt more than saw the movement as Rose folded her
cloak back over her head and disappeared upstairs.

Hearing voices calling his name, Spire mounted the stairs
and stumbled into the light; his fellows took one look at his
face and blanched.

"What's down there?" a young patrolman asked.

"Hell," Spire replied. "Don't anyone move a thing until all
details have been recorded. I want more than my notes to re-
fer to. Get Phyfe down there, I want records of everything.
Every single terrible detail."

Spire sat in the fine chair Tourney had been using and continued making notes. The poor maid had been laid out on a
nearby sofa; a nervous elder officer stared down at her as if
afraid that if he turned his head, she'd stop breathing.

"Is there any other staff?" Spire asked.

"None that we've seen," the officer replied.

He did not know how long he sat there, recording his impressions of the horrors below, before a voice startled him out of his morbid reverie.

"Harold Spire, come with me." He snapped his head up to behold the same well-heeled footman who had been at his doorstep that morning.

"Ah, yes . . ." Spire rose and numbly walked to the door. "The queen's man. Are you here to arrest me?"

"No, sir. While I had a mind to do so, Her Majesty is gracious and commends your commitment to English citizens. But you *will* come with me now."

"Ah. Well. Yes. Lead on, sir."

During the ride, Spire could think of nothing but what he had seen in that hidden cellar and what it reminded him of. He was not surprised to realize that his hands were shaking; his stomach cramped and growled, though the mere thought of food was enough to make him want to retch again.

Buckingham Palace soon loomed ahead, gradually taking up the entire view out his carriage window. The hansom drew up to a rear door and Harold Spire found himself led by the stern footman through a concealed entrance, along a gilded hall, and into a tiny white room that contained only a single item: one fine chair.

The space had no windows, only a door with a panel at eye level. The footman closed the door firmly, leaving Spire alone in the cupboard of a room. "Would someone mind giving me even a partial clue as to what's going on?" Spire called, glad he had restrained from cursing when answer came, as the voice was a familiar one.

"Hello, Mr. Spire," was the reply from the other side of the wall.

Lord Black.

Spire wanted to spill all the information about the case, as

Black had been critical to its culmination, but would hardly do so across a wall.

"Give me a moment, Mr. Spire, if you please." Spire then heard two voices beyond the threshold, talking about him. Neither man bothered to lower his voice; obviously they did not care if they were overheard.

* * * * *

"Humble thanks, my dear Lord Denbury," Lord Black said, bowing his blond head to the handsome young man with eerie blue eyes seated next to him in the lavish palace receiving room. The immaculately dressed gentlemen each held a snifter of the finest brandy. "Firstly, for the use of your Greenwich estate. Her Majesty is most grateful to have a place where her scientists and doctors may be safe and undisturbed as they study the mysteries of life and death."

"Provided your aim is always the health of humankind rather than personal gain, you shall have my support, milord," the young man said, bowing his black-haired head in return. "That house has . . . too many memories," he added. "I love my New York mansion far more."

"Ah, yes!" Lord Black leaned forward with great interest. "New York . . ."

"My wife is a consummate New Yorker, born and raised," Denbury said with a smile. "I see the city as I see her: bold, opinionated, and beautiful. I love it. You should visit."

Black nodded. "I plan to. Secondly, I must thank you for coming here on vague bidding."

"I hate secrets," the young man said in a cautious tone. "After all I've been through."

"Of course." Lord Black spoke with quiet gravity. "So let me be direct with you now. I need a chief of security services for those scientists and doctors and I'd like your . . . expertise in determining character. I understand you . . . *see* it like none other."

Lord Denbury sighed wearily but nodded. Both men rose; Lord Black opened the eye-level panel in the door and bade the other look through.

"His name is Harold Spire," Black said. "What do you make of him?"

The man in question, seated on the velvet chair in the white room, wore a modest black suit. Scowling, he rested his hands in his lap. His green cravat gave the impression of having been hastily tied; it was rumpled and a bit askew. There were smudges upon his suit as if he'd encountered dust or soot and there was a dark stain on his cuff. At a median British height with light brown hair, Spire's average appearance might be gamesome, possibly even handsome, if the scowl didn't make him somewhat of a bulldog.

"What do you see?" Black murmured to his companion.

"Well," Lord Denbury began matter-of-factly. "He's had a terrible day by the look of him. He bears a general white aura with hints of blue, which represents that he means well and is at heart a good man, untroubled and unbiased by exterior forces. He will do the right and moral thing. Provided that is what you want, Lord Black, you and he should not be at cross purposes."

Lord Black smiled as he shut the observation panel. "I assure you, my friend, that I want what is moral, just, and fair."

"I see the same light about you," the dark-haired man replied. "But should those colors change, you'll no longer have my friendship. I'm sorry if that seems harsh, but the trials of the last two years have inured me to niceties.

"Is that all, milord? I've left my dear wife anxiously awaiting her surprise: a trip to Paris. She's impossible when she's impatient . . . and she's never patient," he added with a smile that spoke of the throes of young love.

Black chuckled. "Indeed, you are released and I cannot thank you enough. Safe travels to you and yours."

Denbury bowed his head and strode away, escorted by an immaculately clad footman.

Black turned to his aide. "Tell Her Majesty that Mr. Spire passed the test."

Lord Black hadn't told Lord Denbury that the scientists and doctors stationed at Rosecrest, the Denbury estate, had recently gone missing, along with the security chief assigned to them. If the cable he'd received from a contact in America was to be believed, the Americans weren't having a good time of it either. He had to wonder if the incidents were related, somehow. Impossible as that seemed.

He turned as a rustle of skirts heralded the formidable presence coming his way.

"Ah, Your Majesty." Lord Black bowed low to the diminutive sovereign. Her stern face with its round cheeks was framed in white lace while the rest of her was engulfed in black taffeta, dripping beads of Whitby jet. "Spire has been cleared."

* * * * *

Spire waited, not entirely patiently, for several minutes before Lord Black opened the door and gestured for him to leave the tiny, plain room. Eager to bring the handsome, slender, fine-featured blonde up to date, Spire began, "Tourney, Lord Black—it's done. But what I found—"

Black held up a hand. His tense smile flexed the scar that ran from above his right eyebrow down into his cheek. Spire often wondered about the origin of that scar, but never asked. "Good work, Spire. The queen awaits you. But first . . ."

The sour-faced footman stepped up with a black suit coat in hand. "You look as though you've traversed every layer of Dante's inferno," the man said.

"Oh, just come right out and say I look like hell," Spire muttered, staring at Lord Black. "I *saw* hell. It's worse than anything you could have imagined."

The footman grabbed his sooty coat and slid it off his arms, then muscled on the fresh jacket though it in no way fit. Spire feared he'd split the seams with the least shift of his shoulders, which were far too broad for the fine fabric. The too-short sleeves didn't entirely hide the patch of blood on his shirt cuff. Shuddering at the memory of where he'd acquired the stain, Spire tried to tuck it out of sight. Black nodded Spire toward the receiving room.

He was shown in wordlessly; the door closed quietly behind him.

The surreality of Harold Spire's day was heightened by the lavish setting of Buckingham Palace, worlds away from his life and laughable when compared to the horror of his morning duties. He'd passed around the outside of the building during parades and once had visited the main foyer, but never before had he gained entrance to one of the receiving rooms. It was full of things; lacquered things, mirrored and crystalline things, tasseled and brocaded things. Strains of music wafted into the tall, bright room, perhaps from a ballroom: a string quartet playing Bach. Spire preferred dark-paneled rooms filled with books. And good whiskey. And Chopin. And a coat that fit.

"Your Highness," Spire said, paying due deference to Her Majesty Queen Victoria, who stood facing away from him, hand upon the crest of a large armchair, turned toward a tall window with lace curtains partly drawn. Spire stepped forward, noticing that the marble-topped writing desk beside the queen was covered with maps of New York City and schematics for an ocean liner. A telegraph machine sat silent on the desktop, gleaming in the sunlight.

"Mr. Spire," she began without turning to look at him, speaking in a grand way that left no room for interruption, "I have called you here to give you an appointment. You rose quickly through the ranks of the Metropolitan Police. I've been assured you are fair and just, keen to recognize patterns and aberrations that catch criminals, swift and smooth with your decisions. But perhaps too quick to *spy*."

Spire felt heat rise in his face; he glanced into the golden-framed mirror on the wall next to him and saw his fair skin had colored all the way up to the roots of his light brown hair.

"I was afraid that's what this was about. Please, your Highness, I've personally apologized to the prime minister and to Miss Everhart. A cloaked female utilizing secret passages within a subsection of Parliament does seem suspicious, surely—" He hoped he didn't sound whiny.

"As you know, that was to hide the fact that the P.M. had employed a *lady* as his chief bookkeeper. Imagine the outcry. But this isn't about the prime minister or his employees. You come highly recommended by Lord Black." She turned around at last. Her eyes were shrouded by dark lenses connected by a curving filigree bridge. He must have looked quizzical, because she paused and said, "Lenses cut from a scrying glass, in hopes I'll see the dead."

When Spire simply nodded, the queen cocked her head. "Not *him*, necessarily," she scoffed. "I know what you're thinking."

That the queen still dressed in mourning for her husband, Prince Albert, many years deceased, and entertained all sorts of ideas of how to contact him—not to mention sleeping beside a picture of him and placing out his fresh clothes each day—had become a quiet joke in the realm.

"What am I thinking, Your Majesty?" Spire asked innocently.

"Oh, come now"—she batted her hand in irritation—"it's as if you all think I go about dragging his coffin behind me everywhere I go."

"I thought I saw parallel scratches on the wooden floor," Spire said, gesturing down the hall. "That explains it." He smiled.

The queen tried to scowl but instead coughed a laugh. She removed her glasses, piercing him with a stare. The short, plump-cheeked woman was downright disconcerting when she deployed her steely gaze. She was *Empress,* after all.

"What is *wrong* with you, Mr. Spire? You look dreadful and you need a better tailor."

"I came direct from a crime scene, Your Majesty, my apologies. I thought your gentleman explained—"

"Ah, yes, yes, Tourney and the resurrectionist ring. Tell me, how large of an operation do you deem it?"

"Between the financial speculation and the body snatching, I imagine it may be a wide net. The ledger we found will condemn the ring, though there was a . . ." He trailed off, unsure how much of the dreadful scene to speak of. The Queen simply stared at him expectantly. At last he swallowed back a wave of sour saliva and continued, "A peculiar crest was discovered. . . . Well, it all had a ring of . . . ritual to it, Your Majesty."

The queen snapped her head to the side and it was only then that Spire noticed Black had slipped into the room behind him. "Ascertain that crest," she snarled. "If it remains from Moriel's tenure, I want them all to hang." Lord Black nodded reassuringly. Spire was pleased the queen was taking the matter as seriously as she should.

"Mr. Spire," the queen said, "I am about to tell you a state secret known only to a few. The Eterna Compound was first sought in America after the assassination of President Lincoln. A bold idea, born of grief. I well understand Mrs. Lincoln's woes. A small team of theorists made no progress in their research until two years ago. But now there is a fresh impasse. As I have full faith in *my* realm, I believe we can fix the Americans' mistakes and make the compound viable."

"May I ask what the Eterna Compound is, Your Majesty?"

"A cure for death. A drug that confers immortality. I've had a team compiling information and studying the idea for years."

Spire kept his face unreadable, his skepticism hidden. "And do we? Have the cure for death?"

The queen shook her head. "Our plant within the operation has not reported as scheduled. We hope to retrieve information and material from New York; material that you, Mr. Spire, will safeguard. Other Special Branches of investigation and prosecution will counter various political threats. *Your* division, Omega, will counter the greatest threat of all: a nation that could make its leader immortal. We cannot allow America to gain the upper hand in immortality. I empathize with Mrs. Lincoln but have no desire to confront an utterly impervious American president."

Lord Black stepped forward and spoke carefully. "The British operation is . . . paused. Our facility was recently compromised. You will safeguard fresh intelligence and a new team, in offices that are presently being prepared. You must focus on life and death in a whole new way, Mr. Spire. All other matters of mundane police work must be cast off to the fellows you leave behind at the Metropolitan Police."

Spire reeled. This appointment was a nightmare. The queen had the wrong man. Spire didn't believe a word of any of this. A cure for death? How could he manage an operation he couldn't take seriously? He broached the only comfort he could cling to, the resolution of the horror he'd faced.

"But today's findings were hardly *mundane*; the work not of mere Burkes and Hares but something even more insidious. . . ." Panic threatened to overtake him as the images rose in his mind.

Lord Black stepped close and flashed Spire a look of warning as he poured whiskey from a crystal decanter into a pair of matching snifters. "Material and information will arrive from New York," Black said smoothly as he handed Spire a glass, "and your focus must be upon it, Mr. Spire. I will *personally* see to it that the Metropolitan follows every Tourney lead." From the flash of fury in the man's eyes, Spire knew Black meant what he said and recalled it was Black himself who had obtained the ledger Miss Everhart had given him. More than he'd ever have expected of an aristocrat in the House of Lords.

Spire fought the urge to drain the snifter as the queen delicately lifted a cup and saucer of tea. Then she stung him.

"That you have suffered grave loss and then been betrayed by love, and in such a way as to cost state secrets may be something a man might be ashamed of," the queen began, "but I look upon it as a gift. Your cautious care, a healthy ability to second-guess, a lack of trust, this will all be very valuable. Trust no one. Not at first."

Spire swallowed hard. The queen had most certainly read up on him. His mother's death had been a bit of a media circus at the time, and his father had done nothing to calm the frothing "journalists." Then, *Alice*. He'd been too naive to have imagined that an officer like him, assigned at that time around the Houses of Parliament and surrounding neighborhoods, would have been of interest to French agents. He'd never dreamed they'd employ a *lady*—and Alice Helms, now Madame Lourie, had easily taken advantage of him. He had been a fool and women were a source of woe.

"And so I look at the whole of your history and see the sort of solid man I can depend on, one who has been scarred in all the right places. One must build up scars in war. And we are engaged in a most unusual war here, Mr. Spire. I need you scarred. Sane. And unafraid."

Spire nodded.

"As we speak, all your belongings are being transferred to rooms in Westminster; Rochester Street, lovely accommodations unregistered and unlisted, a vast improvement from your current subsistence," the queen continued casually. "Bertram will give you the keys. You will share your address only with the most trusted members of your assigned team, and only once you have ascertained their loyalty."

"Yes, Your Majesty." Spire bristled but managed to keep his tone level. He was a private man. That persons had been in his home and uprooted his possessions made him clench his fists.

"Lord Black will see to your new offices. Tell your Metropolitan fellows nothing save that you've been transferred. You'll liaise further with a contact at the British Museum."

"With all due respect, Your Majesty," Spire offered quietly, "I cannot in good faith abandon the Tourney case."

"I insist that you do," she replied stridently.

Spire swallowed hard. He would not disobey the queen. Not to her face. Instead he changed the subject.

"Your Majesty, I'm sorry, I have to ask, considering the bent of this commission . . . Did my father put you up to this?"

The queen arched a brow. She was not amused. "Victor Spire?" She scoffed. "Author of penny dreadfuls, Gothic novels, and sensationalist plays? Have audience with Her Majesty the Queen?"

"Ah, no, of course not. Forgive me for bringing him up," Spire said, mustering sincerity, biting back the urge to say that he knew firsthand she had secretly attended his father's latest show; after all, his men had seen to her protection. "But a race for immortality. It sounds like something he'd serialize in Dickens' magazine."

The regent stiffened. "Dare you imply, Mr. Spire, that this position is not to be taken seriously?"

"Of course not, Your Majesty, pardon me," Spire said, bowing his head. "Unlike my father, I have retained appreciation only for the concrete, tactile, apprehendable, and solvable."

"Apply those very principles going forward, Mr. Spire." The queen clapped her hands once. Her serious, jowled face grew even more intense. "Tell your father his last novel was dreadful."

"You read it, Your Majesty?"

"Every word," she said with exaggerated disdain. "Truly *dreadful* stuff."

"Agreed, Your Majesty."

"Good-bye, Mr. Spire. Good luck and do good work."

Spire bowed his head as the regent swept away amid the clicking of beads and the swishing of silk. The sour-faced footman showed him out a different door, first retrieving the excellent, though too small, coat and, with a curled lip, handing over Spire's soot-stained jacket as well as a brass key with a number on the fob.

Stuffing the key to a whole new existence into the pocket of his long, black, velvet-trimmed, fitted coat, Spire couldn't deny he was curious. He could go examine the place, test the walls, see if they'd granted him hidden compartments and revolving bookcases. Hopefully there was a wine cellar.

To leaven his darkening mood Spire lost himself as he loved to do: in the smoky, sooty, horse-befouled, hustling chaos of London proper, reveling in the onslaught of sensory input that drowned out all concerns, doubts, and anxiety. The crashing, audible waves of London always trumped the drumming of the mind; the roaring aorta churning the very heart of the world won out every time over one's own racing pulse. He let the chaos of London in like a man might smoke an opium pipe, allowing the high to carry him about the city on a cloud of stimuli.

Spire trailed a nervous man in a brown greatcoat for two miles simply for the sake of proving he could do so unnoticed. He chose his subject after overhearing him lie to a pretty girl leaning out the window of a brougham—narrowing in on one conversation out of the melee, it was as though Spire could hear a single, subtle line of dissonance in a rollicking symphony. The young man sent the blushing, giggling girl off, saying he was going west. Instead he took off east, stuffing his hands in his pockets, a sheen of moisture over his lip.

It wasn't that Spire assumed everyone was guilty of something, but years of honing perceptions, translating body language, reading movement and expression, ascertaining habits, casting judgments, all made him suspicious of nearly everyone at first glance. Trust no one, the queen had said. Spire had abided by that edict for years, ever since Alice . . . Since her, he hardly trusted himself.

Now he was being entrusted with state secrets coming from the highest channels. Ridiculous ones at that. Should he have said outright that he didn't believe in the supernatural? Skepticism had its uses. If the queen needed him to be a believer, she should have asked him.

That the man in the brown coat went into a jewelry shop and came out with an engagement ring—Spire had leaned against the shop window on Farringdon Road to eavesdrop upon the conversation with the clerk—filled him with a certain joy. He loved to be proven wrong. It didn't happen often enough. And if he didn't treasure those instances when the brighter side of humanity showed its face, he'd have to throw himself in the Thames.

He doubted the sights of that basement would ever leave his thoughts, and offered something of a prayer upward, toward an entity he regarded with as much skepticism as he did anything outside his own mind and body, hoping something about his new appointment might make for the ability to seek out further answers. For what could drive creatures to do such horrific things if they were not possessed, maddened, by the intrigue of life and death?

Regardless of motive or madness, to the point of risking treason, he'd hardly abandon the case.

CHAPTER

TWO

New York City, 1882

The tumult of New York harbor was deafening. There was confusion, concern, even panic on the docks at the tip of Manhattan Island. Ahead of Clara, as she looked out past schooners and ferry boats, lay the first tier of the pedestal that would eventually host Bartholdi's Lady Liberty . . . if New York could ever pay for her. Clara thought with a profound sadness that perhaps Liberty would never lift her lamp high over the water, not if all those warships meant anything.

A fleet of Britain's warships, the Union Jack flying high and proud upon every mast: the world's greatest navy, amassing at the tip of America's greatest city. A dread chill coursed through Clara's veins and she clutched her shawl tighter around her neck.

England would make America theirs after all. A colony it simply could not let go.

The act of a monarchy that could never die.

Never die.

"Wake up!"

Clara's eyes shot open as she bolted upright. The ruffles of her nightdress, which she'd bunched up around her neck during her nightmare, fell back down in a splay of fine layered lace.

Given the words that had roused her, Clara Templeton expected the visitor to be sitting at the foot of the wide bed she had once hoped to share with Louis Dupris. But the visionary

young chemist and theorist had died yesterday, and the voice
was not the visitor's but a renewed urging from beyond. More
was being asked of her than mere living.

She had returned from the park to the Pearl Street town
house she shared with her guardian, Senator Rupert Bishop.
Having written a note stating her instinctual certainty that
something terrible had happened to the team, Clara slid the
sheet of paper under the door of Bishop's study and locked
herself in her room. She'd have ignored his orders that she
never visit the laboratory site if she'd thought anything
could've been done. But the visitor had confirmed her instincts. Whatever the disaster—a fire, an explosion, an unexpected reaction of any kind—she prayed they had not
suffered.

The senator kept late hours and traveled often, his sched-
ule changing on a dime, so despite her best efforts to know
his calendar, Clara wasn't sure when he'd see her note. But
as the secrecy of the commission couldn't be broached by sending policemen to the laboratory, she needed him to decide on
their next steps.

Sunlight streamed in through the exquisite craftsmanship
of the Tiffany glass window of Clara's bedroom, through
glowing, textured milky magnolia petals that cast pale yellowish spots upon her white satin bedclothes. Turning to one
side, Clara stared into the mirror of her rosewood vanity, meeting her own terrified gaze. Waves of dark-blond hair framed
her oval face in a wild mane. With wide eyes that were more
eerily golden than they were green, and her mouth open, she
looked like a mad Pre-Raphaelite painting, Ophelia just before the drowning.

In her hand, a saffron-colored strip of fabric.

A fine silk cravat.

Louis Dupris had left it behind after one of their harried
tumbles of lips and hands and she'd been too fond of him to

return it, instead secreting it away in a compartment of her jewelry box. The amulet he had bequeathed to her and this cravat was all she had of him; she'd fallen restlessly asleep clutching it.

She rose and went to her wardrobe to begin the feminine ritual of donning innumerable layers. She opened her bedroom door for a moment to listen for sounds from elsewhere in the house, but all was silent. That was for the best, lest she spill everything to the senator in one look.

Rupert Bishop gave her everything she needed; he was her mentor and her joy. He'd taught her everything she knew and remained her spiritual counselor. Her relationship with him was complicated and nearly impossible to describe. Once he might have been her Great Love. Epic, sweeping, and all-consuming. But was that this life? She doubted so. Once she'd asked him if he felt whole.

"Frankly, I don't know," he'd mused. "This life is full of fragments. We're all torn apart."

It was not an answer, but it told her enough: she was not what he was missing. She buried her feelings. "Do you feel whole, then?" he asked her in turn.

She shook her head. But until she understood the exact shape of the puzzle-piece holes within, she did not dare pinpoint exactly what might fill them. With Rupert she had to take immaculate care. When all her school and society friends abandoned her at age thirteen, when her seizures started—none wanted to be seen or associated with such an unfortunate—Rupert was all she had. She dared not do a single thing to jeopardize that. Even calling him Rupert often felt too familiar, an intimacy she relished but one that frightened her. And so, as everyone else called him either Bishop or Senator, so did Clara, pressing love for him so deep into the recesses of her heart that it had fossilized.

Who did the visitor mean by her "missing link?"

Clara had toyed once with channeling some of her over-whelming sentiment into something productive. A novel. A memoir. She still *felt* with that ardor that, at twelve years of age, had had her blurting impossible things to powerful peo-ple. But when she tried to put her thoughts into words, the result was unwieldy and read like the scribblings of a naive schoolgirl. No reader would believe the intensity of her feel-ings; none would understand that she was a soul with every nerve ending accessible. Perhaps in childhood, all souls were similarly exposed. But grown persons were calloused; keeping a fragile heart was physically and psychically dangerous. The bounds of human flesh were finite. After all, when dead, the heart was mere flesh. Clara's material world was small, but her spirit was as vast as the sky.

So Clara did not write. Instead, she went to work. Good, honest, busy work; the salve to both emotional deficits and oversensitivities.

In the Pearl Street offices she balanced the books on the Eterna teams' expenses, ensuring fresh supplies of basic chem-icals and minerals, the most modern medical manuals and textbooks of interest, with a budget left over for items of "spir-itual" interest.

When it came to matters "paranormal," she was more di-rectly involved. She interviewed those who reported strange phenomena, then filed the results at the office. She and Sena-tor Bishop kept an eye on theatrical psychics and other spiri-tualist charlatans, warning them when they went too far in taking advantage of the grieving or bored.

Clara occasionally accompanied the senator on campaigns. She volunteered for New York City's ASPCA, a cause the Templeton clan had long championed as friends of the orga-nization's inimitable founder, Henry Bergh. She visited her parents' mausoleum in gorgeous Greenwood weekly, taking the trolley to the Gothic gates and passing the day in lavishly carved stone shade. What company could be more beautiful than those stone angels? She kept herself occupied. She needed no lovers or close friends.

Until Louis Dupris came along as the capstone to the Eterna research team and upended her entire, prematurely spinster-ish, calcified universe.

They had met at a soiree at the infamous Vanderbilt mansion. The details were emblazoned in her memory. She had stepped into a shadowy alcove, deliberately out of Bishop's line of sight, when suddenly an exceedingly handsome, olive-skinned man in a fitted black suit blocked her path.

Clara took a moment to psychically evaluate him and de-termined she was in no physical danger. His piercing hazel eyes bored into her with thrilling intensity. "You're in my way, sir," she said quietly.

"So I am. I've been instructed not to introduce myself," the man began, in a rich, deep voice. "And while I do value my new job as my life, that life would be forfeit if I did not at least tell you that you are, by far, the most interesting crea-ture in this entire room, if not this entire city. Save, perhaps, your guardian, my employer, who insisted you were quite off-limits. This would make any woman all the more fascinating were you not so utterly time-stopping on your own. I under-stand now why the senator is so protective of you."

Clara laughed. "Did my dear Bishop employ you merely for flattery?"

"No, my lady, he employed me for theory and faith. How I might apply spiritual concepts and principles into the quest of immortality as pursued by your department."

"Ah, you're one of ours!" she commented brightly. "You're new. Where do you hail from? Your accent is distinct."

"New Orleans, my lady, a distinct city indeed." He bowed. "Louis Dupris, at your service, Miss Templeton. I hope my overtures do not offend. It may be that I never speak with you again, as I value my work and the senator deeply. But there are times when a man must speak or forever regret the chance, and you evoke that prescient timeliness."

She cocked her head to the side gamesomely, the plumes of her fascinator rustling. "You should come to call, Mr. Dupris."

"I couldn't . . . I can't."

"But you should," she insisted sweetly. He looked uncomfortable. She chuckled. "In secret, then, if you're so worried about the senator's wrath." She batted her silk-gloved hand. "Come stroll with me on Tuesday, through the Greek and Roman relics at our glorious Metropolitan Museum. At two. Tell me about spiritual disciplines I know little of."

And then she'd had a seizure. Right in middle of the Vanderbilts' home.

Whenever too many ghostly voices or psychic phenomena pressed in upon her at once, Clara had an "episode." Generally her body gave her an aura of warning and she would exit a place before any damage was done. Distracted by the party, by Louis, by all the glamour and finery, she'd missed the telltale signs. She hadn't had a "fit" in years and was more mortified than ever by the condition she'd been fighting since the age of thirteen. While she knew she had nothing to be ashamed of, the world wasn't so generous. Especially not at a Vanderbilt party.

Bishop had taken her home immediately and Clara had assumed she had seen the last of Louis Dupris. That she had gone to the museum on Tuesday spoke of her essentially optimistic nature—and her fondness for the museum's marble halls.

To her great surprise, Mr. Dupris was entirely undeterred by her ignominious departure from the Vanderbilts'. He met her at the museum at the appointed time, and at every place and time they could find after that. Happily, the great city abounded with secluded spaces. Cemeteries became their collective haunt as they mused on life and death. Clara sensed that her soul and Louis's had gone round together at least once in the past. He hadn't betrayed or brutalized her then, so why not indulge the blossoming bond in this life?

Louis found her seizures, the aura she saw, the way her senses abandoned her and returned in pieces, entirely fascinating. His acceptance won her trust. He taught her how to block out the spiritual press, lessons born from his own studies of spiritual and theological matters. She had, after his tutelage, been fit-free for two years.

He was her visionary, insatiably curious and confidently ambitious. No matter what other matters called to his attention, he remained enthralled with Clara, and she with him. Now he was dead and she had no way to quantify the grief she felt, no way to show it, for she and Louis Dupris had never even met, as far as the outside world was concerned.

She would have to, she realized, live her current life denied of many things. Her heart hardened. It had to. While she knew, as a spiritualist, that the spirit lived on, death had made her cold. She thought of Greenwood's stone angels and wanted to become one of them.

The Eterna team was dead. Did anyone know, other than Clara?

She tucked the saffron cravat into her corset, against her bosom, and set off to be the center of the presaged storm.

* * * * *

"It was as I feared," said Louis Dupris as he trailed his brother Andre through downtown Manhattan at the crack of dawn, floating a foot off the ground.

Andre tore down Broadway, surely appearing mad talking to thin air; thin, cold air in the shape of his twin. . . . He shuddered. He could not begin to process the horror he'd seen.

"Don't tell me you *predicted* that hell that took you?"

Andre growled at the ghost, a gray-shaded, near-transparent image of his brother. "Your whole team? I can't begin to understand—"

"*Something* was in that house. We were not alone. But what it was, or why our compounds made it come alive, I can't understand. Perhaps, in death," Louis continued excitedly, "I can learn more! Perhaps here I can do more good, in this state—"

"I'd rather you were alive," Andre said mordantly. "That we'd traded places."

"Don't say that, brother," Louis exclaimed earnestly.

Perhaps Louis would have agreed to the switch if he knew the whole truth; that for many months, Andre had been spying on Eterna on behalf of England.

"Perhaps your partner Malachi's rabid paranoia was founded," Andre muttered. "You're right, you were not alone there. You were certainly being watched, and not only by me."

In a fit of overwhelming paranoia, one of the researchers had ordered the Eterna theorists to move their laboratory into his eerily empty town house. They humored him to keep a fragile peace. Louis had Andre store his most precious notes and research in another location, trust swiftly eroding between the once-filial team. Disaster struck the very next day.

Andre would never be able to purge the memories of the Eterna researchers falling to the floor, suffocated by strange, creeping tendrils of smoke, by a presence that Andre didn't wait around to experience for himself. No, Andre did what he'd always done as the black sheep no one spoke about— he ran. But lest he go to his own grave an utter coward, he would do his best to help his brother find peace.

"Today we begin to set things right," Andre declared, brandishing a small envelope. He moved at a harried clip that was not unusual for New York, though his anxiety trumped the speed of the average pedestrian out at such an early hour. "I'll turn this over, then return that damned dagger you stole to New Orleans, praying to all your *mystères* for protection along the way."

"Don't mock the *mystères,* brother," Louis scolded.

"I'll believe in them if they protect me against one very angry woman," Andre retorted. "Of all the people you crossed coming to New York, it had to be a Laveau protégée? *Bon dieu!* I suppose it's only fitting penance I be the one to see this through."

"You're not the irredeemable sinner you think, Andre—"

"But I am!" Andre insisted in a coarse whisper. "I lied to you, Louis! I wasn't interested in Eterna because of you, but for my own interests. You gave me secret refuge and I squandered it. Trust me, I've a lot to answer for. Slates must be cleaned. Yours and mine. But someone should know what happened to you, Louis," Andre stated. "Your sweetheart, perhaps? You adored her, that woman deserves answers—"

"Keep Clara out of it," Louis warned, an icy whisper in Andre's ear, "with her condition, I shouldn't—"

"I'll leave the key. If they're as clever as you say, they can figure out what it belongs to without incriminating me. And then I'll be on my way home, none the wiser for my presence."

Louis's anxiety was unassuaged. "You hid my papers as I asked, didn't you?"

"I left what you gave me at the college," Andre assured. Whether or not he'd be telling his employers about the materials or the disaster, he had yet to decide. He wanted to wash his hands of all of it, be done with spying. But survival first. Strategy second.

Andre stared up at the Romanesque edifice, dark and looming in the early light. Louis's presence was a cold draft at his neck. The living man shifted the envelope from one hand to the other, considering his task. The door was locked. Andre flipped back the thick cuff of his sleeve to reveal several thin metal implements. In mere moments the lock had been picked and the door swung wide.

"Do I want to know where you learned that?" spectral Louis murmured.

"The bad egg survives," Andre muttered.

Charging up to the third floor, Andre threw wide a wooden door to reveal a long dark room whose decor looked more a lady's parlor than an office. Depositing the envelope conspicuously in an empty tray, he sped out again. "Onward toward resolution," he rallied. "And vanishing from the record."

He darted out onto Pearl Street, tipped a wide-brimmed hat lower over his brow and turned back to see Louis floating in front of the building, his grayscale form immeasurably eerie in the misty, waterfront dawn. After a moment, he wafted to Andre's side.

"There's so much Clara and I should have shared," Louis murmured.

Andre shifted on his feet. "You never told her about me, did you?"

"No," Louis insisted. "You came to me in trouble. I never told her I had a twin or betrayed your confidence."

"And I never deserved a brother so good, loyal, and true," Andre said bitterly, for the first time feeling tears well up. He wouldn't tell England another word, he decided.

In the tumultuous, heaving throng, the sheer, maddening bustle that was New York Harbor, Andre made his way through a deep maze of wood and steel, planks, ropes, and sail. One small leather pack slung over his back, a precious ceremonial dagger well-hidden on his person, he wove swiftly to the docks. Louis floating beside him, traveling right through anyone in his way . . . persons who would think him nothing but a breath of cool breeze.

Despite Andre's speed and twisting path, he noticed that a

particular face was never far from him in the throng. Even crowded onto the ship that should have carried him safely away, his desire to vanish was thwarted. The follower spoke to the captain in a soft, upper-class British accent. And stared right at Andre where he stood among the massed humanity on deck.

"Damn you, Lord Black, and your spies," Andre muttered. "Damn you all to hell."

* * * * *

Franklin Fordham lived alone in the stately, Federal-style Brooklyn Heights house the rest of his family had abandoned after his brother's death in the war, his mother having found it impossible not to be haunted by the place. Franklin bore his own suffering like a pebble in his shoe that he never removed. His brother was dead and Franklin hadn't been there, fighting at his side, due to a bad leg. Living in the home they had once shared was a form of penance.

At a sharp rap, he opened the town house door to a most lovely, welcome sight.

There, framed by dappled sunlight filtering through the growing trees behind her, beneath a rose lace parasol, was the woman who had once cut through darkness and saved Franklin's mind, like an angel descending through storm clouds.

Clara Templeton was dressed beguilingly as ever, today all in burgundy; a black-buttoned jacket with fitted sleeves over gathered, doubled skirts, a small black riding hat with a burgundy ribbon set at a jaunty angle on her head. Despite her broad shoulders, she was slight in girth, yet Franklin knew she was capable of great strength. As he looked at a face more suited to a classic painting of an infamous woman from history than to this era's praised softness, he noted that she seemed unusually drawn. The oft-mischievous slant of her pursed lips seemed strained and her luminous green-gold eyes were hidden behind small, tinted glasses.

Not for the first time, Franklin thought that Clara was a magical creature. It wasn't that she was beautiful, though an argument could be made for her unusual beauty, it was that she was lit from within by an indomitable fire, both terrifying and wonderful.

"Miss Templeton," he greeted her with a smile. "To what do I owe this pleasure on a day off?"

"They're dead, Franklin," she said quietly, each word like the faraway toll of a bell. "The whole team is dead."

Franklin stared at her. "What? How? How do you know?"

"I simply know that they are gone," she continued in a deadened tone. "And this morning I had a dream that in the near future the English would invade."

"Well then," Franklin said, turning to the wardrobe by the door to withdraw a lightweight brown frock coat, hat, gloves, and an eagle-topped walking stick. Clara's dreams and instincts were serious business he'd learned not to trifle with.

When he was properly attired and had exited the house, she took his proffered arm; he noticed she leaned upon it more than usual.

"We must do whatever we can *not* to embolden them, as their Empire seeks ever to expand," Clara declared.

"And what would so embolden Her Majesty Queen Victoria as to take on such an ally in trade, finance, goods, and culture?" Franklin asked. "We've never had so cordial a relationship."

"If she thought she could live forever," Clara muttered.

"Aye." Franklin sighed. "That's the crux. Eterna is . . . eternal."

"Perhaps," Clara murmured.

Franklin wished he understood the pain in her voice. Though she undoubtedly would mourn the death of any person, she didn't know the Eterna researchers personally. Why then, was her grief so apparent?

"I don't suppose you've your office key?" she asked. "I'm a bit . . . distracted." Franklin fished in his pocket, making a jingling sound. Clara offered a weak smile. "Always prepared," she said approvingly. "I adore that about you."

Franklin contemplated myriad things he could have replied, but said none. They set off down the picturesque, cobblestone street where young trees, planted within the past few years, were flourishing and fine new town houses were being built. The residents proudly loved their separate city of Brooklyn. When they looked across the water at behemoth, monstrous Manhattan, many thanked their stars for their few blocks of haven.

Clara and Franklin strolled toward the Fulton Ferry landing, beside the vast stone trunks of the nearly completed Brooklyn Bridge. Its Gothic arches towered in the sky—it was the tallest man-made structure on this side of the world, its spiderweb of cables catching dreams and hearts and possibilities in its wire-bound frame. The bridge was scheduled to open next year, on Queen Victoria's birthday, funnily enough—to the chagrin of those countless Irish laborers who built it. The structure would unite two thriving cities with distinctly different identities but perhaps similar obsessions.

The skyline of Manhattan was growing like a brick-and-mortar weed, ever vertically, ever uptown, like a sprawling cobblestone flower over which thousands of ship insects docked and buzzed, dipping into its jagged petals and sailing off again along the choppy harbor currents.

Clara broke the silence. "It's my fault they died."

Franklin shook his head. "You can't think like that."

"I've been trying to convince myself that the government, if it wanted to safeguard its leaders, would have come to this eventually. But Eterna was my idea. I am responsible, at least in part. The child in me wants to hide. But if I do, we may find things stolen out from under us."

They boarded the steam ferry, jostling for a place near the captain's cabin so they wouldn't be pressed shoulder to shoulder. Franklin didn't like to be by the edge and wasn't terribly fond of ships. Clara stared down at the churning East River currents while Franklin looked at the masts of passing ships that cluttered one of the world's busiest harbors.

"Miss Templeton," he began carefully, about to pose the age-old question she wouldn't answer. "Will you tell me?"

Her nostrils flared. "Really?" she said through clenched teeth. "*Now,* Franklin?"

"You promised that when it was truly important, you'd tell me how you found me in that mental ward years ago. The team is dead and I don't understand," Franklin insisted. "All the research we've compiled and still, little to nothing makes sense, I'm at a breaking point—"

"What I know of you won't solve life's confusion," she countered bitterly, "and the team will still be dead!"

"Maybe it doesn't matter to you how you found me," Franklin murmured, tapping his walking stick nervously on the wooden deck, "but it matters to me."

"Of course it matters how I find the important people in my life!" Clara snapped. She sighed, lowering her voice when ferry passengers in plumes, ribbons, and top hats turned toward her agitated tone. "But often telling them kills something inside me, some mystery I've kept alive."

"You like the mystery," Franklin argued. "I don't."

The haunted look bloomed on her face again; Franklin hated seeing it, for it made her seem a thousand years old. She had an air of gravity far beyond her years, much like her guardian the senator; it unnerved him when displayed so plainly.

"You'll learn to enjoy mystery one day, Franklin," Clara murmured. "Treasure it, even. When there's mystery, you might still be wrong. I've been right about too many sad things."

"Your mysteries changed my life for the better and I yearn to know why," he pleaded. "Out of all the people who need help in this world, why me?"

"You still feel you don't deserve it," Clara said sadly. "Because of your brother."

Franklin looked away and shrugged. "I doubt Ed would've wanted me to feel guilty."

Clara looked around her with a heavy sigh. "And on a ship, no less," she muttered, and took a deep breath. "There's a recurring dream where you're always in a storm, on a ship, dangling from a rope, and you're afraid no one can hear you screaming?"

Franklin's eyes widened. "Yes, how did you—"

"Think for a moment about the ship. Do you remember a flag?"

"Yes. White," Franklin said excitedly. "With yellow. A crest. Yellow fleur-de-lis?"

"The standard of the King of France." Clara stared at him and he could feel her piercing gaze even from behind tinted glass. "You were the bosun on that ship and I was your captain. I heard you against the horrid gale; I hoisted you back on deck and you were suitably grateful."

Franklin stared at her; as always, she spoke in an unflinching way about a previous life. She hadn't shared many of them, but the ones she had, Franklin didn't dare question, though he wondered how she could recall details he was unaware of.

"I sometimes visited with Mrs. Lincoln, after Eterna was underway," Clara continued, "and she would ask for news around the country, of those still grieving their dead, of fellow broken souls. Her soul and mind were so wounded, commiseration made her feel more whole. A servant brought in your picture, with a letter explaining how your mind had been wrecked by the loss of your brother in the war. I recognized your picture, because that recurring dream haunted me, too.

When I saw your image, I knew that I had kept that dream so that I'd remember to find you in this life."

"And again rescue me from a storm," Franklin murmured mournfully. "This time a storm of my mind. I wish I wasn't the one who always needed saving." The ferry docked and passengers began spreading like ink onto the shore and up into the veins of narrow, curving Manhattan streets. They followed the current. "Maybe I can save you someday."

"Maybe that's what this life is for!" Clara said with a hollow laugh, hoisting up her skirts and jumping from the deck onto the dock, never letting feminine finery get in the way of an active spirit no matter how much the fashion of the age tried to limit her sex. He stared after her for a moment, then took a few quick strides, limping slightly on his bad leg, to catch up with her.

"If you'll let anyone," he said as they turned onto Pearl Street.

"Beg your pardon?" Clara said, climbing the brownstone stoop of their building.

"If you'll let anyone save you. I've never met a more independent soul in all my life, Miss Templeton. It's like you don't need family, friends, a lover—" Franklin fell silent as Clara scowled at him, snatching the keys from his hand and opening the door, blowing past the first two floors where the Manhattan County Clerk kept records.

Franklin in her wake, she stormed upstairs and threw wide the double doors to her offices. She froze on the threshold. The wide, long office, which might heretofore have been mistaken for a hoarder's den or art museum vault, was *very* clean.

Tall, sturdy wooden file cabinets now stood between her beloved floor lamps of cutting-edge Tiffany studios provenance, their stained-glass domes lighting controversial Pre-Raphaelite-style paintings upon maroon-painted walls above dark mahogany paneling. Metal sorting trays sat upon the three hefty wooden desks in the room, their plain rectangularity a sharp contrast with the curves of the lily pad and peacock-feather desk lamps; more Tiffany.

"Franklin . . ." Clara began, with a rising pitch to her voice as if panic were barely being held at bay. "An eclectic, lived-in, *meaningful* office makes me feel safe and protected. How can I find anything with everything put away?"

"I *organized*," Franklin assured her. "Nothing's gone, merely sorted. You know what mess does to me. I assure you everything is safe. Safer than it was when your towers of paperwork leaned perilously close to the flames of your beloved stained-glass gas lamps. The whole place could've gone up in a minute."

"Where are my window talismans?" she said slowly, stepping into the room and gesturing to the clean, empty panes of her curving bay window where pendants, amulets, gems, crystals, dream catchers, and leaded-glass icons had all floated behind her wide leather desk chair. "I told you not to touch them. They are of extreme spiritual importance and are there because of my . . . condition."

"They were collecting considerable dust," he replied gently, as if afraid to wake a dragon. "And several of them fell, all at once. We can put them back up," he said reassuringly.

"When?" Her voice had grown even more shrill. "When did they fall?"

"Yesterday," Franklin answered quietly, aware of the significance of his answer.

"When the team died . . ." she said with a choking hitch in her voice. "Perhaps it's best, then, that this place is clean."

Her frown deepened as she went to her desk, a great carved rosewood beast at the center of the office. Behind her was the bay window in which she often curled up to take a nap, or read, or simply stare down at Pearl Street; Franklin wondering all the while what was going on in that uncharted mind of hers.

Fishing in a small beaded reticule hanging from a ribbon at her waist, her gloved fingers plucked out a small silver key. Unlocking her center desk drawer, she withdrew a file and set it on her blotter. Her gaze, still hidden behind the small tinted frames, fell upon something further inside and Franklin had the sudden impression of an arrested engine.

Slowly, she sank into the high-backed, thronelike leather chair. A shaking hand pulled out a small, white bit of paper as her shoulders hunched forward, curving slightly over the open drawer, unable to contract more than her corset would allow. She held the folded paper, hands pressed as if in prayer, brought her steepled fingers to her lips, and bowed her head.

"Pardon me, Miss Templeton," Franklin murmured in the strained silence, desperate to say something. "What I said before was too bold, about your life, I don't—"

"Know what's gotten into the polite, soft-spoken partner I once knew?" she retorted sharply. "I don't either. Please go find that man and return him to this office."

"Yes, Miss Templeton. I'm sorry."

"I don't mind being told I'm independent," she continued vehemently. "I am. But when *man*kind thinks there's something wrong with that, I chafe."

"There isn't anything wrong," Franklin said, eager to diffuse her anger, but she bowled over him with a mounting fury.

"You say I act as if I don't need friends or family, are you not my friend? Is the senator not family? And just because I don't talk about a lover doesn't mean I haven't had one." Her fingers reached up beneath her glasses—was she crying? That would be a first for Franklin to see. "Ugh. *Sentiment.*" She tossed the mysterious note back into her desk, closed and locked the drawer.

Franklin had never seen her as anything but a composed coworker; compiling literature on any reference to curing death, chatting with extraordinary—if not oft unhinged—persons, scanning communications, sending ears into the field, keeping an eye out for promising discoveries and innovators. He'd not seen anything truly affect her—not visibly. He knew she trusted very few and kept mostly to herself. For a sensitive, Franklin was surprised at how very steeled she seemed. Perhaps there were infinitely more layers to her than he could have imagined; lifetimes of lessons deepening the magnetic nature of her old soul.

"There now. Am I more human to you?" Clara asked with a bitter smile. "Surely my tears make me more a woman. Quick. Go tell all the men who have ever insulted me, they'll be so pleased."

"Miss Templeton." Franklin looked at the floor again. "I'd never delight in your pain."

He chided himself for pressing her. Clara Templeton liked clever gentlemen with whom she could verbally fence, generally best, and leave staring after her. He'd watched her flirt with countless gentlemen if it suited her cause, and he'd once wondered if she was capable of anything beyond that arch distance. Perhaps that note, whatever it was, proved differently.

"Stop pouting, Franklin," Clara said with a laugh. Her bite never lasted long, a quality that he appreciated deeply. "I know you want to play the rescuing hero to all the world. In due time, surely." She squinted at something that suddenly caught her eye. "Franklin, are we not the only ones with keys to this floor?"

"We are," Franklin replied, following her gaze.

"Then what, pray tell, is *that*?"

Across the room, jutting from a metal tray that was commonly used for incoming correspondence, was a yellow envelope that she was sure had not been there before.

Clara crossed the room, picked up the envelope, and carried it to Franklin's desk. Seizing the engraved letter opener from the fine desk set his mother had proudly given him upon his appointment to "government work," Clara swiftly slit open the envelope, which was bulky at the base.

Glancing inside, in the next instant Clara gasped sharply and dropped both letter opener and envelope. She took a step back as the items clattered onto the wooden surface of the desk. Franklin could now see that the envelope held a key. A dark smear marred the metal surface.

Blood.

Franklin reached for the key.

"Franklin," Clara cautioned. "Don't touch it."

"I'd like to feel useful for a moment," he declared, just before the soiled, black iron key disappeared into his fist.

He closed his eyes, feeling the metal heat up in his palm and the familiar pain flare at the back of his skull. He saw a plain, redbrick town house with brownstone details. A number: fourteen. He heard screaming. He saw plumes of odd-colored smoke from beneath the garden-level door. A man in a black suit came tearing out, holding a kerchief over his mouth, and ran away. Smoke lifted, curling as a dark substance pooled out from under the door and dribbled down onto the landing.

Franklin opened his eyes. He could see that Clara had already guessed where the key had come from. Franklin nodded. "I know where they died."

CHAPTER

THREE

When Spire hopped into the hired hansom that arrived at the designated hour, he was startled to find Miss Everhart already seated inside.

"Don't be surprised again, Mr. Spire, please, it will grow quite tedious," she stated. "I've a good eye for numbers, research, codes, and ciphers. I'll be useful to your team—"

"I am aware of your talents, Miss Everhart," Spire replied cautiously. "Your Parliamentary employers took great pains to ensure you could do your work without bother. I don't think they'd take kindly to your abandoning it."

"Who said anything about abandoning it?" she replied sharply. "We're all doing the work of the British state, Mr. Spire."

"But not all work is meant to be shared. Especially work as dangerous as this."

"I survived thus far." Her tone was steel. "Why else do you think Lord Black put me on as Gazelle but to prove myself to you?"

"Have you been appointed to the Eterna team, then?" Spire asked directly. She nodded. "You'd truly want to work for the man who spied on you?"

She pursed her lips. "At least I know you'd keep track of me."

Spire loosed a humorless chuckle.

He couldn't let the memory of Alice cloud everything,

everyone—a whole gender. He'd need someone like Everhart; detail oriented, dogged, persistent, loyal, selfless. Fond of
work. He hated to think they'd actually have a great deal in
common; he'd set himself up to despise her for the trouble
her presence at Westminster had caused.

"Today we meet Mr. and Mrs. Blakely at the British Museum," Miss Everhart said. "They've been consulting on the
Eterna project for a while now. You'll inherit some 'staff,' as
it were, but Lord Black will flesh out your full brigade and
provide new researchers."

Spire narrowed his eyes. "Whatever happened to the previous ones, then?"

Miss Everhart swallowed and looked away, clearly uncomfortable. "No one knows. They disappeared—all four researchers and their security adviser."

"Lovely," Spire muttered. "The queen could've mentioned
that. Any leads?"

Everhart frowned. "None." There was an uncomfortable
silence. "How is Rochester Street?" she asked finally.

"Does it matter?" he replied with a shrug. "I doubt the
crown would accommodate me if I complained. I'd have liked
a bit of warning, though. And to have taken my piano."

"They moved me, too," she offered. "My cousin and I were
fond of our old place and haven't settled in yet. The trick is not
to feel like property, or like a pawn, as they shuffle you about."

"And how is that coming along for you?"

"I demanded they bring me a piano." She smiled briefly.
"And I'm slightly happier."

At this, Spire chuckled gruffly and the silence that followed
was not tense until the museum loomed before them.

* * * * *

The British Museum, large and cluttered with treasures
collected—stolen—from around the Empire, was a squat,
square, colonnaded edifice that was no gem of architecture.

The real beauty, Rose knew, lay inside, in its ever-growing cache of artifacts. Spire helped her out of the carriage, their gloved palms and arms stiff against each other.

"East wing," she instructed as she crossed the open plaza, passing among strolling tourists and locals. Comparing herself with other ladies who walked about beneath parasols, in floral shawls and frilly hats, she noticed her dark muslin layers trimmed in mauve and black didn't match the warm, bright day. She always stood out so, never quite in season, never on top of a trend. She could care less.

Spire caught up to her as she reached the building. He opened the door for her and she allowed him the courtesy. "Downstairs. Two levels. Prepare yourself," she said, and kept a smile to herself. She didn't have to be psychic to know she would see a few more raised eyebrows from Spire in the following moments.

"For what?" he asked.

"A medium. And her consort."

Spire set his jaw and followed.

On the lower floor, Rose led the way down a shadowed, chilly hall; she rapped upon an unmarked door in a specific sequence, pressed a lever, and a door opened, revealing a cavernous room filled with wall-to-wall tapestries from all around the globe. She had been there before; it was, in fact, one of her favorite places. Though she'd have added a large bay window where she could sit bathed in light, imagining herself strolling through each woven scene, experiencing the many worlds they represented, from religious icons to court scenes to theatrical presentations.

Art was a poultice that soothed her ache to travel. But unmarried women did not travel unaccompanied. Married women might travel with their husbands, but they most certainly did not work, so years ago she made her choice and shoved other longings into the corners of her steel-trap mind.

A round table took up the center of the room, wooden chairs spaced around its circumference. "Mrs. Blakely" sat there, facing the door, her eyes closed. Dressed in royal blue satin and baring more bosom than was appropriate for the hour of the day, her brown-black curls were up in an artful coiffure, a faint rouge was visible on her cheeks. Though she sat in the basement of the British Museum, the woman seemed ready for a ball. Rose had encountered the Blakeleys only a few times and had never seen them dressed in anything less than high-dramatic style.

Mr. Blakely stood nearby, a short, sharp-featured man in a black-and-white-striped linen suit and a blue cravat with a too-large bow, his fingers fluttering constantly. His ticks were offset by an engaging, near-constant smile.

"Mr. Spire, I presume? Hello, Miss Everhart," the woman at the table said, without opening her eyes.

"Pleasure to meet you, Mr. and Mrs. Blakely," Spire said, bowing his head even though Mrs. Blakely's kohl-rimmed eyes remained closed.

"Hello, Miss Knight," Rose said quietly. At the different name, Spire stared at her.

"Spire," the striking woman at the table said, "I sense you're a man who doesn't like to waste his time, particularly not on pleasantries. Good. So let's get a few things entirely clear." Her lined lids snapped open, revealing large, piercing, dark eyes. She almost looked like a doll but her appearance was off-putting, as if the soul of some wizened old regent had been thrust into a young woman's body and was still getting used to the adjustment.

"I am not legally married to Mr. Blakely," she began. "Thus I am not Mrs. Tobias Blakely. Not to you. Within our operations, you may call me Miss Knight. However, I prefer just 'Knight.'"

Spire nodded, taking in the information. "Good then. I go

by Spire and prefer this precedent. Keeps us from becoming too familiar."

"Ah. Then on *that* count, should you possibly spy upon me like you did Miss Everhart, let me make something quite clear. I prefer the company of women in every way. And while kissing a woman may be part of an operation, it is also how I might spend an evening on my own time and should not be a subject of concern or censure. Establishing one's predilections when surrounded by spies saves us all from awkward misunderstandings. You may lower your eyebrows now, Mr. Spire."

Spire did as he was told, donning his characteristic frown. Rose withheld a chuckle. Not a single Victorian soul spoke like Marguerite Knight did in mixed company. At least, no one Rose had ever met or even heard of. Mr. Blakely didn't bother to hide his grin. It was entertaining, Rose had to admit, to see a bulwark like Spire so thrown off guard. And the surprises were only beginning.

"I appreciate your honesty, Knight," Spire said without affect. "Am I to assume you'll be the one giving the orders for our operations?"

Knight waved her hand dismissively. "Oh, no, that's entirely on your head. I find giving orders terribly boring. I'll do as I please and assume it corresponds with our mutual directives." She smiled without showing teeth. "And I'll never undermine you unless you undermine me. So let's not cross each other. Because I'll see it coming." She tapped her temple.

"Well, be sure to tell me," Spire retorted, "just what it is I'll be up to. Free will is so . . . *boring*." While Spire's tone may have been sharp, there was a certain light in his eyes, the look of a duelist ready for swordplay. Knight laughed and Rose heard delight in the sound.

"I would guess you're not used to people like us, Mr. Spire, eccentric and scandalous," Knight began nonchalantly, "you're used to policemen. And Miss Everhart, you're used to clerks and officials, and so if we offend you, well—well, I'm not sorry, but I do believe we can all find common ground. It's not that I think the world should be like me. I'd rather the world not insist I should be like them."

Spire held up his hands, offering no argument. It was Rose's turn to take exception.

"You're talking to a woman, Miss Knight, who managed to gain secret passage into the Palace of Westminster to go to work," Rose said primly.

"And have I ever toasted your accomplishment? I should. I honestly meant to." Knight clapped her hands. "Champagne. My house. I've calling hours on Tuesdays. And don't worry, if it's a concern, I don't seduce coworkers." She flashed a winning smile. Rose opened her mouth and closed it again. "Indeed," Knight added, gesturing. "Often the best thing to do when confronted with someone who says shocking things is to keep silent."

"In this crowd will I ever again utter a word?" Spire muttered. Knight laughed again. "I will say," he continued, "I deem scandal relative and find this age too preoccupied with 'sin' while having a profoundly hypocritical relationship with vice. . . ." He trailed off, and Rose noticed how his determined face went haunted, as if some terrible memory took hold of him.

"Agreed!" Mr. Blakely responded enthusiastically.

Looking closely at their new leader, Knight narrowed her eyes suddenly. "You haven't told your father you've moved or that you've a new position," she scolded. "You'll need to tend to that, lest he write a play about it." Spire opened his mouth and then closed it again as Rose had done. "I am clairvoyant, Mr. Spire. I pick up on things. There go your eyebrows again."

"Get out of my mind," Spire growled, seeming genuinely

unsettled. He whirled on Rose. "Did you tell her about my father?"

"You haven't said a thing to me about your father, what business would that be of mine?" Rose said defensively. Spire scowled.

Miss Knight shifted forward suddenly and said; "Pardon me, friends, duty calls and I must leave you. There's a mummy requiring my attention on the next floor. His spirit is in the throes of anger."

In a rustle of shimmering sapphire skirts and trailing bell sleeves she was out the door. Rose wished she could collect on the number of raised eyebrows she'd seen from Spire since the moment they'd met.

She assumed he'd learn to mask his skepticism entirely, as she had, and become unreadable. She'd certainly felt spun round roughly when Black began training her for espionage above bookkeeping. She'd enjoyed being an excellent clerk; thorough paperwork was gratifying in its precise predictability, a comfort so unlike life itself. Being bid to look at life through a scrying-glass darkly, this was hardly comfortable for her. She knew in her heart where her priorities lay, and she hoped her instincts wouldn't get her into trouble.

There was a cry down the hall in some foreign tongue. Rose managed not to snigger when she saw Spire's jaw muscles clench as he valiantly tried to restore his blank expression.

Mr. Blakely nodded nonchalantly toward the noise. "That would be Sepulcher B3. Troublesome. The prince rearranges the artifacts. We keep telling the curator the funerary items are arranged in the wrong order, I mean, the prince should know, it's his grave, but the museum won't listen. The missus tries to explain to His Majesty that the curators mean no disrespect, but still, it's very disrespectful," Mr. Blakely said woefully.

"What was she speaking?" Spire asked.

"Egyptian," Rose and Mr. Blakely choroused.

"What is she doing out there?" Spire asked Blakely, choosing his words with care. "Does she think she's setting it to rest? Calming it down?"

Mr. Blakely shook his head. "She is a confidante when it comes to spirits. She doesn't see them, only senses particularly anxious presences. She can't set spirits to rest, exorcise, or banish them. I understand that's a different department. But the missus's true talents are prediction and reading. She gets a read on people right quick," Blakely said with simple admiration.

Rose wondered if he had fallen in love with his faux wife, despite her predilections for the female sex. Perhaps if he couldn't have a real marriage, he'd take a fake one instead. Rose hoped that wasn't the case, for that story was a bit too tragic for her tastes.

In her mind, unrequited love was a pointless waste. Either love was present or it wasn't. Her schoolgirl friends had chastised her for practicality, but she'd aced her classes, healthy and safe in a dry bed when they'd failed exams after throwing themselves into rainstorms after being rejected. Hardened differed from practical. The former was full of sorrow but the latter left hope for something to arrive worth wasting time on.

Curious about the "couple," Rose took an opportunity; "How did you meet?"

A wide grin burst over Blakely's face like a beam of light. "Marguerite was in Bath, *persuading* her elderly relatives to leave thousands of pounds to worthy causes such as, well, herself. My . . . show came into town." Blakely turned to Spire. "I'm a performer, you see."

"You don't say," Spire replied in a monotone.

"As fate would have it," Blakely continued, "she had procured the money but was worried about reprisals once her relations awoke from her persuasive spell. She needed a place to hide; I needed another act. She joined my troupe as a psychic and told me to marry her—on the condition that we wouldn't actually marry. She does love a good show," he said, grinning again as if he'd lost all the bats in his already questionable belfry. "Eventually Lord Black, who is fond not only of a good act but of the genuinely psychically talented, found us and made us respectable."

Spire clenched his jaw at the word "respectable." "I understand you were consultants to the previous, now missing, Omega team," he stated.

"Yes, but we worked from here," Blakely stated, "poring over anything of supernatural or immortal interest to add to the Queen's Vault. Lord Black tells me we're to have new offices now that you're with us."

There was a shriek and a crash from well down the hall and more cries in Egyptian.

"As the museum won't do at all, really," Blakely added.

On that note, Spire and Rose departed. At the door of the museum, Rose stopped her director before he walked off into the heart of Bloomsbury.

"Mr. Spire, would you kindly come by Westminster at your leisure later today?" she asked. "We have things to discuss."

Spire clenched his jaw. "Your parliament office, in the place that ought to have no offices?"

"The very one," Rose replied with a prim smile. He nodded.

There, in the safety of her tiny, contained universe, she would put her new director to a different sort of test; one of loyalties and personal conviction. She would see if they were indeed two creatures of the same mind or destined to be at odds.

* * * * *

The Majesty—He would always call himself Majesty no matter what the rest called him—shifted on his small, uncomfortable pallet.

He was hidden away in an isolated, dreary, windowless cell within London's Royal Courts of Justice. Only three people knew the space existed; the guard, who was his ear and mouthpiece to the external world; himself, and Her Majesty, Queen Victoria, who was impressively inscrutable. He harbored hope that she would come to embrace his cause, for surely she could see the damage the rise of the unwashed was doing to his beloved England.

A woman's voice from beyond the narrow set of bars startled him from his lovely reverie of a fiefdom reclaimed.

"Mr. Moriel," uttered in a biting, disapproving tone, signaled the arrival of Her Majesty, who swept into the dim light, her elaborate, expensive mourning garb overwhelming the space. "It has come to my attention that a certain Frances Tourney was running a heinous operation fit for hell, one that seemed to bear your crest of devilry. You were granted a stay of execution, Mr. Moriel, not a *pardon*. You assured me all your society operatives had been turned in."

"They . . . were. Tourney was never a member. He's a dilettante and an ass—pardon me, Your Majesty. Privations such as this do not make for subtle or couth conversation. You're not telling me he actually did something?"

"I'm not going to tell you what he did because it does not befit a lady's lips to speak of. You should have been more careful and given me the names of any and all persons who might have had even a passing interest in your little secret society."

"If I am allowed a writing implement and paper, Your Majesty, I will be happy to set down any and all names that come to mind."

"I'm not interested in vendettas and personal grudges; you seem to have too many of those. Only those who might be capable of the true, unmitigated horror you were so known for in New York and other cities, such as this newly disrupted resurrectionist ring that despoiled the bodies of dead children. Along with other sundry brutal murders."

"Tourney?" Moriel said in disbelief.

"Others were involved, surely. But financed, and *housed*, by Tourney. I want to know the entire chain or else this most gracious stay of execution comes to an end and you will be hung in this dreadful little chamber until you are as dead as everyone in my government already assumes you to be."

"But then where lies your vital, noble search for immortality, Your Highness?" he asked softly.

"We've many resources, Moriel. You're hardly our only asset in our search for the answers to life and death; you're merely the most sickening, a disgrace to the noble line you descend from," the queen said, finality in her voice. She turned without another word and walked away, the sweep of her black crepe gown against the stone covering the sound of her footfalls. Her instructions to the guard echoed in the narrow stone hall. "The prisoner is to have no food for six days."

"Yes, Your Highness," the guard replied.

The queen, exiting, didn't see the guard's wink to Moriel, who smiled sweetly as he was left alone again.

"My upheaval shall unfold in due time," Moriel murmured to the stone walls as if they were listening. "For now, I've pawns to pit against one another."

He shifted the small cot he'd been afforded, revealing a checkerboard square beneath that he'd etched into the corner of the dank floor with a rock. The greasy bones of a rat he'd caught in his cell, peeled open and disarticulated, all with his bare hands, sat in a relative chess formation. He slid a claw toward a femur and knocked it aside with a contented sigh.

* * * * *

A small, withered-looking clerk sat inside the door Miss Everhart had instructed Spire to enter. The man narrowed his eyes at Spire while waving him on, as if he didn't like the fact that anyone without a title had clearance to pass him. Though surely the clerk himself lacked a title, the man's disapproving expression had Spire instinctively straightening his striped cravat and smoothing his gray vest and deeper gray frock coat.

Spire strode deeper into the wing of the House of Lords where everything was gilded and red fabrics were seen everywhere in the furnishings and hangings—as opposed to the carved but unvarnished stone of the House of Commons, where all was trimmed in green. He passed the enormous statue of Queen Victoria, a loving tribute from Prince Albert that Spire found a bit ostentatious and perhaps indicative of a bit of magisterial insecurity. As he trod the fine red carpeting and traversed narrow passages of dark, polished wood carved in regal Gothic form, Spire wondered what Guy Fawkes would have thought of the splendor of Westminster today.

At the end of the passage, Spire stopped to look at the note that Everhart had slid into his palm as they'd left the museum the day prior:

> House of Lords. Before the "not content" lobby
> reaches the peers' lobby, there is a small door set
> within a Gothic arch. Press down on the brass
> plate that looks like it was meant for a keyhole.
> Try to do so when no one is looking. The narrow
> passage beyond will lead you to my tiny fiefdom.

Spire did as instructed. The narrow, nondescript door, which was paneled like the rest of the corridor and almost unnoticeable if one was not looking for it, granted him entry into a stone-floored, undecorated passage that led into a tiny fiefdom indeed. One special room that was no one else's.

He was soon seated in one of the two chairs in his associate's small, cramped, but immaculately organized Westminster office. The members of the House of Lords did not have offices, or clerks for that matter, yet this small room was secretly reserved for Miss Everhart. If it could be called a room. It was really more a closet. Supposedly the prime minister had access to this room by some other hidden passage, but Miss Everhart had not illuminated Spire on that point.

This alcove was the origin of the misunderstanding that had gained Spire the attention of the queen. A great deal of fuss over a space barely large enough to hold two people. Spire knew that Lord Black spent a deal of time in Everhart's office. He wondered how the space managed to contain his Lordship's expansive presence.

The lower five feet of the walls were paneled in dark mahogany; the upper portions were papered in the red of the House of Lords. In addition to the visitor's chair, the room was appointed with a tall wooden file cabinet, a fine writing desk, a leather chair, and an ornate gas lamp. A line of trays marched up the wall at one point, all filled with papers. A richly colored Persian rug was laid over the tile floor; fine writing implements lay upon the desk. Was Rose a member of the aristocracy herself? Spire wasn't sure he wanted to know.

Spire's first examination of the room provided him with more questions than answers, chief among them, where was she?

Then he noticed the note upon the blotter upon her desk, written on the back of a used envelope.

> H. S.—*Am out for a delivery—await me. We*
> *have several things to discuss. R. E.*

In her absence, Spire continued to peruse Rose's office with the eye of a detective. What little space she had was meticulously organized, but he saw no tea service, which rankled as he wanted a cup of tea. He'd expected no luxuries in the House of Commons but he thought surely the House of Lords might have some amenities. . . .

One shelf sported dictionaries and countless books about codes. There was a telegraph close to hand—and something upon the tape. Spire rose, intent on examining it. A noise behind had him turning to behold a cloaked figure he assumed was Miss Everhart, arms full of books and files.

Spire kept his expression unreadable while he prayed all those papers were not for him. She set everything on her desk and steadied the stack before she turned to him, gloved hands pulling back her thin cloak. Her hair was done up tightly, her black dress was simple and utilitarian but still elegant, matching the black of the cloak.

"A little light reading, Mr. Spire," the woman said with a smile. She hung her cloak on an interior hook and gestured to him to be seated. As he lowered himself once again into his chair, he nearly struck his temple on the protruding handle of a card catalogue that took up nearly half the space.

"On what topic?" he asked.

"Immortality. I can give you the highlights, if you like, as they relate to the facts going forward."

"I would appreciate that, Miss Everhart, because if my studies include *Varney the Vampire* I might throw the lot through the window, where it would undoubtedly hit some poor pedestrian on the head and the poor sot could pray for immortality himself." If there was a window, Spire thought.

Rose chuckled as she placed files into drawers of the wooden cabinet that was as tall as she was. "I understand your skepticism, Mr. Spire, truly, but everything in the vault may have its uses for reference." She took a seat, perching upon the lip of the desk with marvelous skill, somehow managing to shift the trapping of bustle that was increasingly prominent in today's ladies' fashion to the side, as if a mere act of sitting were an equestrian event.

"Vault?" Spire furrowed his brow. "What vault?"

"The vault contains our information on all the possible scientific theories on the extension of life," Rose explained. "The Americans didn't invent the search for immortality, of course, but it seems they may have come the closest."

"Did they, though? It sounds like their team may have disappeared like ours did. And who's to blame?"

"The Americans were on to something. Obviously not the right thing, but further than us. For a long time we thought the Americans were solely interested in research, not development. But our embedded contact alluded to several wild, inventive experiments in New York that have far surpassed attempts by our former team. It appears we British were stymied by the more spiritual aspects. Hence these texts, meant to expand the mind." She gestured to the cabinets. "I'll transfer this newly complied material within the week. The vault was moved to the cellar of Kensington Palace after one of our early researchers defected to America."

"America." Spire frowned. "You know, it sounds like we are at war."

"In a way, we never stopped being at war," Everhart countered with a shrug. "But we'll never act like it. America and England will always posture against each other. We share more common interests now than ever before, but those interests shall remain peaceable *only* if our developments in science and industry progress at the same rate."

"You make a mad quest sound almost sensible," Spire said with a slight growl. "But in all honesty, Miss Everhart, when there's more important work to be done, I find this whole commission difficult to swallow."

His colleague flashed him an intense look as she handed him an envelope and placed a finger to her lips. Spire opened the envelope, curiosity piqued, and his heart leaped.

The interior paper read: *Further Tourney contacts for*

investigation. While the Metropolitan's investigation had been extensive, this list of places, persons, and information was new to him. Privileged persons that high society wouldn't want associated with such deeds, whose reputations afforded them more safety and less scrutiny than the average man.

He stared up at her, an excitement matching the particular, engaged light in her prominent eyes. She tapped her ear and glanced behind her toward the wall, gesturing that he keep quiet.

Grabbing the paper and turning it over, he took a long and careful moment to write a question coded in the simplest of ciphers, asking if she would help the case continue in secret. She read, decoded the cipher in her mind, and nodded. The day had improved infinitely and Spire offered Rose the genuine smile that resulted in his turn of providence.

But suddenly the queen's warning to not trust anyone, and Spire's past, darkened him immediately.

He added, in the same simple cipher, a question, holding up the paper to her: How can I trust you?

She stared at him and spoke quietly. "You and I have things in common, Mr. Spire. We are passionate about our work. I love what I do here. And I am honored by my new appointment. Why on earth would I ever put that in jeopardy?"

She took the paper and swiftly scribbled an addition: *For the right cause I will.*

Spire stared at her. A woman. A fairly unparalleled one at that. One he'd have to trust, despite his history and all his discomfort.

He noticed Miss Everhart's eye fall upon the telegraph machine. She plucked a volume from her shelf of code books, flipped to a page marked by a ribbon, then turned the book upside down. She drew the message tape toward herself. For several minutes the little room was silent save for the sound of a pencil scribbling upon her notepad as she looked between book, message, and paper. At last she finished, lifting her head to gaze at Spire.

"Our overseas agent, Brinkman, is on a riverboat southbound, possibly to New Orleans. Either he found one of the scientists from that Manhattan team or he's tailing our spy who was embedded directly in the project."

Spire stood and went to the door. "I'll go share this news with Lord Black and see what else he can tell me about Brinkman." He tucked the file Miss Everhart had given him beneath his arm. Spire paused at the door. "Do you know where I might find his Lordship?"

"At his club. Here." She slid her hand into one of the cubbies of her desk and passed Spire a white card bearing a simple script address. "Give this to Foley at the door. Be persistent." She handed him the decrypted message to proffer to their superior. "If our embedded contact fails us, Brinkman is our key to the entire next step."

"I'll find a safe place for everything," Spire said carefully, patting the Tourney file.

"Please do, Mr. Spire," his colleague replied, weight to her words.

They stared at each other a moment, a great responsibility balancing on a perilous line between two relative strangers. He nodded and exited the same way he'd come.

It took all Spire's willpower not to immediately descend upon every contact the woman had given him. But instead he made his winding way out from Parliament's shadows, through the heart of London proper, to a post box that only he and his trusted Stuart Grange knew of.

Spire didn't mind that his newly appointed lodgings on narrow Rochester Street were bare, it was that anything he did or had on the premises could be watched or seized. So he fingered his key in his pocket as he bowed his head to the balding postal clerk who always seemed to be on duty at this spot. Despite the fact that Spire had used this location for years, he and the clerk never exchanged more than a nod. Still, Spire liked to imagine the man knew he was a part of something important.

Spire opened the box, dropped in the envelope, and returned the box to its cubby, thinking about all the evidence, secrets, and items vital to past cases that he'd kept there at times, far from meddling fingers. But nothing so precious to him now as that list, and Spire planned to be grand inquisitor to all.

But first, a bite of lunch at one of his old, cozy pub haunts. Then, onward to a club where he could never afford the food.

* * * * *

Spire had argued heartily for a good several minutes with the dour Foley—through the shuttered club door—before the ancient man admitted him. Spire entered, noting the doorkeeper's fine coat and tails and his vicious scowl, which Spire coveted for its sheer ferocity. Foley pointed with one crooked finger toward the heart of the building.

"He likes the mezzanine level, Mr. Spire," Foley said.

"Thank you, Foley."

"I didn't give you permission to call me Foley," the man said sharply.

"What would you have me call you?" Spire responded wearily.

"'Sir.' *Foley* comes with time and privilege."

"Yes, *sir*," Spire said through clenched teeth, striving to project respect for the little Napoleon of his club kingdom.

The rich red carpets beneath Spire's feet stood in stark contrast to the building's entirely white walls. Spire headed up a grand staircase that led into a small, private mezzanine-level chamber filled with aromatic smoke from the sort of fine cigars Spire had only read of. As he walked, Spire tried to shed his irritation in regards to his commission, capped by Foley's initial denial of admittance. It seemed "unclassified business" didn't open doors. Couldn't he have a badge or something that deemed him important?

"Spire! Hello, good sir." Lord Black looked up but did not rise from a large leather armchair in what was clearly his section of the exclusive setting; the area around him was strewn with paper, tea leaves, and tobacco droppings.

To his Lordship's right, a deep green frock coat and matching top hat hung from gilded hooks. He sported a black waistcoat with green buttons, billowing cream silk shirt cuffs matched a generous cravat of the same lush fabric pinned with a House of Lords insignia, gemstones glittering faintly in the soft gaslight issuing from cut-crystal wall sconces. The green pinstripe of Lord Black's perfectly tailored trousers indicated a large wardrobe rich in color and pattern.

The average man, Spire thought, had to consider practicality in clothing. Lord Black did not. Spire was well aware of his own modest, dark wardrobe in far heartier fabrics than nobility's silks or satins.

Spire tried to mitigate his biases, as Lord Black seemed to be genuinely interested in his line of work, which was unusual for a member of the aristocracy. He wanted to like the man. After all, to have a friend in the House of Lords was hardly a bad thing, whether Lord Spiritual or Temporal.

Given Spire's new appointment, he wondered if those labels would take on whole new meanings. The spiritual and the temporal: for Spire, these had always been at odds. A desperate desire to believe in the spiritual had led to temporal disappointment too many times for him not to declare empirical evidence weighted against the spiritual. But somehow, Lord Black seemed to manage the two with a certain amount of baffling joy.

The lord's fair hair looked even more blond in the yellowish light, almost angelic, and his bright eyes pinned Spire upon his approach. "To what do I owe this pleasure, Mr. Spire?"

"After a valiant fight with the vulture at the door—"

"Ah, good Foley." Black smiled, revealing one angled tooth. "We'd be lost without our gatekeeper."

"I am here, Lord Black, to ascertain what you believe to be my foremost objective within the scope of my operations, and to deliver a message."

"The queen wants England to have immortality before the Americans do," Lord Black stated. "I thought that was very obvious. America's Eterna Compound is incomplete. Whatever they missed, we must find it first. They were barking up every odd tree. Where they've sniffed, so must we. I am currently vetting new researchers. But our investigators and security services had best be well versed in the realms of the inexplicable. It's why we have our vault. There are many types of science, Spire."

"Only mystics say that. You're a lord. Sir."

"A mystical lord . . ." Black said dreamily, gazing toward the mezzanine's arched beveled window bedecked with stained-glass royal crests.

Spire ignored this. "I need more information about your American operative. Will he return? How embedded is he?" Black shrugged. "Does the man even receive orders," Spire pressed, "much less obey them?" Black shrugged again. Spire cleared his throat, managing to keep his tone level. "You do realize, Lord Black, this vagary makes me uneasy."

"I'm sure it does." The lord smiled. "You're a man who hates uncertainty. But I, my good man, thrive on it!" he exclaimed, lifting one hand in a flourish. "I love losing myself in everything I don't know. Curiosity, Spire! That's what will keep us alive; immortal. *Curiosity!*"

Spire remained unmoved by Black's enthusiasm and handed

over the decrypted message. "Miss Everhart is excellent with codes," he blurted, unable to hide how impressed he'd been.

"Our veritable wizard with ciphers. Blakely is too, in his way." Black smiled mysteriously. "I'll soon prove the full talents of your team to you." Unsettled, Spire opened his mouth. Black continued with a scoff; "I can read you like a book, Spire. You don't discount Miss Everhart because her intelligence is so obvious. You deem the others lunatics." Black finally read the message and frowned. "Oh. One of America's team survived after all and is being trailed."

The nobleman looked up at Spire. "With this news, I don't know when our man will resurface again. He's slippery, with a mind of his own. He gets us what we need, so he's worth the headache."

"Known aliases?" Spire asked.

"He sports variants of what may be his actual name, Gabriel Brinkman, though can we really ever be sure?" Lord Black smiled again, fondly, as if taken up by the romance of a spy's life. "Ask Miss Knight if her gifts offer us a sense of where he's gone off to."

"If my job is security services, sir, with all due respect, I truly doubt a medium is my foremost weapon. A weapon, rather, would be my foremost weapon."

Black laughed, though Spire had not intended to be amusing. "Mr. Spire, let me make something quite clear to you. The nature of your job is multifold. Sometimes you'll have to be a policeman. Sometimes a spy. Sometimes a diplomat. Sometimes a liar and cheat in the name of England. Sometimes a soldier. And sometimes you'll have to be a believer. You're an extremely capable and talented man, but it is becoming increasingly clear that believing is the one thing you cannot do. And that's a task worth working on."

"I will do my job, sir," Spire said, careful to keep a level tone. "Please give me details, names, operatives, everything about Eterna on all clearance levels and precisely what you expect of me. I can do nothing with phantoms, whether I believe in them or not. Good day, milord."

Without a further word, he turned on his heel and strode away. "Try to enjoy your appointment, Mr. Spire," Black called after him amiably.

Spire nodded without turning around. For Spire, there was nothing enjoyable about work at cross purposes with logic, but Black's enthusiasm was something to marvel at.

As Spire stepped out from under the arches of the club, leaving Foley's scowl behind, out of the corner of his eye, he saw a man in a somewhat theatrical cloak approach quickly on the cobblestones. He had a wide-brimmed hat pulled low over his face and his suit was too tight, revealing lines of a muscular body. Spire shifted to evade him but the stranger seemed determined to collide with him.

Spire moved quickly to his right, but not before something landed over his head—a hood, something made of fabric anyway, dark and full of smoke. Spire struck out and felt a satisfying punch land somewhere in the central body mass of the caped man, but someone else dragged him back against the Parliament bricks. He gasped involuntarily and whatever acrid scent was in the hood overwhelmed him and he sank to his knees as everything faded to black.

"You saw . . . how they died . . ." Clara murmured, staring at the bloody key.

Oh, God. That would mean Franklin had seen Louis's death. . . . She'd been shocked at how seeing an amorous note from him she'd hidden in her desk had pierced her like a lance. Her brilliant, seductive Louis, so full of life . . .

"Yes," Franklin said.

Clara was staring at Franklin in horror when the door swung open and they both jumped.

Senator Bishop strode into the room, which immediately felt smaller for his presence.

Dressed in a black frock coat with charcoal trim, silk waistcoat, and gray ascot, he was an elegant study in gray scale. The senator wore his prematurely silver hair longer than was fashionable, usually curled neatly behind his ears, the edges brushing his shoulders. It was rather mussed now, and Clara knew this meant he had been raking hands through it in worry or distress.

Stormy, steel-blue eyes reflecting the silver of his hair, he swiftly drew near to Clara, his sharp gaze locked onto her, examining her with a deep scrutiny that was both thrilling and unnerving.

"Something went wrong," he said quietly. "I can feel it."

Clara nodded, glad he got right to the point. "Yes. I left you a note."

"Ah, thank you, my dear," he said softly, "but I've not been home to see it. The New Jersey caucus was a frightful mess and needed a day's work. Coming in from the ferry, I went directly to check on the laboratory." The senator swallowed hard. "Nothing is there. No one. Perhaps the team moved it? Save for a few old books and equipment, everything is gone."

"I think, sir," Franklin began carefully, "I may know where they . . ."

"Died," Clara whispered, willing herself to keep calm and maintain smooth countenance. "They died yesterday."

"Dear God." Bishop closed his eyes and murmured a little prayer. This afforded Clara a moment to press tears well back behind her eyes, willing herself to drink saltwater down her throat rather than lose her composure here.

"You've a lead?" Bishop turned to Franklin. "Did your gift of past-sight play a role?"

"It did, sir. This key revealed an address," Franklin replied, displaying the item.

"Well done, my good man," the senator declared. Even Franklin was not immune to the senator's charm; he displayed a flash of pride at the compliment.

"I am sure it's where something happened," Franklin added, "but I saw no bodies. We found the key mere moments ago and have no idea who left it for us. It was not here when we were last here. I should know. I cleaned."

"How curious." Bishop fiddled with the knot of his neck-wear, a custom of his when musing. "My contact in the House of Lords has told me English eyes are spying, but what they know, why the lab and the scientists are all disappeared, the origins of this key; I haven't a clue."

"I don't suppose today would be the day you'd care to reveal your contacts? Anything that may have led to this?" Clara asked, an edge to her tone.

"Clara, don't start, please," Bishop said wearily.

Once the Eterna Commission had been put into place, she and Bishop had been relegated to figureheads, nothing more. Bishop was granted more clearance than Clara, though even his knowledge was limited. For Clara, being set apart from the project she had helped birth and allowed no interaction with the theorists or the laboratory, was infuriating. Her resentment of the circumstances had only grown through the years.

"I dreamed the British are coming," Clara stated. "It was one of those dreams; the kind that can't be ignored. So you might want to start trusting me with more information, *senator*."

Bishop turned to her and her breath caught at the sight of his deeply pained expression. He spoke with earnest solemnity. "I take my English contact with a grain of salt, but I always trust your dreams, Clara. And it's true. You're no longer a child. I can only do so much to protect you. Anything I've ever withheld, it's been for that reason alone."

There was a tense silence. Clara wasn't sure whether to feel better or worse.

"We must determine what happened," Bishop continued, breaking the tension with directives. "Keep watch for a certain 'Brinkman.' He's been here a few years. He came to light—and my attention—while aiding a British lord beset by paranormal circumstances. Brinkman is fond of travel. Get your man on the books to look for variants of his name." The senator turned to the door, coat flowing behind him. "Are we going to find this place or aren't we? Come on."

* * * * *

The three were silent as they rode uptown on a swaying trolley car. They hopped off before the car veered towards the open plaza and tumult of conjoining streets that was Union Square, walking west toward Fifth Avenue.

In the distance they could hear the swelling chants of a labor union rally, a coalescing force that took to the open park regularly. Clara wondered briefly what had sparked this protest—perhaps the most recent garment district fire, in which six women had burned to death. Life and death shared such close quarters in New York City. They strolled now along a pleasant, residential block, just a block south of that latest conflagration. Chaos and calm, separated by a street or two.

That was what made working on Eterna somehow plausible in New York to begin with.

Though the day was warm, Clara couldn't stop the shudder coursing up her spine. To defray her fears, she focused on the firm plod and subtle scrape of Franklin's uneven stride. It was a strange comfort, that sound, something so fallibly human. . . .

The air was sweet—well, sweet in that early summer New York way—and laced with a tinge of horse manure. There were no clattering trolleys or rails on this bastion of residential properties. The block was quiet, peaceful . . . and oddly free of pedestrian traffic.

Clara felt the change in atmosphere and knew they drew closer to their destination. Bishop felt it, too—she saw that in the hesitation of his firm, purposeful step, the subtle tilt of his head. The hairs on the nape of Clara's neck bristled and rose.

The Eterna team had usually hidden in plain sight, in various industrial locations where deliveries of goods would not be suspect, but this location was unexpectedly residential.

"What's the address?" Clara asked softly.

"Is anyone listening?" Franklin countered.

The three looked around. Passing pedestrians, the occasional buggy, hansom, or cart. No one seemed interested in them. No faces in windows. No doors ajar. One learned to look for the signs of a city that was listening. New York had much to listen to; it was the perfect place to hide. But it was a city that also might not hear you scream.

A sudden voice rang out from across the street. "Miss Templeton, Mr. Fordham, and Senator Bishop. Together again?" A familiar face tipped into view beneath a bowler hat. Clara sighed, aggrieved. "I've missed you, Miss Templeton!" called the man, who looked roughly near Clara and Franklin's age, late twenties. "Where have you been keeping yourself?"

Peter Green, journalist for the *New York Tribune,* had first encountered Clara during an investigation into grave robbing years prior, and had pestered her ever since. Brown hair poked out from beneath his hat; his dark blue frock coat and a long striped ascot somehow made him seem even taller than he was, with their angular cut and strong vertical lines.

"Nothing about Miss Templeton is any of your concern," the senator quipped.

"What's brought you to this fine neighborhood?" Green asked, ignoring the two men and focusing entirely on Clara.

"You know, Mr. Green," Clara said with a bite in her voice, "that I'm not at liberty to tell you that. As I say every time you manage to run into me."

Green crossed the street to stand near them on the sidewalk, speaking more quietly. "It has to do with your secret initiative, the one that's been years in the works—"

"I will have you arrested, Mr. Green," Bishop stated calmly.

"On what grounds?" the journalist whined. "I'm not trespassing—"

"But you're following us," Bishop interrupted.

"You're flattering yourselves." Green laughed. "I happen to live a block away."

"You do follow Miss Templeton," Franklin growled. "It isn't gentlemanly. You've been warned—"

"If a journalist takes being threatened seriously," Green said, shaking his head, "he needs to rethink his profession. For the record, I follow Miss Templeton because she's interesting and clearly up to something. All the great New York detectives—of which you are not one, Mr. Fordham— rely upon dogged investigative journalists. You should see me as a resource, not an enemy. As for what the senator here is up to, I'm always intrigued—"

"Would you like me to report you to the local precinct?" Franklin asked with a gamesome smile. "I believe Lieutenant Kaminski is on the beat at the moment."

"Ah, Kaminski, good man." Bishop nodded, folding his arms. Everyone glared at Green.

Green sighed. "Can't blame a man for trying to get a story." Seeing he'd get nothing more out of the three, he strolled away, occasionally glancing back. The investigators stared after him until he disappeared around the corner.

"Every good operation needs an irritating, nosy busybody," Bishop muttered with a chuckle.

"Could you not simply mesmerize the man to keep his distance?" Clara asked. Only she and Franklin knew about that particular talent of the senator, who, out of pride, hardly ever utilized his powers of persuasion.

Bishop shrugged. "Tails can keep us vigilant," he replied, then took a breath, looking not at the whitewashed building they'd paused in front of but the next one over. "This one," he murmured. "It's been years since I saw the paperwork, but I think Malachi Goldberg lived here."

The building in question was a dark red brick with brownstone detailing, a basic, unremarkable town house save for the pall of dread that seemed to hang over it. A film of smoke and dust ringed each black-trimmed window frame. The building's cloistered air was off-putting on such a well-lived street.

The feeling the building exuded was one of a held breath. Clara hoped whatever the building wished to exhale wouldn't be too overwhelming. Bishop sniffed the air, squinting up and then scanning slowly down the structure as if he were a building inspector, but Clara knew his consideration was far more spiritual in nature.

"The structure isn't teeming," Bishop concluded. "Something is off about the place, but does it require extra precaution? Clara?" Her name was a request for confirmation.

"Not yet," she replied. "It won't be comfortable, but we can take the time we need."

A fine mahogany brougham passed behind them as they descended the stairs to the lower-level entrance, which was shaded by a black iron overhang that protruded from the face of the building like a mourner's veil. Rivets in the wooden door signaled that a layer of metal had been added. The door bore vague smoke marks that tinged the threshold and added to the general air of menace.

"Open the door, please, Mr. Fordham," Bishop commanded. He turned to Clara. "The moment you begin to feel the aura—"

"If I do, then I will exit," Clara assured him, steeling herself. Neither of these men knew the keening ache in her heart, the fear of what they'd find within, and she could not let on. "I would hope after all these years you trust I'm not cavalier about my condition, but I will not let it exclude me from our work."

Bishop nodded.

Franklin withdrew the bloodied key from his coat pocket and he slid it into the lock. The latch fought a moment before yielding, squealing on hinges that sounded but did not look rusted.

A peculiar metallic scent accosted Clara's nostrils with the strength of smelling salts. The outside light filtering past the shaded entrance revealed a dark hallway with a wooden staircase leading up on the left and a closed door down to the right. The sheet of metal indicated by the exterior rivets had been affixed to the inside of the door and bore, near the handle, a terrible image.

The oxidized print of a hand.

Clara shuddered and forcefully shut down the part of her mind that insisted on imposing horrific iterations of Louis's demise onto this eerie setting. She owed it to his memory to keep herself together. She pressed trembling fingertips to the protective talisman under her bodice and said a prayer for strength.

A great deal of soot and ash drifted about on the floor in the draft from the open door. Clara prayed she was not standing in someone's remains, but had the sinking feeling she was—they all were. That's why there were no bodies. The team all went up in dust. . . .

They stepped into the first room.

"This is the room I saw," Franklin declared.

In a typical home, the space beyond the pocket doors they stepped past was likely used as a parlor, but instead of settees and console tables and genial discussions of the weather, there were slate-topped wooden laboratory tables where coiled gas burners with small-nozzled jets sat between an array of glass containers. There were wooden stools at each station and a scattering of steins and coffee mugs surrounded each place.

Across the room towered a hefty bookshelf that held formidable tomes and various brass instruments that reminded Clara of astrological tools. The long, rectangular room sported greenish satin wallpaper above wooden paneling; the velveteen floral flocking of the paper was the only remnant of the room's past life as a place of teacups rather than tubes and beakers.

The whole of the wooden paneling that covered the lower four feet of each wall was charred in an odd pattern that never rose above the paneling. The greenish satin was unmarked save for the occasional searing lick of flame. The damage did not appear consistent with a normal fire, and Clara had seen many, for New York had no shortage of conflagrations.

The residue on the walls was slightly yellow. The scent in the air was bitter and sour. Sulfuric.

It was hard to acknowledge the presence of sulfur and not think of hell.

Clara wondered suddenly—though not for the first time—if her idea had not been born of a divine and loving God; if it sprang, rather, from some less amenable force.

Bishop had trailed them into the room and now she saw his body stiffen, as hers had within the constraints of her corset. She knew he could feel the distressing vibration of the room just as she could. He turned to her.

"I'm all right," she insisted. "I give myself about ten minutes." Clara timed herself in any place that retained any amount of spiritual charge, joyous or dark. Any emotion could overwhelm in large doses.

Clara and Franklin had a routine when investigating a building or a person. She took notes and retrieved empathic and occasional psychic images, Franklin used his psychometric touch to gather further information. If the person or place raised too many concerns, they would send Bishop with one of his several trusted mediums (all of whom worked completely out of the current fashionable spotlight) in instead.

She was in the middle of the room, withdrawing her notepad from her reticule and studying the windows, which were oddly frosted over when a motion drew her eye. She turned to see that Franklin had gone to the wall and was taking off his glove. The soft beige leather slipped from his hand and he flexed his bare palm. Clara well knew what that meant and she'd never been so scared for him. Not in a place like this. He might never return from what he saw. . . .

Their regular routine did not apply to this place. The signals and cues triggering one of her episodes were not present, but the house itself was like nothing they'd yet encountered.

"Franklin, not here." Clara dropped her notebook as she rushed to intercept him, but it was too late. The terrible secrets within the bricks would reveal themselves.

She watched her partner's body seize up, crumple like a doll, and then seize rigid again, his hand affixed to the wall, palm pressed to the charred wood paneling as if a nail were through it. It was impossible for Clara to bear seeing such a gentle soul in so much pain. Not that she liked seeing anything in pain, but cruel souls in pain proved some satisfaction. There was no glory in this moment, only concern. She wondered if this was how she looked during one of her fits.

"A few glimpses, Mr. Fordham," Bishop cautioned, "that's enough, surely—"

Clara tried to pull Franklin's hand away from the wall. He seized and shuddered, again convulsing on his feet.

Empathy wasn't enough, she could sense what he was feeling but she wanted to see with his eyes. She felt she owed it to the memory of Louis Dupris to understand what happened to him, even if she could hardly face it. Whatever Franklin saw would haunt her dreams and fabricate new nightmarish terrors, she knew. Still, she owed it to the soul of the man she'd only just begun to imagine a future with.

"*Enough*, Franklin," Bishop said, moving near, obviously intent on detaching Franklin from the wall. With his free hand, Franklin shoved Bishop back with preternatural force. The senator reeled into Clara and they both tumbled to the floor, banging into one of the old laboratory tables. Clara struck her head, then lost her breath in a rush as Bishop landed atop her. A rush of undulating energy washed over all of them, like a pungent vapor, and in it was the cry of death.

Clara's impact with the floor kicked up an acrid dust. As she gasped for breath, it rushed, burning into her lungs, she coughed and the room spun and shifted. Damn. An episode. Or was it?

This was immediately different than a fit, nor was it one of her clarion clairvoyant moments. Her body, though free from a seizure's clench, floated in a different reality. Her fits were whirling light and psychic frisson and the occasional message, like a scream from the spirit world, always stressful and traumatic. Her successful clairvoyant moments came when single messages from the spirit world or glimpses of past lives appeared in specific sequence before fading, leaving her able to relay them calmly. This was, instead, a slow, cool descent as if into a darkened pool in a dream.

Franklin and Bishop vanished. The room seemed to lengthen into a long corridor and before her were shadows. Tall, long, human-shaped shadows.

A host of black silhouettes.

"Help us," they chorused in unison: a deep, male tone.

"How?" Clara murmured. "Who are you?"

"You know who we are," they replied.

"The team," she prompted. "Are you the team who died?"

"Find the files. One still knows. One survived."

"What are your names?" Clara said, searching to find any distinguishing characteristics in the black voids, for confirmation of who they were. If one of them was Louis, she yearned to talk to him. To be forgiven by them all.

"We cannot rest until what's wrong is made right," the voices droned.

"Please," Clara murmured, feeling her lungs continue to burn. If this was indeed one of her episodes, it was the strangest and most lucid one yet. "I'm so sorry. . . ."

"Something went wrong here, dreadfully wrong. Find the files. Woe to those who allow this power to fall into unworthy hands. Watch for those who are watching you, for they will come after you."

The silhouettes lunged at her. She choked and turned onto her side.

As she came to, Bishop was folded over her, staring, concerned. Despite this compromising position, it was hardly her first thought to get out of it.

She turned her head to Franklin. His back was against the wall, eyes closed, breathing heavily. The tether was broken. He'd recover, and live haunted. Like the rest of them.

"He's strained but all right," Bishop stated, keeping his focus on Clara. "What happened? Are you all right? Can you hear me?"

"Yes . . ." Her return to consciousness was full and sudden. Usually, during one of her episodes, her senses came back one by one; sound was often one of the last. "Oh, God . . . Did I seize?"

"No. You simply *faded*," Bishop replied. "But who were you talking to? You had a whole conversation."

"You didn't see the figures?" she asked.

"Figures? No, only you." Bishop peered at her, reaching for her wrist to check her pulse. There was an odd, strained pause in this compromising position; neither Clara nor the senator moved. Clara resisted the impulse to reach up and embrace him, murmur his name, tell him everything, beg his help through her grief. . . .

Franklin had roused. His discomfited cough as he stared at Bishop folded so intimately over Clara sobered her. She sat up with the senator's help.

"Shall we share our respective hells of what came over us?" Franklin asked grimly, moving to pick up Clara's fallen notebook and pencil.

"Not here," Bishop instructed, helping Clara to her feet and into the entrance hall.

At the stairs she paused. "We'd be too lucky if the files were *here*."

"What do you mean, Clara?" Bishop asked.

"The Eterna files," she said excitedly. "The team's notes,

whatever is left of the research that drove them to this terrible point. That's what the spirits said, to find them . . ."

Charging up the stairs, she tore into one empty room after another, filled with the urge to do, solve, and fix—a manic insect, buzzing around. The gentlemen followed. But nothing was there, not even a cabinet, let alone a file.

"This place doesn't want us here any longer, Clara," Bishop warned at the top of the first-floor landing. "We've overstayed our welcome."

"Agreed," she called down from the barren third floor. "I can feel a malevolence rising and I know better than to press my luck. My sight has shifted as well, and that's a first symptom."

They left in haste, lest Clara be truly overcome once more.

Spire came to upon the ground, still under the hood.

He recalled the last few moments before he lost consciousness, outside Lord Black's club. Surely someone had seen and reported his abduction. He smelled grass, earth, and chemicals. Through the rough fabric of the hood, he heard murmurs—lots of them. Giggles. Even laughter . . .

An acrid taste lingered on his tongue. But as his senses fully awakened, he realized his hands were not bound, so he sat up and whipped off the hood to find himself in the center of a wide patch of grass.

In a tent.

With an audience.

He was surrounded by a semicircle of benches filled with servants; stable hands, scullery maids, laborers, cooks, and butlers, all pointing at Spire and laughing. Either this was a nightmare or there really was a hell; the blow had been fatal and he'd not been good enough in life to escape eternal punishment.

Confused and uneasy, Spire tried quickly to assess his circumstances. He was under a white-and-red-striped tent with a vast pole at the center. Through a gap in the fabric—an entryway—he could see, in the distance, the soot, smoke, and spires of London industry wafting into the air like a pit of dragons keeping close company. . . . The view was not unfamiliar; neither was the rolling heath he could see through the open tent door: Hampstead.

Though he did not utilize the vast tracts of forest or spacious clearings for sport or leisure as the upper classes did, he had pursued criminals onto the expanse and knew it well.

A few paces behind him, a thick red curtain covered a large wooden dais. Rising to his feet, he felt constrained. A hard plate pressed against his back and girdling bound his middle, some sort of device was hitched beneath his suit coat and waistcoat but above his undershirt. The crowd laughed again. A few apple cores were launched in his direction. Spire dodged as he patted his pockets and found he still had his key and wallet. As he began undoing the many buttons of his coat and vest to examine his rigging, which seemed to include thin belts and buckles running down his sides, the crowd made various suppositions about his activity.

For a horrible moment Spire thought this whole spectacle might be revenge by some of Tourney's contacts. He did not dare say a word until he understood what was happening; he shuddered to think what might be coming next.

The dais curtain was whipped aside to reveal a line of velvet-covered chairs upon the wooden platform, like one might expect for a royal party at a tournament of old. Lord Black, smiling in a self-satisfied manner, was seated at his ease at one end of the row.

Two empty chairs sat to Black's left, and then Knight, seated, splendidly happy in a lavish red gown and golden feathers that made her look a living accessory for the tent. Spire narrowed his gaze, feeling his face flush with fury, but before he could demand answers, a weighty tug at his back launched him into the air.

The crowd roared with laughter. Spire whipped his head around; the back of his skull grazed the thin rope—perhaps it was corded wire—that drew him up toward an elaborate pulley. Spire's dangling body swung above the dais. The crowd laughed again. More projectiles flew and an orange rind bounced off his skull.

Spire glared down at Black, and before he could say a word, the rope went slack, dropping him inelegantly onto a chair. He nearly went sprawling. More laughter. Spire righted himself, then leaned toward Black until his perspiring face hovered inches from Black's shaved, pampered cheek and the brocade collar of the Lord's fine frock coat.

"Explain," he growled.

"Watch and learn, Spire," Black said calmly. Spire returned to undoing his buttons so he could remove the harness, but Lord Black slapped his hand. "Ah, ah, Spire," he said. "All part of the show."

Spire's chastised hand clenched into a white-knuckled fist.

"Ladies and gentlemen," boomed a vaguely familiar voice, "you are gathered here today for exhibition and examination and we aim to amaze!"

A narrow, sumptuous red carpet unfurled from behind their sightline, rolling across the grass and stopping before the great middle pole that kept the tent's foremost turret upright. A tall figure—taller than Spire remembered, perhaps due to his studded black leather boots—stepped onto the carpet. Mr. Blakely.

The foppish creature Spire had met in the museum was now commanding and sure of himself in tight-fitting breeches, a long black silk coat with enormous, red, satin-lined cuffs and tails; the latter flashed like the flick of a toreador's taunt as he strode down the carpet. Atop his head perched a tall, black satin top hat with a silver skull at its prow. A glimmering silver staff topped with a glass ball was crooked under his arm, the shaft held tightly in a black-gloved hand.

"What the bloody hell, Blakely—" Spire growled

"Hush, Spire, you'll ruin the illusion," Lord Black said chidingly.

"The illusion that I'm *not* about to make a calculated strike to Mr. Blakely's jaw?" Spire tried to stand, only to be jerked back down immediately into his seat. The crowd roared with laughter. A swift study showed that the harness had been somehow, while his attention was elsewhere, attached to the base of the seat. He glared at every amused face.

"*Madames et messieurs*, good working folk of this glorious Hampstead Heath, for your appreciation, reunited for this brief command performance in hopes we may impress our patron, Lord Black: The *ciphers*!" Blakely crowed, driving the glass-topped staff into the earth so that it stood on its own. He waved dancing fingers over the glass knob—a jolt of fire burst forth and everyone applauded. Beside Spire, Lord Black clapped his hands with a degree of glee unbecoming a nobleman.

"My faux husband is a jack-of-all-trades," Knight murmured proudly, "and master of many, including chemistry. Engineer of the sleeping hoods, which send you gently into unconsciousness with just the right amount of chloroform—"

"I wouldn't say gently," Spire growled.

"And he is *very* good with fire," Knight added in a coo. "Setting it and containing it. Let me be clear, I don't like fires. But there are times when fires must be set."

Something about her tone made Spire have to hold back a shiver.

Into the open vista between the drawn tent curtains that framed London in the distance, stepped two persons all in black; hooded tunics above crisscrossing bands of leather that kept to the contours of their fit musculature. They wheeled in a tall wooden board covered in another red velvet curtain and positioned it squarely in the aisle.

An accordion began playing a forcefully dreary tune; a

calliope organ joined in. The black-clad performers lifted their heads, revealing simple masks beneath their hoods. Spire recognized the faces as similar to those he'd seen in mosaics in the British Museum, depicting Greek drama. Blakely joined them and the three began dancing to the creepy waltz, switching partners every couple of steps with unwavering precision. Within moments, their waltzing transformed into acrobatics; the three formed a human pyramid, then tumbled into other formations that displayed strength and dexterity.

"My friends," Blakely said evenly, breath apparently undisturbed by his exertions, "Welcome to the edge of the abyss where we, the ciphers, test our human limits."

The accordion and calliope launched into a jauntier, more manic tune.

Blakely bowed low in front of Spire, who clenched his other fist. The one Black had slapped had yet to unclench.

"Sorry for the headache, gov'," Blakely said, affecting a cockney accent he dropped when he leaned in to whisper giddily in Spire's ear. "I wanted you and Lord Black to truly see what we could do! How could you trust us in the field without having seen our *show*?"

Blakely darted to the star at the end of the runner and his voice filled the tent. "Ladies and gentlemen, bear witness! Even gravity cannot best a cipher!" The black-clad figures were suddenly airborne. Spire had spotted the lines of the thin dark rope a mere moment before the pair took flight. The crowd oohed and ahhed while the ciphers unfurled their bodies overhead, performing impressive feats of dexterity.

Blakely wheeled out an empty tea cart. From his sleeve he withdrew a red silk rectangle, whipping its length out over the tray. When he lifted the silk again, three short swords lay upon the previously empty cart. Everyone applauded save for

Spire, who had begun to wonder if Miss Everhart was somewhere amid this nonsense. If she was not, she was the only member of the company missing.

Blakely tossed two of the swords into the air, point first. The aerial performers caught the hilts of the weapons effortlessly as they wound around the center tent pole as if it were a maypole, bouncing lightly off it to unwind again.

One of the flyers pulled on a rope and two trapeze bars swung down within their lithe reach. They unhooked themselves from the weighted wires to hang from the trapezes and conduct a sword fight. They hung from their knees, or from one knee or one arm, occasionally swinging toward the tent pole to bounce off in a dizzying sequence of thrusts and parries.

"Your turn," Blakely said, suddenly close to Spire's ear once again. He offered Spire the third sword just as the former police officer was hoisted out of his chair.

Spire grabbed the hilt and tried to thrust at Blakely's top hat but Blakely nimbly avoided the blade. A roar of laughter from the crowd was accompanied by a few healthy taunts.

A body came swiveling toward Spire upside down, blade out. Spire parried right, casting his opponent's sword aside and setting himself rotating on the wire. Humiliating, of course, but great fun for the crowd, who clearly thought him the clown of the operation.

As Spire turned, he found that behind him was another swinging body with outstretched blade. Spire had to duck to avoid the collision as the cipher swung past him to clash with his previous opponent. Spire bellowed in frustration, lashing out at one black-clad figure and then the other. A glancing blow to one fellow's shoulder, the tear of black fabric, then the inevitable spin that let him cut toward the other's head; that strike was parried.

"I've had quite enough now," Spire called. As soon as he was on the ground he wanted to walk up to Lord Black and submit his resignation.

Blakely snapped his fingers and Spire plummeted, slowing just as he hovered back over his chair, again dropped inelegantly to the ground, stumbling and sliding on a bit of cabbage. The crowd jeered again at inelegance.

Leaping onto the dais with a wide, Cheshire Cat grin, Blakely stabbed at Spire's side and a lock clicked loose. The metal plate against his back slid down, thudding when it hit the chair.

Before Spire could undo the rest of his rigging, Blakely snapped his fingers and the curtain fell from the tall wooden board opposite the dais, revealing Rose Everhart. Bound to the board by hand and foot, she looked every bit as furious as Spire felt. "Oh, good God," Spire muttered.

"When I said I'd help you, Blakely," Rose snarled, "this was *not* what I was expecting."

Four knives sprang into place around her head, twanging as their points were embedded in the wood, flung at lightning speed by one of the masked, black-clad creatures. Everhart screamed. Wild applause roared from the common folk, who threw not a single vegetable at this admittedly impressive display.

With a dance of his hands, Blakely threw a set of fireballs that roared in the air toward the crowd before dissipating. A swing of his still low-burning staff ignited a wire that wound up the tent pole in a sparking flame that changed colors as it rose. Wilder applause. Black made a cutting signal to Blakely, who immediately bellowed:

"Ladies and gentlemen, that will be all!"

There was a general shout of deep disappointment. "Where are the 'orses?" Bellowed an old man in stable-hand garb. "What kind of show in a tent doesn't have a 'orse stunt?"

"A show entirely of the human variety, my good man," Blakely replied charmingly, unruffled. "No offense to my equine friends, but humanity is capable of craft beyond the wildest imagination, and our good patron Lord Black needs *us* to be the very *cleverest* of animals and the most impressive show of all. I hope you have enjoyed our little act on the grand and glorious old Heath where highwaymen once looted and where ghosts still howl upon the moor. . . ."

As the applause began, Knight swept away to stand by the tent door, graciously bidding adieu to the crowd as they bustled off toward their employers' various estates—land that would never be theirs nor the rights of their lineage. Many thanked her for a momentary distraction from their dreary routines.

Spire and Rose stared at each other helplessly across the grassy space as the tent emptied.

"Blakely, get Miss Everhart out of that trapping *right* now," Spire barked as he finally freed himself from his harness. One of the ciphers helped her down. She yanked her arm away from the figure, storming over to take the empty seat next to Spire, glaring at Lord Black all the while.

Everhart made a wiping gesture at her face, nodding toward Spire. Puzzled, he put a hand to his cheek; it came away covered with white greasepaint. So they *had* made him the clown. Growling, he whipped out a handkerchief from the breast pocket of his best—now grass-stained—brown coat and tidied his besmeared face. Finished, he clenched the ruined handkerchief in a greasy fist.

"A circus *act*," Lord Black cried, shaking his head, laughing. "Brilliant for espionage. Brilliant for spying. Magicians make people, items, information, all of it disappear. And the aerial work! Genius! Imagine, Mr. Spire, how useful they'll all be!"

"Were you kidnapped as well?" Spire asked the nobleman.

"Heavens no," he scoffed. "I wanted to see how they

captured someone. Ground, aerial, and chemical assault all at the same time, masked and hooded, quick and seamless; all just as you advertised, Mr. Blakely, thank you. I am most impressed by the show." He inclined his head toward the small man; a benediction of sorts.

Spire doubted Lord Black would dare to be so casual about Spire or Everhart if they too were nobility. An old, old wound—once again, the upper classes used the striving classes for sport—burned low in a quiet, locked-away place in his soul.

The tent was empty now save for the performers and those on the dais. Blakely dropped the tent flaps. Before Lord Black and Spire, the two acrobats got down on one knee and took off their masks and hoods. They seemed familiar, though Spire could not place them.

The male was a gorgeous creature who looked as if he'd stepped out of a Raphael masterpiece; the woman, utterly exquisite, the bulk of her thick black hair tucked beneath a thin black head scarf, large dark eyes, and olive skin. They were in their mid-to-late thirties, perhaps, Spire guessed.

"I started the ciphers in my youth when I broke this gentleman"—Blakely stuck a thumb out at the blond man—"out of our orphanage—really a workhouse—when I was twelve. We survived by performing, by small acts of petty thievery, wherever anyone would take us. Some of us went on to do great things, didn't we, Mr. and Mrs. Wilson?"

Everyone gasped. The Wilsons, Spire thought. No, they couldn't be. . . .

"I thought you died in the wilds of Afghanistan!" Black exclaimed incredulously.

"We'd rather the world continued to think that," the man said, and there was something in his voice that made Spire wonder if he wished that they had.

The *Wilsons*. Mr. Reginald Wilson, a legendary spy who had given the military key victories four years earlier, at the beginning of the war. Then he started fudging information and sending back false leads.

His wife, Adira, was a whole other grand story.

She spoke in faintly Arabic-tinged English, her gaze never wavering. "We have done this because we have no other way to stop running. Lord Black, we need your blessing. Mr. Spire, we ask you to agree to be our captain. We would like to serve the country where we both were born and we dare think our skills are impressive and unusual enough to be of service. Hence the display. One often needs to make a show of things to be able to present the truth."

"Unconventional as we most certainly are, we're tired of existing entirely in the shadows," Blakely stated. "Lord Black, you have been the only one open minded enough to consider us for anything to do with the government, and we are so grateful to you."

"Yes, but Mr. Wilson, you disobeyed your government's orders," Black said sternly.

"Crisis of conscience, sir," Mr. Wilson replied. "Adira and I are tired of the Great Game; the mandate to be anywhere and everywhere, telling everyone how they can or can't do business, the Empire eliminating anyone who got in its way. We thought we'd just stay in Kandahar, make you think we were dead. But we missed home."

"Truth is, we were born to be spies," Mrs. Wilson said with a hunger Spire recognized from when he joined the Metropolitan force. "I never knew life could be so thrilling until Reginald taught me the trade. We *need* to be spies, milord, it gives us strength and purpose. Can we instead bring the Great Game home, to something less deadly and politically muddy?"

"Everything is politically muddy, Mrs. Wilson. And I know you're not naive enough to truly believe otherwise," Lord Black said gravely.

Spire recalled more of what he knew about the Wilsons,

as infamous in England for their romance as their talents, death having thrown wide their sweeping secrets and made them icons. Born in England, Mrs. Wilson was said to be as brilliant as she was striking. Descended of Persian aristocracy, she'd fallen in love with Mr. Wilson while visiting relatives in Tehran, where he was on a mission, and decided to abandon the marriage planned for her.

At Adira's request, Wilson converted to Islam so that she would not have to forsake her faith as well as her family, then the two made it appear she had died in a tragic accident. Married, the Wilsons aided England, providing information gleaned from relations on the outs with the native regime. But, as was the case with many great talents in the confusing moral fog of war, the Wilsons reached their breaking point and wiped themselves off the map.

Sensational novelists had written dramatic accounts of their relationship and tragic end. Reginald's scandalous conversion to Islam would have been decried if he'd lived, but in death the Wilsons' actions were painted with unabashed romantic heroism. His father would be so disappointed, Spire thought mordantly; to find out that the Wilsons were alive after all.

Black rubbed his dimpled chin. "Because you voluntarily went missing in action, thusly insubordinate, submitting fraudulent documents, your identities would have to be entirely eradicated. Your story, your love, your 'deaths' were all famous here. So if you work with Mr. Spire and under my protection, you can never be seen in public as yourselves. Do you agree?"

The Wilsons nodded. Mr. Wilson reached for his wife's hand and squeezed it.

"Did I mention they're damn fine pickpockets to boot?" Blakely asked, producing a basket that contained several items, one of which, Spire noted, was his wallet. Miss Everhart pursed her lips, eyeing a small embroidered bag. Lord Black applauded as he fished out a gold watch fob. In all this elaborate waste of his time, the Wilsons were the only thing Spire could admire, their craving for spy craft as keen as his need to police.

"Also know, Your Lordship, Mr. Spire," Blakely continued, "that I can make sympathetic stain." When Spire didn't answer immediately, the small man added, "There's only one company here in Britain that makes it. But I can. Sympathetic stain, white ink, the words are invisible until you—"

"I know what sympathetic stain is, Blakely," Spire barked. Blakely nodded and smiled again.

"Rest assured," Lord Black said grandly, "I am impressed by all of you. Every talent shall be put to use as I see fit." He glanced to his side and coughed. "As Mr. Spire sees fit, I should say. Well done!" His unabashedly delighted gaze was fixed on the performers once again.

A dark-skinned, white-haired head popped up around the side of the dais, the man's tall form followed, carrying a large accordion like a breastplate. He waved. " 'Ello, Your Lordship, name's Samson," he said in a resonant cockney accent. "If you're 'iring, sir, do let me know if you've need of a musician, will you? I hear Parliament can be a bit of a circus, too."

Lord Black laughed heartily. "Noted, Mr. Samson. Your music was a vital element!"

Samson's brown, full mouth flashed a smile as bright as his white hair. He turned away, packing up some of the cipher materials.

Black turned to Spire. "Was this not an incredible display?"

Spire stared at Black for a long, frowning moment.

"Really, what did you think?" Blakely asked earnestly. "Reggie and I haven't performed together in *years,* but I assure you, I take theatrical quality very seriously, Mr. Spire."

Spire stepped out of the last remaining cord looped around his leg, and stood. "When an operation calls for insanity, now

I know whom to deploy." Spire whirled to Black with a fierce look. "Lord Black, I'm off to *work*. I'll not be giving or receiving orders from a carnival tent."

He stalked off, batting back the thick burlap curtain and nearly running toward carriages tethered in the shade, grateful that his boyhood love of horses and the freedom they offered meant he was an efficient, swift rider and the city would be soon gained. Keeping his rage in check, he unhitched one of the horses from a red brougham painted with the word "Ciphers" in gold and rode the beast bareback to London.

CHAPTER

SIX

Clara and Franklin returned downtown via carriage in utter silence, exiting a few blocks off at the tip of Manhattan's first park, Bowling Green. She didn't press Franklin for what he'd seen. Not yet. The senator had gone to Delmonico's, to meet with campaign strategists who seemed to keep calling hours in fine dining establishments.

Ahead of them as they turned toward their building, leaning against a lamppost at the intersection of Pearl and Broad Street, was a familiar, brown-skinned face beneath a newsboy's cap. The youngster's clothes were not new, nor fine, but very well maintained. Clara and Franklin smiled at the same time.

"Josiah!" Franklin called. The errand boy had a joyful spirit and was their most reliable hire. He beamed and took off his cap, revealing spiral black hair shorn close, and bowed slightly.

"What, why are you lookin' surprised, I'm always here for you!" Josiah said with a little laugh, as if his presence were obvious. He kicked a stone at his feet with a worn shoe that spoke of darting endlessly about cobbled streets.

"I know," Clara said quietly. "It's just nice to see you. It's been a . . . difficult day."

"I am very sorry to hear that, ma'am," Josiah said earnestly. "Can I help with anything?"

"Yes, in fact," Clara said. Josiah lit up. "We need the Bixbys. Remember them?"

"Oh, yes! Why, I saw them yesterday, they were visiting their gran up in my neigh—"

"Hush." Franklin stopped the boy. Josiah snapped his mouth closed. Clara watched a complex flurry of emotion pass over the boy's face.

"Right," Josiah said. The stone got a fierce kick across the cobblestone street.

"Remember what I said about our interactions?" Franklin asked softly.

"People might always be listening or watching," the boy muttered. "I never take the same road twice. And I know the Bixbys can't act around your folk like they've got relatives like my folk. I know. And I won't say nothing." He turned to Clara, visibly struggling to regain his usual warmth.

"I truly do appreciate that you keep an eye out for us, Joe," Clara said, smiling down at him, her heart aching at the hard truths crashing over him like a wave, a separate and unequal New York eroding the foundations of his young life. Rules, spoken and unspoken kept him, and the community from which the Bixbys once hailed, at a disadvantaged, racialized distance both literally and figuratively.

"Of course, Miss Clara," he murmured. She watched the boy bury his truths in a deep, complicated place. "Why do you need the Bixbys?" he asked.

"Ah, you know we can't tell anyone, not even you, exactly why." Clara chuckled. "Just send for Fred Bixby, please. Tell him to check the books for any known *Jacks* and come to me straightaway."

"Someday will you tell me what things like that really mean?" Josiah asked.

Clara shook her head. When the boy pouted, she added: "I would if I could," though she knew that not knowing kept him safer. "Did you happen to notice if Miss Kent came to the office today?"

"No, but I'll send word if you need her," Josiah stated. "I bet she'll be glad for something to do, with Mr. Veil traveling so much and her family disowning her and all."

"Indeed, do send for her then. Did I ever tell you that you were the most useful young man in the world?" Clara asked.

"Maybe. Once or twice." The boy shrugged with a chuckle.

"Never forget it." Clara smiled. "Now, go on with you."

"Right away, ma'am," Josiah exclaimed, beaming as Franklin passed him a bill. He ran off, intent on his tasks.

Back in the office, the first thing Franklin did was to go to a small cubbyhole in the wall, from which he plucked two snifters and a small bottle filled with brown liquid.

"You'll need this when you hear what I have to say. Hell, I need it," he muttered, pouring a generous tot of brandy into each glass. She appreciated that Franklin never made her feel unladylike for her occasional penchant for a strong draught of liquor.

"No matter how hard," Clara said as if trying to convince herself, "it's better than not knowing."

Franklin nodded and drew a deep breath. "The team were all at the tables, working, when the incident began. Five people. Four at tables, but there was someone there who didn't quite belong. Someone hanging back and watching." He paused and looked at Clara. She shrugged and he continued.

"They were putting ingredients into a large glass bottle with a narrow, angled neck and watching for a reaction after each addition. Words were exchanged, but too muddy for me to hear. After a number of items were combined, the compound reacted. There was a bubbling, a little spark. Smoke truly came to life—tendrils rose, reaching about the room like growing vines. The curls of dark gray vapor asphyxiated the workers, one by one, as if the acrid tendrils were strangling hands."

Clara put her hand to the desk to steady herself, trying to not imagine Louis's handsome face distorted in pain.

"They did not suffer long, Miss Templeton," Franklin added softly. "Then everything went up in a strange fire, the result of which we saw in that room. And throughout all of it, there was a dark silhouette against the wall. If it was another person, unrelated to the workers, it was too dark to tell. It was a big black shadow, a ghost in reverse. It stood there after the fire and then faded."

There was a long silence.

Clara clenched and unclenched her jaw. She never wanted to seem weak in front of Franklin, no matter how much she trusted him. She sipped the brandy carefully. The sting was painful going down her throat but she welcomed any sensation that allowed her to in some way share the agony of Louis's demise, even something so mild as the burn of alcohol.

Setting the snifter on Franklin's desk, she pressed a hand to her bosom and felt the slight unevenness of the fabric caused by the cravat she'd stowed against her breast, next to the amulet.

"It was . . . it was a good idea, originally, Franklin," she murmured. "The compound. After the assassinations, Lincoln, then Garfield . . ."

"You mustn't second-guess yourself," Franklin insisted. "The bent of your heart is honorable. People die for good causes." Franklin paused, likely thinking of his brother. "But take heart, Miss Templeton. Someone made it out of there. Someone survived."

Clara didn't dare imagine that lone survivor could be Louis, but something flickered within her. She didn't like that small wick of hope. Small candles, even buried, were too easy to blow out. The cold wind of hard reality always got to them, no matter their depth.

"Now. Your turn. What did you see?" Franklin asked.

Clara sighed and relayed her encounter with the silhouettes. Franklin chewed his lip, considering her narrative. "So, ghosts, then?" he began. "You think they were the spirits of the scientists? Bidding you to find their papers?"

"I'd like to think so. Manifestations come in all kinds, however, these . . . entities were unlike any spirits I've yet encountered. My glimpses of ghosts are shimmers of light, a suggestion of shape and body, and while sometimes I can ascertain words and messages, it's always brief. Any sustained communication triggers a seizure. I am surprised this did not. But who else would they be but the team?"

Franklin shook his head. "I don't like it. How can we know what they mean?"

"It must be something of the team's legacy," Clara replied, as uneasy as her colleague. "We have to find it. The warning was clear that unless we acted, others would act around us."

"Clearly that precise compound should never be made again," Franklin said.

"I doubt it ever can be," Clara countered. "But my vision said: 'If you don't do it, someone else will.' And that doesn't bode well either."

Franklin paused. "True. I do trust our country more than any other. Where to begin?"

"With whoever fled. One of the team? The one watching? One of ours . . . or another's?" She lifted her glass. "It isn't just us anymore. I can tell."

Though Clara barely heard the downstairs door open, she knew immediately who had entered the building. This was no visitor to the government offices below. No, this was the Eterna Commission's own doorkeeper. They received few visitors, but there was the occasional call. Given the nature of their work, it was vital that their receptionist be savvy. Lavinia Kent was a marvel.

"Hello, darlings!" she called up to them.

Clara descended to meet the girl—the *woman*, rather—young as she was, at twenty-one Lavinia was certainly an adult and Clara had to stop thinking of her as anything else. It was hard—after so many rounds upon the globe, everyone felt like children to her. Yet to society, Clara was an aberration, a girl who'd gone to waste. . . . As with most of history, the assumption was that she should be a wife and mother by now. But the fates had other plans for her in this life.

Lavinia was so dramatic that one didn't have to be a sensitive to smell the giddiness wafting from the young woman like perfume. Her elaborate jet-black dress rustled as she entered, artful bombazine layers streaming with black ribbons. A few locks of her deep red hair flew free from her black bonnet, its crepe veil cast back. It might be supposed that the girl was in mourning, but this was not the case; it was simply her fashion.

"Hello, Clara dear," Lavinia said breathlessly, her bright green eyes wide. "I had quite the night," she continued, holding out a bejeweled hand: a band with a shimmering dark stone. "It's a black diamond, isn't it amazing?" Lavinia cooed. "Didn't Nathaniel do well?"

In a breath, Clara banished the flare of jealousy that cracked through her like a whip, echoing through her timelines. "Congratulations!" Clara embraced her friend. "He finally came around?"

"It was pure hell to get there, but I won him in the end," Lavinia cried in a crisp London accent that announced her as a member of the striving class. "It will cost me everything, of course, the very last of Father's favor and the home in Lancashire. But true love is worth it."

Clara nodded. Though she'd not yet been asked for her hand, her past lives understood love comprehensively.

She moaned suddenly. "This means I need to start looking for another receptionist!"

"As if I'd stop working for you!" Lavinia scoffed. "You're my mentor! Well, you and Evelyn, of course." She pressed a hand to her forehead, speaking like a melodramatic ingenue. "I wasn't meant for a life of housekeeping alone!"

Clara laughed. "Few of us are, and yet, you'd think the world has no other uses for us."

"Then we shall tell the world otherwise," Lavinia said with a smile. "Like we've always done. We must stay together, Clara, we need each other's support now more than ever."

The Kents had practically abandoned Lavinia after a terrible mishap with the law. Bishop had convinced Lavinia to work in secret for the Eterna office. Her family knew only that she had a "benefactor;" generally they acted like she didn't exist.

Lavinia had become the much needed bosom friend to take the place of the schoolgirl companions who all abandoned Clara when she did not continue in "society." They'd had many conversations, shared innumerable secrets, yet Clara had never said anything to Lavinia about Louis. So she couldn't even now unburden her heart to her closest female confidante.

"Evelyn Northe-Stewart!" Clara exclaimed. "How is she? Hosting séances for curious girls? She's such a dear confidante of the senator, I thought I'd see her at the house more often, but of late she has been absent."

"I suppose her being re-wed has something to do with that, now that she has a family of her own again. And yes, séances as usual," Lavinia replied. "She has me helping now, with the more unstable ones, considering my experiences. . . ." She looked down at the floor.

Clara lifted her chin with her finger. "What have I said?"

"No shame in the office," Lavinia parroted obediently.

Two years prior, Lavinia's social circle, followers of flamboyant, darkly dramatic actor Nathaniel Veil—now Lavinia's fiancé—had been targeted by a strange chemist. They sought a "cure for melancholy," but the drug he supplied produced wild rages. It was thought the chemist might be a recruit for Eterna research, but the man was arrested. However the event wasn't a total loss, for Lavinia had developed an uncanny ability to judge human intention. She could quite literally smell intent.

Behind Lavinia's post on the first floor of the brownstone were pulls that went to bells informing the upstairs office as to what sort of visitor they could expect. Lavinia would assess a visitor and pull one of the four black tassels. The smallest led to a high-pitched bell signaling a known acquaintance or colleague. The next larger announced a visitor Lavinia deemed friendly. The next meant neutral, and the largest and deepest bell indicated that the company was a liar, a cheat, or potentially dangerous. At this signal, Franklin quickly descended with pistol in hand. This thankfully had only happened with a few drunks.

"Are we expecting anyone today?" Lavinia asked, perching on her wooden desk.

"Fred Bixby," Clara replied.

"Bixby!" the young woman cried, elongating the "y" sound in glee.

Though Lavinia's melancholies were intense, she was an utterly pure soul who felt things lavishly and found dramatic ways to express sentiment. Clara hoped she never lost this quality the women had in common, though Clara had learned to shield herself better. But then, Clara had had more practice; Lavinia was a newer soul.

"What's wrong, Clara?" Lavinia asked. "Something's wrong and you're trying to hide it."

Clara took a shaking breath. "It's the Eterna team. They're all dead, though one may be alive. We don't know who."

"That's terrible," Lavinia breathed, skirting around the desk and flouncing into her chair, layers of black tulle and crepe spilling everywhere. "I'm sorry," she said. "I know I should feel their loss but, not having been given the opportunity to even meet them, I don't."

"Nor do I," Clara replied, lying again and staring at the shelf above Lavinia's desk, which was crammed with notepads, a compass, a replica Egyptian Canopic jar that she used to hold her quills and pencils, and more. Clara's gaze rested on a collection of shards from gravestones, which Lavinia had artfully arranged into a miniature druid ring.

"It wasn't your fault," Lavinia continued. "I know that look, dear, the helpless look you get when you want to fix things you can't. It wasn't your fault. No shame in the office, right?"

"Indeed." Clara patted Lavinia on the shoulder. "Do send Fred up directly, won't you?" Lavinia nodded. "Again, congratulations. Your nuptials shall be the most dramatic, black-crepe-filled affair the world has ever seen. The death of Prince Albert will have nothing on you dears."

At this, Lavinia laughed and Clara trotted up the stairs before her pang of grief deepened.

* * * * *

Wanting a moment alone, Clara asked Franklin if he'd be so kind as to fetch them some lunch from a nearby butcher. He graciously agreed. With him gone, Clara leaned forward, layers of bustle, interior ruffles, and petticoats shifting as she pressed her hand to her sternum.

There, Louis's amulet of protection nestled between her breasts, beside the knot of his cravat. Pressing, Clara felt all the strictures that bound her: rigid bodice bones upon corset bones upon human bones. She slipped her fingers beneath her clothes, fishing past the hooks of her bodice and the thin layer of her chemise, grasping an end of the saffron silk fabric with thumb and forefinger and sliding it from its warm hiding place.

She tried to ignore how the pulling of silk from along her breast felt like Louis's unlacing of her stays . . . but the more she tried to block the warm, passionate images, the more sensations washed over her. He was an inventive, thorough man in every regard; he was the first in this lifetime to leave her feeling as though he could chart her every inch and still seek further discoveries. His thirst for life, and for her, meant his sudden absence created the cruelest desert.

Ducking beneath her desk, Clara shifted a small carpet and lifted a floorboard, then stared down at the small black metal face of the safe set into the floor. She had precious few secrets, but even she needed a secure place to hide them.

A chill abruptly ran down her spine and the hairs at the back of her neck rose on end. The room became dreadfully cold and she saw her breath misting in the air. Generally this indicated that there was a ghost nearby. Her heart pounded.

"Louis . . ." she whispered. "Louis, if that is you, give me a sign. . . ."

There was no sound nor movement. A reminder that she'd never really had anything. Passionate words and caresses, but those too were phantoms in the end. He would never have offered for her, since they were not supposed to even know of each other's existence.

Her shoulders fell. She turned the combination of the dial, opened the safe and tossed the warm yellow silk into the black void, closing the lid on this sensual remnant of her lover, locking it and her feelings away.

Franklin returned with cuts of meat and cheese, and they sat with the day's difficult images and emotions in silence until a cry from the threshold:

"The redcoats are coming! Or, rather, they've been here. Now they're going back and forth!" Fred Bixby burst into the office, carrying a ledger.

Clara was so entertained by him she forgave the start that caused her coffee to spill over the rim of the porcelain cup she had been holding when he'd shouted. Lanky, thin, light-skinned, with short auburn brown hair, what Bixby didn't have in girth or bulk, he made up for in enthusiasm.

"Look," he exclaimed. "The log, here. One Mr. Brinkman. We've seen that signature before, haven't we?"

"It's good to see you, too, Fred," Clara said with a laugh. His energy wiped away the disaster site's lingering chill.

"Oh. Yes. Right. I haven't seen you in, what, a month?" the man processed. "Sorry. Hello!" He waved at them both.

"Two months since we last called upon your services, my friend," Franklin clarified.

The tall man blinked chestnut-colored eyes. "Has it truly been that long?"

Clara nodded. "What has been keeping you busy?" she asked.

"Well, I read the whole collection of the circulating library near Union Square."

"What were you looking for?" Franklin asked.

"Peace," the man replied, staring Clara straight in the eye. Fred was compulsive. A voracious reader and live wire, he kept himself content by constant intake.

"May we all find peace," Clara said softly. "Now, tell me why the British are coming."

"You remember Brinkman, right?" Fred asked. "Our slippery Brit, snooping for years?"

He leaped over to sit in the chair opposite Clara, bumping his skinny knees against her desk. The man was a bloodhound of logs and ledgers, of finding needles in haystacks, an invaluable asset, as America was vast and so was her paperwork. It was a blessing that Bishop had found him and his sister through a mutual circle of progressive Republican activists.

"Do you see this in yesterday's southbound logs?" he said, pointing to a line on a ledger page. "Look how a Mr. *Bankman* appears, an alias of Brinkman, you can tell as there's the same slant to the script, he appears on liners via the same agents who deal chiefly in British interests."

"Good eye, Fred," Clara declared.

"Thank you, ma'am. But this is a man who, it seems, shuttles solely between New York and London. Why would he now travel so far, having bought passage all the way to New Orleans? It doesn't mean that that's where he's going, but the ticket gives him leave to travel the length of the Mississippi. Is there something down there to be aware of?"

Clara ignored the searing pain that seized her at the mention of New Orleans; that magical, mysterious place that had raised Louis Dupris. There could be a correlation: maybe dear Louis was the one who escaped after all. Her heart leaped at the hope.

"Maybe there is," Clara said quietly. "Fred, you're a genius." She closed the ledgers and returned them to the man, who would return them to their rightful owners, the ships' companies. "But do take a moment, breathe, eat something. You're all elbows."

"Will your office be sending a tail?" he asked with a grin.

"But of course, Fred," Clara declared. "Set your sister loose."

Fred clapped and called over his shoulder, "Effie!"

"You brought her with you." Franklin chuckled. "Of course you did."

Clara and Franklin watched Miss Ephegenia Bixby traipse into the room in a modest calico day dress that covered a figure as gangly as her younger brother's. Her brown spiral curls, less red than her brother's, were wound tightly to her head and mostly covered by a lace bonnet. She and her brother both were dusted with a smattering of brown freckles.

As far as most knew, the Bixbys had always lived in Greenwich Village. But Clara, Franklin, and Josiah knew the truth: they used to go home to a neighborhood where the average skin color was far darker, the law less fair, and the opportunities far slimmer. Unfair as Clara thought it was that they felt they had to, the conditions of the country were such that the Bixbys had made a harrowing choice to leave those lives behind and reinvent themselves.

It was something Louis had talked about often. When he imagined a future with Clara, not in New Orleans but in New York, if they dared go public, Louis would continue to pass. . . . Clara clenched her jaw and forced him from her mind.

Effie kissed her brother daintily on the cheek, then turned to Clara.

"'Bankman.' won't be far off yet," she stated, her voice musical and pleasant. "If I take one of the newer express trains, I could catch up to a port of call in a day. Shall I go?" Excitement lit her brown eyes, indicating her happiness at the thought of more adventure than was usually afforded her sex.

Effie was as energetic as her brother, but better at controlling it. The young woman could find anyone. Anywhere. A family of bloodhounds—one for names and paperwork, one for actual persons—and Clara had had the great fortune of utilizing their services in honor of their country. She felt sorry for snooping England, who couldn't possibly possess such unique talents.

"Yes, Miss Bixby," Clara exclaimed. "Please go and foil that bully England!"

When Harold Spire woke, he did the same first thing he did nearly every morning; clear the crimson-drenched image of his mother out of his mind. The human body has a great deal of blood to spill. Despite being moved to new, still unfamiliar apartments, despite the fact that the majority of his modest belongings remained in boxes, the daily routine of wiping horror away remained, unchanged. Something within him had died with his mother, seventeen years earlier. Only police work made him feel as though there was still a heart somewhere inside his hollow body.

But his new appointment was hardly police work and it hardly gave him purpose. Indeed, it was an example of the very thing he'd sought all his life to avoid, having grown up in his mad father's absurd worlds of extremes and ridiculous fictions.

Knight urging Spire to visit his father had struck quite a chord. A woman of the theater, she didn't have to be psychic to know about the disconnect between father and son. The last time Spire had gone for an indefinite time without visiting his father or seeing one of his shows, the man launched a production about filial abandonment. All over London, adverts and plastered playbills announcing the show brightly proclaimed:

My Son, My Son, Why Hast Thou Forsaken Me?—The Truth in Two Acts by Victor Spire.

This angered the junior Spire more than he could possibly express. He got quite the ribbing for it at the precinct, save from his trusted colleague Grange, who had found it in as poor taste as the sensational account Victor Spire had published of his wife's death years prior. That, for Harold Spire, had been the nail in the coffin of paternal affection. The play about the faithless son did, however, ensure that Harold paid *dear old dad* a reluctant visit once a month. His usual interval having nearly expired, Spire had determined today would be the day. Now more than ever, he could not afford light being shone his direction and so he embarked upon the dread routine, lest his father once again expose him to the world.

His whole day, in fact, would be trying, he thought, prematurely weary. After his reluctant visit, he would attend an Eterna "team meeting" at their new offices. Keys had been deposited through the mail slot of his door with a note giving the address—somewhere in Millbank—and setting the meeting time at noon.

Seeing the building where he had been raised, down a curving street just outside the Covent Garden district, always made Spire anxious. Not only because of the violence that had taken place here, but because his father did nothing to deter the air of misery and anxiety that permeated the walls.

He climbed the stoop and tried the lock in the weatherworn door that needed a new layer of black paint. As always, he was surprised to find the locks from childhood unchanged.

"Father," Spire called up the stairs.

"Harry, I presume?" growled a voice.

"Unless you have another son," Spire said wearily.

"Oh," followed by a dramatic moan, then, "I have a *son*, do I?"

Spire sighed. *And so it begins . . .*

Harold Spire ascended the wooden stairs, noting dusty railings, moldering carpet, and wood that groaned beneath his boots. The house's front windows were sooty and there was no lamp or lantern to light his way; everything inside as gray as a London alley. Victor Spire could not keep a housekeeper. Spire didn't know if his father's trouble with staff was due to the widespread knowledge that there had been a death in the building—histrionic folk claiming to see the specter of Mrs. Spire—or to his father's odd temperament. The lack of a housekeeper was probably for the best as Victor didn't have enough funds to employ one anyway.

Two flights up, Spire stepped onto the landing. He heard other footsteps now and studied the half-open wooden pocket doors before him, whose intricate carvings bore the same level of dust as the balustrade. A sweeping flash of red within made Spire squint.

Victor Spire had bought the town house after the financial—though not critical—successes of his first novel and its popular stage adaptation. The home had Gothic tracery and detailing, arched windows with stained glass in deep reds and blues, and was the closest Victor could come to the castle he'd written about in his homage to Horace Walpole, his idol.

The Northernmost Castle had been filled with every titillating thing usually encountered in a Gothic yarn, but with an absurdly high body count. Spire had started reading it before his mother was killed. After, he blamed the novel for the heinous act and moved out of his father's house as soon as he joined the police.

Police work, to Harold Spire, was the antithesis of his father's fantasies. Victor Spire made up ridiculous ways of hurting people and getting on in the world. Harold Spire fought against troubled fools who made such fictions reality.

Spire slid open the doors and entered an empty space with lancet windows of deep-colored stained glass like those described in Edgar Allan Poe's "Masque of the Red Death."

Shafts of color speared into the room but the result was more muddy mess than cathedral of light.

The threadbare carpet that Victor had paced holes in had once been a beautiful Persian rug in an intricate black and white floral pattern. There was little furniture in the room apart from a chair, a writing desk, and a tea tray, yet it was still too much, an over-the-top clash of color and pattern, of hard edges and blurred lines.

At the sound of the doors, Victor Spire had paused in mid-step, his back to his son. He wore a long red satin robe, something Asian-looking, his white hair wild. Unless he had shaved it since Harold's previous visit, his aging father sported a lengthening white goatee. To his relief, Harold Spire had more of his mother's features; a refined, genteel look, comely and stoic, as opposed to his father's hard angles and drooping mouth. It seemed as if the years were turning the elder Spire's face into the tragedy half of the paired masks that had come to symbolize the dramatic profession.

"Harry," Victor Spire growled.

"Father," Spire replied shortly. He hated being called Harry. "The place is looking worn," he continued, standing beside a shaft of yellow light from a bit of jaundiced stained glass. "What happened to that nice box keeper from the Lyceum, one of those long-suffering friends who make up your theatrical circle. Didn't she used to come around and straighten things up?"

"Left for Paris," Victor said, waving a languid, wrinkled hand as he continued walking; his hair took on different colors as he passed in and out of the colored beams of light that penetrated the room. "Why do all the good souls of this earth go to France?"

Spire gritted his teeth and ignored his father's inadvertent jab. Victor Spire likely didn't remember that the woman Spire nearly proposed to had been a French spy. The man didn't take the trouble to know or ask much about his son's life.

"Haven't the foggiest," Spire said, trying to sound dismissive. "I've come to tell you I'm living in Westminster now, Rochester Street. I've a new appointment. I can't say anything about it, the department is classified. So if you come looking for me at the Metropolitan, you won't find me. If you need anything, send word to this address." He placed a card on his father's writing table, adding bitterly; "I can't have you writing another play about a vanished son."

His father made a nondescript sound. Spire wasn't sure it was a response to what he'd said, but considering there was no calculating look in his father's eyes, he felt confident that the man hadn't had anything to do with the Omega appointment. Fate was instead playing a particularly cruel joke. If there was a God, surely this was evidence of His great love of irony.

"Father." Spire sighed. "Would you stop pacing a moment?"

"No," Victor said, sounding horrified. "Pacing keeps me sane."

Spire chortled. "I think that's relative." He found his father's unfailing habit of relentlessly pacing the floorboards, day in and day out, childish and self-indulgent.

His father whirled to face him, red robes jerking to a halt. "Smug. You know, that's what you've become, smug. I hate smug."

Harold stared at his father, wondering when he'd last felt genuine affection for the man. "Smug keeps me sane," Spire replied after a tense moment. A reluctant smile tugged at the corner of Victor's pursed mouth.

"Congratulations on your appointment," the older man said with sudden brightness. "Will you come see my new play? It opens next month."

The consequences if he refused to attend would be as melodramatic and absurd, but far more long-lasting and public than suffering through the play itself. "Yes," he replied simply.

His father beamed, for the first time, showing a flicker of true warmth. "Good then!" He rummaged among the papers strewn on his desk, selected a sheet, and thrust it at his son.

Spire kept his face neutral as he read it: a theater bill, printed in bright red:

AT THE LYCEUM FOR ONE NIGHT ONLY! *A Seventh Wonder of the Dramatic World* by Victor Spire, inimitable author of *The Northernmost Castle*! PRESENTING A STORY OF PASSION AND POISON! OF REVENGE, RUINATION, AND LARGE REPTILES:

THE DEADLY DAMSEL IN DISTRESS:

ONE IMPERILED BUT CONNIVING WOMAN!
THREE MEN!
WHO . . . WILL . . . SURVIVE???!!!

"Lovely," Spire choked out quietly and with great effort.

Perhaps he could convince Lord Black to send his father a note expressing his regrets that "Harold was kept at work." Victor Spire couldn't afford not to be nice to an aristocrat. . . .

"I'll be sure to get you the best seat!" his father cooed. "Or seats, perhaps? Do you have a special lady friend you'd like to invite? I daresay the show is rather titillating—"

"No," Spire replied through clenched teeth.

"Pity," Victor replied, his angular face contorting into an unattractive pout. "Now. Is that all? As you can see, I'm *quite* busy."

Spire stared at him blankly.

Victor tapped his head. "Busy. Busy, busy, busy!" He resumed pacing, apparently immediately dismissing Harold from his mind.

Harold Spire saw himself out, crumpling the theater bill in his pocket and actively not looking at the second-floor doorway through which he inevitably saw his mother, her throat slit and blood streaming.

Much like that poor woman in Tourney's cellar of horrors.

He yearned to set to work on Miss Everhart's list of leads, to check in with his fellows on the force, learn of any new developments in the case, and be bolstered by his men's more sensible natures and pleasant camaraderie. Clenching his fists, he instead made his way toward Omega's offices. He wanted to be there before anyone else, to look around the space prior to the arrival of his ragtag team.

* * * * *

Lord Black, clad in a suit entirely of ivory silk that couldn't have been more in contrast with Rose Everhart's prim, school-marmish, blue linen dress, slid two brass keys on an unadorned ring across Rose's small desk.

A man whose capacity for nuance, detail, and diplomacy was as refined as his joie de vivre was contagious, Lord Black had long ago earned Rose's admiration and care. At his entry into her tiny Parliament office, she had set down her book, a rather poorly written, uselessly sensationalistic, turn-of-the-century review of various occult practices. She had been trying to gain insight into aspects of the Tourney case.

"Henceforth, you'll report here," Lord Black said, pointing to the keys. "You and Spire will be the first ones in. Shall we go have a look, before the others arrive at noon?"

She nodded and rose, allowing him to lead her out from under the grand Gothic eaves of Parliament, recalling how thrilled she had been when she'd watched the clock tower rise, a beacon of the elegant, modern world over the muddy, old river.

They strolled in silence from Parliament to Omega's Mill-bank offices, Rose wishing all the while that she could talk freely to the man beside her. In her private moments, she thought of him as dear Edward Wardwick—a familiarity Lord Black allowed a scant few. Respect between them was mutual; he commended her talents and praised the fact she didn't chide him for choosing work above a family. And he never pressed her toward the same.

Today, she wished not to talk of personal matters but of work. While Rose believed it important to foil America's efforts, even though she was unsure if immortality was possible—she didn't see why she couldn't attend to both it and the Tourney case that seemed to her to represent deep demons of their manic, polarizing age. What if she could prove the Tourney case could give insights into immortality? After all, someone had been experimenting on those poor women and children in some way, and the police had no idea what the goal had been.

Ethical terror took hold of her. If she made a correlation, would the queen condone such experiments, if performed under government supervision? How desperate was the woman? Was she primarily interested in beating the Americans or did she want the compound for herself?

Rose shook herself mentally. For now, Omega needed her and all else would have to wait. She and Black paused near the corner of Horseferry Road and Millbank Street, noticing Spire approaching. His blond-brown hair was mussed by the breeze and he was dressed in modest earthen hues. As she had when they'd met before, Rose noted that his frock coat, waistcoat, and trousers were clean and well maintained but nothing he seemed to take great pride or care in. She wondered if the man owned any hats or if the idea of one had ever occurred to him beyond for warmth come wintertime. He bowed his head in greeting once he caught sight of Lord Black and Rose.

"So. Home sweet home?" Spire asked, taking in the building. Lord Black beamed.

Rose stared at the high-ceilinged three-story dark brick edifice that sat a stones' throw from a couple of breweries. A further stone might have landed in either the massive hexagonal Millbank penitentiary or the nearby holdings of the Chartered Gas Works, equally harrowing and potentially dangerous places. Looking toward the Thames, Lambeth Bridge was directly ahead, curving east, the stately spires of Parliament; a few wharves stretching wooden fingers out onto the river between.

With granite keystones above the wide, arched windows that were the most interesting feature of the building, the edifice looked like what it was, an industrial building with simple lines and an unadorned facade.

Lord Black let Spire do the honors; Omega's director used his hefty iron key to open the large metal front door. The threesome stepped into an open space with doors leading into separate rooms. Like the exterior, the interior was fairly unadorned: brick, solid, angular, save for the immense wrought-iron main stair with a bit of flourish on the balustrade.

The building was gaslit, direct from the nearby Works. At the center of the space hung a great circular fixture that featured the same sweep of elegant wrought-iron around a ring of glass globe lamps. At present the daylight was strong enough not to need it. The curved windows were dressed top to bottom with ivory damask curtains that looked freshly installed, which created a warm, diffuse light in the space.

In Rose's opinion, all this made for a surprisingly pleasant atmosphere. It was so open and modern though in the middle of cramped, cluttered old London. Work spaces were her havens and she placed on them a reverence that others might give cathedrals.

"The whole building is ours," Black stated. "I'm the only one who knows it belongs to Omega. Even the prime minister doesn't know, Miss Everhart, so before you mention it, let's chat about disclosure preferences."

Rose nodded. She'd need her Parliamentary workload altered—decreased, possibly extensively. Black could deal with the whining.

"Is it too much space for so small a team?" Spire asked. "Unless we place the new scientists here? I'd be pleased to have persons I'm meant to guard within my sights."

"As far as I know, that's the plan, though Her Majesty has been known to override me," Black said before turning to climb the stairs, fine boots clanging on the iron between floors, frock coat flapping behind him. "I'll have the treasures of my war room brought up here," he shouted, "and take an office for my own!"

"Would you like to be director, then, Your Lordship?" Spire called after him. "I do have police work I could be doing."

"Oh, no! I'll come and go on my own whims, Spire, I don't want to be director!" The nobleman yelled before disappearing beyond the upper landing.

Rose watched Spire clench his jaw and check a surge of frustration, keeping a calm and capable attitude of command. Sounds from outside heralded the arrival of the rest of the team and there was work to be done.

* * * * *

Spire took a deep breath and tried to take in his surroundings objectively.

The second floor was a wide brick room with the same arched windows and damask curtains, furnished with several long tables and tall stools, desks and desk chairs under the windows, wooden shelving and filing cabinets along the walls and between the windows, and a large, circular table at the center of the room, surrounded by chairs. Considering he'd had to share cramped, cluttered, dark, gloomy offices at the

Metropolitan, the fact that there was bright light and breathing room was at least an improvement.

Then he saw *his* office. An anterior room, partitioned from the open space by tall wooden walls. A wooden door bore a brass placard; fine, noble script, it read:

HAROLD SPIRE, DIRECTOR

This did something to his heart that he didn't expect; this proof that he was trusted unequivocally by the highest authorities in the land. He swallowed hard, a sudden swell of pride and sense of duty that entirely shocked him out of his dismay at how little he'd been a part of the department's decision-making thus far. In the next breath, he was damning himself for his response, which would make it all the harder to go behind their backs and continue on the Tourney matter.

Lying on the circular, central table was a file, labeled in typeset letters:

THE UNITED STATES OF AMERICA'S ETERNA COMMISSION

Frowning, Spire walked over and was about to pick up the documents when the Wilsons exclaimed in sudden unison and everyone in the room—even Spire—jumped.

"Thank heavens," Mr. Wilson cried as he whipped aside a dust curtain to reveal a large tea cart with full amenities and behind it, a small coal-burning stove and a teakettle.

"We are in a civilized building after all," Mrs. Wilson declared. "For a moment I was very afraid." Smoothing her soft scarf, she immediately set to stoking the stove while her husband filled the kettle from a water tank at the corner of the wide room.

Blakely and Knight strolled about the space arm in arm, Blakely guiding Knight. Her eyes were closed; she was quietly asking the building if any spirits were present and listening for a response.

Tucking the file under his arm, Spire called to his team: "I'll be in my office, familiarizing myself with this file. Please assess any security weaknesses of this building. Lord Black will see to the financing of their improvement."

"Yes, sir," Mr. Wilson replied over his steeping tea.

Spire opened the door bearing his name, closed it behind him, and breathed deeply at the beautiful sight before him: a large, oak desk with blotter, inkwells, fountain pens, and a ream of paper, a leather chair, an empty bookshelf upon which sat a crystal decanter of liquor and two snifters. For Spire, peace of mind was hard to come by; work was the only thing that gave him any solace and this simple, quiet space, fit with sturdy, well-made things, entirely without ostentation, this was pure luxury.

He dove into the file. It contained a compilation of the Eterna origin story, a hodgepodge of memoranda; timelines; names of known operatives; newspaper articles alluding to the formation of the United States' Secret Service, under whose umbrella the Eterna Commission had evidently crept; telegraph messages and various correspondence from the past decade.

Andre Dupris's letters were useful: they set the discussions and work of the place in a more human context, not merely fact but a glimpse of life. Spire wanted to know the sorts of people he was investigating; making decisions on facts alone without ascertaining the personalities surrounding a given situation invariably would lead to error. He didn't believe in the endgame of what America was after, or even in the experiments or theories themselves, but he needed to know what drove those involved.

Well, it was obvious what drove America. Empire and conquest. The apple didn't fall far from the tree of Mother England, but over across the pond, the orchard was far more wild and the rules of the land less certain. After their Civil War, the country's military had strengthened, codified, and redeployed westward. Industry was booming. The natives that

hadn't been massacred were driven to far-flung corners of
the nation and America's insatiable appetite for expansion
plumped its borders. It had even dared to invade British holdings in the north early in the century. The loose assembly of
states didn't know when to cool its unruly heels.

While Eterna may have been born out of assassination, it
continued out of the need for dominance on a world stage.
Eterna, in theory or practice, hadn't managed to do anyone
any good, but the legacy of a young girl's impetuous suggestion of immortality lived on to frighten (or seduce) Queen
Victoria.

Spire began to find all of it fascinating. Absurd and stupid, to be sure, but magnetic all the same. He wondered if any
of his team would see Eterna and the political theater in which
they were engaged as he saw it: a grand, posturing, ridiculous dance.

When Spire finished his review and reentered the main
room, he found the team scattered about at various desks and
tables, each with a cup of tea. Knight had laid out a tarot
spread for Mrs. Wilson, who was in turn teaching her the
names of the Major Arcana in Arabic.

Spire seated himself at the circular table and in moments
the others had gathered around him.

"The Knights of Omega's Roundtable," Mr. Wilson stated
as a palpable excitement rose among the team that Spire
couldn't help but notice, even if he was reluctant to embrace it.

"So," Spire began. "What we know of the Eterna Compound is that it was the brainchild of Clara Templeton, who
was a friend of Mary Todd Lincoln, then the first lady, due to
her"—Spire grimaced at the word—"*clairvoyant* tendencies.
After her parents died of tuberculosis, Templeton became the
ward of another spiritualist and fierce supporter of President
Abraham Lincoln, Republican Senator Rupert Bishop. While
Templeton was not a member of the Eterna team, Bishop ap-

pears to have spearheaded the early commission, which was formed shortly after Lincoln's assassination."

Spire paused, resting his hands on the papers before him and waiting for Blakely to pull some magic trick, Knight to start speaking in tongues, or the Wilsons to cite some angle of espionage. But no. They simply listened, taking in the information with the focus and dedication he expected of his former colleagues on the Metropolitan Police. Spire doubted this illusion of an actual, working department would last, but he would enjoy it while he could. He continued, indulging in the dark humor he found in the information:

"The American team consisted of a number of scientists— let's say theorists, since not all seem to have scientific training. First was Malachi Goldberg, a rising star in botany—I didn't know such a mundane field was capable of infamy, but the notes seem to think so. There was Barnard Smith, an American-born chemist with a penchant for putting anything and everything imaginable into test tubes and setting the contents on fire. Bartholomew Feizer, a doctor and evidently a British citizen. Let's look into that," he said to Miss Everhart, who was taking notes. She nodded.

"Feizer was versed in matters of the brain, having been a devotee of the Frenchman, Jean-Martin Charcot." Spire tried not to make a disdainful face while saying "Frenchman," but couldn't help it.

"The team was joined in 1880 by Louis Dupris, a theorist from New Orleans, a believer in the Vodoun principles espoused by his mother. Evidently Dupris took the team to new, *imaginative* levels, allowing spiritual and scientific matters to mingle. He worked closely with Smith, and together the men seem to have begun believing in the existence of magic, purporting that all faiths and all sciences, at their zeniths, create what is tantamount to sorcery. They set about trying to prove this."

Spire drew a thin sheet of paper from the file. "Louis Dupris's twin brother, Andre, who joined Louis in New York, provided England with information on his brother's activities. Last word we have from Dupris is this telegraph memorandum from over a week ago, reporting that Malachi Goldberg was acting odd and paranoid, making the others nervous and suggesting they move locations. After that, Andre did not report as usual. Some disaster befell the Eterna team and all have died or vanished, save one survivor who may be Andre or Louis. Either way, the man is being tracked by our chief American operative, which gives new life to an otherwise dead end.

"We must learn all we can about the site of the American experiments, what officials are involved in providing for and protecting the theorists and in the investigation of the apparent disaster. We must determine which of the Dupris brothers lives and learn all he knows," Spire finished.

"Given the New Orleanean background of Andre and Louis Dupris," Rose chimed in, "it would behoove us to understand more about Louis's Vodoun practices; qualities that may appear in his Eterna offerings. New Orleans is a quilt of culture, a lush city where multiple traditions intersect. Though, New Orleans having been under a particular pressure in the American 'Reconstruction,' I doubt their willingness to support the Union cause." She reached for the file where it sat in front of Spire and drew it to her. Opening the folder, she quickly flipped through to sheets Spire recognized as being information on the Duprises. "Ah. I see now."

Spire raised the eyebrow he hoped would gain him illumination.

"The twins' grandmother was a slave," Rose explained. "The laws enacted in southern parts of the United States since Reconstruction have not made freed black persons welcome, to say the least, though Creoles operate within their own distinct class. I do not know if the Dupris brothers were, as the Americans have called it, 'passing' as white in New York, or how much of their French heritage they parlayed to leverage status, but a Louisiana native working on a northern-based project spearheaded by a Republican administration makes sense to me now."

"I didn't know I was gaining a cultural consultant in addition to an excellent clerk," Spire said with a curt nod of approval.

"Why Andre Dupris would spy for *us*, however," Rose added, "remains a mystery."

"A mystery whose solution I know but cannot reveal," Black said from the doorway. Everyone jumped—no one, not even Spire, had heard the metal stairs give away his approach. Holding a mess of newspapers under one arm, Black clearly delighted in their surprise. "Covert operations means taking care with your feet on iron steps!" he said with glee, reminding Spire that the nobleman sometimes seemed to think this all a game. Very well then, maybe he'd think of it in precisely the same terms.

"Is there some scandal concerning Dupris, Lord Black?" Miss Knight asked, sounding hopeful.

"That's a private matter," Black countered cagily. "We've a tail on him—or his twin—so information is forthcoming." He crossed to the table. "I should tell you that on paper, this building is listed, when it appears at all, solely as a 'records depository.' Should you ever be asked, do not discuss it, send the questioner to me."

He placed the stack of newspapers on the table, saying, "I have arranged for the major dailies to be delivered here, as we oughtn't be out of touch." He squinted at a headline, then looked at Spire. "'Resurrectionist ring's arrests,'" he declared. "Appears your men at the Metropolitan rounded up an orphanage director who supplied bodies to Tourney."

Spire snatched the paper and read the account, proud of Grange and Phyfe. He was disturbed, however, to read reports of suicide among other implicated men, according to their families. However no *complete* bodies of these dead had been recovered, marking a glaring loose end.

"A resurrectionist ring profits off the uses of dead bodies and body parts," Spire said, setting down the paper, which Everhart immediately took up. "Tourney's network may be cannibalizing itself; good for business and no one can squeal. I should make sure Grange knows to—"

"Ah, ah, Spire," Lord Black stopped him, smiling. "Your focus is here." His silk-clad arms gestured around the wide space, his ivory form backlit by soft, diffuse light.

Spire wanted to punch something. With a deep breath he forced himself to remain calm, reassuring himself that Grange was brilliant, he'd do all the same things Spire would do. He could feel Everhart staring at him and his ruddy cheeks burned even hotter.

"Speaking of missing bodies," Spire said through clenched teeth, "that brings up the missing British scientists, Lord Black. How can we in good faith install new men when I've been given no way to sniff out their predecessors' trails?"

"I'm sorry, Mr. Spire, I'd love to discuss those men with you, but there is no trail. One day they were in Greenwich, the next they were not. Nothing was altered or out of place. The men were simply gone." Lord Black fell silent, looking steadily at Spire as if challenging him to pursue his enquiries further.

Spire wouldn't give him the satisfaction. Instead, he asked the team to report on security issues. Everhart, Blakely, and both Wilsons each handed over a sheet of paper. Black, frowning, plucked them out of Spire's hand before he could do more than glance at them.

"I thank the team for its suggestions. I will be sure they are attended to immediately," Lord Black said. "Tomorrow

I'll bring you the scientists' profiles for perusal. The telegraph wires have been installed and the machine will arrive shortly. Who knows, before too long we'll even have electricity!" the aristocrat exclaimed, aglow. "The world is new, my friends, and you are at the forefront of the next great stage of human advancement!"

Everyone appeared caught up in Black's excitement, save Spire and Everhart, who looked worried. Spire took another long breath. It was near the end of the day. His time away from work was still his own, and he'd spend it on that which had always meant the most to him. In this case, more work.

Lord Black swept off, muttering something about contraptions being installed upstairs. Spire heard himself saying vague things to his team regarding aims for the next day and week while his mind raced along other tracks. He hoped his words didn't sound as vacant as they felt, but they seemed to suffice; everyone but Everhart went on their way with no further comment or concern.

"May I walk you home, Miss Everhart?" he asked, trying to sound casual.

"I thought you'd never ask," she said eagerly. On the sidewalk, Everhart glanced up over her shoulder at the window at the center of the uppermost floor. She waved and smiled. Spire turned to see Lord Black leaning out of an open window pane, waving a silk handkerchief as if they were rolling away on a train. "Scratch that, not home, Parliament," she whispered against the warm river breeze. Spire tried to look amenable toward the man. At this, his colleague nearly sputtered a laugh. "Mr. Spire, I'd not even try to force a smile. On you, it just comes out as an obvious grimace."

Spire raised a hand instead, a gesture that could be construed as cordial. "I just don't know about that man."

She replied as they veered toward Parliament. "He's a dear, truly. It isn't his fault you're off the Metropolitan beat. If it were purely up to him, I'm sure he'd let you do both jobs as long as they got done."

"And I would, I will—"

"Pick your battles, Mr. Spire," she said sharply. "I have to every day. If I should be found, I'd best be found in Westminster, as I am expected to check in. And I can do more things from that office than from my home. I just have to be very careful, sending queries tonight."

"Right now we need information as quickly as possible," Spire declared, "and we can't afford to have the whole of Tourney's network be drawn and quartered, traces disappearing before we get anywhere. London makes it all too easy for things to vanish. I doubt any death that had been made to look like suicide actually was one."

"No one is that 'noble' en masse," Everhart agreed.

"They're being hushed, which to me indicates perhaps a secondary ring is involved, with its own interests, which possibly indicates something on a far grander—more terrible—scale."

"How could anything be worse than Tourney's cellar?" she said with a shudder.

"If there were other such places, perhaps?" Spire mused in horror.

"Psychopathic, ritualistic murder isn't cholera, Mr. Spire," she countered with a shake of her head. "It's not contagious. I doubt half if more than a few of the men on that list had any idea what went on. The orphanage director, yes, obviously. But the man who installed the wiring in Tourney's basement? The one whose arm was found by his wife? Likely not. People like Tourney, with resources, may well be protecting themselves, but the rest are most likely hired hands."

"I want to pinpoint them all," Spire declared. "Tonight I must meet with Grange. I'll drop by my old precinct—"

"No, you won't," Everhart countered. "I'll wire your old

precinct from my office, let's not risk your being seen there. Grange can meet you somewhere. Do you and he have a—"

Spire's chuckle stopped her. "Wire 'S.G. to Heorot,' if you please. He'll know."

His colleague appeared bemused. "I assume there's a story behind that."

Spire shrugged. "What would you expect of boyhood friends but that we fought over who pretended to be Beowulf and who Hrothgar? Grange had a Great Dane named Bill that made an excellent Grendel." Everhart laughed. Spire grinned. "Heorot, of course, in later years, became whatever our favored pub happened to be at the time."

"Clearly," she replied with a smile, "warriors and kings need their mead halls."

"Thank you, *Gazelle*," he added. "What's the story behind that?"

Everhart looked into the breeze a moment, wisps of brown hair flying free from beneath her sensible hat. "As a girl I was painfully shy; wasn't one for playing with others. So I pretended to be an animal. Imagine being able to run like the wind," she said wistfully, before offering a little salute. "Until the morrow, Mr. Spire. Go on and fight Grendel however you can."

* * * * *

Stuart Grange was the most welcome sight in the world when Spire entered their favorite haunt, not far from the old precinct, northwest from Parliament's Gothic eaves and the Millbank bricks that ruled Spire's new life.

A bright, freckled redhead, Grange looked an eternal boy despite his thirty years, and was as kind and dependable as when Spire had met him in school. With all the tragedy Spire had endured, a man who remained ambivalent about God, he couldn't help but give something up there thanks for such a good friend.

The jacket of his uniform was hanging from a peg above the booth, his shirtsleeves were rolled up, and he already had a pint in hand. A second pint was resting on the table, waiting for Spire. It was an old habit—first to arrive bought the first round.

"What happened to you?" Grange exclaimed, standing to clap Spire on the back. "We thought you were kidnapped until we received a note from the palace saying you'd been promoted."

"Kidnapped, really," Spire muttered.

Grange chortled. "Don't tell me it's desk work."

"Not exactly." Spire looked around. Everyone was focused on beer, not secrets. "I can't say much other than I'd rather be back with you and the lads."

Grange shook his head. "And right at the critical juncture with Tourney, to lose you—"

"You haven't," Spire countered as they sat. He drank deeply, then proceeded to explain his plan to remain involved, without indicting Everhart directly. Though Grange knew and respected what she'd done as Gazelle, her further involvement was not his to offer.

Grange spoke of his warrants and arraignments, slowed by the spate of "suicides" that Grange found just as dubious as Spire. Knowing that time was against him, he scheduled twice the arrests originally planned. "Though the web, I think, is still wider," he stated.

"I know it is," Spire replied, telling Grange about stashing the list of names to probe.

"I'll look into it. And watch our old box for news and directives." Grange grinned. "Just like old times, going over big heads to get the job done."

Spire leaned forward and whispered, "Be more careful than ever, this big head wears the crown."

Grange saluted, and the dear friends were on their way once

more, unto the breach, living their boyhood pledge, trying their best to keep the monsters at bay.

* * * * *

The important goings-on inside the vast, white stone Gothic grandeur of the Royal Courts of Justice were all but a ghost, the parading pomp of the day vanished into midnight quietude at the toll of somber bells. The peace was entrusted to external posts—night watchmen at the fore and the corners of the palatial holdings. Deep in the complex's interior, down an abandoned stone alcove, one guard kept watch over the tiny, dank, cold gray stone cell bound and fortified by more chains and locks than might have been deemed necessary for one small man's solitary imprisonment.

This was no ordinary prisoner. That he was, in this singular circumstance, the Majesty, Mr. Moriel deemed a credit to his importance.

"O'Rourke," Moriel murmured, "come into the light of this tallow flame."

"Your Majesty?" asked the fleshy, gruff guard. His large body was mostly in shadow but a faint glow from the candle stuck into an iron lantern glanced off deep scars across his broad Irish face.

Moriel deemed the creature who guarded him as unintelligent, an oaf born of the sewers he had once patrolled. Appealing to the man's base nature and promising to provide exactly what the guard wanted—which was to control parts of the city underground—Moriel found the man easily won. The powers of thrall that he had learned from his summoned colleagues had certainly helped tip O'Rourke's allegiance.

Closing the distance between them, the man's barrel chest brushed the bars; then he bent for closer audience with the diminutive prisoner; Moriel reached up, through the bars, and caressed O'Rourke's scarred face. The guard closed his eyes as if deeply pleased.

"I feel vulnerable," Moriel whispered.

"How can I help ease you, milord?" the guard asked, restricting his usual booming voice to match the Majesty's volume.

"I need to clean my slates. How many prison guards stand with us?"

"In the city? Perhaps twenty, scattered in various places. Since your lot has all kinds of folk in 'house arrests' and not in cells at all, the possibility for turning more is always available to you," the man said.

"How wise," Moriel cooed. "I truly do have far more at my disposal than I even ask for." He took a breath. "I can't sleep for fear of what Tourney might say. Sloppy idiot. Cost us nearly the entire underground. He deserves worse than death. I know"—Moriel sighed—"I promised him if anything happened that I'd spread a net for him. He truly was gifted, but I can't let him spill anything further, else it becomes him or me."

The guard bowed his head. "Yes, Majesty. He is a coward for not taking care of himself already."

Moriel murmured a pensive hum of agreement. He tapped the iron bar of his cage with a jagged fingernail. "How many of the names I gave the queen have been purged since she and I spoke?"

"Nearly half, Majesty," the guard replied. He reached out a fat hand and quashed a roach crawling up the wall near Moriel's head, its body falling with the sound of a raindrop into a dank puddle at his feet. "I believe the list is being systematically extinguished, however if you'll permit my opinion, sir?"

"Yes, yes." Moriel waved a bored hand.

"If we kill them so systematically," the guard countered, "mightn't the police suspect the dragon snuffing its own fires and begin to protect them?"

"Then be careful about it," Moriel purred. "And start turning more police to our side. If recruits won't go willingly, convince them with powders. We need to build our army's ranks, lieutenant." One hand shot out to clutch the man's throat; the other fluttered up the round chin and over those deep scars once more. "Tell me. Are the four test bodies prepared?"

"Yes, sir," the guard whispered, standing stock still against the iron.

Moriel smiled. "Good. Ship them soon."

They heard a door open, far down the long, narrow hall. Shift change. The guard stepped away so as not to be seen conversing with the prisoner.

The Majesty shoved his oblong, clammy face against the chains wound around the cell's hinges. "Make sure Tourney doesn't survive the night," he rasped in a saccharine murmur, as if bidding flights of angels to sing his beloved friend to rest.

The guard bowed his head, retreating into the darkness, leaving him with a soft promise: "All shall be attended to, milord."

CHAPTER

EIGHT

Aware she was in that precarious place between sleep and waking, Clara didn't push away the images. They were pleasantly painful, so she indulged them.

Louis lay with her in his Union Square apartment, spacious lodging provided by his government contact. They were lounging atop the duvet of his bed, as they often did after a tangle of lips and hands. Many times they had gone nearly so far as to take her virtue but always stopped short.

Clara remembered other lifetimes, when deflowering meant either death or a very inconvenient child. She'd not trifle with it in this one. They both knew that Eterna, among other things, stood in the way of marriage, so the subject was tabled indefinitely. Well versed in pleasure, their desires did not suffer.

From their conversation, Clara knew she was remembering the night Louis had learned of the death of his foremost idol, Marie Laveau, whose fame as the Queen of New Orleans' Vodoun community had spread far and wide. While he didn't always condone the queen's methods, and certainly not the sensationalized extremes to which outsiders took them, he admired how she had increased the visibility of the faith his mother had passionately instilled in him. His belief system gave him clarity of purpose; he lived in joyful awe of *Bondye* and the *mystères* whom he served and sometimes channeled, ever respecting the animus inherent in all life and every being.

Louis removed an amulet; a bird carved into a bit of quartz

crystal, from around his neck. He unclasped the chain to loop it around Clara's neck, nestling the rock between the curves of her bosom, just visible below the lacy line of her chemise.

"Mother blessed this for me before her death," Louis murmured, fondling a lock of her hair where he'd pulled it back to fasten the chain.

"No, Louis, I can't," Clara protested, placing her fingers over his, trying to stop him. "This is too precious."

"*You* are precious," he said with a smile. "Mother would have loved your brilliant, independent spirit. Take it, so I can share something of her with you and you with her."

Clara accepted at his insistence, letting the cool stone warm against the slight tremor of her heartbeat.

They let tears flow for their ancestors and spiritual leaders, for Queen Marie. They bid the saints be kind and Louis lit candles at his home altar; a colorful, adorned ledge across one wall that filled Clara with a sense of reverence and power.

In this rich memory, Louis gathered her in his arms, breath glancing off her neck, her undone tresses, the bare skin around her open chemise where hooks and eyes had been parted, the avian amulet flying as free as her spirit as he expounded theory that thrilled her deeply as his touch.

"The key of Eterna, *ma cherie*, is to determine the boundaries of meaning. Nothing that may have meaning in terms of life can be overlooked," Louis said, tracing the line of her arm with his finger. She watched his fingertip, reacting to its course, considering the ever so subtly darker hue of his skin against her own pinkish tones.

"Until I came to New York, I believed only in my faith. Not in magic. I am no warlock. My prayers are not spells. My *mystères* are the opposite of demons, whatever popular fetish has warped them into. But I have discovered that magic runs a parallel course, and now believe magic is only a science that has yet to be divulged," he declared. "Meaning has science. Life has science. And we must tie life to meaning in base materials and in spirit and there must be science to this act. No single chemical will prolong life and prevent death, but a holistic compound might result in immortality. We must look beyond the linear and the known and be intimate with mystery."

"The scientist and mystic must live in one heart," Clara murmured, repeating Louis's favorite mantra. He tapped her chest, above her heart, with his finger.

"They must *love* in one heart, too. Indivisible. Else this project is doomed. I'm onto something, something about the vibrations and meaning of certain places that have life and vivacity that have nothing to do with the body and everything to do with soul.

"There's such momentum, my mind hums with a thousand voices urging me forward. I'm doing the great work of the alchemists of old, eternity is within my looking glass. . . ."

Suddenly his expression transformed from pleasant to harrowing, his wonder to horror. A chill took her. This was no longer the same memory.

"You have to keep searching, Clara. Keep searching. What we were doing was not wrong but something went very, very wrong. I don't want to have died in vain."

Face gray, Louis rose and stood at the foot of his bed, his brown trousers rumpled, his white shirt open and undone. His body convulsed and toppled onto her, now stiff and lifeless. She felt the weight of his death.

Clara woke with a wrenching gasp, the protective amulet swinging like a pendulum from her neck. The dream, like a poker, prodded the smoldering fire of her grief but she refused to sob, lest either the housekeeper Miss Harper or Bishop hear her. Her pain had to remain solely her own, and she stifled it yet again.

She wanted to deny that the scientist and the mystic were

ever in league. She vehemently did not want to do what her dead lover asked: to keep searching.

After breakfast she dressed in a cream-colored dress of eyelet threaded with ribbon and went to the office, where she found Franklin leaving.

"I'll be out," he stated. "All day. I need to walk, to clear my mind. Too much clutter."

She understood. After Franklin used his gifts, he was introspective and moody for several days. He often stated that he needed solitude at such times, and preferred walking to sitting at home. Clara wished him well and went to her desk.

"Louis," she said, looking up at the ceiling, "if you are out there, up there, if you care . . . Can you help sort this out? For both our sakes?"

How could she look if she had no idea where to start? She opened one of her desk drawers, hoping to find inspiration in her files. A survey of varying cultural notions of vampirism. Bishop's notes on why ghosts linger and his feeling that it had to do with the living, not the dead. A paper positing that electrical current prolonged life. The tract repeatedly referenced Nikola Tesla, reflecting what seemed to be obsession on the part of the writer, who seemed as touched as Tesla himself.

Genius aside, Clara had seen Tesla at a Westinghouse presentation and had sensed he was a bit unhinged. Still, he was far more intriguing than Edison—his rival in the war of the currents—who seemed a bit of an ass. Clara had found Mary Shelley's *Frankenstein* compelling; she couldn't help but believe in a connection between life and current.

Interviews with mediums and spiritualists she and Bishop deemed legitimate, who were not preying upon the widespread cultural fascination with séances. An odd New York City police case in which a young woman claimed that a young man's soul had been torn from his body and imprisoned in a painting, leaving the body possessed by another.

Here Clara paused, tapping her fingers upon the file. The case was related, at least on paper, to Lavinia Kent's problem with the chemist—and to a series of odd events. Mrs. Evelyn Northe-Stewart and her friends had unveiled a group of experimental madmen bound to a secret society insidious in purpose, though its aim remained unclear. The leader had been executed the year prior, in England. Something about this nagged at her. She thought back to a detail she'd seen at the disaster site, something on the corner of an upstairs floorboard, where lush carpeting had been laid over the wood. . . .

Her thoughts were interrupted by Lavinia, who darted upstairs and into the office, bright eyes wide. "Sorry, Clara. It's . . . Come see. I don't want to touch it. Just . . . come, please."

The ladies descended. Lavinia pointed toward her magpie-like nest of the weird and inexplicable. Nestled amid her collection of séance materials was a small chalkboard intended for automatic writing—a tool for communicating with the dead. In shaking script, two words read:

"C, keep searching . . ."

"It wasn't there an hour ago," Lavinia whispered, shuddering. "No one but Franklin has been through. He'd have had to reach over me to touch it. I haven't moved. What does it mean?"

Clara's heart went to her throat. Was Louis listening to her pleas after all?

Lavinia tried to take Clara's hand. "What aren't you telling me, dear?"

"I can't say, Vin. Someday, maybe, but not today." Clara fled back upstairs, mind racing. She paced her office and wrung her hands, hating feeling helpless when she was a woman of action. How could she search when she didn't know where to begin?

Her eye fell upon the file she'd been considering when Lavinia interrupted her. She thought again about the disaster site.

There was something she hadn't seen. Something she hadn't had time to see, as she left before she was overcome. Her time might be even more without Bishop and Franklin at her side, but she felt she had no choice. She took the bloody key from the locked cabinet safeguarding items of current import, and stormed out the door. Lavinia called her name but she neither turned nor replied.

"I'm searching, Louis," Clara murmured, looking up past brick buildings to blue sky; the breeze of the rivers' confluence at the tip of Manhattan buffeted the eyelet layers of her summer dress. "Wherever you are, help me."

* * * * *

"What have I done?" a voice asked ruefully.

Andre Dupris woke with a start to find his dead twin brother at the foot of his narrow cot. Andre's vision blurred and he felt dizzy; the riverboat was swaying at one pace and Louis's transparent, gray form, floating three feet above the floor, was moving at quite another.

"Go away," Andre mumbled.

"I'm sorry my death is so *inconvenient* for you," Louis said in the same tone he'd always used to chide Andre when he'd overslept after a night of carousing. Maybe the boat wasn't swaying after all—Andre had consumed quite a bit of whiskey the night before.

"I want you to be at peace, brother," Andre mumbled. "We're working toward that. We put your sweetheart on the trail. She'll know something about what happened to you, at least."

"Yes, she's very clever. And she's the only one I trust. But what if whatever was in that place, whatever killed me and my colleagues, goes after her?"

"I don't think the compound has that sort of effect, brother—"

"I don't think the compound alone did it. Something

intervened. We should never have humored Malachi and moved operations. It made everything unstable. I can't wrap my brain around it. Here I thought Smith, constantly setting his vials aflame, would be the death of us."

Andre snorted despite himself. "I did, too."

"I was hoping great mysteries could be solved in the afterlife." Louis sighed, disappointed. "Maybe in some other place, but not here in this great between. I'm no closer to understanding what happened to me, to our bodies, to that space. . . ."

"The 'magic' you and your fellows cooked up is not the key to the universe after all, Louis." Andre sighed. "All I know is that *home* is what's ahead. Where I shall endeavor to fix some of your mess."

"And what about *yours*? Spying for England? If Clara is in danger because of you—"

"Information is all England wants, not your lover," Andre exclaimed, putting a hand to his throbbing head. "What country would let a cure for death go by without interest? Besides, I was trying to extricate myself. I haven't given them any information since the incident. They don't know what happened, or even where, only that I have not reported. When Malachi started acting strangely, I hid your files and all your notes at Smith's old lab."

Louis sighed. "Returning the sacred item I stole from the priestess won't appease her. She'll not easily forgive it, she won't understand. She'll think you're me!"

"Then advise me." Andre shook his head. "You're not helping set yourself to rest. It's like you want to be here."

"I'm *meant* to be here, there's a difference. To save my soul . . . and Clara."

"She got you into this mess to begin with!" Andre spat. "Her *Eterna* is the reason you're dead—"

Louis shook his transparent head. "That isn't true, though I'm sure she blames herself—"

"Go haunt *her,* then," Andre begged.

"I've tried to haunt her!" the ghost cried. "I *can't.* I've gotten near enough to try to talk to her, to touch her, to make her see me, but nothing worked. I tried to leave a message but hadn't the strength to complete it." He floated to and fro, making Andre more seasick. "She's too intense a being. And from spirits, she has to shield, because of her condition. I helped her learn how to do so! And now it's impossible to get noticed. There are so many other energies around her, I can't get through."

"You and your *energies.* Even in death—"

"Energy, life force, it's all the more present after death. That's all that's left of me, a trace of human life left in pulses, vibrations, an electrical spark; I am a mere whisper she cannot hear, talented and sensitive as she is. There's too much noise around her. So many spirits want to touch her—"

"That pretty, is she?" Andre asked with a leer.

Louis bobbed in the air, scowling. "You know, Andre, that you're being watched."

"Yes. A British man has been following me since New York."

"What did you do to involve the British, Andre? In trouble *again?*"

Andre threw up his hands. "Even dead, you sound like Mother—"

"Would you like me to go fetch her?" Louis seethed.

"For the love of God, please don't fetch Mother," Andre growled, tossing back the sheet and pulling on the clothes he'd left lying in a messy pool beside the uncomfortable cot. "I made powerful people in London angry and one of them happens to have an interest in Eterna. It was leverage. I'm a coward, yes. But now I don't want anyone to have anything to do with it. If I could show them how you died—" Andre's voice cracked as sorrow struck. "No one would dare . . ."

Because Louis's ghost was ever-present, Andre hadn't begun to truly grieve. Though Andre had to consider the fact that the horrors he'd seen might have simply cracked his mind open like an egg and that he wasn't speaking to anyone other than his own inner demons.

"Dancing with the devil," Andre muttered as he buttoned his trousers. Louis's stolen ceremonial dagger was hidden inside, in a scabbard lashed to his belt. He tied the neck of his shirt, threw on a vest, and knotted a loose ascot. "The devil was at work in that house and I don't even believe in God or any of your saints.

"I'm going above. Where I can't be seen talking to you." He stormed out and onto the foredeck, still working on the buttons of his vest and trousers.

Of course, the Brit was there, lying back upon a deck chair. Though dark glasses concealed the man's eyes, Andre could feel the watcher's gaze as he crossed to the rail and looked out over the river. Home. He just wanted to go home.

As he imagined once again stalking the familiar lanes and favorite watering holes of New Orleans, a woman materialized beside him as if from thin air. She murmured; "You make a terrible spy."

With a start, he turned to stare at her. Beneath a straw bonnet that curved around her face, held in place by a wide ribbon, her light skin bore a dusting of brown freckles; she had slightly rounded nostrils and tight brown curls. Her blue calico dress with lace detailing was perfect for the weather and nicely made. She was lovely, too, he noticed, and gave the appearance of being upper middle class—not the wealthiest on board, not the poorest. A good way to fit in and go unnoticed.

"You're right. I make a terrible spy," Andre said mordantly. "I never wanted to be one."

"That British gent has had you uncomfortable since New York," she said. "Why?"

He eyed her. "Why should I tell you? Are you a spy?"

She smiled, revealing dimples in both cheeks. "I know for certain that *he* is," she said, gesturing toward the current bane of Andre's existence. "And that he's tracking you. I boarded at your last stop upriver because I'm tracking him, wondering what a British agent is up to on a leisurely, southbound riverboat cruise. So if he's interested in you, then so am I."

"I'm flattered."

"That accent of yours." She spoke with a charming air. "You're trying to put Northern on it, but you're Southern." She leaned closer. "Louisiana, if I'm good, and I'm very good."

Andre raised a brow. "How'd you get so good?"

"You want the truth or a lie?" She smiled disarmingly again. "Usually no one gets a choice, but I'm in a particularly gamesome mood."

Andre smiled despite himself, allowing a bit more drawl to seep into his voice, now that he was found out. "The truth, of course."

"The basement of my home was a stop on a certain railroad to freedom," she began, her voice suddenly haunted. "So I heard every dialect the South had to offer. I grew up scared of everyone and everything. But I hardened, as we have to, and I am not scared of you."

They stared at each other, deeply. "You could pass for white, you know," Andre murmured, giving weight to his words.

"I do," she replied, with the same hushed heaviness. "So could you."

"I do, outside of home. French heritage lends advantage," he said sharply.

"So here we are. A woman and her target, with grandparents of a darker color who somehow drop off the face of the Earth . . . and we go on without them, towards *better pastures*." Her words were evenly clipped.

"Something like that, I suppose. Don't worry, I won't tell anyone."

"You're the one who needs to worry about your status," she retorted. "Not me."

Andre looked her up and down, nodding as she leaned more suggestively toward him, implying with her posture that their conversation was about something else entirely. He felt his muscles stiffen as tension swept through his body. "Are you here to arrest me or something?" he asked. "Do they have lady cops now in New York? I know the big city is full of surprises. . . ."

"I could have you arrested," the woman murmured, "but I'd rather you tell me *why* that man finds you interesting."

"I imagine that's fairly classified."

"Listen," she continued, "at some point that man is going to try to force you off this ship. Where he'd take you then, God only knows." She paused and touched him lightly, keeping up the masquerade. "Where *are* you attempting to go, though?"

"Home," he said, enraptured by this intrigue, despite his brother's chill whisper in his ear.

"Don't tell her about Eterna. I don't know if we can trust her." Andre tried not to look in the specter's direction. The woman shuddered as the air around them dropped in temperature drastically. "But I like her far better than the Brit," Louis added.

Home. Who was he kidding? Andre and his albatross of a ghostly brother . . . Some New Orleaneans wanted both of them dead, though for very different reasons. The fact that Louis was already dead wouldn't stop them from trying to exact revenge.

The woman continued. "Come under our protection." She glanced briefly at her target before her gaze flickered toward the shore and her voice became even softer. "If we get separated, and it's a very good idea that we do, remember Sixty-one Pearl Street. Manhattan. Third floor."

Andre stared at her, trying not to reveal that he knew that address already. Louis, surprisingly, said nothing, indeed, he seemed to have floated off. Ghosts were maddeningly unreliable.

The woman searched Andre's face. "Do you understand?" He nodded. She bowed her bonneted head. Nimble fingers slipped something into his pocket. His hand dipped in once hers withdrew: money. "To get you on your way," she murmured. "My job with you is done." She swept off in a bounce of calico and lace.

Andre thought of his belongings in his cabin—nothing he couldn't replace. On his person was money and the dagger. He looked after the woman, then swept his gaze around the deck. The British watcher had not moved, yet somehow seemed closer and more dangerous. Andre considered the speed of the boat. Studied the distant shoreline.

A chill breeze swept past him as Louis, brilliantly, gave him a gift; managing, with whatever strength a ghost could muster, to tip a passing tray of champagne onto the spy's lap.

Andre dove overboard.

* * * * *

Clara stared at the building on the middle of West Tenth Street. A home, once. Then, a lab. Now?

It looked sick. The shuttered windows seemed to seep, a dark substance oozing around their frames, discoloring the bricks, as if the eyes of the house wept dark kohl down its face.

The sight of the place made all the tiny hairs on Clara's body stand straight up.

She would not have much time at all, if this was how she felt *outside*. She catalogued her symptoms, what might come next, and considered a timeline.

Considering the magnitude of the oppressive energy the building exuded, a sense that had only increased since the first visit, she gave herself three minutes. Not a lot of time to find whatever she had missed before.

She descended the ground-floor stairwell and turned the key in the lock.

Three minutes.

Nearly immediately, the first symptom: the dim light of the entrance hall shifted and her vision swam, the corridor lengthening, then regaining perspective.

The out-of-place thing was on the second floor. She tore up the stairs. Something about the carpet. The corner.

She ran to the room's north wall and opened the shutters, despite the choking dust flying about, choking her.

Streaming sunlight barely enticed color from the worn, sad, floral-patterned carpets that covered nearly every inch of the wooden floor. If this had been Goldberg's house, before the team moved in, why was it so terribly bare? Did he know he was going to die?

Her breath was shorter than it should be, as if a hand was pressing directly on her lungs. Two minutes.

The flap of carpet she'd noticed on her first quick perusal was still upturned, something carved on the wooden board below. She knelt and found herself looking at a picture of an eye.

She lifted the carpet.

And stifled a cry of shock.

There was writing on every inch of the floor, screaming, apocalyptic text. She lifted another carpet.

More.

The words were etched into wood and filled in with either a dark, coppery-scented substance or thick black ooze. Blood and tar.

Countless quotes from the Book of Revelations screamed

up from the floor in a shaking knife's hand, writ beside damning words from other faiths. Some words were written backward; there were phrases in Hebrew, in what looked like Arabic and probably in other ancient tongues, even pictograms in iterations of blood and tar. What she understood damned the faithful of every past age, the present, and times to come, lifting up demons as the only sources of power worthy of worship.

She felt a roaring in her ears, as if she could hear the coursing of her blood in her veins.

One minute.

She lifted the last carpets, confirming that the whole floor was covered with writings of end times. Dancing around the bits of text were hieroglyphs, runes, talismanic symbols, and numbers, numbers everywhere.

In one drawing a huge dragon tore at an eagle; in another, an inverted pentagram pierced the heart of a crudely depicted naked woman. This would be too much to take in even for someone who had no psychic inclination whatsoever. For Clara, it was an assault almost beyond measure. She didn't need to scream—the room was screaming for her.

With a sick lurch, she realized that what she was looking at was terribly similar to an old case of hers, and if that sort of dark, twisted, sick magic was somehow wrapped up in the Eterna Commission, God help them all. If immortality were to be gained on these counts, it would be lived out in a vicious hell.

Whoever had converted this house into a literal book of death had invited the disaster across its threshold.

Thirty seconds.

She backed away, nearly tripping on the folds of carpet, her boot heel sticking in tar and dried blood. She did not think whose blood it was.

Fifteen seconds.

Her eyes began blinking rapidly as everything took on a hazy glow. She stumbled on the second-floor landing and her feet nearly went out from under her, tearing at her petticoat hem. She almost threw herself down the stairs, focusing her strength in her arms as those always failed her last, and half-slid to the first floor, where she hurled herself at the front door.

One second.

Clinging to the doorknob, balancing her strength and attention on her hand, grasping the metal ball, she desperately heaved the heavy door open. Whether she hurtled forward or the house expelled her, Clara could not tell. She dragged her rebellious body up the stairs to the sidewalk, where she collapsed, half on the pavement, half on the steps. The slam of the door behind her was simultaneous with her desperate gasp for breath, knowing that if she lost herself now, she would convulse with no one to keep her from further injury.

Breathe, breathe, she commanded.

She did. Gasping, wrenching breaths.

She was trembling, but shaking was not convulsing, though it was so close. Far too close.

"Miss, are you . . ." A passerby, an elderly woman with a parasol, was staring down at her.

"Fine," she said. "I . . . lost my balance for a moment. Please, leave me be, and don't ever come near this house." Her tone brooked no argument and the frightened woman scurried away. Clara would do the same as soon as she could stand.

She would run very far from that place indeed.

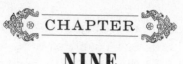

CHAPTER

NINE

Rose Everhart had watched the bullet strike her father's back, pierce his dress uniform, and continue through his body and into her mother, whom he was embracing. He had just received a medal honoring his outstanding naval service. The regal Buckingham appointment room had filled with screams.

That one small bullet took two lives, her father's immediately and her mother's after a scant week.

It would have been the biggest scandal of the age if the truth were told; Everhart being a heroic general and the marquis who shot him being barking mad. . . . It wasn't the hush of it all she hated as much as the soft murmurs of pity that still haunted the halls of Parliament where she worked in the same kind of secrecy that shrouded her parents' murders.

When she'd been asked what she wanted to keep her quiet those eight years ago, she asked to lose herself in "distinct matters of Parliamentary government." Her family was proud and she enjoyed the idea of earning rather than being given charity. The merchant who had been courting Rose at the time, for whom she'd have settled to please—and silence—her mother, found this request amoral. They forgot each other swiftly.

Lord Black had stepped in to handle the whole affair, already pegged, from his first term in the House of Lords, as the foremost man for delicate matters.

The rest of the Everhart family was never told the truth

about her parents' deaths, fobbed off with a tale of a swift mutual illness. Lord Black counseled Rose not to say otherwise, and she obeyed, though the guilt and lies ate at her for some years.

She had quickly settled in to work. From the first, she had loved her job and enjoyed her quiet life alone with her cousin, victim of yet another tragedy. They did well enough on her earnings and were pleasantly established in a house provided by the government.

The Tourney case had struck this old nerve. She'd had her fill of mad, overprivileged murderers. Yet she would not turn away. Neither, she knew, would Spire. Lord Black had given her information about Spire's past that Rose was certain Spire would not wish her—or anyone—to know. His life's trajectory was not dissimilar to hers, yet she could say nothing to him about that.

Weary of waking with the assassination in her mind, Rose resolved to pray with her parish priest about her nightmare, to see if such mental scars could be healed or the images replaced with more pleasant memories. Could anything of peace erase such horror? Negativity and sorrow held a weight that joy did not. How could something less traumatic balance upon the scale?

If only her twin hadn't died, she'd have someone to share the burden with. She'd always wondered what happened to the soul of that stillborn sister and what her life would have been like had they both lived.

As she stepped onto the otherwise unoccupied Millbank office, a familiar clicking whirr sounded. A telegraph machine had been installed, as Lord Black had promised, along with a desk stocked with paper, envelopes, and writing implements. Rose opened the thin cipher book that was always on her person—every dress she owned had an adapted pocket for it sewn into the bodice—and went to work on the message.

Lord Black entered almost silently while Rose worked and soon presented her with a cup of tea with a hint of sugar, just how she liked it. She was too engrossed in her task to thank him.

There were two messages. The first was not good news. The latter was terrible news from her most reliable news desk contact, whom she regularly appraised on matters she wanted immediately brought to her attention. It took every ounce of Rose's willpower not to cry out or shudder in revulsion at the information. She tucked the message deep into the pocketed fold next to her code book.

Rose heard the front door open and shut and footsteps on the iron stairs.

Black was staring at her from beside the tea trolley, where he was preparing another cup. She would have to say something.

"Brinkman lost his target," she stated finally.

"What about Brinkman?" Spire asked, striding into the room.

Lord Black handed Spire his tea and Rose took advantage of the pause in conversation to pick up her own cup. "You're welcome," Black said with a pout.

"What?" Rose and Spire both asked, befuddled.

"For the tea," Black muttered. "I'm a *lord,* I'm not supposed to serve. I was being nice."

They blinked at him; Rose wasn't sure whether he was joking or not. He wasn't even supposed to be there, she knew there was an important vote on in the joint houses.

"What happened?" Spire asked.

"Whatever Brinkman was following, he lost it," Rose said. "He pledges to regain the target and to send us materials from the disaster site." Rose turned to Black. "Do you have another contact in America we might use, milord?"

Black shrugged. "Not that I know of, but the government

has many operatives I don't know about." He grinned. "I can enlist Omega to find the ones I'm *dying* to meet!"

Rose sighed. "Lord Black, *please* don't send any of us out on another wild goose chase after those people, they don't exist."

Spire stared from one to the other, eyebrow quirked in that way that Rose already knew indicated curiosity.

"Ghosts, Mr. Spire," Lord Black explained. "The ghosts of this age elude me. I've been told by Her Majesty that specters are handled by another department."

"Ghosts? Another department?" Spire's vague contempt at this idea was thinly veiled.

"It's the strangest thing;" Black continued. "Her Majesty spoke about it falteringly, as if searching for a missing memory. It's a terrible mystery. Of course London has ghost stories," he added, lounging on a nearby stool in a position that made the chair look more comfortable than it was. "And séances have their time and place, but something else is going on, I just know it. So keep your eyes out, Spire, for this other department. I *must* meet them!"

"I'll be sure to send them your way," Spire stated dryly.

"Yes, but today—new scientists!" Black cried. "Profiles are waiting in your office, Mr. Spire. I'm off to Parliament! I should make an appearance for a vote now and then." He swept to the door. "Tell that wily Brinkman to hurry everything up!" With iron-echoing footsteps, Black proceeded out the front door.

Spire turned away, stalking to his office. Rose thought about running after him to tell him the unfortunate news she'd concealed from Black, but if the rest of the team came in and saw her emerge from Spire's office . . . it would appear wrong. The Omega team were hardly the arbiters of propriety, but Rose had to be careful not to allow anything to become too casual. Such would only hurt her and her reputation, of which she must take great care if she was to retain her position.

Propriety was most inconvenient because it was about what was seen and how it might be construed; never about the simple truth. Spire was able to overlook the fact that she was a woman for the sake of the greater task at hand; Tourney—and then Lord Black—forced them together and in less-than-usual circumstances. But Spire didn't have to consider the same things she did. As a man, he wouldn't receive the same scrutiny, needn't be as circumspect.

Her superiors could never have any reason to think her immodest. Honor and absence of scandal was critical.

Miss Knight entered, looking distracted, in a shimmering, bustled turquoise gown. She gave Rose a brief nod before gliding to the desk she'd taken for her own, where she perused a letter she drew from her reticule. The Wilsons walked in quietly and took seats in the rear of the room.

Spire stalked out of his office, carrying a stack of papers—likely the profiles Lord Black had mentioned. Rose tried to catch his eye, so he'd see there was something she needed to say, but he was engrossed.

Spire spoke as he distributed materials to the team. "We need to know everything about the new scientists, their habits, what to be suspicious about. Wilsons . . ." As he called them, they stood. "Inspect homes, habits, family. It looks like these men are all bachelors. Learn everything; make note of everyone who goes near them. We must be able to immediately recognize something out of place or added. Considering the unknown fate of the previous scientists, we can't lose more. Remember to keep a low profile." The Wilsons nodded, folded the papers out of sight, and exited as if dismissed from rank and file in a military operation.

"We also need a doctor on call." As he crossed to hand Miss Knight a sheet of notepaper, he walked past Rose. She tried to touch his elbow but he was too far away—she would have to reach, and that would be noticed.

Fluttering her satin-gloved hands over the list, Knight made a disdainful face. "Boring. None of them will do. None creative enough. Still, I'll examine them." She tucked the note in her bosom and turned to Rose. "Miss Everhart, will you come give a less flamboyant opinion, one that Spire will respect more than mine? Don't bother objecting, Mr. Spire," she added. "I'm not offended."

"With your permission, Mr. Spire, I shall," Rose said, willing him to see, with eyes that bored into him, that there was news at hand. But he was not a psychic. Perhaps if she were out she could excuse herself to follow up on that damned wire on her own. . . .

"As you wish," Spire replied. "Miss Knight, where, might I ask, is Mr. Blakely?"

The tall woman shrugged, turquoise fabric rustling as she replied casually, donning a fanciful headpiece that trailed ostrich feathers; "I've no idea, he's not my husband."

Rose watched Spire clench his jaw. While she generally found Knight entertaining, she did not envy Spire having to direct such personalities, and on a day like today, everything irritated. She threw her gray wool half cloak over her shoulders and fixed a simple riding hat atop her head; a practical piece of fashion in stark contrast to Knight's plumage.

"I'll go ahead and hail a hansom," Knight called over her shoulder as she exited.

Spire watched the woman go and Rose seized her chance.

"Tourney's dead!" she cried in a harsh whisper. "Found torn apart in his cell. Blood *everywhere*."

"Damn it all," Spire seethed, balling his fists, a groan of anger growling past clenched teeth. "Anyone who he indicted, then, will likely die in the next round and the trails will go still colder. Their network can't be this endless, or have such power at their command!"

"It's maddening," Rose wanted to shout. "Even if the Crown threw all their resources to us, even if we were given leave to fully take part in the Metropolitan case, is this beyond all of us?"

"I feel it's the tip of the iceberg," Spire said woefully, then brightened. "Grange has the list you crafted, and it's far more comprehensive than what my boys were given clearance to investigate. Grange said they were doubling arrests, and will have to do more now, under the guise of protection."

"But as Tourney was killed in his cell, prisons aren't any safer," Rose countered. "Not that I'm not glad the bastard is well and truly dead," she added.

"Hear, hear," Spire agreed.

"You should advise Grange to bring more officers than he thinks he needs," she suggested. "Armed, even."

"Indeed." Spire sighed. "What a bloody mess." He lifted the file in his hand. "And now this. This man is on our list of possible theorists and on *your* list of Tourney leads."

"I know, Mr. Spire, I compiled these documents," she stated, offering him a prim, proud smile. "I assume you will take a look at that man yourself."

Spire clapped her on the arm like he might have done one of his Metropolitan colleagues. This gesture of respect warmed her heart and they were each off to their respective races. Time was most certainly of the essence.

* * * * *

Knight was right, Rose soon realized. The medical men were boring, ill-suited, and far too annoyed at being questioned by women. Even before Knight gave her psychic impressions, Rose didn't like the reception they received. The physicians were accustomed to prestige granting them automatic appreciation from women; they leered openly at their female visitors.

"Miserable, the lot of them," Rose stated after they crossed the last off their list.

"I've the solution," Knight declared brightly. "A Russian man. Zhavia. He's delightful. Perfect for our merry little band. He saved Blakely's life back in our circus days. We owe him honest work. With discrimination being what it is, he's struggling."

"Discrimination?" Rose asked, curious.

"He left Russia during a pogrom against the Jews and hasn't found Anglican England entirely welcoming. Even Disraeli couldn't live as one."

"Disraeli's father converted," Rose said, perplexed.

"My point exactly," Miss Knight declared. "This country has an issue with tolerance—with allowing people to be who they are, believe what they believe, love who they love." Her own personal choices undoubtedly informed her statements. Rose did not interrupt nor argue.

Zhavia lived in a second-floor run-down flat on the South Bank. Miss Knight knocked on the door and shouted, "Bones, my love!"

There was a chuckle from inside and the door was flung wide by a man who looked like what Rose would expect of a wizard from a fairy tale. Petite, with distinct, wrinkled creases on his forehead and around his mouth, indicating heavy thought and equal laughter, Zhavia was the very picture of Merlin; though his beard and hair were both long and black, save for a few white hairs around his temples. His head was topped with an embroidered red velvet cap that matched his full-length, red velvet robe, which brushed the threadbare carpets beneath their feet. When he saw Miss Knight, his wizened face became youthful with joy.

"Sorceress!" he cried, his voice deep and accented. He embraced her and kissed her cheek. He bowed his head to Rose. "What brings you here, though you are most welcome?"

"I'd like you to convince Miss Everhart here that you're the right man for a job."

Zhavia ushered the women into the main room of his flat. He offered them seats in carved wooden chairs at a small table. "Give me a moment!" he called as he ducked behind a curtain.

"Sorceress? Bones?" Rose asked with a gentle smile.

"Zhavia finds my gifts impressive. Around him, I admit, they're unparalleled. He helps me see sharper, at a longer distance," Knight said reverently. "As for Bones, you'll see."

The wizardly man returned, carrying three small, beautiful, gilded glasses filled with hot tea. Rose lifted the glass to her lips. As she did, Zhavia stared with a disturbing intensity at her wrist and murmured in Russian.

"Beg your pardon?" she asked. The man just smiled, his gaze fixed on her fingertips.

"Bones," Knight said cheerfully. "Zhavia is obsessed with the magic of the body. He likes to recite the names of the bones, muscles, and tendons that make a movement happen. In Russian, of course."

"Well . . . that is unique," Rose said. She looked at Knight nervously, disconcerted by Zhavia's unwavering focus on her hands. "I'd hate to sit next to him at an orchestra."

Knight chuckled at this, then sobered as she added, "He was a special physician dispatched to several nobles in Kiev. One of them alerted him to the pogroms. Ugly stuff."

At the word "pogrom," Zhavia's eye twitched slightly. "You'd think," he said with sarcasm, "with all the money those fine families of Kiev invested in my education, having plucked me from my shtetl after word spread about my gifts, that

they'd want to keep me somehow, perhaps change my name
and hide me. But no, it seems that no one wants my people,
no matter how talented."

Miss Knight lay her hand on his where it rested on the table and the tension in Zhavia's shoulders eased at her gentle
touch.

Rose began asking questions. They could not directly al-
lude to the nature of Omega, but they wanted to get a sense
of fit, competence, and potential conflicts of interest. Miss
Knight always asked the final question. She had explained to
Rose that it was at this moment that she put her special talents to work and learned the most about the person being interviewed.

"What do you think about immortality?"

Zhavia arched a thick black brow and twirled a lock of
his beard between thumb and forefinger. "Man will always
quest for it," he replied pensively. "Man always has." There
was a long pause as they waited for Zhavia to add to that
statement. He did not.

"Do you have an opinion about that quest?" Rose
prompted.

Zhavia shrugged. "Whatever man cannot help but quest
for, as a doctor, I am . . . how would I say . . . called. Like
prophets of old. To seek out the quest healthfully. Intelligently.
Humbly, if that's possible . . . Though I doubt determining the
length of life should be in mankind's hands at all."

Rose glanced at Miss Knight. This was the most thoughtful response they'd received. The other men laughed, stared
at them as if they were mad, or discounted the idea of immortality outright. The women nodded. The choice was very
clear.

Knight and Rose made a warm exit, saying they'd be in
touch.

Once seated in the hackney Knight hailed, the woman

pounced with a vehement query. "What are you and Spire up to?" Knight demanded. "You're up to something and I cannot get a read on it, it's driving me mad."

Rose narrowed her eyes, a righteous fury flaring within her. How did she dare? "Why wasn't Blakely in this morning?" Rose countered calmly. "What are you two up to?"

The women stared each other down. Rose might not have Knight's purported psychic gifts, but she was whip smart, had good instincts, and was *not* in a mood to be either questioned or trifled with.

Knight smiled suddenly and spoke brightly. "I won't say if you won't say."

"Provided we never endanger each other or our team," Rose clarified, "let us keep our secrets. Because they are very important."

"Perfect," Knight agreed. "It clearly is important, as you're able to block it from me, which means it is entirely none of my business. I respect that, Miss Everhart. I truly do."

Rose nodded, trying not to feel overwhelmed by new parameters of psychic disclosure. To calm her racing heart and mind she looked at the passing scene: ship-masts bobbing in the muddy waters of the Thames, fires of industry churning along the riverbanks, spouting filmy smoke into the sky and dimming the already gray day. London was a study in charcoal.

"Secrets aside, Miss Everhart," Knight said earnestly, "one of the reasons I wanted you to accompany me on this little outing, is that there's something I need to tell you."

"Do I want to hear it?"

"It's something you think about often. And what I have to say might save your life."

"Then by all means . . ."

"Your stillborn sister," Knight began matter-of-factly. "You've always felt something was missing, and you wonder about that spirit." Rose felt her stomach drop. This woman truly *was* gifted. That was hardly public knowledge. Knight closed her eyes as she continued.

"Someone is tied to you who may be looking for you. If it is that twin soul, she didn't come along immediately, but waited. For what, I don't know." Knight's eyes opened again, piercing Rose. A hand descended onto Rose's shoulder as if latching on with talons. "You've always been together. Male or female, one life to the next, you've always been siblings. But not this life."

"Why not?" Rose asked tentatively.

"Do you truly want to know, Miss Everhart?"

"Yes . . ."

Knight exhaled slowly through flared nostrils before speaking. "Because this time, if what I sense goes unaltered, she may mean the death of you."

Rose swallowed. That was not what she'd been expecting.

"I'm sorry," Knight murmured. "Like Dickens's ghosts, 'These are but shadows. That they are what they are, do not blame me.' But, also, again in his words, they are shadows of things that *may* be only. You're missing something, yes, but I'm not sure I'd be in a rush to find it. *Her*." Her earnest empathy turned suddenly into preening pride. "There. See? Not bad, eh?"

"Brilliant, really. Th-thank you," Rose managed. They rode in silence back to Millbank.

* * * * *

The chemist, Stevens, had a shop on Commercial Street in the East End. Spire had arrived by hackney, though the driver raised an eyebrow at the destination even though Spire offered him a bill before entering. The man's expression said volumes about the assumptions he was making.

If there was one thing Spire was looking forward to as the Metropolitan Railway expanded underground, it was the ability to travel in mass anonymity, without commentary or permission. He wondered if a stop would ever be put in near poor Whitechapel; when digging the tunnels, they might find hell itself. For now, the Metropolitan's steam-powered carriages only traveled through the finer and financial parts of the city.

Though the whole concept of cloistered subterranean rail made him painfully claustrophobic, Spire had made the underground journey many times since the rail had opened when he was still a child. He was proud of London's cutting-edge innovations in transit. He'd make claustrophobia take a backseat to efficiency any day. But if he needed to travel east, for now he was most beholden to his own feet or a reliable horse.

He watched the city change from regal to ragged. Stepping out at the intersection of Commercial and Hanbury Street, Spire's eye fell upon STEVENS'S APOTHECARY, writ in careful gold paint across a glass window, which was doing its part to hold down a section of the street attempting to present a finer exterior.

He entered the small street-level front that sold various herbal remedies—mostly to women, in Spire's experience, and mostly laudanum. A bell clanged above the door, announcing him. Directly ahead, a gaunt, mousy-haired man in a leather apron stained with dark fluids stood behind a glass counter where powders in vials and crystallized salts nestled between mortar and pestle sets.

"I'm looking for a Mr. Stevens," Spire said, tipping his cap. "Pardon me, Dr. Stevens, actually." The man stared at him blankly. His eyes were reddish and ringed with dark circles and he needed a clean shave. He did not seem well.

"What for?" came a gruff reply at last. The hard tone was American. Eastern.

"Just a few questions," Spire said genially. "Dr. Stevens, I presume?"

"And you are?" Stevens scowled. Possibly a New Yorker?

Spire had worked hard with his colleague Grange to detect accents, but America's vast variety often foiled him and he didn't get much chance to practice. Now more than ever his ear needed to be sharp.

"An officer of the law," Spire said in that friendly tone natural to him only when trying to converse with potential suspects. He flashed the Metropolitan badge that he was so thankful Her Majesty hadn't demanded he turn over. Provided he and his team were diligent, he hoped neither she nor Black wouldn't think to ask for it later.

"I have lawyers," the man said nervously, glancing out the shop windows, narrowing his eyes at every passerby as if they were suspect.

"Hopefully you've done nothing to need them," Spire replied, already hating the man.

"I just want to be left alone," Stevens pleaded.

"Where in America are you from, Dr. Stevens?"

"East Coast," he replied after a moment.

"I've family in New England," Spire exclaimed. "I'm dying to visit them. I adore America; can't get enough of the place. Do you miss New York?"

"I didn't say I was from New York," the man barked defensively. Spire smiled, trying to hide his brief triumph.

"What brings you to England, Doctor?"

"Work."

Having closed the distance between them, Spire leaned casually on the glass counter. "Does the average herbalist in a small East End shop need a retainer of lawyers? I assume you've used them before? Too many 'cures' not cure a thing?" Spire said, holding up a display bottle with a stopper whose label proclaimed it to be a sure cure for "hysteria."

The man busied himself, sorting bottles in a cabinet behind him. The glass vials rang against one another as he moved them, revealing that his hands were shaking. "Yes. I have had suits brought on me, but been acquitted."

"When was that?"

"About a year ago."

"Here in England?" Spire pressed. "Who in the East End could afford to bring a suit against you?"

"To be perfectly honest," the man said wearily, turning back to face Spire and leaning on the counter, "I don't remember much about the whole ordeal over there, sir. I was fairly drugged." For the first time, Spire thought he was telling the truth.

Over there. A suit in New York. Acquitted, then fled or brought to England.

"Do you know a man named Tourney?" Spire asked casually.

The response was immediate and firm. "Never heard of him."

The detective maintained his conversational tone. "You haven't heard about his arrest and the horror show found in his basement?"

Spire watched Stevens gulp hard. "No. Doesn't sound pleasant."

Leaning across the counter, Spire was nearly nose to nose with the now sweating Stevens, all geniality vanishing. "It was hell, Mr. Stevens."

Hatred sharpening, it took everything in him not to reach across the counter and throttle the chemist. But he had to be exceedingly careful. He had no proof to tie this man to Tourney, though his instincts were certain of it. He was also not supposed to be in this shop in the first place, or asking these questions.

Stevens kept looking around—out the window, around the shop. But no one was there.

"I . . . You should go, sir. My . . . lawyers said I should never talk about it. About anything. You should go."

Spire shrugged and presented the man with his card, which bore two addresses. "If you think of anything you'd like to share, please write and send it here." He tapped the first address, the post office box held in Grange's name. "Or go to this place. These days, I'd suggest the latter."

The second address was that of a district safe house that Grange had told him had been arranged for this case. Stevens stared at the card without touching it. Spire set it on the glass countertop. Spire wanted to press the chemist, to break the man, especially in so fragile a state, but he was constrained by circumstance.

He thought of his new commission and looked at Stevens again. The man's eyes were glassy. Perhaps he indulged in the opiates he sold. He certainly couldn't become one of Omega's theorists, Spire thought, wondering how his name—and the others—had been suggested for Omega in the first place. If any of the others were like Stevens, he was not only unimpressed, but frankly frightened for Omega's entire operation.

It was past time to leave. There was nothing more to learn here.

"Be in touch, Doctor," Spire said, turning to him at the door and offering a thin-lipped smile. "Sooner rather than later. Tourney was found dead in a prison cell painted red with his blood. *All* his blood. You may want to pay that safe house a visit and think hard about what you'd like to say. Been a lot of 'suicides' recently around this city. Never know whose throat might be slit next."

The unmitigated horror on Stevens's face was unmistakable. Spire felt a flash of triumph at the sight.

The clang of the shop bell was a herald of the sooty, fouled East End air that hit Spire like a blow as he stepped out of the shop and narrowly avoided a cesspool. The noise of the city was at its most chaotic, dire, and desperate in these parts.

He knew the area well; though it had not been his jurisdiction, he had traversed it often with trusted colleagues. The lack of communication between police precincts had been the foremost bane of Spire's existence and he had been determined to try to build bridges between departments. He'd have to leave that legacy, like so many things, to Grange.

He mused on all that remained to be done, walking at an impressive clip and weaving dexterously through the constantly bustling, teeming, terrifying city. Once he no longer felt twitchy with repressed energy, he hailed a hackney. While Spire wouldn't have minded crossing the whole of London on foot, he couldn't be too long missed.

Spire had the cab drop him a few blocks from the Millbank offices so he could return on foot and determine if he had been followed. As he approached the door, unwatched, he saw a portly man in a top hat and half cloak descending from a fine carriage in front of the old mill. Scowling, the man raised a meaty fist, preparing to knock. Spire intervened.

"May I help you, sir?"

The man whirled to face Spire. His eyes were small, his expression nearly a caricature of disgust, as if the mere act of standing were unbearable. "Do you work here?" the man demanded in a huff, mopping beneath the brow of his brown top hat with an embroidered kerchief. Taking an immediate dislike to the fellow, Spire assumed he'd be trouble.

"I have business here," Spire replied. "Are you here to see someone?"

"Lord Black," the man replied, the timbre of his voice as unpleasant as his face.

Spire used his key to open the door. "If His Grace is here,

he can be found at the top of the stairs. You're welcome to check," Spire said, gesturing the man inside and pointing up. "Have a nice day." He breezed past him on the stairwell.

The man gasped and clucked his tongue. "Rude."

Spire opened the door to his team's floor and closed it swiftly, cutting off any glimpse the interloper might have of their workspace. He heard pronounced huffing behind him and slow, heavy tread up the echoing stairs.

"We've found a fascinating doctor," Everhart said in greeting from her desk as Spire, warm from his journey, took off his frock coat. He hoped she didn't mind a waistcoat and shirtsleeves.

"Good." He looked around the empty office. "Knight come back with you?"

"No, she's gone to the museum, to examine new arrivals," Rose replied. She'd chosen a desk near one of the windows; the light made for easier reading. "How did your visit—"

"There's a man here to see Lord Black," Spire said, his interruption a warning. "And he doesn't seem pleasant."

There was an echoing iron clomp on the stairs, accompanied by pronounced huffing. Their door was suddenly flung wide. The sweaty man with a bulbous nose stood at the threshold, his cloak thrown over his arm. His fine suit had been tailored to accommodate a pronounced paunch.

"Lord Black is not in! Who are you?" the man demanded.

"You, sir, are in *my* building. Uninvited, as far as I know. Here, I ask the questions," Spire stated. "You have yet to introduce yourself." Out of the corner of his eye, he noticed Everhart turn away.

"Lord Snitt," the man snarled. "Colleague of Lord Black, involved in financial . . ." He trailed off, staring across the room. Spire shifted instinctually to stand in the man's line of sight.

"I am Harold Spire, director of this branch. I doubt you have clearance to question us. If you have an issue with this reply, please alert Lord Black and he will assist you."

The man gestured with a fleshy hand, calling across the room: "Miss. Turn around."

Rose swiveled around, expressionless, sitting primly, hands folded over the file in her lap. She gazed steadily at the man and said nothing.

"State your business, Lord Snitt, else I'll have to ask you to leave," Spire said, taking a step toward Snitt, making the space between them that much more tense.

"I am here," Snitt said in his whining tone, "to do as I have on many missions before: determine what my government wastes its money on. And a question for any department, classified or no, is what is a *woman* doing here?"

"She works here," Spire stated. "Not as a housekeeper or drudge, but as a capable employee. Now if you don't mind, we all have to get back to work, even our little lady friend here," he finished with an edge.

"An unholy travesty, that a woman should be in the working company of the stronger sex." The sour-faced lord seemed bent on humiliation, as if reminding Everhart of her inferiority was the whole of his joy. "I shall tell the prime minister to stop this nonsense at once. . . ."

"Oh, you'll tell the prime minister, will you?" Everhart said, standing suddenly. "Not if I get to him first, so he can reprimand your indulgence in *incivility*!" she snapped, hastily scribbling something on a piece of paper as she spoke. "If you're truly interested in wasteful government spending, Snitt, I can tell you, you'll not find it here. I know. I've seen all the numbers."

Everhart strode toward Spire, pressed the paper in his hand and stalked out. Without looking at it, Spire tucked the paper in his pocket. He didn't blame her for walking out. But it left the huffing nobleman staring at him as if expecting an answer. Or validation.

"Lord Snitt, the prime minister is rather fond of Miss Everhart," Spire said with a venomous smile. "You'll not find any sympathy for your case there. I'd leave it be."

"Oh, we'll see about that," the gentleman said before turning and harrumphing out.

Alone in the office, Spire opened the small paper whose rapid script was barely legible.

"Tell Black of mortal offense if he looks for me. Investigating last three names."

Spire wanted to laugh out loud, to cheer the brilliant woman. But the part of him that had been hurt and betrayed kept cool, focusing instead on his part. He needed to meet with Grange and excuse Everhart to Lord Black.

Taking advantage of Omega's telegraph machine, Spire sent a wire to his old precinct, then charged out toward the exclusive club near St. James's Park. The place was within comfortable walking distance of his new home but a whole world and class away.

* * * * *

After a fresh argument with Foley, his mortal enemy, Spire felt ready to face any kind of slight as he explained to Black what had happened with Snitt.

"Why are you coming to me with this, Spire?" Black asked, swirling his snifter of brandy thoughtfully. "Why didn't she?" Spire's whiskey sat untouched.

"Offended, she plans to take time away from the office. Believe me"—Spire gestured behind him—"I'd not battle your troll at the bridge if she didn't send me here to say so."

The nobleman ran a hand through his blond hair. "Rose is not a sensitive woman. She's endured more thoughtless affronts to her sex than I can count. Perhaps Snitt was a last straw. Even the prime minister made an insulting comment about women in front of her the other day."

Spire hadn't considered until now if Miss Everhart had actually been wounded or if she had seen Snitt for the ass he was and dismissed his words accordingly. He wondered how much she didn't mention, how much she bit her tongue in a man's world.

"I've worked hard to ensure our Rose feels supported," Black continued. "So either she's reached her capacity for callous commentary or she's up to something she doesn't want us to know about." Lord Black grinned. "I hope it's the latter. I love surprises."

Sipping his whiskey at last, Spire itched to ask for Black's blessing on further investigation, but didn't dare risk it. He pinned high hopes on Everhart's ability to remain favored.

"How did she get her appointment in the first place, sir?" Spire asked, genuinely curious.

Lord Black considered Spire over his snifter a moment. "Her parents were shot by a madman." He waved a languid hand. "It was hushed up by the Crown as the murderer was a relative. The appointment was given out of pity, since she'd asked for something to *do*. She became invaluable. But, I warn you, if she so much as smells pity, she'll reject it."

Spire understood this more than he'd let on. So he was surprised by Black's next words.

"It's why I picked you both for the division." Spire stared at him. "*Death*. Who better to guard the secrets of immortality than those whom death has wronged, by striking prematurely and unjustly? I know about your mother—"

Spire interrupted, his voice low and vibrating with anger. "You know nothing about me—"

"But I do," Black interrupted in turn. "And I'm right. I've a keen sense of what drives people, Spire. It's how I've gotten where I have. Unlike most of my peers, I don't rely on my status to propel me through the world. I've advanced in a calculated manner, largely by reading people's motivations." He swirled his brandy again, holding it before his face and staring into the liquid as if he were some hag crouched over a crystal ball. Spire resisted the urge to knock the snifter from the man's hand. "Were it not for your mum, you'd not have joined the police."

Spire rose stiffly to his feet. "Death happens to everyone, Lord Black. No one is spared it and no one is *special* because of it."

Black simply smiled, further maddening Spire. "It's something you should embrace, this destiny of yours."

Spire went to the door, fisting his hands into his frock coat pockets. At the threshold, he turned back. "You've got a knack for playing God, sir," Spire said quietly. "With due respect, you should leave that to God. You know, the man responsible for death."

Black kept smiling. Spire turned and let the gilded door of the club's mezzanine slam, damned if he cared if it was a sign of low class.

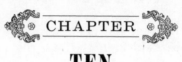

TEN

"You will not see her!" Louis insisted, floating alongside his twin as they again wove through the winding streets at the tip of Manhattan Island. "I never told Clara about you, for your safety, and that's best. Not to mention the sight of you may grieve her unduly. You'll leave Smith's address and go."

Andre chafed. "The woman on the boat offered protection, wouldn't she want to—"

"Explain yourself to the senator, then, and leave my Clara out of it," Louis barked.

Andre again stared at the brownstone building marked 61. New York swirled and buffeted around him as if he were a tree and the populous were leaves in a breeze. He looked behind him nervously. He was sure American interests would serve him best. Perhaps vague stirrings of patriotism were awakening in his heart. More likely he was driven by the same healthy sense of self-preservation that had gotten him this far. After spending most of his life running away from things and getting himself out of sticky situations, he was faced with something inescapable—his brother's death.

He'd decided to throw himself on the mercy of whoever he found inside, hoping their first instinct wouldn't be to cause him harm.

Preparing to knock, Andre glanced through one of the glass panels in the door and spotted a young woman, dressed all in black, performing some sort of strange dance in the entrance hall.

Red hair poked out in unruly wisps from beneath the dancer's crepe hat. Louis had said Clara was a blonde so Andre felt it safe to proceed, knocking upon the glass. The woman froze, then stared at the door, piercing green eyes boring into him even through the glass.

When she opened the door, she did so only to the width permitted by the chain locks he saw gleaming in the gap between door and frame.

"And you are?" the woman asked, unsmiling. Andre was not put out; he'd had worse greetings.

"A woman on a boat told me to come here for safety," he said quietly. "A British spy was tailing me. He wanted information."

Her lovely face appeared unimpressed beneath her black hat. "Hmm. What kind of information?"

"I should probably tell that to some sort of officer of the law or department official," Andre said carefully. "Do you know where I might find Senator Bishop?"

Her entrancing, bright eyes narrowed, assessing him further. Then she shut the door, but only so she could unfasten the chains and beckon him in. She held a thin black stick in one hand.

Andre stepped into the hall. The woman held up one hand, stopping him.

"Pardon me," she said. She flicked her wrist, and with a whipping sound, the small black stick became a full baton that she ran over Andre's body: first one arm, then the next, down one side then the other, up one pant leg and then the next. "Do *not* get the wrong impression," she said, even as Andre's senses thrilled. He glanced at her hand. A ring. Yet she was all in black, perhaps the poor chap was dead.

"I'm unarmed," he said softly.

"I don't take anyone's word for such things," she countered, boldly sticking one gloved hand into each of his pockets, smiling primly the whole time. Apparently finished with the physical exam, she stepped back and studied him.

The sharpness of her gaze made him feel like he was being picked apart by a vulture. Perhaps, in her mourning, all men represented loss. . . . No, that wasn't it. She was summing him up.

After a moment, she seemed to come to a conclusion. She turned to the bell pulls hanging behind her and tugged on one rope. Andre heard a bell ring upstairs, then the sound of a door opening.

"Send them up," a female voice called.

The redhead flashed a toothy smile. "'Some sort of officer of the law or department official' will see you now."

Andre felt a cool draft on the back of his neck. Louis spoke, "*Bishop*. Tell the receptionist where to find my work and ask for Bishop. Then get out."

Andre offered the redhead his most charming smile and bowed his head before climbing the stairs, ignoring his brother's ghost.

On the third-floor landing, a thick wooden door stood open. Waiting on the threshold was an intent young woman, broad-shouldered but slight. Her stature would have been awkward had she not seemed older than her years, an impression borne out by her distinct features and piercing eyes that were nearly golden. Magical. Her dark blond hair had been done up in artful braids, though wisps were coming free. Captivating.

Why was she staring at him like that?

She grabbed him and with surprising strength, dragged him into the room, closing the door behind them. Startled Andre realized he was in some kind of office. Out of the corner of his eye, he saw Louis floating outside, beyond an open window. Though the woman was dragging at him, Andre focused on his ghostly brother, whose expression conveyed frustration and anger. Louis appeared to be trying to move into the room but was unable to pass a small, carved talisman that hung from the center windowpane. Likely it was meant to keep his kind at bay, Andre thought.

"Louis," the striking woman choked out. "It *was* you who survived!" She threw her arms around him and kissed him passionately.

Oh. Trouble. Or perhaps wonderful. This could solve everything. Well, for him, at least.

This amazing woman must be Clara Templeton.

"Darling," Andre breathed, returning the kiss. Healthy self-preservation also had its unexpected delights.

"*You cad!*" his dead twin cried. Furious, the spirit managed to slam the window closed, startling Andre out of Clara's embrace.

* * * * *

Clara reeled. Her darling . . . Not dead . . . She gasped for breath and embraced him again, suddenly very thankful Franklin was not there.

Louis drew back to look at her. His dark eyes looked haunted; his skin, with its warm hints of brown, looked darker than usual under the eyes. "You saw where it happened. It's important you know that."

"Yes," Clara breathed. "And while there I was very affected by a message. From spirits, who spoke of files to find—"

"Yes!" he said excitedly. "Detailing elements of the compound, that's what I need to tell you!" Clara warmed, though the joy on his face looked a hair different than she remembered. She imagined the harrowing events he'd survived had taken their toll.

"Not only that, Louis, but something was *in* that house. Markings on the second floor, carvings across the floor, it's similar to a case from a couple of years ago, I think there was a curse in that house. . . . That may be what caused the disaster."

"There was definitely something terrible at work in that place." Louis shuddered, shaking off a memory. He pressed a piece of paper into her hand. "Take this, it's the address where Lou— where *I*— stowed some of our most important work. Go quickly, before anyone else finds it. I can't stay, I may have been followed. I don't want to let anyone know I'm alive but I'm afraid I'll need protection."

He shifted a bit in her arms—making Clara realize that she was still clutching him. She broke away, hand pressed to her lips and cheeks flushed. "Yes. Yes, of course, I'll . . . We'll fig-ure something out. I dare not tell the senator about us . . . about our . . ." Tears threatened to fill her eyes. "Oh, but you're alive," she exclaimed, pressing herself against him once more.

Louis bit his lip before speaking quietly. "It's good to see you, too, dear. But . . ."

"Of course, of course. Go. I'll retrieve the files. Stay low, hide, Louis, and I'll find a way to make sure you're protected. Whoever followed you, the British agent, will be very per-sistent—"

"Oh, I don't doubt it." He moved onto the landing. She followed him and pulled him into another kiss, but he resisted, holding himself away from her. Her heart fell and she drew away to hide her blush. "I'm sorry," she murmured.

"Don't be," Louis said quietly, an odd guilt on his face. "I'll stay safe and come again when I can."

He stared at her sadly for a moment, then raced off.

Clara ran back into the office and to the window—when had she closed it? Through the lace curtains she watched Louis dart down Pearl Street. How could he be alive when every fiber of her being had felt him die?

Her entire world, which he'd upended when he defied

Bishop's orders and spoke with her, then overturned again by his death, was in turmoil once more. Her head throbbed at a sickening pace, in time with the pounding of her heart.

How was Louis still alive? What had saved him?

Yes, he seemed different, but who would not be? Clara brushed aside her unease as a natural response to believing someone dead and then discovering that that was not true.

If she found Louis's files, would she suffer as the Eterna team had? Perhaps the whole gruesome business should be put to rest and never taken up again. Yet she could not set the task aside—her love had set the work before her and she had to complete it.

While she yearned to go directly to the address he'd given her, she knew that would be unwise. She hated her limits but ignoring them would make everything worse. Considering she'd barely escaped Goldberg's home safely, she needed her guardian now more than ever.

Clutching the paper Louis had given her in a fist, Clara started for home, still in a daze. She ignored Lavinia's inquiry as to her visitor's identity. When the skies opened, she protected the paper Louis had given her in trembling hands and darted the last block to her stoop.

The senator had a mug of coffee in hand and was poring over a legal document in his study when Clara charged in, dripping wet, and blurted: "Two things. The files. I've a location. And West Tenth Street. The building. It's . . ." Her teeth were chattering despite it being a warm summer rain.

"Clara, sit, please." He guided her to a chair, then picked up a velvet throw and placed it over her shoulders before perching on the edge of his desk. "Take your time. You've seen a ghost or two. I know that look."

"I have, of sorts." She took a deep breath. "The disaster site. I went again." She held up a hand when he opened his mouth. "Don't chastise me, it's done and I'm fine . . . but I won't examine a questionable site alone again and tempt fate. Something was in that house. Something terrible was bid to enter. You'll have to see it. Remember that case two years ago that introduced us to Lavinia?"

Bishop nodded.

"One of the locations Sergeant Patt showed me then was similar to what I saw yesterday. Ritualistic in the worst way. The floorboards of the entire second floor were etched with quotes. I've encountered that sort of apocalypticicism before, but never in this combination. I can't help but think those two are related."

Bishop rose. "I'll have a look."

"No. This first." She offered him the paper Louis had given her. "I received this. From . . . an unnamed source. It should lead us to the missing Eterna materials."

Bishop raised a disapproving brow. "You, a trained and seasoned professional, are following an anonymous note? You don't think that has *trap* written all over it?"

"No, I don't, and I have my reasons."

He looked sharply at her but she did not explain. "Why are you only telling me a partial truth?" he asked warily.

Clara pursed her lips. "You don't like not knowing everything either, do you? Welcome to my world, *Senator.*"

Bishop pursed his lips right back at her and she realized she'd probably picked up the gesture from him in the first place.

"Come on, then," Bishop said, striding briskly out the door and down the carpeted stairs.

She shed the velvet throw and followed, trailing lace-gloved fingertips down the carved maple balustrade. Her clothes had begun to dry and she no longer felt as cold. Bishop plucked his hat, a fine summer frock coat with embroidered detail— one she'd given him as a gift the year prior—and a silver-topped walking stick from the wardrobe by the door. He studied her for a moment, then handed her a floral shawl which had been hanging from a peg next to a line of top hats.

"Thank you, Rupert," she said, wrapping herself in the soft fabric.

He smiled. "You just called me Rupert. It's been 'Senator' for a while now. You've been in a formal phase, I suppose." He winked at her.

Clara blushed. Her fondness for him was a hardy flower she could never pull up by its roots.

They walked the half block to the carriage house, Bishop helping her into his fine black hansom. He gave Leonard—their favored driver, as he didn't give one whit about anyone's personal life or the odd hours they kept—the address from the note, and they were off.

The destination was on Forty-ninth Street: Barnard Smith's old laboratory in the natural chemistry department of Columbia College.

During the trip, Bishop's piercing stare threatened to provoke Clara to say more than she wanted. To avoid him, she stared out the window at the undulating tumult of New York. Pedestrians from every walk of life, in every class of dress, flooded the streets in rippling waves. Most wore dark hues but Clara spied the occasional pop of bold color, an errant red capelet or blue frock coat that bobbed about in the sea of people swarming the brick, cast-iron, and carved stone shores of Manhattan.

"From what I understand," Bishop began casually, "it wasn't until Louis Dupris came on in 1880 that the researchers gained ground. He must have been very gifted. It's a shame we never really got to know them better."

Clara concentrated on sitting very straight and focused on an errant thread on her lace glove. She took a calculated risk and went on the attack. "And why not? I wasn't given leave to know them at all.

"The Eterna idea was mine," she pressed, "the implementation was yours. Why give it over to Justice Allen? A nice man, but he has the supernatural inclination of a lamppost. I don't believe Eterna was taken from your oversight. You must not have wanted it anymore, which has left me, as a woman, *doubly* ignorant on the legacy of that night with Mary Lincoln. You can give me the same pat answer you always do about the distance kept, but I'll keep asking until I hear something I believe."

Bishop chuckled.

"It isn't funny." Clara glared at him. "Don't patronize me."

"I'm not laughing at you Clara, I'm simply very proud of myself," he said earnestly. She narrowed her eyes at him. "I've raised just the woman I'd hoped you would be."

She folded her arms and glared, nostrils flared. "And that's all due to you, of course, I don't suppose I might be thought to have played some role in my own development? No, surely not. Men are responsible for every machination of the world, women simply stand there gaping as they are formed by the hands of their betters," she hissed. He beamed at her. "Stop dodging me, Senator Bishop!"

"Back to 'Senator' again," he countered bitterly, as if wounded, then sighed and spoke more softly. "Clara, truly, I began to distance us from the team for the simple reason that I knew Eterna would attract all types of potentially dangerous energies. Psychically, it's better that you and I are out of that fray. From what you saw in the lab, you know I'm right.

"I thought a man like Allen," Bishop continued, "trustworthy but hardly sensitive, was better suited for implementation. But perhaps I was in error. Maybe lack of psychic understanding became a vulnerability. I haven't the foggiest comprehension of what Franklin saw in his touch, or the exact dark nature behind the carvings you glimpsed. But I do know you and I could not have stopped what killed the team." He looked out the window as the carriage came to a stop. "And we have arrived."

Clara's heart was racing, frustrated that Bishop made everything sound so sensible.

At the open quadrangle at Madison Avenue and Forty-ninth, Bishop handed Clara down from the carriage. "We'll be back, Leonard, my good man," Bishop called brightly.

"Yes, sir," the driver replied as if he could have cared less.

The college loomed across a wide stretch of mid-Manhattan Island, an impressive amalgam of large, dark brick, Gothic buildings.

Clara was enamored of the grand setting, the school whose legacy traced back to the mid-eighteenth century when New York was still a British holding. Its immense power and prestige had only grown since King's College had tossed off its monarchial name to don Columbia. She wished she'd had a university education rather than a succession of boarding school and private tutors. She knew, as she looked around at the fine gentlemen parading about the stately library in crisp, dark suits bespeaking means and influence, that she, like all women, was unwelcome here.

Bishop spoke gently, his gifts uncannily picking up on her mood. "It is my hope that soon, Clara, you won't be the only woman standing within these blocks," he said. "And I'll do whatever I can in the legislature to assure it."

"Thank you, Rupert," she replied quietly, grateful that he could acknowledge what an outsider she felt and how unfair it all was. At the sound of his name rather than his title, he smiled once more.

"The School of Mines," Bishop stated, leading her past the library toward a vast building erected eight years prior. He peered into a window that looked in on an office rather than a classroom, then strode to the nearest door, under a pointed-arch eave. Inside, a placard at the end of the long hall read, ANALYTICAL AND APPLIED CHEMISTRY.

"Perfect," Clara stated.

They soon came to an open office door, where they looked in on a fastidious-looking man with neatly trimmed mustache and graying brown hair in a tweed coat. He was reading at a fine cherrywood desk. Clara stepped up beside the senator as the man within looked up past wire-rimmed spectacles.

"Hello?" he said cautiously.

"Greetings," Bishop said brightly. Clara saw his gaze flick over the nameplate on the door. "Professor McBride, I presume?" The man behind the desk rose, nodding. "My colleague and I are with the Secret Service. We're looking for some paperwork."

McBride's eyes went wide. "Secret Service . . . Isn't that for counterfeiting? We're just chemists here."

"We're looking for papers recently delivered here," Clara added, ignoring the confusion on his face, guessing he was wondering why she had been referred to as a "colleague." "Relating to Barnard Smith? Who might we speak with in that regard?"

The man went pallid. "Ah. Yes. Those. I was told someone might come for them. Good. We had to lock the box away in Barnie's old office."

"Why?" Bishop asked.

The man looked away with a nervous laugh. "Because it kept moving on its own."

"Then it's certainly what we're looking for," Clara said sweetly. The man looked even more uncomfortable. She would have to add poltergeists to the list of Eterna effects.

"Can you . . . please, take it with you?" the professor asked. "Mr. Smith was beloved of this department, but this is a gift we'd like to return."

"We shall take it," Bishop said.

"Oh, good, then follow me," McBride said. They stepped aside to let him lead the way, which he did swiftly.

Bishop turned to Clara, murmuring, "After perusal I'll bring this to the depository. No haunted objects inside your office, lest all the talismans and wards I've collected for you through the years be rendered useless."

Clara did not object. The team stored objects of interest deep below a bank vault in the heart of the financial district. Years ago, when Clara had gone there to stow away some exorcism equipment, the residual psychic and spiritual energy amassed in that cellar space had almost instantly brought on a seizure. She had not been back since.

McBride stopped after a few doors and fished a key ring out of his pocket. He flipped past several keys before finding the right one and opening the door. "When Smith retired six years ago, he donated an extensive library to the college, under the orders it be open to all students. Women as well," he added; Clara could feel him trying to overcome a deep discomfort at her presence.

"Barnie was a dedicated man in that regard," McBride continued. "His daughter died a year into his tenure, and because of her, it seems, he became more devoted to women's minds than this college was and is ready to accept."

"I'd adjust your antiquated minds if I were you, professor," Bishop said sternly. McBride glanced sheepishly at Clara, who smiled sweetly.

"You can't keep us in the Dark Ages forever," she stated, stepping into Smith's office.

Floor to ceiling books; what a haven, was her first thought. One large stately window shed daylight through white curtains; a small stone fireplace on the east wall was a dark maw. There was no sign of wood or ash but the mantel framed a few glass containers with burn marks on them. Clara held back a smile, remembering Louis's colorful tales of Barnie's tendency to use fire in his experiments.

McBride pointed at Smith's wooden desk. In the center of the blotter was a cardboard box banded with a leather strap.

"That box was brought in a little over a week ago by a young Frenchman. He gave strict orders that it was only to be turned over to an American who came asking for it. He had a healthy distrust of the British. What that has to do with the notes of a chemist I'm not sure. What has Barnard been up to? Sounds a bit more intriguing than academia," the professor said with another nervous laugh.

"That's what we're here to find out," Bishop replied smoothly. "He's . . . gone missing and we're hoping what we find here will help us."

"Oh, goodness." McBride frowned. "I consider Barnie a dear friend; please do let me know if I can be of service."

"You already are," Clara assured, reaching into her reticule for one of her cards and passing it to the professor. "But if you think of anything else, anything strange you noticed in your last encounters with him, drop by those offices. Either I or my colleagues will take your testimony."

Out of the corner of her eye, Clara noticed the box slide ever so subtly toward her on the desk. Eager to prevent a more obvious demonstration, she snatched it up in her gloved hands and passed the container to Bishop. Even in that brief contact she could feel the box's contents trembling. Louis and Barnard must have infused a great deal of their essence into the material.

The room was cooler than it had been when they'd entered. If she were a betting woman, Professor Barnard Smith would be haunting his office for some time to come. This might be useful to them.

"Thank you, Professor McBride," Bishop said, tipping his top hat. "That will be all."

"Who are you again? I know you're from the government, but . . ." McBride's voice trailed off as the senator leaned toward him. Clara could feel the pull of Bishop's mesmerism, like a magnet.

"Don't worry about that and don't ask any more questions, Professor, it's all confidential. However if the British come sniffing, be a dear and alert us, will you? This isn't King's College anymore, it is indeed Columbia and we've our American interests to preserve. And while we're chatting, professor, what do you think about *Barnard*? Sounds like a fine name for a women's college. You should get to work on that."

"Yes, sir," the professor said, somewhat dreamily.

Clara grinned and kept stride with Bishop as they left the building. She knew McBride would soon shake the lingering, dazed thrall of the senator's unusual ability. Bishop had once explained to Clara that he wielded it infrequently lest he become addicted to the power.

"Not everyone is meant for our work, are they?" Bishop shook his head as they crossed the quadrangle to their waiting carriage. She laughed, feeling his kind yet commanding personality counteract the dread chill that so often accompanied their missions.

Once in Bishop's stately carriage, heading back downtown, he slid off the leather strap and opened the box. The first item he produced was a leather-bound diary, which he handed to Clara before turning his attention to the papers under it.

The cover was plain, but she could feel that the book weighed more than it should—an additional density that was metaphysical in nature. Opening it, she immediately recognized the script and her heart fluttered. This was Louis's book! She scanned for her name in a panic and did not find it.

No, this was Louis's work diary, filled with essays on nature and the spirit. Her gaze fell on sweeping, beautiful passages of theory and limitless possibility; he drew parallels between scientific relationships proven in nature and the interaction between his spiritual core and the *mystére* intercessors of his Vodoun faith.

Much of this, Clara remembered with a fond blush, he had shared with her in impassioned odes. Clara skimmed further and saw more of Barnard Smith's theories of the natural sciences coming into play. Louis and he had developed the idea of every city and place having a specific spiritual energy that was harnessed by its material surroundings. They had speculated on how this might protect those who lived within its localized sphere.

Bishop offered her the three sheets of paper he'd been looking at and reached for the diary. The slightly crumpled pages were also in Louis's hand, Clara saw; they seemed to recapitulate the theory of the diary as a sort of recipe:

The theory of Eterna in Spiritual Materialism is as simple as it is profound:

Seven ingredients are an ideal combination.

Separate: inert.

Combined: potentially the compound, and that which keeps this uniquely ours, American.

From these distinct, live cultures, the tether to a long life begins.

Herein are three distinct examples of our localized compounds.

The Power of Protection unfolds as follows:

THE DISTRICT OF COLUMBIA—Our nation's capital: The Heart of the Matter

BASE MATERIALS:

Capitol building soil, soil from the great Architect sites.

Air from within sacred triangles.

Water at the center of sacred circles.

POSSIBLE ADDITIVES:
> *Fibers of founding documents.*
> *Bullets from all American wars.*
> *Final step: Burn with fire.*

Clara looked up. "What do you make of it?" she asked.

Bishop rubbed his clean-shaven chin, considering. "The first page is a good bit of Masonic flattery," he said. "But that's D.C. There's no changing or disputing that, and if Dupris was indeed the mystic he seems, with Smith interested in the organic, those rites and sites would have their significance. When I next return to Congress, perhaps I'll collect the items listed."

Clara examined the next two pages.

NEW YORK—The Economy and Engine of the Matter
BASE MATERIALS:
> *Take from the most charged place of the city;*
> > *where the striving meet the gods.*
> *Soil of the harbor; cross—waters of the world.*
> *Mix with the air of the center of the city.*
> *Find haunts. Add item from scene.*

ADDITIONAL CHARGED ITEMS:
> *Bone shards from Potter's fields.*
> *Stone from Trinity churchyard.*
> *A Wall Street dollar.*
> *Final step: Burn elements collectively.*

SALEM: An Old Wound of the Matter
BASE MATERIAL ELEMENTS:
> *Take from the most charged place of the city.*
> *Soil of the harbor.*
> *Mix with the air of the center of the city.*
> *Find haunts, take elements from site.*

ADDITIONAL CHARGED ITEMS:
Stone from the witches' graves or properties.
Piece of Literary legacy or other historical
importance.
Final step: Burn elements.

How fascinating; how tied the ingredients were to the United States, to Americana. The team evoked patriotism by limiting the scope of their work to within their country's borders. Which was brilliant, in a way, as how on earth could that be useful to those who spied for England?

"Well," Bishop mused, closing the diary, his gray-blue eyes alight with excitement. "I wonder, when's the next train to Boston?" When he was spontaneous like this, he was hard to resist—but it wasn't his powers at work, simply his natural charm. He gestured at the papers Clara held. "Let's try one. We can collect a New York sample any time, and I'm in the mood for a bit of adventure. Are you game for a day trip to Salem?"

"I . . ." Clara cocked her head at him. "What do you mean . . ."

"I want to truly understand this," the senator replied. "The principles Dupris and Smith are outlining are clear, though they leave ingredients to instinct.

"Instinct isn't a formula, but I think I'd recognize the most charged place in a city," he said with confidence. He pounded on the roof of the cab, slid the small window close to him open and shouted up at lackadaisical, amenable Leonard. "Lenny, Grand Central Depot if you please."

"Yes, sir," the driver replied in his usual monotone.

"If you'd like to come, I'd enjoy your company," Bishop said with a winning smile.

Feeling a little twist in her stomach—one she hadn't felt in a long time— Clara breathed deep against the stays of her corset. Withdrawing a carved wooden fan from her reticule, she used it to cool her face, beads of sweat blossoming on her neck beneath her soft lace collar.

"Why are you doing this, Rupert?" she asked quietly. Surely he wouldn't want to resurrect Eterna, knowing how dangerous it was.

"Men died for this. The least I can do is try to understand it," he said. "I feel that I ought to follow their lead in a place where I will be unbiased by my own interests and history. This island and the District are too familiar, too tainted. Let me be an objective eye to theory in quiet, charming old Salem."

"Witch hunting aside?" Clara asked with a raised eyebrow.

"Adds to the charge of the place," Bishop commented, "and it's an important part of this country's history. The diary says that Smith hailed from Salem originally, which may be part of why he insists on the power of the town."

"I do want to value those who gave themselves to a little girl's wild idea," Clara agreed, "but if the compound is dangerous—"

"The ingredients alone can't be toxic," Bishop interrupted. "It's what was in that house that killed those men. I will go and see what you saw. Whatever experiment was enacted at the time reacted to what was already within. That's a separate issue, I believe. What Dupris and Smith have set forth here as localized magic, we can test in a safe, neutral environment."

Clara swallowed hard. She needed to bring up Louis, to ask for protection for him. But for some reason when she opened her mouth, his name would not leave it. She remembered the silhouettes bidding her to find the files. Surely she had their number right, and Louis should have been among them? Everything felt confused.

They alighted at bustling, tumultuous Grand Central Depot, the heart of New York, pumping baggage and people into the bloodstream of the country. Clara wondered if any other space was such a nexus of possibility as a train terminal. As always when she was swept through its doors, inside she saw the breadth of New York City on display in the waiting rooms and on the platforms. Tall top hats and long, tailored lines of frock coats next to the gathers and folds of bustled skirts, slim waists, and plumed heads; excited children darting around steamer trunks and waving their caps at uniformed train crew; other passengers in plainer clothing, carrying simple sacks, carpet bags, or cardboard cartons tied with twine.

Soon she and Bishop were seated in a private compartment on a train bound for Boston. Once Clara had shifted the layers of her green skirts until she could sit comfortably and press her corseted, bodice-boned back against the cool wood of the train car, she took the chance to catch her breath and assess her feelings. She discovered that she was thrilled with the impulsive journey, the suggestion of danger—but at the same time, nagging dread crept up her spine like a spider.

The Boston express took only a couple of hours to span the distance between the cities. East Coast trains hummed at top speeds, with brilliant efficiency unmatched in other parts of the country, but it was true that the whole of America could be revealed to a savvy traveler in a matter of days. In Boston, they made a smooth transfer to a smaller line that crossed idyllic open countryside.

Once they neared the historic port town made internationally famous for witch hunting, Clara dared to address one insect in the web of her nagging, spidery concerns.

"Would you resurrect the commission entirely? New theorists, starting over?"

Bishop looked at her for a long moment. She couldn't read his expression. He was maddeningly enigmatic; she could never quite pinpoint him despite knowing him so well.

At last he sighed and said, "The disaster has made me

rethink things. Perhaps I've been too hands-off. I'd rather be at the foreground rather than another politician with no hand for the spiritual."

"Why not leave well enough alone?" Clara asked. "Does Washington even want to continue with Eterna at all? Or do they press because England has come snooping?"

"I think England was always snooping, but they've found something. Or someone."

Clara's dream of England's warships weighed on her. She worried for Louis. But she agreed with Bishop on this point: if others were sniffing about, and if Washington demanded a continuation, she wanted to help make decisions. Nothing about Eterna should be left to bureaucrats.

"It should surprise no one that the queen wants the cure for death," Clara said. She, like Mrs. Lincoln, had suffered the premature loss of a powerful spouse. Unlike the first lady, Victoria was a person of power in herself: the empress. Clara could understand why these women desired a route to immortality, yet she was beginning to feel the cosmos should have final say.

"Please, Rupert, you must keep me informed with regard to how Eterna will progress from this point on. I do have a right."

"You do," he agreed. "And I will."

Clara confronted his steely gaze, his eyes as luminous as the shimmering silver of his hair. "Do you promise?"

She could see him sharpening his conviction as he replied; "I do."

Exiting the little station in Salem, Clara paused to get her bearings. Harbor towns have a charge about them, a heartbeat. She felt a strong thrum here in Salem; it was quieter than the throbbing pulse of the Empire city.

Beneath that rhythm Clara felt an undercurrent, one she recognized immediately. She understood, now, exactly what

Barnard Smith had meant. Salem was a compelling place, and she'd wager that there was one thing all similarly compelling cities had in common: the number of spirits inherent to each. Salem—like New York—had a good deal of them.

That made sense. If you were looking to extend life, why not look at places souls refused to quit?

"On, where instinct leads," Bishop said, offering his arm. She took it, resting her gloved hand upon his black sleeve.

They broached the heart of the town; a mixture of fine homes, the occasional manufactory, and a smattering of civic buildings lay just behind the waterfront. The senator led her first into an apothecary shop where he procured a small leather doctor's bag filled with six small glass bottles, each with a rubber stopper or cork. They were ready for their hunt.

Senator Bishop had the best instincts of anyone Clara knew when it came to power—not the newly created electrical kind, but spiritual and natural power. He knew their sources, their patterns and flow, like he knew the beat of his own heart.

Moving away from the homes that rose in waves along the hills, from the port's wide agricultural and pastoral spaces, Bishop led her out along an earthen pier, one of several jutting into the sea. The mid-day sun was bright, yet Clara felt shadows looming.

At the end of the pier, stood a square brick lighthouse about three stories tall. Its octagonal glass crown was bordered by a railed walk. Beyond the lighthouse, the pier jutted to the left and came to a precarious, sharp point like the prow of a ship. Bishop set the leather bag of vials down by the lighthouse and strode to take a stand upon that point, frock coat whipping in the generous wind of the sea.

In top hat, boots, and sweeping coat, he was a grand vision: an old sea captain, an elder god. Other lives once again blinked past Clara's sight as the seagulls above cried out or laughed. Elder songs sang in her heart. She had often been at sea; so, it would seem, had he.

The port was too shallow for the new steel-hulled ships, so the town had sought other industry. Old shipyards and maritime factories turned away from the language of wood and sail toward more modern industrial fare, though ships' masts, like barren trees in winter, still marched up and down the harbor line, quivering gently with the rhythm of the waters. Grand homes speckled the shore opposite; in the distance, Clara spied islands.

The wind took a sharper turn, knifing through her, leaving a sense of devastation behind. Clara could see Bishop react: he cocked his head to the side as if catching an odd scent. His fine top hat nearly flew off his head in a sudden and forceful gust. Opening her mouth to ask whether the change was more than a shift in the weather, she felt as though a hand abruptly closed about her throat.

Bishop jerked forward as if pushed, nearly stumbling into the water. Clara cried out, past the constriction in her throat and grabbed at his coat. The well-tailored garment held fast though he strained against it. Clara dug her heels in; her slight weight, made greater by urgency, was somehow enough, allowing Bishop to regain his balance and reel away from the suddenly hungry-looking sea.

Grabbing him by the arm, Clara turned and made as if to walk back toward the main roads that led to the heart of the town. The darkness they'd encountered had life; it was ready to pull someone under. Spirits found spiritualists a particularly receptive audience and tended to seek them out. Bishop and Clara both knew that if they were together, it was impossible for spirits not to notice them.

Sounding quite like himself, Bishop said, "If you give it a moment, you can listen past the first wave and hear other music. Unless you've any of your symptoms?"

She shook her head. "The spirit tide is strong here, powerful and full of stories," she stated. "But momentum is not malevolence. Let's take soil. This place is worth noting. Just . . . not so near the water, please?" He smiled as they ducked back around the lighthouse to retrieve the doctor's bag.

Clara kept her weight firmly against the ground, carefully positioning her feet so one heel was always dug into the earth. She took a small vial out of the doctor's bag and brushed a tiny bit of soil from the base of the lighthouse into the glass tube. She corked the container tightly before returning it to the bag.

Bishop nodded in approval. "We're done here." He held out his arm and she again took it. She breathed deep; spiritual upheaval aside, the waterfront, and pleasant company, were invigorating.

"Where next?" Clara asked as they set out upon a road that led away from the harbor.

"To a witch's property," he replied. "I toured it once. Was profoundly affected. Defined my aims, really."

"Oh?"

Bishop spoke grandly, gazing about at the town. Clara drank in a story she'd never heard. "I was twenty-three when I came here and heard the stories. I had been drawn to politics in part by those tales. If judges could condemn a woman to death during those trials, if ours is such a puritanical age . . . what if hysteria reduced us to that again?

"In the case of this particular woman, it seemed to me that the townspeople were shocked she did not remarry after her husband's death, shocked that she wore colored garments, shocked that she wished to control her own destiny. I suspect they wanted her assets as well." He looked down at Clara; he was a head taller than she and seemed in that moment to tower over her. The fondness in his eyes nearly took her breath away.

"I had recently taken you on as a ward," Bishop continued. "I already knew your gifts, your strong, bull-headed nature. If you had lived during the witch trials, you might have been deemed a one of them even if none knew of your gifts. Your refusal to be a shrinking violet might have been enough."

Clara loosed a delighted laugh. "You went into lawmaking so that you could save me from a witch trial?"

"I am sharing something deeply sentimental and you demean my kindness!" Bishop scoffed with mock pain. Clara laughed again, rising on tiptoe to kiss his cheek. This seemed to mollify him.

"I'd like to bring back a little of that poor woman's apple orchard," he stated. "The land is quite haunted. Her anger lives on. And rightly so."

After a few minutes' walk, they came upon a few brick and wooden buildings and an open patch of land—an oddly unpopulated spot, still near the main part of the town. There was no marker to delineate the area, but when Clara stepped onto the open grass, sound seemed to distort and the hairs on the back of her neck stood on end.

"I honor you," Clara murmured. The feeling that she was being closely watched abated. Sound sharpened to its normal parameters once more. Clara was not surprised by this reaction: all most spirits wanted was to be acknowledged and respected.

They took a bit of soil, then stood there for a long, quietly reverent time before turning away. Clara forced herself to ignore the immense sadness and anger that hung in the air above the field, lest it drag her into empathic despair.

"The witch trials became bigger than one person or one instance. Those transcendent sins became Salem's great penance as the crimes took on immortal consequence. I bet that's the kind of local power that Dupris and Smith came to realize was necessary for Eterna."

Seeking the next element, Clara and Bishop returned to the bustling town center and strolled along the fine green. Clara bought an edition of Nathaniel Hawthorne's collected works and Bishop procured an eighteenth-century coin from a small museum center. They were drawn inevitably back toward the water.

Rounding a curve, they were treated once again to a view of the sea and the darkening sky beyond. Drawn to a wharf, where the soil shifted to rock from dirt, Bishop bent and gestured for Clara to hand him another of the glass containers within. He knelt at the water's edge. After what had happened before, Clara moved instinctively to his side and took hold of his coat.

"My anchor," he said over his shoulder with a smile before collecting a vial of harbor water. Clara felt her emotions twisting at his simple fondness. As he set the water sample in the bag, she couldn't hold back any longer, finally blurting the confession.

"Louis Dupris is alive." She felt the words land heavily between them. "He came to the office, briefly. That's how I knew about the files at Columbia." This was not the time to reveal their romance.

"Alive?" Bishop said incredulously. A cool breeze swirled around them, blowing the layers of her skirts and the tail of his coat. "Why didn't you tell me?"

"He didn't know who to trust," Clara insisted.

"He doesn't know you," Bishop said warily. "Why would he trust you?"

Clara bit her lip. "He was looking for you but was desperate to go into hiding."

"You trust me, don't you?" Bishop said, confused and obviously hurt. "I don't understand why you didn't tell me right away!"

"I'm sorry, truly. Everything is . . . a bit much lately." This at least had the virtue of truth. "I'd just been to see that house of horrors. I was reeling, Rupert. Please understand."

The senator eyed her, surely knowing that wasn't the full story, but let it go at her gentle insistence. "It is wonderful that someone survived," he offered. "How?"

"He didn't explain," Clara said, shaking her head. "Brinkman tracked him but Effie caught up to the boat and convinced Louis to turn back. We didn't know Brinkman's target was Louis Durpis when we sent Effie after him. She informed us that he jumped overboard when the shore was near and the water shallow, and I assume he took swift trains to return to Manhattan. He told me about the files and fled."

"How can I protect the man if I don't know where he is?"

"Perhaps he will resurface," Clara said, knowing that neither she nor Bishop could count on that. "We have his material; why not let the dead stay dead? I have a terrible feeling about all this. We're in so deep and I don't understand all the levels to this hell."

A dark shadow passed over Bishop's face and he lifted his gloved hand to run a leather-covered finger fondly over her cheek. Her elder instincts, from all the lives of her past, had her aching to turn her cheek into his palm for comfort. As always, she fought those old familiarities.

Bishop shook his head and spoke quietly. "If I'd have thought your brilliant idea would ever have caused you so much pain, I'd have laughed off your bold notion as the ravings of a child drunk on the need to be important in Washington." He chuckled. "Levels of hell. Now you're talking like Lavinia or her beau, Mr. Veil, or a member of his 'melancholy society.'"

Clara smiled despite herself.

"I'll speak to a police contact and ensure a safe haven is prepared against Louis's return. I look forward very much to speaking with Mr. Dupris. Local magic," he said with admiration. "It's fascinating and I'd like to commend him. A whole new direction to consider. And a brilliant safety measure."

"In that magic tied to America would be useless in England?" Clara offered.

"Precisely!"

She gazed out at the darkening sky's beautiful colors. "Are we staying in Salem tonight?"

They traveled together often, always staying in adjoining rooms. Now that Clara was grown, when people saw them together, most assumed them married. Bishop was unruffled by this, but it made Clara blush; her pasts stirred within, like a ghost waking in a house it had neglected to haunt.

"It's been quite a day and I doubt we'll catch the last train to New York," Bishop replied. "Best to rest in Boston."

Silence descended again as they walked to the station, hastening their pace when they saw plumes of steam rising in the sky.

Once boarded, again taking a private compartment, Bishop set the Hawthorne volume, the old coin, and the other gathered ingredients on a wooden tray lowered from the wall. He stared at them with a mad scientist's delight.

Clara frowned. "Rupert, here? Please don't let fascination or excitement rush—"

"I want to see if there's anything to this. Even a little shudder of life," Bishop stated. "We should do so here, where the air is still Salem air. We've not much time. Look with more than just your sight, Clara," he urged.

Aware of what that meant from many a séance and spiritual connection, she sighed, and nodded, as he would not be dissuaded.

Taking a larger, empty flask from the doctor's bag, Bishop opened the window and briefly sung the uncapped container outside: air. Then he dropped in the coin, added a bit of soil, a drop of water, and scraps from the Hawthorne volume, tearing out the first and last line of *The Scarlet Letter*. He closed the flask and shook it briefly.

There was a small surge of smoke, a waver and glistening of light like the strike of a flint, an exhalation of essence. At the sight, Clara held her breath; Bishop drew his in sharply.

What if something like that was the last thing Louis's team had seen?

"We're on to something," Bishop breathed.

"*Louis* was on to something," she corrected.

"Genius. So simple. But this is a spark, not the whole. To keep life in a dying body, there has to be fire. But this could be the match to set the whole thing alight." Bishop looked at the flask, now quiescent, with shining eyes.

Clara slid gloved fingers up and down the windowsill, watching Salem roll away, worrying her lip with her teeth. "So Eterna will resume, then?"

"It must," Bishop replied. "This is *real*, Clara, not just theory anymore. And as much as I don't want us at the center of it, I don't want Washington to take it away from us."

"I don't want more death on my hands!" she said. "On my head. My heart—"

She stopped before she let any more emotion slip. Her cheeks went red. Bishop raised an eyebrow. She turned so that the brim of her prim little riding hat and the curl of hair down her cheek barred him from seeing her face.

"I'm going to Washington next week," he said slowly. "I'll make sure that I am appointed direct superior on all Eterna proceedings. Not Justice Allen, me. And I will mitigate the risks, no worrying your head or your heart—"

"But you must not keep me in the dark," Clara exclaimed, surprised by her own vehemence.

Bishop seized her gloved hand in his larger one. "I will keep you close."

She reeled from more than the feel of his hand wrapped

around her own. Politics made her instantly distrustful. She was reminded of the unease that had plagued her when her idea was first taken over, after that night with Mrs. Lincoln. Poor Mary. The former first lady was so fragile, her grief so difficult to bear, that Clara had not visited nearly enough.

"Dear Mary is ill. . . ." Clara murmured, certain Bishop would know who she was talking about. "We must pay her a visit before it's too late.

"I need to do so many things, help so many people! But I'm so tired. After so many lives, Rupert, isn't it understandable if I'm simply *tired*?"

"My burning heart," Bishop said with a gentle smile, and she realized he meant not his heart, but hers. "Yes, it's understandable you're tired." Moving to the seat beside her, he opened his arm in an invitation for her to fall against him.

She stiffened instead. "Don't."

"Why not?" he said with an exaggerated pout. "Don't you love your old man anymore?"

Clara scowled and felt a sharp point drive deep. "You're not old. I'm not letting you die."

"Ah now, none of that," Bishop chided with a chuckle. "The Eterna Compound is for leaders, not us. You and I need to be keenly aware of that if the commission continues."

She knew that it had to, despite her feeling that Eterna should be abandoned without a backward glance. Now that England was involved, that was impossible.

Clara forced her shoulders to relax and decided not to fight the urge to lay her head upon the senator's shoulder. They didn't say another word until Boston.

In Clara's opinion, Boston was a poorly laid out town whose residents had a tendency to be obnoxious. Perhaps this was New York bias, as the rivalry between the cities ran deep. The hotel near the train station was fine enough—Bishop knew at least one concierge in every major city due to his governmental travel. So their amenities were first rate, their late dinner was well prepared, and their discussion of Republican Party politics was intriguing, but Clara's agitated nerves longed for rest and familiar settings.

Bidding Bishop good night, she eagerly shed all her layers and wrapped herself in the soft robe the hotel provided. In cooler comfort she lay alone in her small room, forcing herself simply to breathe as she stared at the white ceiling with ornate plaster detail.

The sinking suspicion that their situation was about to worsen would not quit. She focused on her breath until sleep overtook her, refusing to indulge even one of her spinning thoughts.

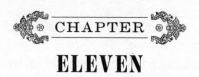

It was nine in the morning and Lord Black was seated in Spire's office, holding a snifter of liquor he'd served himself from one of the bottles Spire had found in a small cabinet during his first inspection of the place. Spire hadn't had occasion yet to touch the stuff and had assumed that since it was in his office, it was his to proffer, but Lord Black seemed to treat the Millbank offices as an extension of his residence, or perhaps his club.

Spire had just arrived for his day's work and found Black installed in the chair facing the desk. He hoped he was not in trouble.

"Good morning, my Lord," Spire said, bowing his head curtly and taking his seat. "You're—"

"Here early and already drinking?" Black sighed wearily. "It's been a day, Spire, it's already been a day and it's not even ten. Let's talk about this." Black passed a telegraph across the table to Spire: a sequence of numbers. "Miss Everhart will be able to tell us what it means. It's in cipher from Brinkman, his call numbers are here at the top, zero-zero-one."

"As I told you, Lord Black, Miss Everhart may not be in," Spire said carefully.

"Unacceptable. Go bring her back," Black said crisply. "She'll either be at Westminster or home, twenty-two White-hall. Go tell her I said stop pouting."

"Yes, sir, I shall. I'll bring this along for her to crack," he said, tucking the message into his jacket pocket and practically bolting out the door.

Perfect. He and Everhart could confer in private and if anyone wondered why they were both missing, well, he was sure Lord Black would cheerfully enlighten them. Given the hour, he decided to try Everhart's home rather than her Parliament office.

He enjoyed the brisk walk east, on the way poring over every detail of his conversation with Stevens so that he could share it with Everhart. Together they would determine the types of background searches to conduct on Stevens and others on the Tourney lists, to see the full scope of the pattern.

On the street opposite the vast Whitehall complex of state was his destination; a Tudor-style beamed building with rooms above and a pub upon the ground floor—a common state of affairs, as there were pubs every hundred paces or so.

A woman in mourning opened the side door in response to his knock. She was soft-featured, with haunted, frightened eyes.

"Hello, madame. I am sorry for your loss, whatever it might be. I am here to inquire of Miss Everhart. Is she in?" Spire asked.

"One man. Average height, dark suit. Broad shoulders. Dark blond hair, receding at sides. Not handsome. Not ugly. Determined," the woman stated, running down Spire's physical particulars before vanishing, leaving Spire baffled and alone at the open door.

Wondering if he should be insulted by her odd assessment that he was an average-looking, albeit determined, gentleman, he stepped into the small entrance foyer. A slightly worn carpet ran the length of the dark wood floor and up a narrow stair directly to his left. Spire saw the woman in black ascending the stairs. When she reached the landing, she sat down upon a low stool and looked through the window at the street. He could hear her murmuring, describing the passersby as she had Spire himself.

He closed the door behind him and shifted upon the runner, considering. Then, "Miss Everhart?" he called, his voice echoing through the narrow town house.

"Mr. Spire, is that you?" came her voice from above.

"Yes," Spire shouted. "I'd have had the woman at the door announce me—"

"Ah, don't mind my cousin. She never recovered from her husband's death, an awful affair. However, she reports everything she sees outside our house. So at least I always know if I'm being watched," Rose replied loudly. "The quality of her descent has its uses, however, it does make for awkward introductions."

"Do forgive me for not sending word," Spire called, wondering why she did not appear. "But there's another message. Lord Black said I should bring you back to the office. He said to stop pouting."

Everhart laughed. "I am not pouting, as you well know. I'll decode the message, then you and I have further business. I've made some progress, though not as much as I'd like. Once I am dressed, of course. Give me a moment."

Spire stopped wearing a hole in the entrance-foyer carpet once she mentioned getting dressed. He was not used to dealing with ladies in business matters. "Ah. Yes, Miss Everhart, of course. Sorry. Take your time."

Moments later—impressively soon to Spire's mind, though he had little familiarity with how long it took ladies to dress— Rose appeared at the top of the stairs wearing a lace-necked blouse, a vest, and a utilitarian wool skirt with only a slight bustle, all in complimentary blues. The fabrics seemed as fine as they were tailored. Never ostentatious, Spire knew that even from short acquaintance; she was modern and well kept.

"I try not to dress in frills that take too much time," Rose said, descending toward him, "and living without a staff, one must make do. I wish it were acceptable to wear practical items, like riding habits, daily." She gestured Spire into the small first-floor parlor and followed him in.

"For what it's worth," Spire replied, "I don't give a damn what you wear." He lowered his voice. "Your cousin, should she overhear us—"

"We'll walk back to the office and use that time to discuss Tourney matters. Give me the message."

He fished in his pocket and handed over the paper. "Brinkman," Spire stated, taking a seat in a cushioned chair at Everhart's nod, though she did not sit. "I want to know exactly what he's doing and what he's about. Our operation relies too much on him and he's a stranger to me. Under whose exact orders is he operating? Do I send a spy to spy upon our spy?"

Rose looked at the sheet, then picked up a nondescript leather-bound notebook lying on an end table. She sighed, irritated. "Brinkman is the only one who uses a *thoroughly* redundant cipher. To your questions, the man is a pet of Lord Black, and has been for years. I've no idea of their history as Edward is—Lord Black—is cagey about a lot of things."

"So I've gathered. Does our every move revolve solely around Lord Black?" Spire said, unable to keep a bite from his tone, though he was curious as to the familiarity she'd let slip.

"Mostly. And Her Majesty, of course. They are the sun and the moon of our sky, Spire, and you must be careful not to fight the heavens. There is freedom in staying in favor."

She spoke with enough gentle warning that it gave Spire pause. Remaining favored, it seemed, was one of Miss Everhart's greatest skills. It was one he'd do well to learn from.

"Noted," he replied.

His colleague passed a rounded settee to take a seat at a lacquered, inlaid writing desk, drawing a pen from her buttoned sleeve as if it were a knife. She gestured toward a wheeled tea-tray set against the wall. "The teapot should still be hot. Would you be so kind, Mr. Spire, to make me a cup while I decipher? Pinch of sugar." She set immediately to work, scribbling on a sheet of paper randomly drawn from atop the cluttered little surface.

He rose after a long moment, staring at her flying hand and her mess of a desk. It was odd, Spire thought, for a woman so fastidious at work to have such a cluttered desk at home.

"Make *yourself* some tea, Mr. Spire, if you won't make me a cup," Everhart added. "But please don't stand there hovering, it makes me nervous." She looked firmly at him; he turned to the tea cart and busied himself with pot and cup.

"You're wondering about my desk, I see," she added. "The papers are at exact angles and in precise order; any alteration would instantly alert me that someone had come snooping."

"That's most sensible," Spire said, relieved. He handed over a cup of tea—with a pinch of sugar; Rose thanked him. She was finished with the cipher before his own tea had finished steeping.

She read aloud: "Will send material from last known location of American scientists. Have promising leads. Permission to interrogate." She set the paper down and looked at Spire. "Whoever he was tailing must have lost him quickly or had help. Brinkman never tells us directly where he is, but I assume he's back in New York if he's going to the American researchers' location."

"Lovely," Spire muttered. "A roving, rogue operative." There was a long silence. "You know, Miss Everhart, for what it's worth, Lord Snitt is an ass, I hope that won't—"

"Deter me in the least?" Rose smiled. "Men like him only strengthen my resolve."

"Good then." Spire nodded. "Tell Brinkman to pursue whatever he's interested in, and suggest he try not to make it obvious to the Americans that it's *us* asking the questions. Blame the French."

Everhart smiled. "Why the French?"

Spire grimaced. "They should not, as a species, be trusted. Determine the scope of Brinkman's plan and if he will work alone. I don't want an international incident on my hands."

"Indeed, Mr. Spire." She set down her cup, rose, and swept out to the entrance foyer, drawing Spire in her wake. "To the office?"

"To the office," he agreed. "We've persons of interest to discuss."

"Indeed we do."

En route, they caught each other up on their respective investigations. Everhart agreed that Stevens was critical and hoped he'd be sensible enough to turn himself in and in so doing, perhaps save his own skin. As for her interviews: one had been recently killed by his wife in a "domestic dispute" that everyone doubted was true. Another revealed a company used in shipping and manufacturing that might be a cover for insidious materials; this, she felt was critical.

* * * * *

In the dank shadows of the cell deep in the Royal Courts, the Majesty, Mr. Beauregard Moriel, the *rightful* Duke Masparian—not that simpering imitator, damn him to the eternal hells—could not allow himself to luxuriate in daydreams of his coming reign. He had to remain focused. He could not jump ahead and ignore the myriad details of the present. That's what had gotten him into trouble before, what had gotten him captured.

Being imprisoned was a horrid setback, he'd been sloppy

with trivial old vendettas that had curtailed his momentum. He had to forget avenging petty injustices and instead dive into what the Fates demanded of him, taking great care never to disappoint the summoned again. They could never see him weak.

When his pet arrived for his appointed round, Moriel salivated not for the moldering bread but for reassurances.

"Is it done, O'Rourke? Tell me, tell me," the Majesty murmured, reaching between the iron bars and clasping the guard's hands in his.

"It is, milord, it was said Tourney's cell was awash in crimson, that there was no blood left in the body, every drop painted the walls."

Moriel sighed, all the rippling tension in his body easing in a wave of peace. "It was done by host bodies, yes? My summoned have done so much for me, I need to make sure they are well taken care of, that they get the trophies they so richly deserve."

"Oh, yes, milord, I doubt a human alone without the augmentation of the Summoned could accomplish such incredible acts otherwise. And yes, trophies have been taken of all the deceased."

"Make sure all my morgue men get their tokens and consecrate them," Moriel instructed, his fingernail dragging up the guards large forearm to peel open a scab on the man's wrist, watching closely as a droplet of blood bubbled up. "In order to wake the bodies overseas, I need a powerful lot of pieces. My men all know this, of course, as do my summoned, but, knowing that you're keeping tabs on all of it, O'Rourke, my good man, it simply"—Moriel sighed and clasped the guard's large face in his small palms—"brings me such peace of mind."

"Of course, milord," the deep-voiced guard reassured. "All shipments, once they are fully consecrated and prepared, shall begin to be sent to the same port via the usual society channels unless compromised."

Moriel nodded, his voice soft and musical as he placed a length of chain over his small, barrel chest as if it were a ceremonial sash. "Sweet, sweet America, where our sun shall never set."

Their return to New York was blessedly swift; their conversation light and general. At Grand Central, they parted, the senator to visit the disaster site and Clara heading for her office.

"Where on earth have you been?" Franklin barked, glaring up from his desk as Clara charged into the room, carrying Louis's diary, the papers, and Bishop's doctor's bag.

"Bishop and I went to Salem."

Franklin frowned. "Salem, Massachusetts? Whatever for?"

"Witch hunting," she said brightly. Franklin stared at her. "I received information on where to find some of the team's work," Clara said, finding a place for Louis's writings in a file cabinet.

"Bishop and I went to Salem," she repeated. "We were testing localized magic." She set the black leather on her desk and sat down.

Franklin took a deep breath and spoke in measured syllables. "Protocol is to tell your partner if you leave on a mission."

"Sometimes things just come up, Franklin." She sighed. In truth, she hadn't even thought of notifying him; Bishop's energy and her own desire to know what Louis had discovered had swept her along.

On her way in, Clara had stopped and asked Lavinia to bring coffee. The redhead's arrival leavened the mood, as Lavinia regaled Clara and Franklin with her fiancé's latest adventures. He'd been mistaken for a body snatcher when he was, in fact, being a good Samaritan at the Denbury clinic in London. Clara and Franklin contributed anecdotes about their own Burke and Hare cases. Morbid humor was one of their strong suits.

"Oh, earlier, Clara, I intercepted someone on your behalf. Peter Green, the journalist who is always after you. He wants to take you to the opera," Lavinia said with a grimace.

Clara laughed.

"Is that your answer?" Lavinia asked. "Do I write: 'She laughed'?"

"No," Clara snickered. "Write: 'She laughed at you, sir.'" It was Lavinia's turn to laugh.

"That's cruel," Franklin said in a chiding tone.

"Then you go to the opera with him," Clara snapped.

"I know he's irritating," Franklin said sincerely. "But you don't have to be mean."

"He doesn't have to be a pest!" Clara insisted. She turned to Lavinia. "Tell him no, dear."

Lavinia pouted. "That's no fun at all."

"Yes, but I need to keep up my"—Clara gestured in the air, searching for the word—"what do you call it?"

"Karma?" Lavinia smiled fondly at her dear friend. "Yes, Clara, love. But he's annoyed you often enough, even karma will allow you to be as direct as you need to be with the man."

"Perhaps so," Clara said. She turned to Franklin. "When men start affording more rights to women, maybe we'll be nicer to the ones we don't like. But for now, I know that I myself am too busy trying to preserve my rights and faculties to take care of a man's fragile ego."

Franklin knew he was outnumbered and outgunned, and said nothing.

Clara spent the rest of the day poring over the file she'd kept on the earlier case that was similar to what had happened at the Goldberg house. She was right, the carvings had been very similar; in addition in the prior circumstances, what looked like a door had been etched into a wall, undoubtedly bidding something terrible to enter.

She hadn't seen such marks at the lab; perhaps Bishop might find it, or something else she missed in her haste to escape her oncoming episode.

How could the chemist responsible in that case have anything to do with Eterna? He was in jail.

No.

She discovered a later addition to the file, a little sidebar clipped from a newspaper. The bastard had been acquitted. Perhaps there was more of a network than the police had originally thought.

Franklin slipped out at some point without her notice. Late in the day, Lavinia came up to ask if Clara needed anything. Clara refused and told her friend she could leave whenever she wished. Sitting alone in the office, Clara realized she was hoping Louis might come by. It was the safest place for them to meet.

Focused intently on research she'd pulled from the file cabinets, she didn't even notice it had grown dark beyond the reach of her desk lamp.

"Miss Templeton," came a voice from the shadowed part of the room. Clara started in her chair, spilling now-cold coffee. That would teach her to leave the lights off after dusk. She subtly put her hand below her desk and took hold of the grip of the pistol secured there.

"Come with me," said the voice. It was a low male voice, not one she recognized, and had an American accent, though that was easy enough to counterfeit.

Clara spoke slowly, keeping her tone level despite the shaking of her hands. "I do not casually obey disembodied voices in the darkness."

"Come with me," it repeated.

"You'll have to be more convincing." She detached the pistol from its wire, steeling herself not to wince at the little click of the release.

"You don't have an option if you value your life," the voice said.

Clara fought valiantly to keep her body calm, taking a deep breath. "Clearly I do have an option. You're here for a reason, likely information. Which you won't get if I'm dead. How about you introduce yourself like a gentleman?" She gestured to the chair opposite her.

A figure stepped into the small pool of colorful light cast by the Tiffany lamp on Clara's desk. Tall, thin, and dressed entirely in black, shirt, suit, and all; his dark hair was slicked back, tight to his skull. His face was completely concealed by a simple papier-mâché mask—black, lined subtly with gray—that made for a hollowed, spectral visage.

He held a pistol firmly in a black-gloved hand.

"And at gunpoint, no less. Certainly no gentleman," Clara scoffed, though her heart began pounding at the sight of the weapon. Likely he'd shoot her before she could even bring her pistol to bear. "I hope you know I don't just go walking off with strange men in masks who come creeping about my workplace," she said through clenched teeth. "I am expected elsewhere by important persons. So you really ought to treat me with respect. For starters, by putting the gun down."

"I am respecting you, Miss Templeton. Any good man worth his salt would respect you. However you are in possession of knowledge that I need and I know you will not give it to me under friendly circumstances, thusly I am pressed to ask in this manner. I seek your files. All of them."

"This is an office," Clara retorted. "There are many files here—"

He cut her off. "This is an office born to investigate a cure for death. Let's do away with the games and the stalling. I assume you've a weapon trained on me but given your position, it's highly unlikely that you will strike me if you fire. At least I hope you've a weapon, I'd be so disappointed otherwise."

"I do," Clara said evenly. "And I am a good shot."

The man clicked his tongue. "As am I and right now I'd get you first. So let's try this again. Come with me."

Clara thought quickly. England. Surely this was England's doing. Maybe Brinkman had gotten something out of Louis. She prayed her lover was all right.

"I was raised with the notion that if a stranger attempts to take me anywhere against my will," Clara said, "that I ought not trust a word he says, and that I am to make noise and struggle."

"If you make noise or struggle, I'll simply shoot you, hop out the window, and shimmy up the rope already placed for my escape," the man countered, all as if they were talking about something quite mundane, not kidnapping or murder. "Bring your hands up—*without* the pistol—and rise from your desk. Come with me. Your friends have also been abducted, if that changes anything," the man added casually.

A jolt of terror ran through her. "Who?"

"Your partner with the bad leg. Your dear senator. And Mrs. Northe-Stewart, who hosts so many séances. I thought she'd be very useful. They are all assembled, awaiting you."

The man with the gun hadn't mentioned Louis. Or Lavinia. Surely that meant they were safe. But if any of the others were hurt, Clara would never forgive herself.

Panic must have been visible upon her face, for the intruder said, in a voice that seemed sincere, even if it was a good act, "They are alive, I promise."

"Who do you work for?" Clara demanded.

The man merely shook his masked head, the shadows

shifting menacingly on his false face. He came closer, making silent progress across a room where usually the floorboards creaked with every step.

She abruptly realized that there were lengths of dark fabric in the hand that wasn't holding the gun—likely a blindfold and some kind of binding.

"Miss Templeton, for the last time, place your pistol upon the desk." When Clara shifted forward, the abductor asked: "What are you doing?"

"Detaching the pistol from its moorings," she explained falsely. In truth, she was pulling the knife from her boot.

"Don't try anything. And don't bother screaming either. Save your voice. I used a chemical on the girl downstairs, so she can't hear you."

Clara growled, her protectiveness of loved ones flaring more violently than thoughts of her own safety. She had hoped Lavinia had left for home before this creature's arrival.

"She'll be fine," he said dismissively, waving his pistol nonchalantly. "Just a hell of a headache in the morning."

Clara felt sick to her stomach. For Lavinia, being assaulted might trigger a relapse into fear and paranoia. Clara's mind raced in search of escape. She visualized the trajectory of her knife, the speed at which she might be able to move . . . He was a mere foot away. . . .

Now or never.

Spinning, Clara wielded the knife in her right hand, drawing it up in a cutting block as she tried to knock her visitor's gun hand to the side, away from her body. The assailant's gun fired into the floor and Clara started at the noise. Her knife grazed the man's forearm but made contact with something hard, like a leather cuff, which prevented injury.

The kidnapper grappled for Clara's wrist but his glove slid off a band of satin on her sleeve—Clara swore in that instant she'd only wear slippery fabrics from now on. She drove her elbow upward and there was a crunch as she struck his cheek, crumpling the papier-mâché mask against his jaw.

He grunted at the impact, then growled and clamped his hand onto her forearm like a vise. No help from her satin blouse now as she tried to jerk away from his iron grip. His mask had fractured; a pattern of cracks radiated like a spiderweb from the point of contact. The thin white web made him all the more sinister.

Twisting Clara's wrist up behind her back, the attacker turned it sharply and she cried out in pain. She could feel him winding something—a thin rope, perhaps—around the wrist he held and stood up sharply, attempting to throw her chair into him from the force of her movement. The back of the chair pressed against his leg and he shoved her down into the seat, pressing the barrel of his gun directly against her head. She shivered at the touch of cold steel.

"Miss Templeton," he said; she heard a slight change in his voice, likely from his swollen jaw, "I admire your courage and pluck, truly. I'm sure I could introduce you to my employer, who would be most happy—"

"Go to hell."

"Oh, we'll all see one another there. It will be quite the soiree. Place your other wrist behind your back, please."

She did not move.

"Your hands, please, Miss Templeton," the man said wearily. "I am asking nicely when at this point I'd rather have shot you."

Clara debated a moment. With the gun against her skull, there was no move she dared risk. She could tell that her enemy's patience was dangerously at its end. She did as he'd asked and the intruder bound both wrists.

"I am sorry," he said as he worked, sounding sincere. "Though I shouldn't be, with that hit you landed. I've a handsome face beneath this mask, thank you very much. I don't like doing this to a lady unless she asks me to. Begs, really. But that's pleasure. This is business."

Clara tried to hide her shudder of revulsion but doubted she was successful. Panic made her want to retch.

"Would you rather be unconscious, Miss Templeton? That is the alternative. I have more of the lovely concoction I used on your receptionist. It will render you entirely motionless and unaware."

Clara shook her head. "N-no."

If what he said was true, then the only people who cared she existed were no more able to help her than she could help herself. Clara pledged to have more friends who might be concerned if she vanished, if only the Good Lord would see her out of this unscathed. Secret operations are no good if your life is a secret kept and lost in the bargain.

The coarse black blindfold went over her eyes and was tied roughly. Her abductor threw something over her shoulders— perhaps the black cloak he had been wearing—and put the hood low over her face, hiding the blindfold. A silk lining brushed her cheek. Well, at least it was a fine cloak.

Going down the stairs, bound and blindfolded, was difficult. Clara nearly tripped over the ruffled layers of her petticoat at every step but she wasn't about to ask her captor for any kind of help. She took everything very slowly.

At the door another binding came out and was roughly tied around her mouth. She growled. "The carriage is just outside," he replied calmly as she struggled away from the dark burlap strip, chafing her skin as she did.

Clara prayed harder than she'd ever prayed in her life; that she would arrive at her destination and see the people she cared deeply for, alive and well. They were an intelligent breed. Surely with all of them against . . . how many would they be against? Surely they would survive. . . .

Her mind reeled and rattled, body shaking as the abductor took her arm and bid her step up into the carriage. Even the horses seemed nervous, she heard them stamping and shaking their heads, jangling the hardware of their bridles. Morbidly she wondered if the air around her was buffeted by the wings of the angel of death, the wake of Eterna wreaking horrible effect. . . .

They were off. Uptown. Over. Taking Broadway. The busiest, most populated route anywhere. Why didn't he take the river? She pressed her shoulder against the door. Felt for the latch. Locked and she couldn't unlatch it. She shifted herself, propping herself upon her knees, fumbling with her free fingertips at the latch. She undid it. Oh, it couldn't be that easy. . . . As she pushed on the door, she felt resistance. Something was holding the door in place from the outside.

She tried to count the blocks traveled. She'd been along Broadway in every kind of traffic. Their passage paused for streetcars, she heard dings and shouts of passing carriages or irritated passersby. She shook back the hood on the off chance the carriage window curtains were open and someone would be struck by the appearance of a blindfolded woman in an uptown carriage. . . . She pressed her face to the glass and felt muslin curtains against her cheek. Clearly this was not the man's first abduction.

A turn to the right. East. Several blocks at a quicker clip. Another turn, to the left. Fourth Avenue. She'd have thought she'd be taken into the sordid parts of town where the police dared not tread; the Lower East Side, not the Upper. But then again, crime occurred in the finest parts of town, too, it merely wore different clothes and operated more quietly. She heard the chug and scream of steam trains. They were near Grand Central, adjusting their route to bypass the depot itself. The elevated rails of Lexington Avenue squealed and hissed, one block to the east.

The horses picked up speed, then made an abrupt turn,

whinnying. Clara was jostled inelegantly across the cabin, there was a loud clatter as the horses crossed onto rougher cobblestone. The noise bounced off closer quarters and the cab came to a stop. She shuddered, wondering what would come next.

She was grabbed by the elbow as the door opened. She still heard traffic and the clop of horses, but the streetcar bells were farther. A side street, not an avenue.

"Go on," the abductor growled, pulling her down and shoving her forward. Clara nearly fell up stone stairs. Through the fabric of her blindfold she was aware of a dim light. A key sounded in a lock and a door creaked open. She was urged across a threshold, her boot touching down upon thick carpet with the soft squeak of wood beneath. Whatever light had been outside was not found inside. She heard the wooden slide of pocket doors upon their groove. Was this someone's home? She could hear angry voices, ahead. Her friends? Hope and relief surged in her veins.

She could tell when they first glimpsed her: heard Franklin's distinct gasp of breath, Bishop's sad sigh, and clear words from Evelyn Northe-Stewart who ordered the escort to "get his dastardly hands off her or she'd cut them off herself."

If she had to be taken hostage, at least she had good company. Her hood and blindfold were removed, revealing a lovely parlor, lit only by a pair of sconces, gas jets trimmed low above a fireplace where embers gave off an eerie, molten glow.

Before her sat her friends, in chairs around a circular table. Their shoulders were all awkwardly back, indicating they were bound like her. The abductor shoved Clara into a chair next to Evelyn, with an empty chair on her other side. Bishop was across from her, with Franklin next to him. The table was covered in a black satin cloth; a small, brass bell rested at the center beside a single lit candle. The satin was wrinkled, it hadn't been there long. The bell was of the type used in séances to call forth spirits, to change the sound of a room, to pick up on the vibrations of those across the veil. . . . Was this to be a séance, then, conducted under duress? A séance by force?

Clara began to look about the room, trying to take in the entirety of the situation.

Another man was brought into the room, bound like the rest of them. Clara's heart seized and sunk in a dizzying, sickening tumult.

"Louis . . ." she murmured. He looked at her sheepishly, his usually warm eyes rimmed with guilt. What did he have to be guilty about? Across from her, Bishop clenched and released his jaw almost imperceptibly. Louis was placed in the last empty seat, to Clara's right.

Beyond the table, Clara saw a large wooden arch leading into another wing of the house. The space was deeply shadowed; she could barely make out a figure in an angled shaft of dim light.

Someone spoke from the darkness: the voice of her captor. But it was now deeper, accented differently. Clara couldn't pinpoint it exactly, vaguely French? Why didn't he save the trouble and speak in his British accent? It was likely the infamous Brinkman himself.

"I'm sure you've wondered why I've brought you all here—" he began.

"It has something to do with Bishop's work," Evelyn interrupted sharply. "And you need me to preside as medium, which is where I assume this Louis fellow comes in. I'm clairvoyant, I've worked that out. But why you need *all* of us here is what I cannot comprehend, it's terribly inefficient and potentially dangerous to you to have this many variables. We're a very *variable* crowd, after all," she concluded.

"Information," Clara supplied. "On the Eterna compound. Whatever we know."

"Indeed, Miss Templeton," their captor stated.

"Bishop is a damn fine medium on his own, why me?" Evelyn asked.

"You're better at hearing spirits directly, the very best there is, we're told," replied the voice. "We don't have time to take chances with spirits who won't talk or with mediums who can't hear." Clara watched Bishop scowl and Evelyn fall prey to the flattery for a moment before she copied her old friend's sour expression.

"You'll be asking about the location of all Eterna evidence and the last known locale of the team, of course," the voice from the shadows replied. "If we simply came to you directly, I doubt you'd be forthcoming. And there have been some new . . . wrinkles of late."

Clara watched Louis shift uncomfortably in his chair.

"Name of the departed you wish to contact?" Evelyn asked angrily.

"Louis Dupris," said the shadows.

Clara sputtered in confusion. "But Louis is right here," Clara said, nodding toward him. Evelyn turned to Louis, then sent a questioning look toward the invisible speaker.

"No, he isn't," said the disembodied voice. "Will you explain, or shall I, *Andre?*"

There was a terrible silence. "Andre . . ." Clara said slowly.

"Yes. I am Andre Dupris. Louis's twin brother," Andre murmured.

The strained pause that followed was unbearable. All eyes were on Clara. She blinked back tears. "I . . . didn't know . . ."

"That he had a twin brother? Few did. But he does. *Did . . .*" Andre cleared his throat, his low voice trembling, "He never spoke of me. None of my family did. I brought only shame to them. But he was a good brother to me. And for what it's worth, he loved you very much."

The first tears she'd allowed herself to shed for Louis Dupris fell, in public, and Clara was helpless to wipe them away, hands bound, humiliated, furious. She could not bear to look at Bishop, not wanting to see the surprise on his face. She was not supposed to have known Louis Dupris at all, let alone well enough to have been loved by him. Bishop would be offended by her lies, pained by her secrets. And she couldn't blame him.

"Why," Clara nearly growled, "did you let me believe—"

"Because I am a selfish bastard and in the moment, I thought it might protect me, keep me safe."

"Ask Louis the questions," the voice from the shadows said angrily. "Save the parlor theatrics and petty dramas—"

"You brought us all here, you'll have to deal with the events of the night, however they unfold," Bishop barked. "You don't have hearts, but try to have a moment of respect."

Clara couldn't look at her guardian but this response was kinder toward her than she'd have expected.

"I'm fine," Clara said, putting steel into her voice. She hated to be thought vulnerable in this; one of the most terrible moments of her life. It was her worst nightmare, shocked, grieving, and publicly humiliated in front of people she deeply respected and cared for. Her heart and mind were in such pain, she didn't even know where to begin to sort the mess.

"Please make contact, Evelyn Northe-Stewart," insisted the person in the shadows.

"And ask what, exactly?" she spat. "Perhaps I should ask *your* name?"

Their captor chuckled. "Call me . . . Faust."

"As in dealing with the devil?" Clara growled.

"Aren't we all?" Faust countered airily.

"No, *we* are not," Franklin stated flatly.

"Certain information from the beginning of your commission," Faust continued, "is well known because I've had my eye on you for a while. Your security systems leave something to be desired and the locks on your file cabinets are laughable.

You really should tell your government to invest in better safeguards.

"But awhile ago all your theorists left their laboratory for an undisclosed location. So. Firstly: please ask the dead where he died."

Clara could feel everyone, herself included, bristle at the rude, callous manner.

"Did you hear that, Mr. Louis Dupris, or do you need to hear it in my voice?" Evelyn asked the room. She closed her eyes. There was a very long, tense silence before she spoke again. "Someone is present. I can feel them, but I cannot hear a word." She opened her eyes and looked at Bishop. "Rupert?"

Clara was always surprised to hear his first name from anyone else, however those two powerful spiritualists had known each other for longer than her lifetime. The senator shook his head.

"I . . . I know why you're not hearing anything," Andre Dupris said quietly. He turned toward the shadows. "It's because of Miss Templeton. Louis told me he can't get close to her, can't communicate with her. He's tried, but there's too much interference. She's too powerful or something, too guarded, there's too much that wants her attention, she has protections—"

"That's enough," Bishop said, watching Clara. Her stomach again lurched in a terrible, nauseating roil. She felt them all staring at her again and wished she could take what had been said as a compliment rather than another knife wound to her heart.

"Remove her," Faust growled.

"No!" Clara shrieked, pulling against her bonds. "Let me stay. I need to know—"

"We are here for information, Miss Templeton," Faust continued in a threatening rumble.

Another masked man in black pulled her out of her seat.

Her friends—even Andre—cried out in protest. "Silence!" Faust bellowed. Everyone shifted in their chairs, eyes lit with angry fire.

The voice in command continued: "Anyone who stands in the way of communication must be removed. And if our resident mediums cannot do their duty, then Mr. Dupris, the living had best get some answers out of his brother."

At that, the sconce at the back of the room guttered and went out. "That's promising," Faust added with a chuckle that made Clara want nothing more than to punch him directly in the throat.

"Let me listen from another part of the house, then," Clara begged. "Will that work?"

"I don't know how he operates," Andre said with a shrug.

"You're useless," she hissed. Andre stared at her, not refuting, not angry, just haggard and tired, as if he hadn't slept a wink since his brother died. Maybe he hadn't.

"Take her to the balcony!" ordered Faust. "If still no contact, toss her out into the night!"

"If you hurt her, we will kill you, mark my words," Bishop assured calmly, bright eyes flashing, straightening his broad shoulders in defiance.

"Painfully and slowly," Franklin added.

"We can torture you eternally," Evelyn added for good measure.

Clara's heart surged with affection as her friends issued their threats. Andre Dupris looked at her apologetically. Useless . . . liar. She wanted to slap him. Oddly, she had never known how violent her urges could be until she was denied the use of her hands.

"Information!" the voice in the shadows bellowed. "Will you bloody get on with it?"

Bloody. A Britishism if she'd ever heard one. Unless it was meant to throw them off.

She was dragged roughly back into the entrance foyer and forced up a grand staircase of carved wood. All the gas lamps in the place were set at eerily low levels. Her feet caught on the hems of her skirts as she climbed the stairs; she felt and heard the tearing of the cotton petticoats and her muslin and satin outer skirts. After every stumble she was dragged along more forcefully. The British, she concluded, were truly damnable creatures.

They reached a landing that looked out over the parlor, a bird's-eye view looking down over the circular table where her friends sat captive. Only then did Clara truly appreciate the towering ceiling of the space; how much wealth the building represented. The brute shoved her onto the balcony and she tripped, striking the substantial balustrade and knocking her breath quite out of herself for a moment, heart hammering against her corset stays.

A breeze rose in the room that was not naturally possible, it was ghostly. Her heart ached for the man who was present but who could never get close to her again, living or dead. She cursed Eterna in all it had given and then taken away.

"Your work, Mr. Dupris," the emotionless voice prompted from the dark.

Clara could almost hear the murmurs of the silhouettes from the disaster site, feel them breathing down her neck. . . . Perhaps there was more hidden information than England knew of. Perhaps since their Pearl Street offices had already been breached, they ought to have left that moving box in Smith's office. No, it had been dying to get to them. They did, as the British operative suggested, need better security. A lot would change if they got out of this alive.

There was a long pause. Evelyn bowed her head before offering a reply. "Louis Dupris says he cannot account for his work. He gave his files to the justice who was his superior."

"I don't think that's entirely true, Mr. Dupris," was Faust's response. He snapped his fingers and the masked man suddenly pressed a knife to Evelyn's throat. From the darkened shadows, there was a click; Clara saw a gleam of something metallic in her attacker's hand. "This pistol is aimed at your brother's heart, Mr. Dupris."

"Louis doesn't know where the Justice left them!" Evelyn cried.

"You *have* to believe us, please," Andre begged.

"What was in the papers? If he can tell us, then we'll have the knowledge, which is all that we are looking for, really," Faust stated. "Knowledge. That's not harmful, now is it?"

"It's too complicated," the medium moaned. "Too many particulars. He doesn't remember. The mind is blurred in death, he can't translate it all to me here." The woman snapped her head toward Faust in his shadowed realm. "It isn't like I'm receiving a letter or a telegraph here, you know," she growled.

"Well then, all the more reason to find his work," Faust stated. "Who is the Justice?"

There was another flash of metal and Clara held her breath as a second gun emerged from another point in the shadows, this one trained on Franklin's head.

"Allen, you bastard! Justice Samuel Allen," Bishop barked. "He resides in Riverdale."

"Is this true, *team*?" the voice asked with dripping sarcasm. "Is your dear senator telling the truth in this, Templeton? Fordham? Otherwise your medium will lose a finger."

"It is!" Clara cried, in concert with Franklin.

"And will the documents be coded?" Faust pressed.

Silence. Clara wondered at this. She knew that Allen likely possessed a great deal of information on Eterna, but doubted it was everything. Louis was playing a good game here; deflecting a search away from them. More tears fell from her burning eyes. For a moment, she did not know what was worse: that he was dead in truth, or that he was present but blocked from her even in death.

"Sympathetic stain," Evelyn offered finally.

Faust called into the shadows. "Find Allen, search everything he owns or touches, bring a solvent to decode the papers." The unseen person who received those orders could be heard scurrying away, followed by a slam of the hefty front door.

"Now. Onto our next quest," Faust declared. "Where was the disaster site?"

No one said anything. Clara debated shouting out the answer, to get this terrible ordeal over with, but paused. Why would they want to know that? And could she say any address instead of directing them to the right place? A whooshing sound came from another dark corner and everyone, including Clara, screamed as a knife twanged into the wooden balustrade near her head. Who *were* these people?

"The disaster site, if you please," the villain demanded.

"Stop threatening us," Bishop barked. "It's childish. Play like gentlemen. We know a British agent has been looking into our operations. If you're agents of England—"

"Ah, no making assumptions about us one way or another," Faust warned.

"What do you think you'll gain?" Clara shouted down at Faust. "The compound is a failure. Nothing but disaster. Why would you—" The guard who had dragged her upstairs now silenced her with a punch to her gut, proving that layers of boned corset and bodice did not make for very good armor.

The punch had her reeling—but so did her newest realization: *someone wants it as a weapon.* She gasped for breath and fought off the pain of the blow. What if *that* was the point? Not prolonging life—bringing death. That was all their research had been good for, thus far—death. She nearly retched upon the exquisite carpeting.

"There are uses for this research and everything that has been achieved with it thus far," Faust stated smoothly. "No one country or one person should have access to your findings."

Clara found herself again shouting, this time from her knees through the railing, recalling the memory of holding Mrs. Lincoln's shaking hands in her childhood grip. "The Eterna Compound was born of a specific situation for a specific need; born of Lincoln's death! England has no right! Only Americans can understand what this country went through!" Clara felt tears well up again and the guard leaned close with a threatening arm, hissing at her to shut her godforsaken mouth.

"Clara, dearest," Bishop called, "you can't explain anything to people like these, don't waste your breath." He glared into Faust's shadows. "Fourteen West Tenth Street, though you'll not find anything there. Just the ravings of a madman scrawled onto the floor."

"Only death remains there, Louis says," Evelyn murmured.

"Oh, I'm sure I'll find it enlightening," Faust assured them smoothly.

The murmurs from her vision again swarmed about Clara. If anything related to Eterna became a weapon, she'd truly never forgive herself. Before she could muse further, she was dragged downstairs and thrown back into her chair next to Andre. Her captor swiftly tied her into place once more.

Faust emerged from the shadows, the spiderweb cracks from where she'd struck him becoming visible in the dim light. He murmured in her ear, though it carried ominously through the room. "Until we meet again."

Everyone around the table stiffened at that terrible promise. Clara stiffened her spine.

"At which point," she said with an icy edge, "I'll be inclined to kill you."

"Thank you for your cooperation," Faust said as he

retreated under the arch. From the sound of it, he was followed by his operatives, who had remained almost completely unseen throughout this odd and dangerous audience.

Andre had just allowed his shoulders to fall in relief when Clara's abductor grabbed him by the shirt collar, tearing it as he hauled Andre to his feet. "You're coming with us, Mr. Dupris. *Someone* wants to see you."

There was a sudden wind in the room. The bell in the center of the table fell over with a jarring clang, the black tablecloth whipped about as if in a whirlwind, and the dim gas lamps and the candle upon the table all guttered and went out, casting the entire space into darkness.

"Don't threaten a man when his dead brother is in the room," Evelyn said quietly.

There were sounds of scuffling, fighting, heavy breath, the chair overturned, a punch, a heaving grunt and groan, and running feet.

"After him!" came Faust's cry.

Clara's heart surged; she'd root for a liar over their captors any day. The door slammed, closely followed by the sound of glass breaking and more running. It was unclear who had bested whom.

Silence fell. The house was completely quiet, eerily so.

"Did they just leave us here?" Franklin seethed.

"Yes. It would seem they did," Bishop replied.

"Not that I'm not glad to be alive, but why didn't they kill us once they got the information they needed?" Evelyn asked.

"Because they don't want international relations to go *entirely* to hell, though I'll be sure this goes straight to the president," Bishop said, shaking his head. "They'll want to track us. To see who goes where. Someone has to get to Allen!"

"The moment we're free, I'll wire his clerk and go myself, Senator," Franklin stated.

Franklin turned to Clara with renewed determination visible in his voice. "I've a knife in my boot," he said. "Miss Templeton, you're nimble . . . can you—"

"I can try," she said, lifting her chair with her as she stood. To her surprise, the sconces fluttered back to dim life, providing just enough light for her to avoid running into the table or any of her friends, though she repeatedly stumbled over her torn skirts. The chair shifted uncomfortably on her back as she advanced with small steps. The rope chafed at her wrists until it finally broke the skin—she felt the ache increase to a sharper pain at that point.

Nearing Franklin, she turned her back to him, then shifted carefully to her knees and leaned to the side. The chair legs rasped against the floor as she groped awkwardly behind herself. She felt a warm trickle of blood over her palms as her hands fumbled at the top of his boot.

Clara nearly dropped the knife as, fingertips slick with blood, she slid the blade from the slit in the leather. Evelyn clucked her tongue sadly. "Oh, Rupert, she's bleeding! Darling, that was my favorite of your dresses," she added sadly.

There was a thud as the knife slipped from her bloody hand. "Damn," Clara cursed, shifting to pick up the knife from the floor, knowing more blood was soiling that favorite gown. At last she was able to offer the knife to Franklin. He plucked it from her hands and was wonderfully efficient with it. His own binding was undone in mere moments, then moved swiftly to release them all.

"Go to Allen now," Bishop instructed. "Lose anyone who tails you. Use any Washington privilege you must to get there quickly. Put the Bixbys on alert." Franklin bobbed his head but did not move, staring at Clara. She realized that he was waiting to be sure that she was all right, so she nodded and tried to offer a smile. The attempt assuaged him and with one empathetic glance, he was off like a shot.

Bishop came over to Clara, his cravat undone. He picked

up the knife Franklin had left on the table, sliced the fine silk in half, and without a moment's hesitation bound up each of Clara's wrists in the expensive gray fabric. She found herself rendered breathless by the ministrations of her guardian.

He offered Clara a fleeting touch upon her cheek before moving to examine Evelyn's wrists, but the medium seemed to have fared the best of them and pronounced herself well.

The front door burst open and several uniformed police officers appeared in the doorway, limned by the light of the exterior gas lamp.

"You're under arrest. . . ." one of them said meekly.

"No, not these," countered another firmly—a man of higher rank, perhaps. "These were the abducted ones." This resulted in confused milling about on the front stoop.

"Let me straighten them out," Evelyn growled, charging past the men and disappearing from view. Clara could hear her sharply demand to speak with the highest ranking man on the premises.

"These are the ones I called you to *save*," insisted a familiar voice. A figure in a long coat appeared at the threshold.

"Mr. Green?" Clara exclaimed at the sight of the journalist, his presence only making her horrid night worse. "What are you doing here?"

"The opera," he replied.

Vaguely Clara remembered Lavinia mentioning the journalist's invitation, earlier that day. "I declined," Clara said coldly.

"No, Miss Kent told me to just wait outside," Green replied, sounding hurt.

Clara sighed. "She was being cruel to you."

"Yes, I gathered that after the first couple of hours," Green said, nodding. "But I noticed your light was on. So I kept waiting, as I assumed late hours were kept for a good reason. When you came out, I was standing in the shadows and I saw what was happening, so I went to alert the authorities." His eyes widened as Bishop moved into the light. "Oh, Senator, you were brought here, too? Hello, sir. Quite the story, this is!"

"One you will not be telling, you downright creepy young man, else I'll shut you and your whole paper down," Bishop said. He stepped toward Green, positively towering over him. "While I appreciate your bringing the police, if you value your life, do not follow my ward—my treasure—ever again, lest you have a whole Congressional caucus breathing down your neck. Despite how charming I seem, I can get very nasty if need be."

Clara and Green blushed at the same time. Clara assumed Green was discomfited, but she . . . *treasure*. Their little adventure on the train had brought back old words of affection, as beautiful and painful as ever.

"Is that understood?" Bishop asked.

"Yes, sir, understood. I was trying to be fastidious and patient. Not *creepy*," Green said awkwardly. "If any of you want to give an altered testimony to the paper, anonymously, you know we'd take anything—"

"Leave," Clara demanded. Visibly crestfallen the newspaperman exited. Watching through a front window, Clara saw him dart after one of the police officers, notebook in hand.

Bishop exited the house as well, Clara assumed to control both any press or police reports and for a moment she was alone in their parlor prison.

She inched back into the darkest shadows the room offered. Whose home it was—and how foreign operatives gained access—would have to be investigated.

"Louis, if you're still here . . ." she murmured, tears flowing freely once more, "I loved you, too. I am so sorry we never got a proper good-bye. . . ."

She paused, but the room was too warm. There was no ghost.

He was gone. Truly gone.

His loss was a knife, sharper the second time.

Some part of her had known Andre wasn't Louis. But that didn't help now that reality truly sunk in and she had no reserves. That she had not allowed herself to properly cry for Louis was a disservice at this breaking point as she dropped to her knees, exhausted and wracked by sorrow and the aftermath of fear.

She placed her bound, bloodied wrists to her face and sobbed.

A few moments later she felt strong, familiar hands on her. The next thing she knew, she was cradled in Bishop's arms. He carried her out of the house through a rear exit, then sat with her, on a bench on the veranda, holding her patiently as she wept, her head on his shoulder.

"I wish you'd told me about him," Bishop said quietly, with some hesitation.

"I'm sorry," she choked through tears.

There was a long silence before Bishop spoke again. "Let us thank the Lord we're alive. And let us beg the Lord for further strength to bear all that must be borne."

He kissed her forehead and, easing her out of his hold, set her next to him. Clara slumped against him, spent.

Evelyn charged around the corner of the building, an officer trailing her. Her voice was sharp as she spoke to him over her shoulder. "If you and your colleagues cannot accept that I was kidnapped and forced to hold a séance then I have nothing further to say, but leave me be." The scolded officer sighed and slunk off in the other direction.

She stormed toward Clara and Bishop, her noble face contorted in consternation. "I do wish the New York Police Department would start employing mediums. I'd get taken so much more seriously."

"You were amazing tonight, Evelyn," Bishop said gently.

"I've never been more proud. No other woman could have been so brave, resilient, and strong . . . you and Clara are a credit to your sex."

"Fantastic, then go back to Washington and get us the vote," Evelyn growled.

"I'll continue to do everything in my power," he replied. "It shouldn't be as hard as it is."

"Welcome to my world, dear," Evelyn said with a sigh. "Listen." Her voice dropped as she took a seat beside them. "I picked up an undercurrent, a whisper, during our little *session*."

Bishop and Clara stared at her. She continued, "Forty-nine, thirty-three, forty-four, thirty-three," she said, frowning slightly. "And something about a necktie? The numbers could be the combination to something. The tie, I've no clue. Ring a bell?"

Bishop shrugged.

Clara said nothing, but dread enervated her once more. How in the *world* had Louis Dupris, her dear, dead lover, cracked the combination to her personal safe?

* * * * *

"Gabriel Brinkman"—that wasn't his real name, of course, even his old friend Edward Wardwick, Lord Black, didn't know that particular truth— approached the infamous address on Tenth Street in the middle of the night. It was, he saw, a rather charming, civilized part of town, the street lit by fine gas lanterns, an idyllic place unaware of the morbid fate of those who had labored there. His jaw still hurt from where that spritely woman had elbowed him.

A younger, happier him would have had to find time to court her.

But he was not a young buck anymore and he was not happy. In fact, the man known as Brinkman was a haunted shell, and the soul within that husk was withering away, tortured every day by hell itself.

His contacts were already taking care of Allen, he couldn't be bothered to tag along on that particular adventure. His present preoccupation had the potential to yield more interesting results, and he was the sort of man to follow his interests above all. He was quite sure New York City would prove the key to everything, and, hopefully, release him from bondage.

He watched the building for a long while from one corner of the intersection. It was late, hardly anyone was out. But those few passersby he saw inevitably crossed the street, avoiding the address in question, stepping away as if an invisible barrier prevented their feet from coming too near the space. Carriages and delivery carts seemed to speed up as they passed it from the street.

Next he sized up the town house from across the street before crossing toward it. The saplings that had been planted along the street offered him little cover, but the brownstone overhang that made the garden level entry into a sort of portico put him entirely in shadow save for those directly crossing the sidewalk behind him. As the place itself seemed to divert curiosity, he felt safe enough.

He wished he could bottle whatever deterrent was in the air and sell it to every spy ring in the world. He'd never have to pick a lock again, he could simply lay on some tropical isle. . . . But no, that was one thing those who used and abused him and his family could never take away; he *loved* picking locks.

In one preternaturally swift motion he flipped up his wide black collar, revealing a sequence of gleaming metal picks slid into the seams. Unerring, he plucked out two thin spikes with subtle hooks and picked the lock on the door with a skill that any thief or spy would kill to possess.

Entering, Brinkman noted the oxidizing hinges, which appeared to have decayed at an abnormal rate given the struc-

ture's age, flaking rust onto the charred wooden floor. He drew
a small lantern from his bag, struck a match, and lit it. The
rectangular glass fixture reflected light enough for his task.

He bent to peer more closely at the floorboards. Near the
threshold he spied a blackened mark in the shape of a human
forearm and outstretched hand—or, rather, the shape of their
bones—as if a person had been reaching for the door. If the
imprint of *bone* was burned upon the floor, that would indicate a spectacularly terrible way to go—

Brinkman stopped his mind from imagining further, nodding slowly at the sight rather than shuddering at it. He had
been desensitizing himself to the sorts of sights he'd be seeing with increased frequency.

A small bit of gaslight from the street filtered in through
windows whose shutters were just enough ajar to offer dim
yellow swaths into the space.

Stepping slowly from the entrance hall with its peeling wallpaper and singed wood paneling, he crossed under the arch-
ing wooden beam, past open pocket doors revealing the wide,
main floor room beyond where any partitions had been
removed to allow for a high, molded ceiling and an open
space. He took in the scene of tables and various mysterious
equipment, the repeating, curving patterns of odd charred
markings like the pattern of waves making undulating patterns in sand.

He bent with his lantern swinging slowly from his hand, a
small, boxy leather bag filled with glass bottles at his side. The
only sounds in the room were the soft tread of his leather
boots, the gentle scrape of his heavy brocade frock coat against
the floor when he bent low, and the flick of his pocketknife
as it opened in his palm with a flash of silver.

He worked quickly, moving from one end of the room to
another with his pocketknife out and working in small flur-
ries, scraping bits of residue and film off the floor, the surface

of the tables, any lingering broken glass, odd substances crystallized in spiderwebs. . . . Residues and ash, powders and dust, he separated the collections into different vials and bottles. What had happened to the bodies of those who died there was something Brinkman tried not to think about. He was fleetingly glad the light wasn't bright enough to reveal if there were any further impressions of human bone upon the floor.

There was an empty shelf at one side of the room and behind it, the shelf lending the wall a bit of shadow, was a carving into the wood paneling and up onto the flocked wall. A rectangle, about the size of a door. He knew that well.

"Ah," he said.

He looked around the floor once more for other markings. He climbed the second floor and saw the thrown-back carpets.

"There's the madness. So. One of the scientists was turned," he stated, descending the stairs. "I don't like that I didn't know that. Or who poisoned him."

If he couldn't control the ebb and flow of operations, he didn't know how he could continue on. If the scale was greater than he could fathom, at any point he could be ripped from the equation and the soul that depended on him would be lost forever. He forced back a wave of frightened despair.

As he reached the landing of the entrance hall, the jaundiced light filtering in through the shuttered windows was immediately extinguished, as was his lantern. Brinkman took a long breath and withdrew a box of matches from a deep pocket that held a number of useful items and small weapons. Striking a match, he saw six silhouettes blocking the door. Roughly human sized and shaped, not entirely touching the floor.

Brinkman smiled. "Hello again, old friends."

He wished he didn't understand who and what he was dealing with, the forces driving him, constraining him to make concessions to England for the sake of an innocent life. . . . .

The air around him sighed with a low hiss that ebbed and flowed with something of the feeling of language, the temperature plummeted. His next exhalation caused a cloud of vapor.

"If you are trying to communicate with me, I do not understand you. But allegiances are very clear and you've nothing to fear from me. I am going to be on my way and leave you to your unfolding destiny. May I pass?"

One silhouette shifted, giving him a narrow path of exit.

He crossed between the shadowy forms, every hair on end, moving slowly out of the building, casting not a single glance behind him. He did not slam the door but allowed it to shut behind him slowly. He did not race up the steps to the sidewalk, though he wanted to run fast, hard, and far. He thought about what was clanking in his bag as he moved stiffly toward Fifth Avenue.

Those poor sots in those messy, unorganized, inconsequential New York and London departments had no idea what they were in for. There was no way for all this to end but in war. And no one was the wiser. Not yet. None of them would be until it was much too late.

* * * * *

Andre's penchant for fistfights had come in handy there in the dark. He could feel the chill presence of his dead brother freezing the already cold sweat on his skin.

"Thank you, Louis, for saving me," Andre said as he ran. If not for Louis, Andre would likely have been carted back to England to face Lord Black and the many powerful people Andre had angered and offended in that delicious city.

"You're welcome," the ghost replied. "Now you must do something for me."

"Something more?" Andre cried.

"What you left in Smith's office was only part of the work," Louis explained urgently. "His spirit came to me, in the perilous half sleep that happens in this purgatory I'm in. He hid some of his chemical compounds from me. They went into our final mixture but were ingredients I had not recorded. Smith also concealed some of Goldberg's material from before he went mad.

"He did not wish the entire compound to ever be listed in a single document. Leave Clara a note to go back to Smith's office. There's more to find there."

"What about the material at Allen's?" André asked.

"Old files with work from previous theorists who long abandoned the project," the spirit replied. "If England knows about those tests, so be it. We have to throw them something to scrabble over, like vultures. Clara is the only one I trust, not even Bishop, no one else. There must be more power in my work than I even know, to have gotten this much attention—"

"That's what those numbers were about? Her safe? I nearly blurted them out. But Louis, I need to hide—we need to hide!"

"We have time for this, Andre. You've the advantage here, you must do this."

Andre spied a healthy mare tied to a post near a sort of gentlemen's club where the men were dressed well and the women were barely so. He grabbed the horse from its hitch and took off at a gallop despite cries of protest and a shout of "thief!"

He drove the horse hard, nearly running over pedestrians and almost crashing the poor beast into an oncoming carriage. Pearl Street was won in a surprisingly swift bout and Andre leaped off the animal and ran to the front door.

He tried with his pick to unlatch the lock but his nerves only jammed the knob, so in his haste he broke the pane of the front door with his elbow, reaching through the jagged glass to unlock it. Before bounding up the stairs, he paused for an instant to consider the redheaded doorkeeper slumped in her chair. Andre hoped she wasn't dead but knew he didn't have time to find out.

As Andre ascended, the grayscale draft of his brother gave instructions. "The material is in Smith's office fireplace, up the chimney. Tell her only she must know!"

"Always with the fire." Andre chuckled despite himself, writing out what Louis requested.

"Now to the safe," Louis continued, "below her desk, below the carpeting."

"How do you know the combination?" Andre asked, genuinely curious.

"I watched her, place an item of mine—the only one she had left of me—in that safe. In that moment, because she held something that had belonged to me, I could get close, though I could not speak, couldn't move anything to let her know I was there." Louis's voice was plaintive. He recited the combination and Andre opened the safe.

It was the work of mere moments to toss the paper within, close the safe and conceal it once more, then flee.

Finding himself conveniently near the tip of Manhattan Island, Andre hurriedly planned his further escape. Used to having to escape at a moment's notice due to angry wives, husbands, or creditors, he tended to have money sewn into his clothing and hidden in his accoutrements.

He stowed onto a cargo clipper making a night run across the river, desperate for constant movement. Not sleeping, he barely ate or breathed, unable to relax until the train he boarded in New Jersey had cleared Ohio and he was confident none of his pursuers were following.

Andre still intended to return to New Orleans, to put to rest some of the dust that his dead brother had unwittingly kicked up, but he wondered now if he wasn't being chased by more than British spies.

Something else had been going on in the house where he

and the others had been held that night. Something had been lurking in the shadows. He'd sensed it before, in Goldberg's home, and before then, back home, in Lafayette Cemetery. He'd found his brother there at dawn, drenched in blood and unable to remember what had happened to him during the night. Louis had always been a bit haunted, and paranormal things loved clinging to him. He was, Andre supposed, a bit magical. But that hadn't saved his life. His precious *mystères* hadn't intervened, then or now.

Andre had set sail for London the day after he found his brother in the graveyard and years had passed with no contact between the twins, until he was dragged back into his brother's sphere by England itself. That he had been under the thumb of England was laughable anyway—that damn, fool, uptight, moralizing, hypocritical country. He longed for the days when a libertine might be left well enough alone. Well, they were, if they were well-placed enough. That was the trick, wasn't it: placement. How you were born. *Who* you were born.

"What have we gotten ourselves into, brother?" he asked the cold patch of air beside him as he sat in the back of a train car full of sleeping people, hat low over his olive-toned face.

"I'm not entirely sure," came Louis's whisper. "Whatever it is, it's just gotten worse. Something is afoot in this country that wasn't here before. The priestess back home knew it. She and her colleagues were trying to warn me, trying to create new prayers, new wards, demand of the spirits some answers. She said that something ugly had 'opened up' in this country, and if we weren't careful, we'd be slaves to it. All of us."

Andre shuddered.

"I'm going to go back to New York, Andre," Louis said, his ghostly form receding. "I need to watch over Clara. Good-bye, brother, take care of yourself."

In the next breath, before Andre could say good-bye, Louis vanished.

Andre felt hollow, and terribly alone.

Out of the corner of his eye, Andre could have sworn he saw what looked like an entirely opaque, man-shaped shadow standing at the head of the carriage. But that was surely a figment of his weary imagination. Andre was tired. Dead tired.

* * * * *

"Do you promise me you're not putting on a show of being all right?" Bishop asked Clara as the hired carriage turned onto Pearl Street.

"I'll be fine, Rupert," she said. "I'm tired. Abductions are so exhausting," she added, trying for a light tone.

"Would you tell me even if you did need help?" he asked sadly.

"I would. I will, Rupert," she said, staring into his eyes. "I don't want to keep things from you. It wasn't fair. . . ."

Her guardian was inscrutable as he helped her out of the carriage, taking care of her wrists. They'd gone to the offices to see if Louis's diary and the other papers were still in the file cabinet. It would be a few moments' walk home after that.

Walking up the steps, Clara noticed the broken glass at the door.

"Lavinia!" Clara whirled back to the senator. "She was drugged by the bastard. In the tumult, I forgot."

Flinging the door open they rushed in to find her crumpled at her post in a splay of black fabric, red hair tangled in the beads of a fascinator whose feathers were now broken. Oh, Lavinia's rage would be palpable when she woke and saw her accessories had been sundered. Bishop straightened her in her chair, trying to rouse her.

"Wait here with Lavinia, I'd like to fetch one of my talismans," Clara said, her feet already on the stairs. In her office, she lit the candle in a mirrored lantern with shaking hands, then whirled around the room to make sure nothing lurked in what had previously been shadow.

Closing and locking the door behind her—she did not care to replay her abduction—she darted to her desk. In an instant she had opened the safe, using the so-familiar combination Evelyn had picked up from Louis.

A piece of paper. Like magic, like a ghost; suddenly and unexpectedly there, lying atop the precious bit of fabric that had once belonged to her Louis.

She snatched it up and read the words, seeing the difference now between this handwriting and Louis's. It was up to her and her alone to gather more of the Eterna files. Louis didn't want England—or whoever was behind their abduction—to know about this. Not Bishop either.

She memorized the information, trying to calm her racing thoughts. As for the Eterna Commission . . . she should have tried to stop it long ago, before the project had become steeped in death. Irony, when it was a search for life.

Unsure she could convince Bishop to understand why this mad pursuit had to end, she deemed it best to take certain matters into her own hands.

In that moment Clara decided she would destroy and bury the whole lot, everything she had, including Louis's cravat. There was no body left to bury, but she would honor him as if there were.

Whatever Eterna had done to them, it wouldn't ever happen again, so help her God.

CHAPTER

THIRTEEN

Deep within the Royal Courts of Justice, Moriel's pet lieutenant made sure the other guard—there were only two—had left before drawing close to the narrow bars to deliver a message.

"Interrogation of American operatives was successful," the large guard murmured to the small, balding man curled in the shadows. "Too easy, even."

The Majesty clucked his tongue, a fervor cresting as he spoke. "People are easy to best. What concerns me is the *material*. Our summoned were blocked from gaining further ground even though they were directly invited in by the Jew scientist I had poisoned and thusly turned. So my chief concern now is if there is a ward in play. There may well be. And you know, my friend, that a ward is *unacceptable*." Moriel seethed, pacing his cell.

"That's what must be stopped, the trail thrown cold as ice. Neither team can gain such a shield. Are samples from the site en route as ordered?"

"Yes, Majesty; three vials in secret, to our royal seat, where augury will determine the precise nature of the incident, and if a ward was indeed present or no. One vial will be sent to England's governmental division."

"Make sure the one is intercepted. In detonating, change the sample's properties to be unrecognizable," the Majesty said firmly. "The American and British teams will be at each other's throats, each of them thinking the other is responsible for all ill deeds done. Make sure someone targets one of England's team—throw them off the trail, derail them toward other magics, away from ours. Understood?"

O'Rourke nodded. "Understood."

"Go, out with you," Moriel shooed him.

"Yes, sir." The guard scurried away.

Moriel turned to his immaculate cell. He'd cleaned up the rat; his little game of bones. It was a childhood comfort and it soothed in such a place as this. But as he'd find a way out of this dank pit soon, such behavior wouldn't stand in high society. He would soon have to sacrifice his indulgences and instead regain the sort of subtle, gentlemanly grandeur expected of his status.

As he ascended, he'd need to leave gore to others; his predilections would have to carry on without his direct hand in the entrails. He smoothed his prison garb, lifted his hands and brought them down upon his head, feeling the weight of a future crown he'd wear forever.

* * * * *

Miss Everhart passed along the latest message. Decoded, it briefly described kidnapping Eterna associates and conducting a séance. A detailed account would be wired when time provided.

Spire didn't trust a word of it. "Absurdity of the premise aside," he said, shaking his head, "kidnapping several operatives and keeping them in a room together . . . Who was he working with?"

Everhart shook her head. "This says alone. I'm sure when he sends the full account there will be more details. Only so much can be done over telegraph wires."

"He couldn't have managed that alone, no matter how talented he or Black think he is," Spire said, looking at his team, gathered in full in their Millbank offices. "So why specify working alone if it's implausible? Who else is he protecting? What other operatives do we have there?" he asked, exasperated. "Is there more Lord Black is withholding from me?"

"I truly do not know," Everhart replied.

Spire stared at the second half of the decoded message: "Material in hand will be sent by swiftest packet. Please advise route."

"Is the material safe to possess or transport, whatever it is?" Mrs. Wilson asked. "It obviously didn't bode well for the Americans that engineered it. Are we putting British lives at stake by bringing it here?"

"Brinkman survived to send the message," Knight countered with a shrug of red-satin-decked shoulders, "so whatever it is, it is somehow contained."

"Well, we need to work out a route to ensure the safe arrival of whatever is sent to us," Spire said.

"Concerning the route, if you would, Mr. Spire, give us somewhere with height," Mr. Wilson requested politely.

Spire nodded, already thinking how to accommodate their skills. Their "circus act" aside, he remembered something about the Wilsons' legendary exploits as reported in the papers; a particularly impressive extraction of an operative using rappeling.

"Living there, we know Longacre like the back of our hand," Mr. Wilson suggested.

"Awfully busy," Spire stated.

"Midday, between lunch and close of businesses," Mrs. Wilson countered. "It's busy but manageable."

"All right, then, but I want everyone there. The Americans may be aware that there is material coming, and surely after the abduction we're on far less friendly terms than we were. We'll be lucky if there is not a forthcoming diplomacy issue."

"That's the beauty of their own secret development team,"

Everhart stated. "They don't want anyone to know about it either."

* * * * *

In New York City, on a pallet in one of the empty rooms he kept about the island and used in an unpredictable rotation, Brinkman awoke alive and with all his limbs intact. Because of this, he was granted permission to proceed from the greater of two masters. From the lesser he would be receiving his next instructions.

As far as his supervisors knew, his mission would unfold from here as planned.

To have called himself Faust was not inaccurate. He was beholden to the devil. The beast's crafty claws had dug deep into the only thing that he cared about in this whole world. Shirking off both the chains of guilt and the paralyzing reason why he was constrained into this double-agent capacity in the first place, Gabriel went to work.

Dressed as if he were a middle-class merchant, he left his temporary lodgings on the Upper East Side, carrying with him two small packages bound with twine. Inside, painstakingly packed, were the securely closed vials he'd filled on Tenth Street.

One vial would be sent to London via the channels Lord Black and his company would provide. As far as they knew, it was the only sample taken at the disaster site.

The rest of the vials would go to a factory in New Orleans that neither the Eterna nor the Omega office knew of.

The long stroll down Lexington, accompanied by the screeching music of the elevated rail, terminated in a telegraph office near Union Square. A new clerk, whom Brinkman didn't recognize, handed him a waiting message. Brinkman tipped his wide-brimmed hat and stepped again onto bustling Fourteenth Street, maintaining his casual, strolling pace, one that was more measured than that of the average bustling New Yorker.

To send packages, he used any of several post offices scattered about the city, where British agents were in place. Today was all about efficiency, so he went to the closest one, eager to get the material out of his hands. While he was not a superstitious man, there was enough empirical evidence to suggest that his current business came with some cost. He'd decided to limit his exposure.

Brinkman gave his contact the transportation information he'd received from Black's people, and warned the young man with all proper doom and gloom that if he bungled the job he'd likely die. Mr. Brinkman then washed his hands of the whole ugly business for a while, off to investigate a few matters of his own interest that bore no country's allegiance, just that of his own burdened heart.

Clara slept for nearly an entire day after the abduction, a fact she learned from Miss Harper when she finally awoke, feeling very disoriented, after a sequence of restless dreams filled with shadows. She asked the housekeeper for tea and something simple to eat, and the woman seemed happy to make quite a fuss over her.

It seemed to take forever to dress, even in garments suitable for home. Her mind seemed reluctant to work and only slowly cobbled together full memories of the abduction and its aftermath. She felt hollow, lonely, and confused.

She suspected Bishop would watch her closely for a while, which would make it difficult to return to Smith's office, but Clara could not come up with a plan to evade him. At length she drifted down to the parlor with a novel in hand; Harper kept bringing her tea and plates of food, some of which she nibbled on.

The bright spot in the day came when Bishop came home and attended to her wrists. As he approached, supplies in hand, she smiled at him gently. Her wrists bore nasty burn marks and cuts, but thankfully hadn't become infected.

He knelt before the cushioned chair where she sat in a diffused ray of sunlight through floral lace curtains and began tending to her with careful, sure hands.

"Thank you for your ministrations, Rupert," she said after

a long moment. "I know you've so much to do with the legislature soon in session, so I appreciate—"

The look he gave her was so intense, eviscerating, so pained, it cut her breath from her. "If anything ever happened to you, Clara, I don't know what I'd do. The abduction . . . made me wonder. I pray to your father every day, I ask his spirit if I'm doing right by you. He's never once responded to me. How do I know, then, if I'm—"

It was her turn to stop him short by swiftly leaning down to kiss his forehead, her breath glancing off the gentle creases of his brow. Her lips lingered there as she murmured:

"Wonderful, you're *wonderful,* Rupert. I am *so* lucky to have you."

He released his kept breath and leaned his forehead into her, the slope of his nose pressing against her chin. For one paralyzing moment, Clara wondered if he would tilt his face up further, meet her mouth with his . . . but they both remained still, though Clara could feel his fingers trembling where his bandage dressing had paused.

She was overwhelmed. She thought of Louis and the lingering pain of her wrists was nothing compared to the whole of her ache for him. Yet the energy between her and Bishop in this lifetime had never been so charged. For an instant, she truly let herself wonder for the first time why he hadn't courted and married someone during the nearly two decades they had known each other.

They both pulled back at the same time, as if breaking from a reverie.

"Just . . . promise me that you won't keep secrets from me again," he said, keeping his voice neutral as he finished with one wrist.

"Can you promise me the same?" she countered softly.

He looked up at her again, his gaze steeled now, vulnerability gone. He slightly shook his head. She tilted her head to the side with a gentle look that spoke of their impasse. He finished her second wrist.

There would have to be secrets.

She owed it to Louis not to betray his wishes, to find the rest of Smith's material and keep quiet about it. Tying off the plaster, the senator rose and bowed his head to her, preparing to exit.

"I need to know what's happened," Clara called after him, rising from her chair. "If Franklin has found Allen, Rupert, you can't cloister me here."

"You need a day to rest," Bishop countered, trying to maintain a gentle tone, but his insistence made it strident. "I cannot have you in that office until further safety measures are installed."

She reached out a hand and touched his shoulder. "You did promise not to exclude me."

Bishop sighed. "Once I've confirmed that Franklin has returned safely, I suppose . . . If I know you won't be alone there, I won't palpitate with worry. Come along, then. I know I can't dissuade you. We'll have a look. I need Franklin's update as much as you do."

Clara smiled and nearly dragged Bishop down the street. Lavinia's chair was empty—the young woman had been instructed to stay home and her infamous actor fiancé had even stopped touring to be by her side.

"Thank goodness you're here and all right," Bishop said upon catching sight of Franklin at his desk. "I'm sure you've some tales to tell."

Fred Bixby was also present, waving at them from his small desk that was covered in papers. "Good to see you, too, Bixby," Clara said.

Bixby nodded then returned to his work, using one finger to stab at a ledger line and follow it across the page.

"Indeed I do," Franklin replied, then brought a cup of coffee to his lips. He looked like he hadn't slept since the abduction.

No matter what she decided to do with Smith's information, Clara felt it was now more important than ever to tie up loose ends. To arrest those who had abducted them, to keep further plots from brewing. One by one, all Eterna's ghosts, living or dead, would either pay for their misdeeds or be set to rest.

Franklin spoke quietly, having a hard time looking at Bishop. "Is Lavinia all right?"

"Recovering in the arms of her dear Mr. Veil, so I hear," Bishop replied. "He made quite the dramatic entrance into Evelyn Northe-Stewart's home, asking after her. I'm sure he'll incorporate the incident into one of his shows. How is Allen?" Bishop pressed.

Franklin's jaw clenched. "Dead . . ."

Bishop and Clara both made exclamations. "Those bastards," Bishop cried. "They killed him?"

"No," Franklin said quietly, a bit dazed. "At least, I don't know. He's said to have died in an asylum."

"Beg pardon?" Clara asked. Only a few months ago she'd seen the man at one of Bishop's campaign events, as kind and boring as ever.

"Committed!" Bixby cried, startling them. "Just like I'll be if I don't find out something about that damned house you all were dragged to! It's like it's not even *there*!" Ascot undone about his neck, mustache unkempt, he jumped up and darted to the office door. Not finding records of things that should be recorded was Bixby's worst nightmare. "I've another hall of records to examine," he called over his shoulder as he headed down the stairs. Clara and Franklin blinked after him a moment.

"I guess that's where we stand on the mansion investigation," she said.

"Go on," Bishop barked. "How did Justice Allen die?"

"Found him hanging in his cell this morning," Franklin murmured with a shudder. "Having tied pieces of his clothes together for a noose. Seems Allen suffered a breakdown directly after the Eterna incident. No one was informed, he lived alone with only his housekeeper and I haven't found any relatives who either knew of the breakdown or who would have had him sent to that dreadful asylum. The staff there said he'd come in voluntarily."

Stunned, Clara managed to ask, "And what of our paperwork? The files, whatever the British would be looking for?"

"I searched the house, at least in all the visible areas, while the poor distract housekeeper was trying to be helpful. I told the precinct officer who arrived to watch the house for activity. The housekeeper said that the judge had burned many things in the fireplace. Surely whatever he had of Eterna went up in smoke. There was a file on his desk that I believe pertained to us but it was covered in overturned ink and entirely illegible."

Clara sighed. "Did you see his cell . . . were there any signs . . ."

"His body had been taken down by the time I got there. Nothing obvious in his cell. Nothing I could derive from the guards. I asked to see his body in the morgue and was denied."

"Is there even a body at all then? Could it have been a ruse?" Bishop asked.

"That would be my hope, sir," Franklin replied. "I just don't know what to make of it all. I put the local authorities on the alert and asked them to let us know what they find."

Clara wondered, morbidly, if everyone around Eterna suffered an ill fate . . . How long before all of them met their ends?

"I've got to get to work. And get to the bottom of what

happened," Bishop growled, storming off. He turned at the threshold, staring from Franklin back to Clara. "Don't let each other out of your sights. That's an order."

"Yes, sir." Franklin bowed his head. "And I am sorry about Justice Allen."

"Thank you," Bishop said, his cold tone softening as he glanced at Clara. "Loss is epidemic these days." She looked away. "So we must be more kind and gracious than ever to those who remain."

She offered the senator a soft smile and he exited.

Thanks to Franklin, Clara soon had a cup of coffee in her hand. She sank deeper into her chair, layers of muslin, ribbon, and lace rising up around her like the crest of a wave. Franklin rubbed his fingers against the firm line of his jaw.

"So what to do now that the trail of the rest of the research has gone cold? Do we try to summon Mr. Dupris again, if that's even possible? Another of the scientists?"

Clara shifted uncomfortably in her chair.

"I'm sorry," Franklin murmured. "That wasn't very thoughtful of me."

"It's fine," she said coolly. "Go on."

"I'm going back to the Goldberg house," Franklin said, and got to his feet.

"To do what?"

"I assume our abductors went snooping, considering they wanted to know where it was." He flexed his hand, the hand that could see into the past in a way that still made Clara marvel at its magic. "I'm going to see what I can see."

"Indeed, that's very sensible. While you're there, will you look to see if there are other carvings I missed on the first floor? Perhaps anything on the walls?"

"Aren't you coming with me?" Franklin held out an arm. "You dare not go in, but you ought to be nearby. We'll catch hell from the senator if we split up."

Clara thought for a moment, then rose. She'd see Franklin to the site. As Lavinia did not live far, she'd tell him she was going to visit. Instead she'd go to Columbia. Moving to a cabinet by the office door, she procured a small carpet bag.

"Going on a trip?" Franklin asked warily.

"In case you find something interesting to take away," she replied.

As they rode a jostling trolley uptown, Clara's instinct to withdraw and say nothing was powerful, and thankfully the car was too crowded for them to talk openly about anything.

Always cautious of her condition, Franklin accepted her declaration that she would go no closer to the house than the corner of West Tenth and Fifth Avenue. She warned him of the carvings and eerie omens within.

"The senator will flay me if he knows I let you go—"

"I'm not a child, Franklin," Clara snapped. "I appreciate everyone's care, but I'll visit Lavinia and then go straight home. Tell me tomorrow what you find."

He acquiesced and parted from her, not even noticing that she retained the bag she had brought ostensibly for his use.

* * * * *

Professor McBride was not in his offices in Columbia. The few students or staff who passed Clara gave her disdainful looks, despite the fact she was dressed in fine layers of lace-trimmed muslin, with pearl buttons down her bodice and sleeves, an artful feathered straw hat, and lace gloves. All markers of her place in society and certainly nothing threatening. Just—and it pained her to think this—out of place.

The light flow of traffic was also to her advantage when she stood before Smith's office, trying the door. It was no surprise that it was locked. Clara withdrew two of her hairpins and set to work.

She'd practiced lock-picking on all the doors of Bishop's house when he wasn't around to notice, having decided that in her line of work it would be a very handy skill. It had indeed been one of the most helpful things she'd ever learned. As she shut Smith's door behind her, she felt the cool draft and knew that she was not alone. Far off, she felt the first hint of a headache, but felt she would be safe for some time yet.

One of the glass beakers in the small fireplace was alight, smoke curling in small wisps up the shaft. Clara was quite sure no one had dared enter this office.

"What's this, Mr. Smith? A hint? Please remember I'm here to help and I am on your side, and I honor your life, your loss, your legacy," she murmured quietly. The cold draft that had been directly upon her seemed to dissipate. If that was Professor Smith, he was giving her a wide berth.

She went to the mantel and bent, one hand keeping the skirts of her favorite cornflower blue dress well clear. With the other, Clara picked up the iron tongs from the set of fireplace tools. Collaring the smoking beaker, she moved it and its low-burning contents, which appeared some kind of soil or coal mixture, onto the marble-topped mantel. She took care to position it where it could not fall onto her head or her skirts.

Trading the tongs for the poker, she stuck the implement up the chimney and traced its tip along each side of the square shaft until the pointed tip jostled against something metal. Removing the white gloves she had no wish to ruin, she reached up and found a rectangular tin.

She pulled on it gently but it did not move. Clara shifted position to look up into the shaft. The object seemed to be hanging from a nail. Lifting the box disengaged the hook that had secured it to the nail and she was able to retrieve the sooty box and set it on Smith's desk.

Wiping the box down with a handkerchief plucked from her sleeve, she shook it and heard papers shifting. That was enough. Clara deposited the box in her small carpetbag, wiped her hand, and replaced her glove.

"Thank you, Mr. Smith," she murmured to the room. "If you can hear me and you see my Louis, tell him . . . that I miss him," she said, swallowing hard.

Grasping the bag's wooden handles, she listened for footfalls at the door. When there was utter silence, Clara set Smith's door to latch lock behind her and slipped out again as unannounced as she'd arrived. Her hint of a headache receded as soon as she left the room.

In the hackney home, Clara rubbed her temples, the starched lace of her cuffs scratching irritatingly at her cheek, wanting to think but feeling like she was standing in a sinking quagmire.

She wanted to sit with papers and dream, like Louis. Darling, truly dead Louis; still dreaming and inventing, even as a spirit. Perhaps he was dreaming more purely than ever, being pure energy, devoid of a body. . . .

Clara felt on the edge of some breakthrough; she felt something tingling at the corners of her brain, something she had missed. She did not want the Eterna project to go forward but she did want to understand what drove Louis, what drove all of them to unveil the secrets they discovered. She wasn't interested in the science or medicine of it—it was the spirit of the work that captivated her.

Stepping back onto Pearl Street, she took a deep breath; the evening had begun to settle though the city never truly did.

Lamplighters did their work on some streets while electric lamps flicked to life on other blocks. Clara thought for a moment about the mix of the old ways and those that would likely soon become commonplace. New York was forever a city in transition, always striving, moving forward, trying to save time, save hours, save life. . . . She felt that she was poised in a similar place, trapped between old and new, surrounded by her many past lives but seeking yet another future. Clara shook herself out of her reverie.

Something caught her eye. Someone.

A young man—he couldn't have been older than sixteen—stood across the street, wearing a modest brown suit and trousers. He was standing directly under an electric street lamp. Cocking his head slightly to the side and taking a wide stance, he stared at her hungrily. Improperly. She narrowed her eyes and fixed a stern expression on her face, descending the small stoop to the sidewalk.

As she turned toward home, she saw the lamp gutter above the young man. In the flickering light, she seemed to glimpse human silhouettes floating around him . . . dark, opaque silhouettes, like those that encouraged her to find the files.

The light blew entirely, with a pop that made her jump. Clara hastily turned away, lest she be thought rude, staring at the boy. She also turned away because something about the young man's face and those black, smoky shapes terrified her.

Everything that caught her eye of late seemed haunted. So, thusly, she was haunted.

Something clicked into place within her mind.

She thought about the single defining characteristic of the papers listing three city's respective magics. Each had their own regional components, items to create a sense of boundaries for the compound, that it be tied to this country's soil and governance. But then there was one recurring theme. One word, even.

Charge.

That was it; the idea nagging at the corners of her mind.

Bishop thought that meant something spiritual and Clara knew he was at least partly right. But *charge* had many meanings and connotations.

They were not far from Thomas Edison's Pearl Street dynamos, wonders of the modern world. She suddenly felt called toward their electrical whirr . . . their *charge*. And called toward someone who created in her a spark.

She opened the door to the home she and Bishop shared together, intent on asking him whether electricity could also be a factor in overarching Eterna theory, preferably over a nice, long, lovely dinner.

Behind her, all the lights on Pearl Street went out.

That's the trouble with electricity, Clara thought. Can't be relied upon.

Nor could her emotions, flickering like an unstable bulb. It was clear almost immediately that the senator wasn't home. She went upstairs to her room. Moments later she slipped a note under the door of Bishop's study so he would know she was home safe, then locked herself in and penned notes in her diary, making lists, fleshing out a plan that she hoped would help set everything to rest. . . .

Eterna was full of the restless living and the restless dead. It needed to die once and for all. If England wanted to pursue a literal dead end, then let them be the ones damned for it.

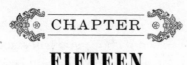

CHAPTER
FIFTEEN

Spire watched Everhart as she stared out the window of the Millbank offices onto the teeming, jostling narrow waterway of the Thames, the next duty upon them. He wondered if she felt nervous.

He felt frustrated. Grange and the Metropolitan had managed to keep several people in custody and alive; trials would be held regarding the Tourney business within the month. But Tourney himself was dead, and most of those still alive knew very little. Spire practically burned with desire to question them, to determine if they knew more than they'd revealed, but that was impossible, and not only because he was no longer on the force.

The Omega team had been busy: communicating with Brinkman in a flurry of wires, preparing the route for today's exchange of material, vetting the remainder of the new scientists, and making sure the facility was ready for them and secure.

* * * * *

"Are you a believer, Miss Everhart?" he asked, moving to stand with her by the window. "In the supernatural?" he clarified.

"Does my answer really matter to you?" she asked. "Would it change anything?"

Spire stared at her. "No. No, I suppose it wouldn't."

"I'm not," she replied. "Not really. But, I should say that

if certain elements of this work prove themselves, I will believe them when they do. I hope you will respect that."

There was no possible response he could make to that declaration, Spire realized.

The clock struck. It was time for them to take their places.

"Are you ready?" Spire asked. She nodded.

Spire had to assume the rest of his team was in place. Unease gnawed at him, as if he could've created a better plan if he'd thought a little longer. Too late now. But was putting Everhart right into the thick of things the best call? Lord Black had rejected Spire's request to delay in order to prepare more thoroughly, insisting that Brinkman's material be sent on the first mail packet possible.

Thankfully he'd have Grange and Phyfe on hand—he'd been allowed to use a few trusted Metropolitan contacts. This comfort countered his unusual sense of dread.

Miss Everhart cleared her throat, the sound stirring him, and he looked up to find she was at the door. "Are you coming?"

Spire joined her at the threshold, glad she did not seem to have the doubts he did, chiding himself for worrying about her ability to accept a bloody suitcase.

* * * * *

Rose didn't think she had any reason to be nervous, yet she was. She shifted in her boots, feeling the gentle sway of her thick layered skirts, then realized she should stand still, lest nervous movement be a tell. At the turn of the quarter hour, a large black carriage drawn by horses accessorized with green and silver feathered plumes barreled across Longacre as if the dogs of hell were nipping at its heels. Though the carriage and its haste were as expected, the vehicle's speed was so at odds with the generally lazy pedestrians that Rose thought some passerby would surely take notice.

She detached her arm from Spire's and walked toward the

vehicle, which slowed as she approached. The driver tipped his hat—again according to plan, the same plan that had dictated her outfit: a fine green dress and a black crepe hat, which driver and passenger would look for.

The carriage's window curtain was drawn, but Rose glimpsed the shadow of a single figure within. She drew near. The window opened and the person inside—still unseen save for black gloves—offered Rose a small, black, leather-bound, rectangular case.

As Rose reached for the case, something flew at her from the alley directly behind the meeting place. Something slammed into her. She felt a shock wave of pain; a fistful of dread pummeled her gut and everything faded to black.

Spire watched Everhart approach the carriage, which had appeared precisely on time. While he did not relax, he was reassured that all was going according to plan.

Time seemed to slow as a figure appeared as if from nowhere and knocked Miss Everhart to the ground. Two of his armed agents rushed forward, one attempting to untangle the two tumbling figures, the other at the carriage, battling for the case.

In the instant, Spire understood why the Wilsons had requested a high vantage point. Two lithe, masked persons in tight breeches and form-fitting frock coats rappeled down from an upper balcony, landing effortlessly on the roof of the carriage. Spire assumed it was Mr. Wilson who nimbly tossed himself beside the driver, who looked to be preparing to jump from the vehicle, and held him in place.

The smaller one, likely Mrs. Wilson, went after a black shape that had flung itself from the opposite side of the carriage cab and was running down an alley.

How could they have been compromised? And by whom?

Fury seethed in his veins as his mission unraveled like a thread pulled by a speeding bullet. If anyone died because he hadn't taken his duties seriously enough . . . He ran to Grange, who was bent over Everhart.

"Give her to me," Spire said. Her limp form was transferred into his arms.

Glancing up, Spire saw a flurry of motion around the larger Wilson and the immobilized driver, as if they were being covered by a great piece of thick black fabric, or as if something was preventing the light of the sun from reaching them. Spire thought of the strange moment in Tourney's cellar when the shadow had left the chained body.

In the next instant, the darkness lifted, Mr. Wilson was thrown off the carriage, and the driver slumped, unconscious. The horse screamed and stamped, bridle clattering, but miraculously did not bolt. Phyfe, who was masterful with beasts, was standing before the mare, being stern and soothing all at the same time.

"Secure the vehicle," Spire barked, shifting Everhart so he could hold her more comfortably. A glance into the cabin through the broken window revealed a dead body. But there had only been one person inside the carriage—so what was Mrs. Wilson chasing?

The carriage was still. Spire risked a closer glance. The body was that of a well-dressed gentleman with a look of horror on his face. His mouth was hanging open, and his general expression reminded Spire all too forcefully of the look of the dead children when that dread shadow had passed over them.

An odd, sparking light could be seen within the carriage, emanating from an object of indeterminate nature on the seat beside the dead man. At the sight of that strange, greenish-yellow hue, instinct surged within Spire.

"Run!" he barked to his men and suited the action to the word, holding Miss Everhart close to shield her from what he suddenly knew was about to happen.

The explosion was most unusual. An odd burst of fire, a

whip of sickly colored, yellow-green flame that reeked terribly of sulfur. Acrid smoke filled the air; Spire could feel the back of his scalp burn where the vapor kissed it, smell his burnt hair. He dashed around a corner, away from the offending gas.

Sulfur . . . the report documenting the Eterna incident had mentioned sulfur. . . . Spire stumbled farther down the alley before slumping against the bricks and coughing, trying not to drop Miss Everhart into the puddle of indiscernible liquid at his feet. Thankfully she was not heavy and Spire was not weak, though the scent and air around him made him feel unbalanced.

He managed to walk a few paces farther into the alley, avoiding the thickening, brick-bordered shadows, and found a rear stair landing. Here, he set Rose down, then sat next to her, keeping her limp arm around his neck to steady her. Her eyes were fluttering madly.

A black-clad figure rounded the corner of the alley. Spire drew his pistol from his pocket before recognizing Blakely, who was dressed in his least flamboyant attire, save for the bright turquoise kerchief he held over his mouth and nose. Spire lowered his weapon.

"I'm fine," Spire said, "and I think she's just stunned." He coughed. "What the bloody hell *was* that?"

"It would seem we were intercepted, sir," Blakely replied, pulling down his protective kerchief.

"I am *quite aware* of that, but by whom?" Spire narrowed his eyes. "Blakely. That whole scene, the explosion, seemed an awful lot like something of yours."

"Sir, I'd never! I swear, Mr. Spire, I will see the day when you trust us!" There was fervor in the man's voice.

Spire clenched his jaw. "How are my men?"

Blakely turned to look back into the haze. "Examining the wreckage."

Shifting Rose's weight, Spire rose. "Stay here. If she worsens, shout," Spire commanded, and strode toward the scene of the incident.

As he stepped out from the alley, his nostrils stung from the still-acrid air. He whipped his own handkerchief from his breast pocket—a white, embroidered piece given to him by his father as a birthday present—though it arrived in the wrong month—and placed it over his face. His scalp was still tingling and he hoped the smoke wouldn't cause him to lose any hair.

He walked over to look again at the bodies. The driver appeared asphyxiated. His Metropolitan partners were pacing about the scene.

"Grange," Spire barked. "How was this man killed?"

"The two in black from on high. They were yours, right?" his friend asked. Spire nodded. "Well, one landed nearly upon the driver, but didn't choke him. Dunno what did."

"One person was seen running off, correct?" Spire stated. "But I only saw one figure in the carriage, and that man is dead, too, so who ran away?"

"Your folks in black went after whoever left the carriage," Phyfe replied. "Is the lady—"

"Alive. Keep quiet about this or I will have your heads. Until we know the nature of the explosion and what caused it, if the newspapers leap to paranormal conclusions, I swear, it's your heads that shall roll."

"Understood, sir," Grange replied. "We *are* aware that your operations of late are covert."

Spire held his breath as he looked into the carriage, for the sulfur scent was strongest there. He reached gingerly past the broken glass of the window to open the latch of the door, then leaned into the vehicle to examine the scene more closely.

On the seat opposite the open-mouthed body lay a crushed glass vial surrounded by a spray of fine powder. The sample.

"I don't know what happened," Mrs. Wilson said when pire approached. "I thought we were chasing a man but then seemed as if the figure vanished, leaving only shadow. We went into some kind of disorienting black fog. I got dizzy but Reginald was in the thickest part."

"We'll get him to a doctor. Miss Everhart was injured as well."

Where the hell was Knight with the doctor who was supposed to be on hand in case something went wrong? Why couldn't anything simply go smoothly in this department?

"This seems hardly government work," Mrs. Wilson said. "Did the Americans sabotage the handoff? Perhaps to avenge the séance our operative forced on them?"

Spire shrugged. "Blakely needs to assess the shadow; see if there was something manufactured about it. Like whatever the hell he puts into those damn hoods of his."

Blakely appeared at the entrance to the alley. "Zhavia's here."

Spire returned to Everhart to find Knight and a wizardly looking man who Spire assumed was Zhavia, hovering over her. About bloody time. He didn't have the energy to rail at them. Once further medical personnel were on the scene and Spire felt confident his Metropolitan associates were keeping the carriage well tended, he withdrew. As he so often did while on a case, he looked up at the sky, replaying the incident in his mind, trying to see things in the moment that he hadn't seen before. But the scene remained stubbornly diffuse; his usual keen investigative eye was cloudy.

"Dear God," he murmured. "Not liking my appointed post is one thing, but if it has rendered me useless of talent, God save me from this purgatory and swiftly grant me haven in different pastures. I am ill-suited for this expanse."

* * * * *

Compromised and likely of no use. Not that Sp
was of consequence anyway. Yet the substance ha
thing, so he couldn't dismiss it outright as an u
breath. Unless all was a staged distraction . . .

"Well, bollocks to immortality, eh?" Grange sa
the space beside Spire. "*Mortality* compound, thi

Unless there had been a secondary explosioi
was meant to destroy the sample. That was perhap
likely explanation. He examined the burn mark:
the leather of the carriage seat was pocked aroun(
tered vial.

"Who did this?" Phyfe called from his position l
body of the driver.

Spire and Grange answered at the same time, "Tl
icans."

"Why?" Phyfe demanded.

"Because we had something of their work," Spire
"And I would imagine they didn't want us to have it
ever it even was. Who else would care but those resp
for its provenance?"

Phyfe shrugged. "We can't be the only ones curious
immortality."

"Just the only ones stupid enough to give it any resou
Spire muttered. "Give me everything around this carı
Don't let it move. I want tracks, I want the whole of this
mapped out and every last detail catalogued, please. B
records than they're used to keeping over at headquartei
you don't mind." His colleagues nodded.

He took off after the direction of his aerialists and sc
found the Wilsons, still masked and hooded for anonym
where the alley opened up into a dank brick courtyard tl
hardly caught any of the light of day. Mrs. Wilson was ben
ing over her seemingly unconscious husband. All this fuss fi
what was supposed to be a simple handover of material?

Compromised and likely of no use. Not that Spire believed it was of consequence anyway. Yet the substance had *done* something, so he couldn't dismiss it outright as an utter waste of breath. Unless all was a staged distraction . . .

"Well, bollocks to immortality, eh?" Grange said, invading the space beside Spire. "*Mortality* compound, this."

Unless there had been a secondary explosion, one that was meant to destroy the sample. That was perhaps the more likely explanation. He examined the burn marks, the way the leather of the carriage seat was pocked around the shattered vial.

"Who did this?" Phyfe called from his position beside the body of the driver.

Spire and Grange answered at the same time, "The Americans."

"Why?" Phyfe demanded.

"Because we had something of their work," Spire replied. "And I would imagine they didn't want us to have it, whatever it even was. Who else would care but those responsible for its provenance?"

Phyfe shrugged. "We can't be the only ones curious about immortality."

"Just the only ones stupid enough to give it any resources," Spire muttered. "Give me everything around this carriage. Don't let it move. I want tracks, I want the whole of this area mapped out and every last detail catalogued, please. Better records than they're used to keeping over at headquarters, if you don't mind." His colleagues nodded.

He took off after the direction of his aerialists and soon found the Wilsons, still masked and hooded for anonymity, where the alley opened up into a dank brick courtyard that hardly caught any of the light of day. Mrs. Wilson was bending over her seemingly unconscious husband. All this fuss for what was supposed to be a simple handover of material?

"I don't know what happened," Mrs. Wilson said when Spire approached. "I thought we were chasing a man but then it seemed as if the figure vanished, leaving only shadow. We went into some kind of disorienting black fog. I got dizzy but Reginald was in the thickest part."

"We'll get him to a doctor. Miss Everhart was injured as well."

Where the hell was Knight with the doctor who was supposed to be on hand in case something went wrong? Why couldn't anything simply go smoothly in this department?

"This seems hardly government work," Mrs. Wilson said. "Did the Americans sabotage the handoff? Perhaps to avenge the séance our operative forced on them?"

Spire shrugged. "Blakely needs to assess the shadow; see if there was something manufactured about it. Like whatever the hell he puts into those damn hoods of his."

Blakely appeared at the entrance to the alley. "Zhavia's here."

Spire returned to Everhart to find Knight and a wizardly looking man who Spire assumed was Zhavia, hovering over her. About bloody time. He didn't have the energy to rail at them. Once further medical personnel were on the scene and Spire felt confident his Metropolitan associates were keeping the carriage well tended, he withdrew. As he so often did while on a case, he looked up at the sky, replaying the incident in his mind, trying to see things in the moment that he hadn't seen before. But the scene remained stubbornly diffuse; his usual keen investigative eye was cloudy.

"Dear God," he murmured. "Not liking my appointed post is one thing, but if it has rendered me useless of talent, God save me from this purgatory and swiftly grant me haven in different pastures. I am ill-suited for this expanse."

* * * * *

The knowledge that Rose was in pain was surpassed by the roiling potency of the dream world in which she found herself; a shockingly rich, spectacularly horrific mindscape.

She stood in a long, vaulted stone corridor with pillars marching into shadow; a diffuse gray light filtered in through Gothic pointed arches. Between each arch she saw a cloaked figure, opaque and black. Shapes and shadows, the height of a person, with what seemed a head and shoulders, they flickered strangely if she looked too hard at them, as if they were not solid but human-shaped voids cut into the fabric of this reality, cold nothingness. . . .

At the end of the hall appeared a lithe, elegant woman in a white, shimmering, gossamer ball gown. Dark blond hair trailed in waves past her broad but slender shoulders; her face was pale, her features obscured by the golden light that seemed to surround her. She was a welcome brightness in this place of dimness.

The woman walked slowly, painstakingly slowly, carrying a large golden chalice in each hand. Rose heard a soft breeze echo through the seemingly limitless corridor . . . perhaps it wasn't a breeze at all but whispers that vibrated from the black, disconcerting semblances of human form?

The warm light stretched back along the woman's path; Rose noticed that in the woman's wake trailed thin, translucent images of herself in endless iteration, as if the woman shed a ghostly echo of herself every few steps. But each image was slightly different—different styles of dress and hair, different, dimly glimpsed faces. All felt familiar to Rose, as did the whole place in which she found herself, though she could not say how or why.

Focusing on the bronze-haired creature who led the procession, Rose realized that the woman was blindfolded. As the woman drew closer, Rose tried to take a step back but found she could not.

Thankfully the cup-bearer stopped a few paces away. Rose studied the woman, trying to engrave the image in her memories. The figure—and each of her iterations—bore a sword at her waist. Arms spread wider than her hips, she cradled the bowl of each chalice in one palm; the stems descended below her hands and ended in carved bases.

The cups were etched in beautiful, curling script and bordered in intricate filigree. One word upon each.

Mortality.

Immortality.

The woman's arms began to shift slightly, almost imperceptibly, up and down. When one arm raised, the other lowered. Rose put the imagery together: Blind justice with her sword; the chalices in each hand represented the scales.

One cup began to drift higher with each movement, and to curve toward the woman's face.

Mortality.

The breeze, no, it was clearly murmuring voices, grew louder.

Rose wanted to speak but though she could feel the movement of her mouth, no sound emerged.

The cup neared the woman's lips, then fell away, then returned, closer than before. A sad, terrible inevitability gripped Rose and she felt tears stream down her face.

Something Knight had said about her long-lost sister suddenly rattled through her mind: "She may be the death of you."

The cup of mortality was at the fair woman's lips.

Her arms flailed out, sending the chalices flying, spilling their black, liquid contents. When the goblets hit the ground, they shattered as if made of glass and fine golden dust exploded into the air. The sword fell from the woman's side, landing with a terrible, echoing clatter.

Justice—if it was she—burst into flame.

The women in her wake did as well, a procession of immolation, instantly becoming an inferno as if made of dead, dry wood.

They screamed, their many voices united in agony.

Rose wailed as the luminous figures were transformed to ashes in seconds, kept screaming—hearing herself, now—as the cinders swirled in the air like gray snow.

She writhed, trying desperately to shift her feet, but stood as if rooted. She closed her eyes against the filthy air, choking on tears and ash.

When she opened them again, the black, empty forms swarmed upon her and the world was bathed in an unearthly, terrifying, deafening darkness.

Rose came to consciousness with a start in a blindingly white room furnished only with her bed, one wooden chair, and a small metal table bearing medicinal jars and a water basin.

"Where am I?" she asked as she sat bolt upright; the small room swam around her sickeningly and she collapsed back onto the bed. The surface of her skull seemed bathed in burning pain.

A white-capped nurse, dressed in a starched white apron over a plain gray dress, entered through the open door. She must have heard Rose from outside the room.

"You're at Saint George's, ma'am, on a private floor," the nurse said. Rose was shocked. She was at one of the finer London hospitals, mere paces away from Lord Black's home at the corner of Hyde Park.

Those treated here were often aristocracy or members of the government: MPs and lords for the most part. Suspecting the prime minister and Lord Black had ensured her place, she was grateful they were so good to her.

The young nurse checking her scalp bandage was likely a student of Florence Nightingale's legacy. Miss Nightingale was Rose's great hero, though she deemed herself too shy for the great social reforms the groundbreaking woman had created. Rose hoped she would someday grow brave enough to open the doors of business and politics for female clerks, operatives, investigators, and advisers, as Miss Nightingale had done for women in medicine.

She became aware of a tingling on her head as the nurse pressed a fresh bandage to a sore spot on her scalp. She reached careful fingers to the side of her head, then drew them away holding a clump of hair. Her small noise of alarm roused a calm smile from the nurse.

"Yes, my dear, you suffered a burn on part of your head. Smelled a bit like sulfur. I am sure it will all grow back in time," she said reassuringly, though Rose was not convinced. Lovely. Losing her hair before it had even gone gray. She prayed to God that if he let her keep her hair, she wouldn't curse him any longer for the few gray hairs she'd found near her temple.

"Once we're sure you're rested and remain without infection you can go," the nurse said. "We found nothing else wrong with you, though I'm sure you've got quite the headache."

Headache indeed, Rose thought, but was relieved nothing else was wrong. Being fussed over made her nervous. As the nurse continued to tend to her, Rose distracted herself by trying to remember the last things she had seen and done before darkness took her under like a wave.

Just as she had reached for the case, she felt herself fly through the air. Her vision had become blurred and full of stars. A gargoyle-like face loomed over her, staring at her so intently that it seemed, in that dreadful moment, that it would suck the very life out of her. Shadows surrounded it, black silhouettes shaped like people—like the figures from her dream, dark and menacing. She remembered hearing murmurs: "Destroy their work. Lest it be the death of you . . ."

What had she seen—a man or a monster? Or had it merely

been the effect of her head colliding with the cobblestones? As much as her rational mind was sure it was fancy, her gut instinct, which was rarely wrong, told her otherwise.

A figure at the door made her stomach drop.

Harold Spire stood at the threshold, hat in hand, looking tired. He bowed his head to the nurse. "I'm . . . with the police," he said quietly. The nurse looked to Rose, who nodded, and the young woman exited with a small curtsey to Spire.

"Hello, Mr. Spire." She forced herself into a sitting position, glad they'd left her in her clothes—or perhaps had put them back on after examination—so that she was still presentable, though soot-stained as she was. "They said as soon as I'm no longer dizzy, I can go home. Thank goodness. I hate hospitals. Not that I've ever been in one as a patient until now. What did I miss?" she asked.

Spire entered the room and explained what he'd seen.

"Do we think the Americans are responsible?" Rose asked.

"I don't know what to think," he replied with a sigh. "We couldn't apprehend anyone. The dead driver and his passenger remain unidentified and there's no eyewitness accounts due to the smokescreen that seemed to cover the whole area.

"It must be the Americans, but I don't know why they bothered. To them, Eterna was a failure, so why would anything from the site be relevant?"

Rose narrowed her eyes, pensive. "Perhaps part of the principle of the compound is residue. What is left behind. That in and of itself, the very process, has life."

Spire shrugged. "That'll be for the new scientists to determine."

"Would you mind escorting me home to Whitehall, please?" Rose asked.

"Indeed. I'll have a carriage brought round," Spire assured her. "Zhavia and Knight wanted me to tell you they were sorry they were not at your side the moment you fell. As it happened, Knight doubled over herself in the next street over, at their post. Zhavia said Knight experienced your strike simultaneously, in parallel with you. For whatever that is worth."

"It's worth the fact that the woman is, truly, a gifted asset, Mr. Spire," Rose replied softly. Spire shrugged and exited.

After he left, Rose shifted forward slowly, less dizzy than when she first woke but still a bit queasy. The nurse appeared, checked her head, fussed over her a bit, then looked her straight in the eye. "I'm sure you'd like to go off with your gentleman friend, but are you—"

"Oh, we're not, like that," Rose stammered, blushing. "I mean, he is my employer."

"Are you up to it?" the nurse continued, either not interested or not believing her. "You'll have to be able to walk to the door without assistance before I let you go."

Rose took a deep breath, squared her shoulders, placed her stocking feet upon the floor, stood up, and walked to the door. She did not tell the nurse that she felt lingering pain in her head and that her vision tracked oddly, that it was an effort to stay upright and on a straight path to the door. She was happy to return to the bed and sit long enough to put on her shoes, but she was ready to leave.

Spire was waiting in the receiving hall beyond. He offered his arm and she deigned to take it. They descended to the street level at a careful, steady pace.

"You have not shared your perspective of the incident," Spire said once he'd helped her into the waiting cab.

It took only a few moments to relate the events—omitting her dream, of course.

"Seems we all saw shadows," Spire mused once she finished, staring out the window of the carriage with a furrowed brow.

The rest of the short ride passed in silence. At her home, Rose climbed out of the carriage on her own before Spire had the chance to disembark. "Until tomorrow, Mr. Spire." She bowed her head.

"Take as much time as you need to recover, Miss Everhart."

"I am as eager to unravel this madness as you are," she replied. "I beg you not to let this incident make you question whether or not you'll have a woman on your force. I'll see you in the morning, Mr. Spire, and thank you for escorting me."

"I've many things to question; I'd rather your position not be one of them. And you are welcome, Miss Everhart," he replied.

She closed the carriage door with a capable smile, ignoring all her aches and pains.

Letting herself into her home and ascending the stairs slowly, wincing from her bruises, Rose allowed herself to smile. She was alive, and had proof that someone would notice and care if she were gone. The basic, human desire for community was served. Still, that feeling of the missing link, which she had confessed to Miss Knight, remained, and something about her nightmare made that hole inside her ache.

At the top window, her cousin was at her post. The day's count was rattled off.

"Sixteen gentlemen. Twelve working class. One middle. Three upper, walking to hail hansoms. Fourteen ladies. Four were with the accounted for working-class men, one was alone; whore, the rest were doubled up with other women."

"Thank you, Minnie dear."

"And one very pretty lady in a very fine dress with a feathered hat. Stood staring up. For a long time."

"Miss Knight," Rose murmured.

Whether colleagues cared if she was alive or dead—until now, she wouldn't have placed much importance on it. Work, and working, mattered. But suddenly those relational qualities were vital, in fact; who cared made all the difference.

She took a deal of time getting out of her clothes and into her nightdress. Her corset hadn't been laced tight but removing it reminded her of her bruises. Layer by layer, hook by hook, it was only now that she noticed several of the fixtures were torn. Likely from when she fell. Somehow this upset her more than the scrapes on her skin.

Moving to the window and opening it, easing onto her window seat, Rose watched the bustle of London below. Her nerves were raw and her senses strained; she felt every creak of the house, every vibration of the floorboards beneath her satin-slippered feet.

The moon was bright above the steepled tops of London, countless tendrils of smoke wafted up from innumerable hearths as clouds raced over the moon's silver face. The sky, full of movement and wondrous excitement, was mesmerizing. Rose realized with a start that she was no longer sitting, but had gotten to her feet.

Judging by the moon's progress, she'd been standing at the window in her nightshift for a full hour. Bright swaths of moonlight lit her white room so brightly it glowed. A full moon. A wind-whipped sky. The stuff of Rose's guilty pleasures.

She'd never admit to anyone that she read Gothic novels. But the sentiments of such books allowed her to experience the extremities of emotion she knew she would not experience for herself. Feelings swept over her like the wind that pushed the clouds and toyed with the moon, penetrated the layers of her clothing and kissed her skin directly.

Danger had its pleasures—in fiction. If she were living in such a tale, she'd be worried. The incident with the carriage was making her rethink everything. Careful what you indulge in, perhaps. Careful what you romanticize, perhaps. It might come true.

Just as she was wondering if sleep would come like a lion

or lamb, she drifted toward a gentle darkness. Another odd dream. Perhaps her subconscious was waking to new senses. . . .

She was standing at her window—if her window was a tall, wide lancet high in a castle. The moon was bright and silver, her robe luminous, her hands ghastly pale as she stretched them out before her. Wind wrapped around her, kissing her flesh with cool moisture.

Unsure what she was reaching for, she knew it was something delicious, inviting, and dangerous; as delicious and inviting things so often were.

Something sweet and seductive called to her from the darkness, in a voice she recognized but could not understand . . . a male voice with an undercurrent, as if a symphony accompanied his whisper.

There was a soft pressure upon her wrist, as if someone gripped her there, but she saw nothing. As the pressure gently increased, the whisper ceased, replaced by something lower, a purr or a growl.

When morning came, Rose's usual sharp awakening at first light was a sluggish rouse. Turning onto her side was painful; she felt heavy and ponderous. Her awareness of her bruises came to life as a punch to her ribs. Secondarily, she noticed a fresh ache in her wrist.

Bringing her arm close to her face, she saw two small puncture marks upon the inner side of her wrist. The skin was not inflamed, nor were the wounds bleeding, yet she was sure those twin holes had not been there before. Perhaps she'd injured herself somehow. . . .

Rose looked at the window frame and from her limited vantage point saw no immediate protrusions or traces of blood. However, the window, which she was sure she had shut and locked the night before, was slightly ajar.

The moment she sat up, the room spun, sending her back

down again. Her body felt entirely made of lead. She looked at the puncture wounds. She thought about the penny dreadfuls playing in Covent Garden. The *vampir* was all the rage.

"No," she said thickly. Even her tongue was not cooperating. "No, no, no, no . . ."

She tried to get out of bed. She couldn't.

To her distress, Rose realized she was unable to go to work. Her cousin wasn't able to carry a message. How was she to let anyone know she was ill? With one great heaving motion she threw her legs off the side of her bed. Her feet made a hard thump when they hit the floor and she was terrified by how little she registered the impact, by how numb her limbs felt.

An attempt to stand ended with her landing painfully on the floor. Her lip split. She tasted copper, but dimly, as if all her senses were dulled.

If she still had blood to spare, then she hadn't been bitten by a vampire. Indeed, they didn't even exist. The wounds were insect bites, surely. From a spider.

What would Spire think if she mentioned the possibility of a vampire? While she wasn't the skeptic he was, vampires would strain anyone's credulity.

It took everything in her power to drag herself inch by inch to the threshold of her bedroom. From there, she tried to call out, but her cousin's name emerged from her mouth as a numb, inelegant wail.

Her head swam miserably. The tip of her cousin's head came into view as Rose slowly, agonizingly, drew closer to the stairs: unkempt mousy brown waves beneath an askew lace cap. As the world once again grew dark around her, Rose sincerely hoped fainting into unconsciousness wasn't becoming habitual.

* * * * *

Spire arrived to find Knight back in the Millbank offices perusing some of Everhart's files on the paranormal. Blakely was nearby, sniffing, poking at, and dividing some sort of powder on the small, smooth metal table that he had claimed as his space, working to determine some of the chemistry of the event. The short, thin man was dressed in a surprisingly simple suit considering his usually flamboyant tastes, and Knight had followed his lead in wearing something simpler. It was as if the events had sobered all of them, right down to their fashion.

"Where's Rose?" Spire barked. "She said she'd be in this morning."

"She suffered quite the fall, Mr. Spire," Blakely replied. "I'd not expect—"

"I wanted her to stay in and rest," Spire exclaimed angrily. "She's the one who wished to go on as if nothing happened."

Mrs. Wilson entered in a simple black dress with a brimmed hat with a tulle veil atop the head scarf that tucked her hair from sight. "Reginald is recovering," she assured, seeing that everyone had turned to her expectantly. She added, to Spire, "What's our plan?"

"I'd like to investigate the scene around the incident," Spire stated. "To see if there were details I missed or if anything is still lingering there. Blakely?" Blakely looked up from examining the powder. "You'll attend with me. I'd like to think, because of your theatrical perspective and experience with crowds, you'll see things that others do not. Don't prove me wrong."

Blakely nodded, scooping the powder into a container before rising and standing stiffly as if at attention.

"I know the street very well," Mrs. Wilson added. "I might notice subtle differences we did not see in the thick of the smoke and trauma."

"Let's get to it then, we three. Knight?"

"Miss Everhart," she replied. At Spire's nod, she swept out the door to check on her colleague.

* * * * *

The carriage itself had been taken into government holdings and placed in a stable behind the Millbank offices, where it would be examined. Longacre should have been going about its business quite normally.

That was most definitely not the case.

The air was freezing cold though it was high summer.

A crowd had gathered around the intersection where the altercation had taken place.

Spire, Blakely, and Mrs. Wilson paused on the fringes of the crowd. Blakely and Mrs. Wilson began to make their way around the group while Spire surveyed those who stood before him, who were staring as if entranced by the very air.

The watchers seemed to represent the whole walk of London life, as if anyone passing had stopped in their tracks to stare, a bit slack-jawed. People seemed to be murmuring something about spirits and hauntings.

Irritated at the forced pause in his investigation, Spire began to make his way toward Blakely and Mrs. Wilson, who had reached the other side of the street. There was a flurry of movement as six persons on horseback charged into the center of the seemingly mesmerized pedestrians. People shouted, horses whinnied, and chaos erupted on all sides.

The six dismounted. Spire studied them—three men and three women, apparently adults but there was something odd about them, a youthful fire and at the same time something older, ancient even.

A tall man, all in black, held court in the middle of the group, staying each horse by merely holding up his hand in front of each animal. Black cloak billowing about him, black hair buffeted by a wind he himself seemed to be creating, he gestured for his fellows to gather around. Clearly, the leader.

The six formed a circle in the center of the lane. The wind rose, tugging at clothes, hats, and hair. Spire swore there was some sort of odd light hanging about the imperious looking fellow who had first attracted his attention. He considered the other five: one man wore a priest's collar, one blond woman seemed a bit more ragged, perhaps working class. Another woman was severely and plainly dressed, like a school matron. All six seemed to be focusing on something above the street, though Spire saw nothing in the air.

He wondered suddenly if this wasn't perhaps that *other* department. He heard soft chanting from the group. Yes. This was Lord Black's mysterious, ghostly department!

A lean, blond, sharp-featured man in ostentatious clothing dropped his gaze from the heavens to the gathered crowd. He began waving his hands at them, gesturing them away.

"Off, off, off you go," he said in a casual, foppish tone. Those watching began to look away and wander off, still looking dazed. The blond gentleman, who looked like a misplaced royal, turned his back to his fellows, who seemed to be addressing the air itself. Spire shuddered briefly at a cold gust—the whole of the lane was frightfully chilled. When he looked again at the circle of five, he saw an unmistakable ring of pale blue light around them. The stormy, dark-haired leader gestured with both hands, as if conducting an invisible orchestra.

All around Spire, people continued to turn and walk away—even Mrs. Wilson and Blakely.

"Excuse me, you are not dismissed, get back there," Spire barked at them. They did not respond, simply disappeared around the corner along with many others.

"Excuse me, sir," the blond man called. It took a moment for Spire to realize the man was addressing him.

"What the bloody hell is going on here?" Spire barked as he approached. "This is the site of an investigation—"

"Indeed, sir, and you're not the only ones investigating. What you are going to do now is turn around and walk away," the man said calmly, giving Spire a wide, sharp-toothed smile.

Spire set his jaw and stepped forward defiantly, closing the distance to something less than polite and staring directly into the man's pale blue eyes. The other fellow kept waving his hands about as if he were casting off insects. The crowd of watchers had thinned to next to nothing. Spire growled his response, "I work for Her Majesty's government."

"So do we," the man replied, his smile transforming into a goofy grin as if he were most delighted with himself. "*If* by 'Her Majesty' you mean an ancient force from long, long ago that far outranks Queen Victoria, long live her and all. But the restless dead are indeed *our* jurisdiction, sir, so leave us to it, will you? You've no choice. And you won't remember us even if you try. . . ."

"You are that department!" Spire cried. "The ones Lord Black was banging on about!"

The man's bright eyes narrowed. "Someone . . . knows about us?"

"Yes, well, no," Spire muttered. "My superior has said that when it comes to ghosts, there is a rumored department that no one really knows about."

"Ah. Yes. Well, that would be us," the man said, and made an exaggerated bow.

"Don't chat them up, Withersby," shouted the leader in a reverberant baritone, his dark eyes blazing. "Wipe them and get them out of our way!" The man seemed to strike the air and if Spire wasn't mistaken, the air shimmered. The temperature seemed to be rising to more comfortable levels.

"Yes, your royal eeriness," called the blond, evidently Withersby. He winked at a pretty, dark-haired woman in the circle; she was shaking her head at him and chuckling. "This is why no one really knows about us. Now be a good dog and run along. . . ."

He waved a languid, long-fingered hand very close to Spire's face.

Harold Spire wandered amiably away from Longacre. For the first time in a long while his face was not contorted by a furrowed brow or a stiffened scowl. A pleasantness had come over his mind. He almost smiled at the gentle warmth of the day. His thoughts wandered. It was a wonderful day in this wonderful city. . . .

He'd visited the scene of the incident and had nothing to report. Nothing at all odd had happened. He'd dismissed Blakely and Mrs. Wilson . . . hadn't he?

Wasn't there something he should tell Lord Black? Something that had made Spire think of him?

No.

Everhart. Spire should go and check on her. That's what he'd been meaning to do. It was only courtesy, after all, to stop in and see her.

* * * * *

The first sensory tether Rose had, climbing out from the dark pit, was her hearing. Someone in the room was murmuring in Russian.

Oh, she thought as she swam toward awareness, struggling to gain purchase. Zhavia. He'd come after all. She was in bed again. And she had help.

How had Zhavia known to come? Rose thought back to the last thing she remembered: crying out for her cousin. The acuity of her memory was somewhat of a curse, for even if her body was compromised and uncooperative, her mind was too focused for its own good. She often wished she could be a mind alone, floating out in the world, and not be troubled with a silly body and all its trappings. Especially a female one with all the limitations decreed upon it.

But Minnie couldn't have known to fetch Zhavia in particular. Miss Knight must have sensed something and sent him.

Her eyelids refused to lift and Rose again cursed her body for not being cooperative. But she realized what she *didn't* want to see when she opened them: Spire staring down at her harshly.

Her voice was raspy but worked. She croaked her question: "Who's there . . . ?"

"Vasily Zhavia, Miss Everhart," came the thickly accented reply. "Can you open your eyes?" He followed this request with a long, softly murmured string of words in Russian. Rose assumed that he was declaiming the muscles needed to raise an eyelid. Zhavia's uncanny habit, which had garnered him his nickname of "Bones," remained off-putting; Rose rolled her eyes in their sockets, but the lids remained as heavy as lead.

The doctor repeated his Russian phrases and somehow, Rose felt her muscles begin to respond to her wishes. Maybe his mutterings weren't merely a list of bones and muscles but some kind of spell, willing her to move.

Slowly, like drawing back a thick curtain, Rose opened her eyes. Zhavia bent over her. His long black beard, his robelike coat, and his hawklike black eyes marked him as something magical. Perhaps her supposition that he cast some sort of spell wasn't entirely far off. Of course, Omega couldn't have a normal doctor. Only a wizard would do.

"I need . . . office." Rose struggled to speak more quickly. "To go. To office. Spire."

"Spire? You want to see Mr. Spire?"

"No!" she choked. "Don't want . . . him to see."

"Ah, yes, you don't want him to see you like this lest he think you a weak and inconsequential woman, not suited to the work. Of course. Well, he won't see you then. But you cannot go anywhere. Not like this." Grateful she was understood, she smiled at him. He leaned close. "Can you tell me what happened?"

"Ever since . . . incident. I've been . . . off. Seeing things, shadows." She shuddered uncontrollably and the act hurt.

"What happened before you called for help?"

"Bad dreams. Hurt wrist. Couldn't move."

Zhavia's attention focused sharply. He picked up her arm and hand and turned them gently revealing the delicate tracery of blood vessels on her inner wrist. Her hand sagged limply in his. The puncture marks remained, though drastically faded.

The doctor's prominent brow furrowed. His dark eyes widened, then narrowed. Rose was in no way reassured by the expression on his face.

"That's odd," he murmured. "Changes my initial assessment."

"Which was?"

"Vampirism."

Bloody hell.

"No." Rose tried to shake her head. "Don't exist."

Zhavia wrinkled his nose. "Bah! Of course they do. Not in the sense you may think. Not in nightmares or stories to scare children. But creatures that drain people? Oh, certainly.

"At first, I thought, that perhaps you had a particularly"— Zhavia struggled for the right word—"fond mentalist. Draining you too much. Easily remedied.

"But this is different. Especially with the marks. And your weakness. Abnormal."

The idea that anything related to this could be normal was disturbing enough. Before she could ask what to do next, he set her arm back onto the bed.

"Must think."

He sat thinking for a very long time. So long that Rose nearly drifted off to sleep, her anxiety drowned by her body's overwhelming apathy.

Suddenly he shot to his feet, shouting; "Demons!"

"What?" Rose started.

"Mmm . . . But the point of entry. Of contact. No . . . perhaps . . . Mmm . . ."

Zhavia furrowed his brow and sat down again. This time

his silence continued until Rose's eyes closed. If there were further exclamations, they did not rouse her.

When she opened her eyes again, she knew time had passed; the light had tracked farther down her wall. And someone different was nearby. Spire. Her cheeks went red.

"Hello, sir, this is not how I wish to be seen." She managed to shift into a sitting position against the pillows.

"I wouldn't wish to be either," he replied. "But I wanted to see how you're doing."

Rose debated a moment about what to say. She surreptitiously glanced at her wrist and saw that it was not bandaged. In fact, it looked healed entirely, but the color of her skin was slightly off where the marks had been. She realized that something had been painted over the wounds. A cosmetic. Like stage paint. Zhavia was trying to mitigate how it might appear. Bless that strange wizard.

"I wish I could offer you a suitable explanation, sir," she replied at long last.

"What is Zhavia's prognosis? I couldn't get a thing out of him." Rose quirked an eyebrow in question and was rewarded with a tiny smile from Spire. "He was in the parlor with your cousin when I arrived. He was speaking to her in Russian and she was responding in numbers."

Rose nearly laughed at that, with what breath she could muster. Communication. What a strangely compelling human need.

What had Zhavia said before she slipped into darkness? Demons. It would seem demons were on the table, but were possibly ruled out due to some issue with "point of entry," whatever that meant. Spire might send Zhavia packing on the spot if Rose said any such thing so she chose her words carefully.

"He isn't sure," Rose replied. "Did he say anything to you?"

"Just that something sought you out. Something that wanted you to know it was there."

And that's when Rose realized, with the sort of sinking knowledge that brings with it an impossible dread, that the wound on her wrist wasn't an odd dream, an insect bite, or any other far more welcoming and plausible explanation.

It was a warning.

"Mr. Spire," Rose murmured. "I'd like to come to the office with you."

"I'm not sure you're in any condition to do so. Zhavia said you shouldn't be out of bed. Mr. Wilson seems to have had less of an . . . exposure to whatever knocked him cold, he is recovered. But it would appear you're going to have to take greater care."

Rose looked away, clenching her fists. "I hate this." Her cheeks grew warm as she tried to impress upon him the importance of her words. "You must understand, Mr. Spire. Work gives my life meaning. Work is, truly, what I live for."

Spire nodded but no feelings showed upon his face. "I respect that, Miss Everhart. I feel exactly the same way." He paused for a moment. "We received full details on the interrogation of the Americans."

"I insist on being present for the reading, Mr. Spire," Rose insisted.

"Oh, I daresay you'll be the only one able to decipher them. I'll come with a carriage in the morning. In the meantime, rest well."

"I will," she said. "Thank you, Mr. Spire."

She prayed she would not be worse off in the morning from whatever plagued her.

CHAPTER

SIXTEEN

So as not to be caught in a lie after her Columbia venture, Clara sought out Lavinia, who was very glad to see her. Sensing that Lavinia needed the company, as her infamous fiancé was in New Jersey giving a performance of his flamboyantly Gothic show, Clara invited her friend over for dinner. Though she was not much in a mood to entertain anyone, her heart heavy and conflicted, the distraction of a female friend might do her a bit of good.

When they exited the trolley car a few blocks from Pearl Street, the gas lamps were beginning to be lit, The electrical lights, however, were misbehaving.

Sparks flew everywhere. If there was anything electrical, be it wiring or lighting, residential or commercial, anything along Pearl Street, including Edison's dynamos, was sparking like some sort of firecracker.

"Now what does one suppose this is all about?" Lavinia breathed.

"Haven't the slightest," Clara whispered in turn.

People were running along the street; flapping frock coats, lifted petticoats, hats askew. A fire had started in a building not far from the Eterna office. Part of Clara wouldn't mind seeing the Eterna office burn, but even as she thought that, a rush of nostalgia for the building proved once again that her mind and heart often existed at odds.

Thankfully the raucous clang of a fireman's bell meant that a brigade had been alerted. There was a great deal of money in lower Manhattan and capital had to be preserved. If they were farther uptown, she'd be far less confident of the survival of the block. Her and Bishop's town house, farther down and across the street, was in no danger.

In the midst of the chaos Clara saw a young man in a brown suit, standing still, arms out as if embracing something invisible. His gaze was fixed on Clara. Unsettled, she was reminded of the intense gaze of the man she'd seen below the guttering streetlight. Surely, this was the same person—he had the same build, the same wild hair. . . .

A carriage with a tank and hose barreled around the corner, startling Clara and Lavinia both. The two women stepped back into the shadows.

After a long moment of silence, Clara replied, "Thank you for being strong, my friend. After everything we've been through in the past week, I hope you know how much I value you. The city is full of strange dangers, and it seems we're bearing witness to so many."

"I'd die without adventure, even if adventure kills me." Lavinia chuckled.

Leaving the crowds on Pearl Street behind, Clara took Lavinia on a shadowed route home, entering the town house through the back door. The housekeeper was nowhere to be seen. Clara knew the woman was prone to worry; perhaps the fireman's bell had drawn her out into the street or sent her into a dead faint.

In either case, Clara prepared a light supper for herself and her guest. They ate in the parlor, watching the bustle on the street. Eventually the senator arrived home, tense, storming in, but the moment he saw the ladies in his gaslit parlor, he breathed a sigh of relief.

"Seeing the chaos out there nearly gave me a heart attack. I'm so glad you're here. It would seem there's a problem with the electric. Dangerous stuff, that."

"Don't worry for us, Mr. Bishop," Lavinia said brightly. "We're survivors."

"That you are," he said with a smile.

"When do we lose you to Washington again, sir?" Lavinia asked.

"At the end of the week," he replied. Clara stared at her tea. Lavinia made a pouting sound. "I've an appointment with the British embassy, as I plan to make them look rather bad to their own kind. I want there to be some kind of resolution after what we suffered." He peered at Clara in the dim light. "Are you all right?"

"Yes," she said as convincingly as she could. "It's only that I . . . don't know where anything stands."

Not Eterna and what it represented, not her heart, not her work, not her losses . . . Nothing . . .

Bishop only nodded and ascended to his study.

She didn't want to lose Rupert to D.C. and yet with him here, could she truly put everything to rest as she desired?

When the hour grew late, when the senator was in his study and Lavinia had been sent home in a cab, Clara retreated to the privacy of her own room. There she opened the metal box and began to go through the papers. Some were other examples of localized, city-based magics; others were indecipherable chemical notations and equations. There was an illustration of a ceremonial dagger being used to cut into organic compounds so that the blessed energy of life could burst forth.

At the bottom of the pile lay a daguerreotype of a young girl, marked Eliza Smith, age nine.

Of course Smith might have wanted to preserve something so innocent and lovely. . . .

A whisper in her mind began to taunt, to second-guess. Or perhaps that vision was speaking to her . . .

"You'll fade. Lost. Unknown. Unnoticed."

What was the desire for immortality but that very fear? And yet, did Clara not know, more than most, how powerfully the spirit lived on?

"No one will ever know," the shadows murmured. "No one will care if you die, so why not take up the mantle and reject death?"

Unflinching, Clara looked deeply into the shadows of temptation and replied: "The world cannot recognize, quantify, or assess the whole of me, nor can it ignore me. I am all the lives I have lived. I shall outlive my own life. I blaze, an eternal torch. The burn you see upon the interior of your eyes when you close them is my aura. It does not fade, even after this body has decomposed. I do not need immortality when my spirit has always lived it."

With a derisive snicker that seemed somehow to lack confidence, the presence retreated.

Clara went to sleep, her moral center undeterred by the dark lure of her own brainchild.

Having renounced the tempter, she woke the next morning more rested than she'd perhaps ever been. She looked in the mirror and felt strong, determined, much more than the lost soul that she'd glimpsed right after Louis's death, a mad Ophelia in the glass.

"While I have the flame of life in this body, for this time," she said to herself and to the heavens, "I shall burn."

The following morning, Franklin sketched on a wide pad of paper at the office. He showed her the picture: a man's head, neck, and shoulders. His coat collar was flipped up and the sketch showed what appeared to be tools stuck into it.

"When I put my hand to the exterior of Goldberg's building," Franklin explained, "I saw an operative pick the lock.

Beneath his collar was an amazing array. In his coat—genius! This is what he looked like." He turned the page to reveal a second image: a handsome, dark-haired man with distinctive features. "I put my hand down on a table in the laboratory room and saw him scraping residue off everything, putting it into glass containers. Must be Brinkman or Bankman."

Clara nodded. "England's operatives, it seems, want to determine the properties of what went wrong. They must think it will help them correct the problems within their own research. We need to be on the offensive, Franklin. Why don't we have spies in London doing the same as Brinkman and his lackeys did to us?"

Lavinia brought up the morning paper. Pearl Street's electrical explosion had made the front page, in a bylined story. Clara and Franklin examined the article, which referred to a "voltage aberration" and cast doubt and blame upon the whole of electricity. Something didn't make sense to Clara: the incident had occurred outside of Edison's edifice, but the level of the surge simply didn't add up; it was like a conductor of dynamo levels was out there on the street, uncontained. Meaning something else had caused it, an external force.

"An external force," Clara breathed. "Like what happened to our team. An external force in that house."

Edison's firm claimed the incident was evidence of sabotage, another twist in the ongoing "war of the currents" between Edison, Tesla, and Westinghouse; a nasty affair involving patents, theft, lies, explosions, electrocutions, one-upmanship, vast sums of money, and more than a bit of genius. And most certainly sabotage.

Clara remembered the face of the man she'd now seen twice: when the lights flickered, and again the previous night, close to the conflagration on Pearl Street.

Sabotage.

Whatever malevolence was let into the Goldberg house, it was sabotage.

The abduction and directives from Louis had derailed her, but she would talk to those who were involved in the similar case from a few years ago. If she recalled correctly, one of the chief culprits involved in the parallel case had been mysteriously acquitted and sent to . . . London.

She plucked the file again to see if memory served her and sure enough: a chemist named Stevens, acquitted and somehow extricated. Last known address was in the East End of London.

"Damn you, England," Clara muttered, staring out her window onto Pearl Street. "If you want to go to hell, don't take us with you. We threw you out long ago and we'll do so again. What you're doing to us won't go unanswered. But you'll not get anywhere with our material. I'll see to that myself."

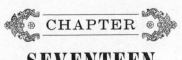

CHAPTER

SEVENTEEN

Seated in her parlor, Rose was writing down the details of her dream about the woman she dubbed "Justice" when Spire was announced by Minnie's unceremonious cataloguing. Rose closed her notebook and set down her pen.

"Ready for the office today, Miss Everhart?" Spire asked at the parlor threshold.

"Absolutely, Mr. Spire, thank you for coming for me," she replied, though her confidence was a lie. She felt drained, like something had latched on to her and was sucking the life out of her.

Harold Spire gave her a brief smile before installing her in the hackney and climbing in after her.

As their journey began, the tree-bordered avenue of Hyde Park was suddenly transformed into a long row of tall evergreens; the light of day was replaced by the dark of deep night. Ahead, a vast house, reminiscent of Austen's Northanger Abbey, stood atop a hill overlooking howling moors. The moon was bright and the terrain was oddly luminous.

Between each tree at the side of the road floated a black, human silhouette. Rose's blood ran cold. When she looked again toward the vast structure, she saw something that hadn't been there a moment earlier.

A figure in flames stood in the portico.

Rose blinked and was again in Hyde Park with the buildings of London on either side. She was glad she hadn't screamed like in her fiery nightmare. But this was not a dream. She was most definitely awake.

So. Dreams were becoming visions. Well, that was a new development. Or, perhaps, whatever had started happening to her during the ruined handoff was also rotting her mind.

She sat silently and gave no sign of what had occurred. Beside her, Spire seemed oblivious; he continued to watch the endless flow of energy and persons that were hallmarks of London.

At the office, Rose greeted her associates with a little curtsey and was welcomed with the usual niceties. Tea was served. Then Rose was handed a stack of documents that had safely arrived from America on a later boat, in accordance with Spire's orders.

Knowing that they were waiting for answers, Rose silently set to work. As she finished decoding each item, she passed it to Spire. Though her focus remained on the sheets yet to be deciphered, she was aware that the translations made their way throughout the group.

In the end, it took an hour of work before the full report was revealed; everything Brinkman had recovered and discerned in his investigations, including having perused what Eterna paperwork he found in the American offices and all the details of the forced séance.

Knight was the first to offer insight after a long, uncomfortable moment. "These are pieces of a dynamic, complicated puzzle. And it seems clear to me that out of everyone, it's Dupris's puzzle to solve."

"The spy or the scientist?" Mr. Wilson asked.

"Theorist," Spire said. "Don't call these people scientists—"

"Louis Dupris was the visionary and the linchpin, in my opinion," Rose offered. "He had a relationship with the founding inspiration, Miss Templeton. Their affair was revealed during the séance, poor thing."

"But why his and Smith's notion that American air and dirt would aid immortality, you've got me," Spire stated.

"Spire," Knight said in a teacher's tone that Rose could see plainly irritated Spire. "Localized magic is what it is. And very clever, too. We could not use that same compound here. It would be meaningless. There are tricks and there is magic." She gestured to Blakely, who wiggled his fingers at Spire in a little wave, making a coin disappear. "Tricks. But what they're wielding? That's *magic.*"

Spire blinked at her a moment.

"It's no secret that you're a skeptic, Mr. Spire," Knight continued. "I do not care whether or not you believe me a gifted medium and psychic. I know what I can do. However, I foresee that your utter rejection of this mission will, if you're not careful, cost at least one of us our lives. So I suggest you at least entertain the possibility that there is more to the world than you can see. When you close your mind and accept the blinders put onto you by empirical evidence alone, you may miss a more fantastical, but still probable solution."

Rose was surprised to catch Spire's fleeting glance, almost as if he was checking for her response before making his own. She tilted her head slightly, to indicate that to her mind, Miss Knight had a point.

"I will consider your thoughts, Miss Knight," Spire said with calm that Rose found impressive.

At that moment, Lord Black burst in, waving a wire in hand, placing the telegraph sheet before her.

"My good citizens and most formidable civil servants," Black began. "It would seem we need to send you, or operatives of your choosing, to the great Empire City."

"New York?" Blakely asked excitedly.

"The very place. Besides all the clues you can gather on the ground about Eterna," Lord Black began, "there is also one Mr. Francis Mosley attracting attention. It would seem Mr. Mosley can manipulate direct current. Electrical current. With his own body. It's said the young man hasn't aged a day in years."

"Ah, so that's of interest, of course," Spire said. Rose was taking notes. "*Longevity.*"

"Well, yes," Black said. "Extension of life falls within our purview. And he's British."

Spire sighed. "Of course he is."

"So he has become a person of extreme interest," Black added.

The whirring of the telegraph machine drew Rose to its side like a siren.

Blakely made a steeple with his fingers like the villain of one of those penny dreadful dramas in Covent Garden. "New York needs a circus!"

Spire scowled. "New York *is* a circus. And who said I was inviting you?"

Rose, decoding the latest message, dropped her pencil. With difficulty, she managed to neither scream nor faint. It took all her strength to walk over and hand Spire the paper. Her hands were shaking as he took the message from her and read it.

"Good God," he gasped. "A shipping manifest examined by a British mail-packet operative has revealed four immaculately preserved bodies. Thought to be our missing scientists. Port of arrival: New York Harbor."

Jaws fell open throughout the room. Lord Black stared at Spire and Rose realized that perhaps for the first time in his life, the nobleman was unsure of the next step.

Spire, however, clearly was not. There was a light in his eyes. He cleared his throat and spoke authoritatively, emboldened.

"If dead British bodies have been shipped to New York City, why, that changes everything," he cried. "Damn those little upstarts. By all means, ciphers, pack your bags. Give the circus that is Manhattan a circus of your own. The Empire further infiltrates the Empire State."

Often epic and prophetic, sometimes memories from previous lives, Clara's dreams tended to be interesting. She jotted some of them down in journals, but kept the books hidden.

This dream in particular needed to be remembered.

She was walking up a long pebble-strewn lane that was bordered by short hedgerows that grew higher until tall evergreens towered on either side of her. She did not feel she was being chased but whatever she was walking toward was important, she could feel it in her bones.

Her destination became visible: a vast, dark, Gothic-looking manor, all stone and turrets and sharp angles, the whole expanse luminous under a half-moon over which clouds raced in a strong wind as if fleeing from danger.

A dark-haired woman stood at the end of the lane, wearing a lovely dress the color of the evening sky.

Clara could not make out the woman's features, and though she strode on, she gained no ground. The house and the woman remained impossibly far away.

The waiting woman raised a hand, palm out. A gesture that clearly said, *stop*. Clara paused.

In the next instant, everything, the trees, the manor, the woman, all burst into flame.

Clara woke with a start. The dim light in the room told her it was not yet dawn.

A female figure sat at the end of her bed, dress and hair of an indeterminate color. Backlit by a bit of stray moonlight, her features were entirely shadowed, but Clara knew at once who it was. The visitor.

"Oh, God," Clara said. "What terrible thing is about to happen now?"

"I'm always glad to see you, too, dear," the figure chided. "I presage nothing this time. This time I am merely a messenger. What's missing isn't what you think."

"What's that supposed to mean?"

"You'll know. All your lives, Clara, something's missing in this one and it isn't what you think. *Who* you think. You're missing a critical companion."

Her mind still muddled by the dream, Clara was not sure what to think.

"Are you an angel?" she blurted.

"I am whatever you wish me to be," was the reply.

"That gives me too much power."

"That is a most sensible answer, Miss Templeton!" The woman rose. "It isn't the search that will damn you but what's *done* with it.

"Do not trust voices without specific provenance. Look for your missing piece. Without it, you can't possibly weather the storm ahead."

Message delivered, the visitor walked out the door. Clara heard her soft tread down the hall, heard the front door open, then close with its usual gentle click—so there was something corporeal about the apparition. But no one else in the house stirred or gave any sign of having noticed the trespasser.

Fully awake, Clara wrote down the particulars of both the dream and the visitation. Do not trust voices without specific provenance. The silhouettes, perhaps. Who or what was the missing piece?

She dressed and made her way to the office the moment the sun rose high, noting that there were new locks on the front door. The glass panels of the door and the first-floor windows were now protected by iron bars. Security guards had been posted around the perimeter of the building and the gentle fiction that the structure was a repository for city records had been done away with. Bishop had promised new security measures and he was a man who got things done.

After admitting her, Lavinia handed Clara three new keys—two for the front door and one for the office door, which had also been fitted with a new lock.

Upstairs, Clara sat stewing at her desk, thinking about her dream.

In this life, in any of her lives, the crux of the matter always came down to one thing: the people. Those she cared about and who cared about her made all the difference; life or death. So who was her missing piece and how would she know? Was it life or death for them, too?

The clock chimed half past nine when Franklin burst through the door in a beige frock coat. Lavinia was right behind him in a rather absurd black bombazine mourning dress, bringing their morning coffee and a Western Union Telegraph envelope.

"Fred Bixby dropped this by earlier," she said. "He said it's from Effie."

"Thank you, Lavinia," Franklin said, bowing his head. The redhead returned to her downstairs post.

"I've been to the tailor," Franklin began proudly. "About that lock picking set I saw in my vision, sewn into the coat. I *must* have something of the like. Miss Carter is going to help me. She's the costumer at the Astor Theater, I've seen her work in person and it's exquisite. So is she. I'll tell her what I'm commissioning is for a production."

"Well that's nice," Clara said. "If we're going to do this kind of work we ought to have finery and toys."

They shared a smile as Franklin opened the envelope and

began to read the wire. Clara saw his pensive expression turn into a scowl. He examined the letter closely, holding it to the light, then brushed a substance over the paper. Other words appeared. "From Effie," he announced.

"Whatever evidence our abductors took gleaned from a visit to Tenth Street, was taken to England but there was an altercation over the material. Our English contact isn't sure where the material has gone, even his source seems vague on the subject. So the London group in charge of tracking Eterna may be at a loss, just as we are."

"How does Effie know all that?" Clara asked.

Franklin shook his head. "It would appear she's gone to England herself and has been snooping. She must have tapped Bishop's elusive contact there."

Clara laughed despite herself. "Clever girl. She's precisely where we'll need her." Clara's smile turned into a scowl. "I doubt England's at a loss. I think they may be in deeper than we are, and darker. I believe they sent either an asset or did something to Goldberg's mind to turn him. That house is evidence, as is Stevens's extrication to London.

"All to sabotage our team and our efforts. Let their parroting 'commission' be as lost as we are. Damn this work. Do you think we're doomed to hell for what we've done?" she asked sincerely.

Franklin shrugged. "For asking questions about the boundaries of life and the permanency of death? No, I don't think we're doomed or damned. But if it taxes you, strains you, then walk away, Clara. No one is forcing you to be here.

"I want many things in this life, Miss Templeton. For you to be happy is one of them."

She stared at him. After a moment she smiled. "What a thing to say, Mr. Fordham."

His cheeks colored and he looked at the floor.

"I can't walk away, Franklin," she added. "As for what makes me happy? The trouble with life, liberty, and the pursuit of happiness as goals is that the first two are so clear, the latter, so vague."

Fred Bixby came running in, dressed in a vest, rolled shirtsleeves, and a bowler, looking like he'd seen a ghost.

"Bodies. In boxes. Bodies in boxes," he blurted. "Four of them."

"Pardon?" Franklin rose to his feet.

"Someone sent the English scientists here," he said, trying to calm himself. "The dead ones. My source at the shipyards sent word that bodies from England's own Eterna Commission were sent to these shores."

"Who did this and how does anyone know who they are?" Clara said, shocked.

"Some strange things were in their boxes. Caskets. Whatever. I wired Bishop's contact in London, who confirmed that they had gone missing and were presumed dead," Bixby replied.

"Where are they being taken and can we intercept?" Franklin asked, putting on his coat as he was never one to be seen in shirtsleeves outside of work.

"The city morgue, of course," Bixby replied.

"I'll tell Bishop if he's home," Clara said, sweeping out the door. "Otherwise, we'll have to wire wherever he is. He might have to delay his return to Washington."

* * * * *

The senator was not home. According to the housekeeper Miss Harper, he was out drinking with congressional colleagues. Thus Franklin could go and ruin his night with news of dead bodies.

With all the new information, with the game getting ever more dangerous, she had to do what she could to protect what was left of their team. After painstaking thought, she concluded having any of the Eterna material at all, even Louis's papers, was dangerous and damning. Smith had given her a hint in leaving something burning for her in his office.

The clock struck quarter to midnight. It was time.

Clara had asked Lavinia for help and thankfully her friend hadn't asked why but agreed straightaway.

Lavinia's task was to engage a police officer in conversation. This particular police officer patrolled near Trinity Church and Lavinia was to keep him occupied and facing down Wall Street. Josiah, their trusty errand boy, had been paid handsomely to distract the officer who patrolled the back lot. After fifteen minutes they could resume their regular activities. That was all Clara had told them.

Clara donned her favorite sporting skirt, seeing no scandal in the garment's separate legs, which she carefully tucked into the tops of a tall pair of boots.

She waited until Miss Harper had made her last rounds downstairs, then cast a black cloak over her head and, clutching a black bundle in her arms, darted out into the street.

Always a brisk walker, she made quick headway over to Broadway and the mouth of the church, a small Gothic building whose edifice had been rebuilt countless times since its founding. In a shadowed patch between gas lamps, Clara launched herself over the iron gate, grateful for her trouser-like apparel. The last thing she needed was to have her skirts caught up on a graveyard fence.

A small pack slung beneath her dark cloak, she scurried among the old stones, having already decided on a fitting patch of earth between Alexander Hamilton's grave and that of the Mulligan brothers, members of General Washington's infamous Culper spy ring.

So much of her work and life was focused so near to addresses central to the first spymaster's operations and those of his associates. She couldn't have ever predicted there'd again be such espionage between her city and England, but the reality was upon them all and they needed to be better equipped for the fights to come.

Hamilton's pointed obelisk of a grave was easy to spot in the dim evening light, which was augmented by gaslight and the electrical lighting that was cropping up downtown. She kept low, where the shadows still clung, as she slipped past the tomb's pale, nearly white stone.

Dropping to her knees, Clara removed her pack and reached a gloved hand inside for the trowel. Working quickly, she pried up divots of earth, careful to keep the sod intact on top, then dug, pausing at any sound that might indicate she'd have to run, glancing about to make note of a good hiding place among the eighteenth-century stones and slabs.

She felt like she was digging up layers of hopes and dreams, of innocence and altruism, of pasts and mitigated futures. She wanted to bury sentimentalism in exchange for a more stoic, steeled self. Her heart, that unwieldy instrument, pounded hard. There was no going back from this precipice.

"*This* is why me," she murmured, hoping the visitor could hear her. She paused to inspect her work—the hole she'd created was about a foot deep and as wide as the span of her hips. It looked large enough. "I am forcing a turn in the road, no longer sitting on the sidelines. Some ideas should have never left the ground. So into the ground I return it."

She upended the bag, tumbling all the papers she had of the late Eterna work into the pit. The sheets glowed white in the dim light as they shifted and fell, order and organization disappearing.

Clara had raided her own office safe before going home that evening. Thus, she would be able to completely rid herself of anything related to Eterna, including her last reminder of Louis Dupris, whose soaring ideas should have seized the world by the throat and left it as breathless as he'd been able to make her. Clara plucked the cravat from where it had lain warm against her bosom and set the silk in her lap. She thought about removing the protective amulet but couldn't bring herself to part with it.

Rummaging in an interior pocket of her cloak, her shaking fingers managed to find the small rattling box of matches she'd stowed there. Striking a match on the ornately decorated box, a flame flared to life. As the fire blossomed, her eye caught a phrase on the topmost sheet.

The Power of Protection.

She grimaced. What good had magic done the team, after all their diligent work?

A night wind rustled the few trees above her, at least, a breeze was what it seemed at first, but the fabric of her cloak did not buffet in the air. As she paused, listening, the sound seemed more like the murmuring of voices. The match went out.

Clara muttered a curse and lit another. It, too, was blown out. Then another, and another. Four matches, all extinguished, as if by a precisely aimed breath. The air around her had grown noticeably chill.

Before she could wonder if she was not alone among the graves, sparks soared into the sky in a wide and impressive arc above Pearl Street. Whatever electric lights had been on in that block, street lamps or indoor lighting alike, went dark.

"Charge," Clara said thoughtfully, realizing that she could no longer ignore or forget this word. There were shouts and running feet and suddenly she did not feel so confident about her business in the graveyard. She also could feel a flickering at the corner of her eye, and a bitter taste in her mouth.

She needed to work quickly. As her vision shifted slightly at the edges, she knew an episode was on its way. So that's why she was so cold. Damned ghosts. And damn the effect they had. They must be trying, all of them, to get at her. . . .

She did not strike another match. Instead, she buried the bag, the papers, and Louis's saffron cravat, which she carefully placed on top of the rest. At first she shoveled dirt into the hole with her hands, wanting to cry and retch, wishing she could give him more ceremony. But she was already testing her luck. She had a minute at best.

Clumsily with the trowel, her limbs already growing numb, she scattered the soil, then tried to set the grassy patches back in place as if assembling a puzzle. Her gloves were thin enough that touch guided her in trying to make the ground even; without the electric lights from down the block it was almost too dim to see and she didn't dare light a lantern.

Her body failed her. She fell, began seizing, and everything went dark.

* * * * *

Louis Dupris floated above the graves, breathing heavily, for the moment relieved. She couldn't hear him crying. "No, Clara, no! Our magic is a ward! You'll need it in the days ahead, the house was compromised but the ward is necessary!" He had begged her, willing her to understand the full scope of what he was only beginning to comprehend, to no avail.

But he'd managed to muster enough power to blow out each of those matches.

The compound was indeed a type of cure, but not in the ways they thought. There was more than one force trying to control this game. Louis, from his precarious spirit-world vantage point, could see great forces shifting like volcanic land masses at cross purposes.

Somehow he had to let Clara know that while he didn't want anyone else to know about his work, it couldn't be destroyed. She was the *only* person in the whole living world he could trust, the only one he dared tell his realizations. And he couldn't communicate with her.

Andre had fled. Louis was on his own. But not alone.

It would seem the rest of New York's spirit realm felt threatened, too.

In Trinity Church Yard, at the mouth of Wall Street, if one were inclined to see spirits, one would have seen a massive horde of them, from the Colonial eras and the early years of the city's century. Floating, nearly substanceless, like feathers in the breeze, they were drawn, more than a hundred, to that small plot at the base of Manhattan Island. They hovered, transparent, staring down at a slightly uneven patch of earth, and at a woman scrabbling over a grave, a woman at the center of a great storm.

"Get back," he warned them. "Don't overwhelm her. Leave her be, it isn't good for you all to be here." They floated in a swarm, not paying any attention to him.

They were staring at Clara, begging for her intercession, begging her to listen to them, all concerned that their own spiritual apocalypse was at hand. Half of the specters pointed at the harbor, shrieking that the devil was nigh. Louis was beginning to understand that what had happened to him was the beginning of an invasion. That nothing and no one, living or dead, was safe from what was coming, bubbling up from under the surface like blood seeping out from under the edges of a cracking scab.

Clara tried to steady herself on the ground, her breath coming in ugly gasps.

"Stop, don't you see what you're doing to her?" Louis screamed. "Get away!"

He watched in horror as Clara, his vibrant love, fainted dead away at his floating feet, shivering and shuddering, and though his spectral form bent over her, he could not touch or help her.

"Clara!" Louis cried. "Someone help my darling Clara!"

If one could hear spirits, what a horrible racket.

Louis Dupris wasn't the only one with his spectral mouth in a wail around Clara's unconscious, shuddering form. All of New York's ghosts were screaming bloody murder.